"*Guilty Until Innocent* is a fi... legal drama. By turns movin... this terrific tale of redemption and justice will stick with you long after the final page."

— RICK ACKER, BESTSELLING AUTHOR
AND VETERAN ATTORNEY

"*Double Indemnity* is another winner from Robert Whitlow, one of my favorite authors. The taut suspense builds until the likable pastor is falsely accused of murder, and his new girlfriend, an attorney, has to solve the case. Highly recommended!"

—COLLEEN COBLE, *USA TODAY* BESTSELLING
AUTHOR OF *THE VIEW FROM RAINSHADOW
BAY* AND THE ANNIE PEDERSON SERIES

"A rich and compelling story of family, faith, and friendship with just the right dose of legal thriller, *Relative Justice* is a winner."

—*SOUTHERN LITERARY REVIEW*

"Robert Whitlow's legal expertise shines in *Relative Justice*, a story of patent infringement and illegal gains, but it's his characters who will steal the readers' hearts. Katelyn Martin-Cobb, her husband, Robbie, and his family face trials that allow them to heal old wounds and forge new bonds. Whitlow's fans are sure to enjoy going along for a memorable, roller-coaster ride."

—KELLY IRVIN, AUTHOR OF *TRUST ME*

"*Promised Land* is a book about coming home. Of becoming settled in your spirit and your relationships. With layers of intensity, thanks to international intrigue, moments of legal wrangling, and pages of sweet relationships, this book is rich and complex. A wonderful read."

—CARA PUTMAN, AUTHOR OF *LETHAL INTENT*

"This tense legal thriller from Whitlow boasts intriguing characters . . . One gripping chapter leads to the next . . . Readers will have a hard time putting this one down."

—*PUBLISHERS WEEKLY* ON *CHOSEN PEOPLE*

"If you're looking for a book with unexpected twists and turns that delves into the cultures of Palestine, Israel, and their peoples, you must check out this engaging novel."

—BOOKREPORTER.COM ON *CHOSEN PEOPLE*

"A legal thriller written from a contemporary evangelical Christian worldview, *Chosen People* presents intriguing, well-rounded characters, thought-provoking moral dilemmas, tense drama, and several surprising plot twists."

—*MYSTERY SCENE*

"My verdict for Robert Whitlow's *Chosen People*: compelling, realistic, and inspiring. Robert combines the intensity of a legal battle against terrorists with a poignant depiction of Israel, with all of its tensions and grandeur. As a lawyer who handles cases for terrorism victims, I loved the realism of the novel and felt deeply the joys, disappointments, and triumphs of its characters. But the matters of the law were eclipsed by matters of the heart—faith, love, and hope in the midst of despair—this is where Whitlow truly shines."

—RANDY SINGER, BESTSELLING AUTHOR OF *RULE OF LAW*

"Whitlow writes a fast-paced legal suspense with amazing characters. There are twists and turns throughout, and a number of unexpected surprises to heighten the suspense. Whitlow is an amazing writer and he touches upon delicate topics with grit and respect."

—*RT BOOK REVIEWS*, 4 STARS, ON *A TIME TO STAND*

"Whitlow's timely story shines a spotlight on prejudice, race, and the pursuit of justice in a world bent on blind revenge. Fans of Greg Iles's *Natchez Burning* will find this just as compelling if not more so."

—*LIBRARY JOURNAL*, STARRED REVIEW, ON *A TIME TO STAND*

"Part mystery and part legal thriller . . . Definitely a must-read!"

—*RT BOOK REVIEWS*, 4 STARS, ON *THE WITNESSES*

"Whitlow's characters continuously prove that God loves the broken and that faith is a lot more than just showing up to church. [This] contemplative novel is a fine rumination on ethics, morality, and free will."

—*PUBLISHERS WEEKLY* ON *THE WITNESSES*

"Attorney and Christy Award–winning author Whitlow pens a character-driven story once again showcasing his legal expertise . . . Corbin is highly relatable, leaving readers rooting for his redemption even after family and friends have written him off."

—*PUBLISHERS WEEKLY* ON *A HOUSE DIVIDED*

"Christy Award winner Whitlow's experience in the law is apparent in this well-crafted legal thriller. Holt's spiritual growth as he discovers his faith and questions his motives for hiding his secret is inspiring. Fans of John Grisham will find much to like here."

—*LIBRARY JOURNAL* ON *THE CONFESSION*

GUILTY
UNTIL
INNOCENT

ALSO BY ROBERT WHITLOW

Double Indemnity
Relative Justice
Trial and Error
A Time to Stand
The Witnesses
A House Divided
The Confession
The Living Room
The Choice
Water's Edge
Mountain Top
Jimmy
The Sacrifice
The Trial
The List

THE CHOSEN PEOPLE NOVELS

Chosen People
Promised Land

THE TIDES OF TRUTH NOVELS

Deeper Water
Higher Hope
Greater Love

THE ALEXIA LINDALE NOVELS

Life Support
Life Everlasting

GUILTY UNTIL INNOCENT

ROBERT WHITLOW

THOMAS NELSON
Since 1798

Guilty Until Innocent

Published in Nashville, Tennessee, by Thomas Nelson. Thomas Nelson is a registered trademark of HarperCollins Christian Publishing, Inc.

Thomas Nelson titles may be purchased in bulk for educational, business, fundraising, or sales promotional use. For information, please email SpecialMarkets@ThomasNelson.com.

Scripture quotations are taken from the Holy Bible, New International Version®, NIV®. Copyright © 1973, 1978, 1984, 2011 by Biblica, Inc.® Used by permission of Zondervan. All rights reserved worldwide. www.zondervan.com. The "NIV" and "New International Version" are trademarks registered in the United States Patent and Trademark Office by Biblica, Inc.®

Publisher's Note: This novel is a work of fiction. Names, characters, places, and incidents are either products of the author's imagination or used fictitiously. All characters are fictional, and any similarity to people living or dead is purely coincidental.

Library of Congress Cataloging-in-Publication Data

Names: Whitlow, Robert, 1954- author.
Title: Guilty until innocent / Robert Whitlow.
Description: Nashville, Tennessee : Thomas Nelson, 2025. | Summary: "Justice has been served . . . unless the accused is innocent"—Provided by publisher.
Identifiers: LCCN 2024041390 (print) | LCCN 2024041391 (ebook) | ISBN 9781400344475 (TP) | ISBN 9781400344611 (HC) | ISBN 9781400344482 (epub) | ISBN 9781400344550 (audio download)
Subjects: LCGFT: Detective and mystery fiction. | Religious fiction. | Novels.
Classification: LCC PS3573.H49837 G85 2025 (print) | LCC PS3573.H49837 (ebook) | DDC 813/.54—dc23/eng/20240909
LC record available at https://lccn.loc.gov/2024041390
LC ebook record available at https://lccn.loc.gov/2024041391

Printed in the United States of America

24 25 26 27 28 LBC 5 4 3 2 1

To those who fight for justice and never give up.

But let justice roll on like a river, righteousness like a never-failing stream.

AMOS 5:24

PROLOGUE

The air-conditioning in the Blanton County Courthouse was fighting a losing battle against the oppressive July heat of the eastern North Carolina summer. Joe Moore pushed aside his light brown hair, wiped beads of sweat from his forehead, and rubbed his hand on his pants. He was wearing a blue suit that his mother had purchased for the final day of the trial. Early that morning, she'd brought the clothes to the jail, including a freshly ironed white shirt and a yellow tie.

"I wish you were putting this on for church," Myra Moore said when she placed the neatly folded clothes on the table in the room where prisoners met with their families.

"For my funeral," Joe replied morosely.

"Hush, don't talk like that!" his mother said, a tissue tightly clutched in her hand. "Mr. Clark says he's going to explain everything to the jury in a way that they can see you're not guilty."

Joe stretched out his lanky legs and lowered his head for a moment before forcing himself to make eye contact with his mother.

"Mama, you've heard the testimony and seen what's been introduced into evidence. I'm going to be convicted. That's how I'd vote if I were on the jury."

"I hate the drugs, but it's not in your heart to kill someone," Myra replied in a determined voice.

Joe knew it was pointless to argue. Guilt was irrefutable. His presence at the scene. The bloody knife. The fingerprint evidence. The crystal meth in his system. His history of fighting when high. The blood of the victims on his clothes, and worst of all, the photographs of the bodies.

"Who's going to be there with you?" he asked.

"Sissy and some of the cousins. Hopefully, Aunt Vi will make it. She was feeling puny after yesterday. I need to be surrounded by my people."

"Please don't scream if it goes bad."

Tears streamed down his mother's cheeks. "Don't ask me not to care!"

"I know you care, maybe too much."

His mother reached across the table and grabbed Joe's right hand tightly with both of hers. "That's not possible."

Joe sighed. "Do whatever you feel in the moment."

"When God answers my prayers for you to be set free, I plan on shouting, 'Hallelujah!'"

Being on trial for murder someday had seemed unlikely after Joe graduated toward the top of his high school class and enrolled in the local community college. As an elective in college, he'd taken a criminal justice course. Much of what had taken place during the trial matched what he'd studied in the course. But a huge gap separated the words in the textbooks from the reality of Joe's experience. He understood why the overwhelming majority of criminal defendants either pleaded guilty or were convicted. The resources at the government's disposal were immense. Resistance appeared futile. There'd been no plea deal. Joe's appointed lawyer told him a prosecutor's political career was made on high-profile convictions.

Joe again wiped away the sweat that now threatened his soulful brown eyes. A potbellied bailiff entered the courtroom, followed by the twelve-person jury of seven women and five men. Joe's lawyer had been pleased with the jury selection. Joe wasn't clear on exactly why. At the prosecution table sat the district attorney and Norris Broome, the chief investigator in the case. Inside Joe's pocket was a Bible verse his mother had slipped to him when she entered the courtroom. He'd not taken it out to read it.

"All rise!" the bailiff announced.

Joe stood but didn't turn around. He could feel the presence of his mother and sister in the row behind him. A double murder case was a huge event in Cranfield, and the courtroom was filled with spectators. The prominence in the community of the two victims, especially the young woman, had increased the local fascination.

"Be seated," Judge Brinson said in a deep, thick Southern drawl.

Rustling could be heard across the room. Joe forced himself to breathe. The absence of hope he'd expressed to his mother that morning had found a few live embers when he listened to Tom Clark's closing argument. The young lawyer gave an impassioned appeal. The evidence was grim, but there were unanswered questions and no direct eyewitnesses to the stabbings. Perhaps it was enough for what the judge had described to the jury as reasonable doubt.

"Have you reached a verdict?" the judge asked.

A man in the front row stood. "We have, Your Honor."

"Please announce the verdict."

The foreman, a local building contractor, looked down at the indictment in his hand and cleared his throat. "On count one, we the jury find the defendant, Joseph Moore, guilty of murder in the first degree of Cheryl Drummond."

Joe heard his mother gasp and then groan. He clenched his hands tightly at his sides.

"On count two, we the jury find the defendant, Joseph Moore, guilty of murder in the first degree of Martin Brock."

"Was your decision unanimous?" the judge asked in a matter-of-fact voice.

"Yes, Your Honor."

The judge looked toward the defense table. "Any exceptions to the verdict from the defendant?"

"We reserve those for a motion for a new trial and appeal," Tom Clark responded.

"The defendant will remain in custody pending sentence," the judge said, banging his gavel.

As he was led from the courtroom by two deputies, Joe knew he should look back at his mother, but he couldn't force himself to do so. His shame was too great; the agony he knew would be on her face too painful to see.

CHAPTER 1

Joe rested his head on a smooth rock and dozed off. It was 12:30 p.m. at the Lower Piedmont Correctional Center. He'd stretched out on ground checkered by uneven patches of shade provided by a small stand of pine trees at the eastern edge of the vegetable garden. His best friend, a Black inmate named Ray Simpson, with whom Joe shared the same birthday, had selected a nearby spot for his midday siesta. The fourteen prisoners in the work detail had finished a lunch of bologna smeared with yellow mustard on white bread, dill pickles as thick as the end of a hoe handle, and potato chips from bags that expired months before they arrived at the prison. They washed down the meal with water from white plastic containers. When they left the main prison compound at 7:00 a.m., the containers held equal parts ice and water. By noon, the June sun in the sandhill region of North Carolina had turned the ice to liquid. But the water was still cool enough to refresh their parched throats and replenish some of the sweat lost during the morning's work.

After eating, the work crew was allowed thirty minutes to talk, rest, smoke, or chew. Joe no longer smoked or chewed. Because the crew worked within the confines of the medium-security-level facility, no guards accompanied them to the field. A hundred yards beyond the eastern edge of the garden was a ten-foot-tall chain-link fence topped with graceful coils of glistening razor wire. Twenty feet beyond that fence was another barrier just like it. Watchtowers manned by armed guards provided clear lines of sight from multiple angles. The men assigned to garden duty weren't flight risks. Working the four-acre plot of ground was a coveted assignment. Not only did the men perform productive work, but they also got to enjoy the first ripe strawberries and eat sun-warmed tomatoes. Even though he was incarcerated for murder, Joe had transitioned from a maximum-security facility after six years behind bars. He'd been a model prisoner. Good behavior brought benefits. A significant number of the men at LPCC had also been convicted of violent offenses, but when not under the influence of alcohol or drugs, they wouldn't necessarily stick out as potential convicts at a Sunday school picnic. Joe fell in that category.

When he lay down, Joe positioned his straw hat so that it provided an extra layer of protection from the sun. The battered hat covered his face all the way to his chin. He folded his hands neatly across his chest on top of the broad orange stripe that ran down the front of his dingy white overalls. An equally broad orange stripe ran down the back side of the overalls. Beneath the overalls, Joe wore a plain white T-shirt. His clothes were stained from reddish-brown clay mixed with sandy soil.

Joe had been using the rock pillow ever since it emerged from the ground when a tractor plowed the garden in preparation for the spring planting. It was amazing how the soil continued to produce a harvest of stone. The men on the crew had started calling the pillow "Joe's rock." It made Joe think about the patriarch Jacob, who once used a rock as a pillow at a place where heaven opened and a ladder reached down to earth. So far, Joe's rock had only served to keep his head off the ground.

Seventy-five days earlier, the men had planted okra, bush bean, and lima bean seeds in cold frames built on the north side of the garden. They later added tomatoes and a special section dedicated to seedless watermelons. The earlier plants were maturing in the field. The okra plants were covered with light green pods. Fried okra would soon be on the menu for supper in the prison dining hall. Joe liked okra dusted in cornmeal and fried in a cast-iron skillet. The crunchy little pieces were like candy. He felt a tap on one of his black boots. He twitched it to the side. A second, more insistent tap followed.

"Joe, are you awake?" a voice asked.

"I am now," he replied, pulling the hat away from his face and sitting up with his legs crossed in front of him. "I was dreaming about a plate full of okra."

"That's not a dream," said Deshaun, a muscular Black man in his late twenties who'd recently come to faith through the influence of the men on the garden crew. "We'll be eating it tonight."

"And in a couple of weeks we'll have stewed okra and tomatoes," Joe said. "There are blossoms on the tomato plants."

Deshaun sat on the ground beside him. The younger man was serving a sentence of 120 months for robbing two convenience stores and a liquor store in a single night. No weapon was involved. Deshaun was arrested less than a quarter mile from the liquor store. He pleaded guilty.

"My wife served me with divorce papers," Deshaun said, hanging his head.

Joe frowned. They'd been praying for Deshaun's marriage in the Bible study and prayer group held in the building where both men stayed. The young couple had two sons in elementary school. Joe had met Kiesha once when she came to visit. She was a shy, quiet woman.

"I knew it was coming," the younger man continued. "One of my uncles found out she's been stepping out on me. I know ten years is a long time to wait, but she's stuck by me for over two years, and I thought we were going to make it."

"Just because she filed papers doesn't mean she'll go through with it."

Deshaun glanced over his right shoulder at the area where the rest of the men were relaxing. Ray let out a snort that signaled he was sound asleep.

"Maybe, but I can't take that chance," Deshaun said in a soft voice. "I believe I can stop it. My older brother and one of my cousins are willing to pay a visit to the dude she's seeing. They're big boys and should be able to scare him off."

"You don't want them ending up in a place like this," Joe said, shaking his head. "That's not going to solve anything."

"Oh, they'd just talk to him." Deshaun looked away. "Or knock him around a bit without really hurting him."

"Let's go at it another way."

"We tried praying."

"Pray and act," Joe said.

"What kind of act?" Deshaun asked with a puzzled look on his face. "We're locked up in here."

"Promise me that you won't turn your brother and cousin loose. Not yet."

"What do you have in mind?"

"Let me talk it over with Ray and get back to you later this evening."

Deshaun stared across the field toward the metal fence. He closed his right hand into a fist, then released it.

"Okay," he sighed.

———

The phone on Ryan Clark's desk hadn't buzzed all morning. That wasn't surprising. He'd been working at the law firm for only two months, and all significant communication about cases was funneled through his boss. Ryan had met with a handful of clients, but only when Tom Clark, Ryan's second cousin once removed, was also present.

Tom was a gregarious, friendly man who liked to help people and accepted a broad array of legal matters, even those that had to do with areas of the law in which he had little or no experience. One of his mantras was "Don't turn a case away too quickly. You never know where a million dollars might be hiding!"

Ryan didn't know Tom very well before joining the firm. They'd rarely talked at the biennial reunions of the extended Clark family in Fayetteville. Tom and Ryan's father were close in age, but the families never socialized or spent time together while growing up. Tom and his wife, Karen, had no children. Ryan was thirteen years old when Sam Clark, his father, died suddenly in a drowning accident. Tom attended the funeral and made a point to pull Ryan aside and offer to help in any way possible. Tom followed up his words with a condolence card repeating the same message. Ryan called in the favor fifteen years later and drove to Cranfield for a job interview, even though he doubted the offer remained valid.

Ryan was the third associate hired by Tom in the past eight years. All the others had either been fired or moved on. Ryan knew the employment history of previous attorneys when he accepted the job offer, but his own career had reached the point of no viable options. At the moment, he was deep in the labyrinth of the secured transaction provisions from the North Carolina version of the Uniform Commercial Code. It was a topic he'd not thought about since passing the bar exam three years earlier. He rubbed his eyes and ran his muscular fingers through his short, sandy hair. A knock sounded on his door.

"Come in!" he called out.

"Ready for a lunch break?" Tom asked, patting his ample stomach.

"No, I brought an apple from home and plan on working straight through on the UCC question. I know you need a memo before the end of the day."

"I wasn't serious about that deadline," Tom replied with a dismissive wave of his hand. "Tomorrow will be soon enough. There's someone I want you to meet."

Ryan had learned to pin down the senior partner when a deadline was involved.

"What time tomorrow?" he asked.

"Ten thirty," Tom replied. "I have an eleven o'clock meeting with the client. Thirty minutes will be plenty of time to review your research."

"That will work," Ryan said, getting up from his chair.

At five feet ten, Ryan was the same height as his cousin but without the extra weight around the middle. A varsity tennis player in college, Ryan was a defensive specialist who won a lot of matches by frustrating and wearing down more aggressive opponents. Tenacity in the face of adversity had been one of his strengths, but his sketchy employment history since law school had worn him down. For the past few months he'd occasionally struggled with anxiety attacks.

"An apple isn't a meal," Tom said, putting his arm around Ryan's shoulder. "You're doing a fantastic job and deserve a nice luncheon."

Ryan hoped the compliment was genuine. The majority of his interactions with his new boss had been positive, but there had been a handful of negative outbursts.

The town of Cranfield was the county seat of Blanton County. The community of twelve thousand people was only a ninety-minute drive east of the city limits of Charlotte, but the difference in culture and pace of life was as stark as if the two locations were a thousand miles apart. The main economic engine for Blanton County remained agriculture. For decades tobacco was king, but soybeans were now more common, and chicken houses had increased in popularity.

Ryan and Tom walked down a short hall decorated with photos Tom had taken of pastoral scenes in Blanton County. The lawyer especially liked old tobacco barns with faded wooden sides. The law firm occupied a two-story 1940s-era house that had been converted to office space twenty years earlier. Tom owned the building. The extensive renovations had included hardwood floors, crown molding, and expensive furnishings. An oriental rug covered the reception-area floor. The seats and couch were soft leather. Outside, the yard had been meticulously landscaped and featured a parking area with brick pavers.

"Nancy, we'll be having lunch at the club and won't be back for a couple of hours," Tom said.

Nancy Coltran, a smartly dressed gray-haired woman in her late fifties, was a personal friend of Tom and his wife and served as receptionist and bookkeeper.

"Don't forget you have an appointment at one o'clock with Sean Patterson," Nancy said.

"Reschedule it for later in the week," Tom said. "He's wanting an update when there's really nothing to tell him."

As they proceeded out the door, Tom turned to Ryan. "Remind me to give you the Patterson file when we get back to the office. It needs a fresh set of eyes before I take any more depositions. Our client wasn't candid about the facts when he hired me, and I need to figure out the best exit strategy for him and the law firm."

Tom could be as quick to terminate a case as he was to initiate one. They got into his cream-colored Cadillac.

"Who is it you want me to meet?" Ryan asked as he buckled his seat belt.

"You'll find out when we get there. Enjoy the suspense as much as you will the buffet served at the country club on Monday. The prime rib is outstanding."

Ryan loved beef. He wasn't picky. It could be prime rib, steak, or a well-seasoned hamburger.

"The other time you took me to the country club they served a seafood medley," he said. "I liked it."

"You needed a nice meal after they let you go at Summers, Donovan, and Rangel."

Upon graduating in the middle of his law school class at Chapel Hill, Ryan landed a job with a big firm in Raleigh. That job lasted nine months. A research memo he prepared failed to identify a judicial precedent in California adverse to their client's position. The issue was crucial to the case even though the lawsuit was filed in

North Carolina. As a result, the lawsuit was dismissed with pre-judice by the judge. The client suffered a loss of five million dollars in potential revenue, and the law firm faced a legal malpractice claim. If he'd been at the firm longer, Ryan might have survived. But he was little more than a glorified summer clerk and the damage was too great. Firing him made the law firm's management appear proactive. The managing partner, a gruff man in his late fifties, stood over Ryan while he cleaned out his desk. Ryan then endured a walk of shame to the parking deck. Fortunately, his wife, Paige, had a steady job working remotely for a government contractor based in Reston, Virginia, but her income was barely enough to pay basic bills.

After being out of work for six months, Ryan was hired by Summers, Donovan, and Rangel, a smaller law firm in Durham that specialized in commercial real estate law. One of the senior partners was a woman who wasn't actively involved in the interview process. For reasons unclear to Ryan, she immediately started criticizing his work to his face and behind his back. He applied himself diligently in an effort to overcome her negative opinion. Things seemed to get better, but a week after he celebrated a year at the firm, the woman fired him. He later learned that she wanted to hire the daughter of a friend to replace him. A six-month period of unemployment marked by multiple rejections followed. Two job terminations so close in time produced a barrier that seemed impossible to overcome. Ryan considered trying to find a corporate job other than with a law firm. As a last resort he contacted Tom. When his cousin offered him a job at half the salary of the associate position with the law firm in Durham, Ryan accepted immediately.

They reached the entrance to the Western Hills Country Club. The club boasted an eighteen-hole golf course and six composite-surface tennis courts. Ryan hadn't played tennis since arriving in town and wasn't sure he wanted word to get out that he was a good player. After competing at a high level, he wasn't interested in hitting the ball back and forth with a novice.

"Didn't you play tennis in college?" Tom asked as they passed the courts. "There was something about it on your résumé."

Ryan suddenly wished he'd scrubbed that information. "Yes, but not much during law school."

"Maybe Daniel Milton from the district attorney's office will be in the dining room. He's always looking for a tennis partner. If he's there, I'll introduce you. It never hurts to have a friendly face at the courthouse."

Tom drove down a tree-lined avenue and turned into the parking lot. The clubhouse was a stone-and-wood structure with large Palladian windows on the front. They walked up three steps to the double front doors. The entrance to the dining room was directly in front of them. Tom signed in at the host station.

"I'm almost maxed out on my food allowance for the month," Tom muttered as they made their way into the room filled with tables covered with white cloths. "When you calculate the monthly membership fee, it's not a very good deal. We're at table twelve."

The carving station for the prime rib was to their right. There were four chairs at table twelve. No one was sitting there.

"He should be here by now," Tom said, glancing around. "He's never late and gives me a hard time when I am."

A waiter wearing a white shirt, black pants, and a straight black tie took their drink orders.

"I'm not going to wait," Tom said after the waiter left. "I'm starving and want to get a cut of meat from the center."

They made their way to the prime rib table. Tom looked toward the entrance to the dining room.

"There he is," he said.

A short, slightly built man with dark hair and a friendly smile on his face approached. He was wearing an open-collared shirt and cream-colored pants. He shook Tom's hand.

"Ryan," Tom announced, "this is Charlie Drummond. He's the law firm's biggest and best client!"

"No need to broadcast it all the way to Union County," Charlie replied, the smile remaining on his face.

Charlie extended his hand. Ryan noticed a large gold ring on the client's right hand and an expensive watch on his left wrist.

"Nice to meet you," Charlie said. "I understand you and Tom are kinfolk."

"Second cousins once removed," Tom answered.

"How does that work?" Charlie asked. "I can never keep that straight."

"We share common great-great-grandparents and great-grandparents who were siblings, but I'm one generation older than Ryan," Tom said. "His father and I were born in the same year. Isn't that right?"

"Close, but actually he was two years older than you," Ryan replied.

"In a family as large as ours, it takes a book to keep up with the details," Tom said with a laugh.

Tom led the way back to their table.

"Charlie owns and runs a bunch of businesses," he said. "Farms, rental property, an industrial park."

"Thanks to my family," Charlie said. "My grandfather got the ball rolling. I just nudge it along."

"That's too modest," Tom objected. "You've grown everything a bunch."

The waiter took Charlie's drink order. They again made their way to the carving station. Charlie stood next to Ryan.

"Where do your folks live?" he asked.

"My mother is in Burlington," Ryan replied. "My father died when I was thirteen."

"Cancer or heart attack?"

Ryan cleared his throat. "No, drowning accident."

"I'm sorry to hear that," Charlie said, then paused. "I had an older sister who died young, murdered when she was twenty-five."

CHAPTER 2

One of Paige Clark's requests when she and Ryan moved to Cranfield was a home office with a view. Growing up in Colorado, Paige loved vistas like Chasm Lake with Longs Peak in the background. Nothing like that existed east of the Mississippi River, and the greatest elevation change in Blanton County was two hundred feet. When she and Ryan found a modest house to rent, Paige had to settle for a small patch of green grass, a Japanese maple tree, and a row of daylilies against a wooden privacy fence.

She stood and stretched. Paige had just completed a two-hour video conference call with her group discussing a multimillion-dollar bid to provide staffing personnel for a medical assistance program geared toward lower-income families in Pennsylvania. With a degree in English composition and literature from Rice University, Paige worked as an editor to clean up the grammar and style in documents that ranged from narrative sales presentations to scientific specifications. Several of the faces on the screen belonged to technically savvy people who didn't understand the difference between a phrase and a clause and couldn't define a gerund if their life depended on it. Paige had separated her two computer monitors so she could occasionally look out the window. A bird had built a nest in the maple and flew over to feed her chicks. A wet nose nuzzled Paige's leg.

"Ready to go outside?" Paige asked Sandy, the couple's Soft-Coated Wheaten Terrier.

At the word "outside," the dog's head shot up, and she jumped back and forth. It was a sunny day. Because only the upper half of her body was visible during the conference call, Paige was wearing a nice blouse, but from the waist down she had on shorts and sandals. Her reddish-blond hair barely touched her shoulders. Even though she was only five feet four inches tall, Paige didn't have a problem keeping up with Ryan when they jogged on the beach or went for a hike. She'd started climbing mountains as a teenager and before going to college had summited multiple fourteen-thousand-foot peaks. She followed Sandy into the small area enclosed by the wooden fence. Her phone vibrated with a text from Ryan:

> On my way to lunch at the country club with Tom.
> He says it's a surprise. Not sure what's up.

As soon as she read the text, Paige felt a knot in her stomach. Tom inviting Ryan to lunch didn't sound like the prelude to firing him. But after what had happened at the other two law firms where he worked, Paige couldn't keep from worrying. Her father jumped from job to job as part of her chaotic upbringing, and she didn't want to repeat that pattern. Paige's parents had been divorced for years, and despite Paige's best efforts to stay close, they grew apart when she left for college. Now her mother's focus was on Amy, Paige's younger sister, and Amy's two little boys.

Inside the house, Paige fixed a lunch of spinach salad topped with chicken they'd grilled the night before. Through the small window above the sink, she could see the trees that lined both sides of the street in front of their residence. It was peaceful and quiet. A FedEx vehicle stopped in front of the house, and a uniformed young woman walked up the sidewalk. Sandy let out a sharp bark at the sound of the doorbell. Paige opened the door, and the woman handed her a small, lightweight package.

"Thanks," Paige said.

"There's more coming," the woman replied, "but it hadn't arrived at the terminal when I left this morning. I may see you later."

Paige took the package into the kitchen. She suspected what it contained but didn't open it until she finished her salad. Taking a knife from the utility drawer, she sliced through the packing tape. It was a box of pregnancy tests. Paige and Ryan weren't trying to have a baby, but she'd suffered an adverse reaction to birth control pills, and on three occasions during their four years of marriage she'd wondered if she might be pregnant. To their relief, each test showed negative. The couple wanted children someday, but their circumstances, especially Ryan's unstable job status, hadn't been right to start a family. Rinsing her plate and putting it in the dishwasher, Paige then went into the house's half bath located in the hallway that separated the main bedroom from the living area. Two tests later, she emerged with a shocked look on her face and a pair of positive test results in her hand.

The prime rib proved to be as good as Tom had predicted. Ryan wanted to ignore the side dishes of garlic mashed potatoes and steamed broccoli with cheese sauce, but it wouldn't have been polite to focus exclusively on the meat.

"Oh, there's Danny Milton," Tom said, looking past Ryan's left shoulder. "Charlie, you know Danny, don't you?"

"Yes, we're in Rotary together."

Tom motioned for the man to come over to their table. Danny was a tall, lean six feet plus. Everyone stood to greet him. Tom introduced him to Ryan.

"Ryan could have been a tennis pro," Tom boasted. "He played on the Furman team in college."

Physically fit, Danny looked to be in his late thirties or early forties.

"We played Furman when I was at Wofford," Danny replied and mentioned the name of a former Furman coach.

"He left before I arrived," Ryan said.

"Maybe we can hit it around one day. Unless you're burned out. After graduation, I didn't want to pick up a racket for several years. Tennis had stopped being fun and had become more of a job."

"I had a similar reaction."

Danny leaned over and lowered his voice. "And I didn't want to play guys who were only interested in taking a game off me and boasting about it, even though they lost the set 6–1."

Ryan chuckled. Taking out his phone, he shared his contact info with Danny.

"What's your style of play?" Danny asked.

"My nickname was 'Backboard,'" Ryan answered.

"Perfect," Danny said and smiled. "My game is 'hit one shot from the baseline and charge the net.' We could have some fun."

"Absolutely," Ryan replied.

Danny patted Ryan on the shoulder. "I'll let you gentlemen get back to your lunch."

"Nicely done," Tom said to Ryan when they were seated. "Don't wait for him to invite you. Take the initiative."

Tom and Charlie took over the conversation. The client had several legal questions. Ryan received a text from Paige asking him about lunch, and he sent her a photo of his plate. Tom suddenly stopped.

"Ryan, are you getting all this? Because I want you to help me provide Charlie with answers."

Ryan quickly exited his camera. "Not yet, but I'll make some notes in my phone."

Leaving his broccoli untouched, Ryan entered the gist of what he thought the client wanted them to find out. Most of it had to do with commercial lease issues.

"Does your lease have a provision for force majeure?" Tom asked.

"You drafted it," Charlie replied.

"Right, right. I'm sure it's in there, but we'll check when Ryan and I return to the office."

Charlie excused himself to go to the restroom. Ryan returned to the carving station.

"Any possibility of seconds?" he asked an older man who was wearing a tall white chef's hat.

"I think I can spare a morsel and still have enough for the staff to eat lunch," the man replied with a smile.

"No," Ryan immediately said and held up his hand. "In that case—"

"I'm joking," the man answered, lowering his voice. "We know how much to cook to make sure there will be leftovers for the kitchen."

Ryan walked back to the table. Charlie had returned, and Tom was talking on his phone.

"If it's really an emergency, I'll come now," he said, then listened for a few seconds.

Ryan cut into the meat and took a bite.

"Okay, I'm on my way," Tom said, ending the call.

Ryan reluctantly pushed his plate away and prepared to get up.

"I have to drive to Scotland County and meet with the family of a client who had a brain hemorrhage last night and died this morning," Tom said. "He changed his will not long ago, and two of his children didn't know they'd been cut out of the estate. They're trying to get the police involved."

"The police?" Ryan asked in surprise.

"The sheriff is friends with one of the folks who's upset and is asking questions."

"Family relationships can be the toughest," Charlie said.

Ryan stood up.

"There's no need for you to tag along," Tom said.

"I can drop Ryan off at your office," Charlie volunteered. "That will give us time for dessert. They have rum-spiced cheesecake today."

"Ryan, you have to try it," Tom said. "Sneak out a piece in a to-go container for me."

After Tom left, Ryan took another bite of his prime rib.

"Thanks," he said.

"No problem," Charlie replied. "If we're going to be working together, I want to get to know you separately from Tom."

The workday for the prison garden crew ended at 4:00 p.m. so that the day's harvest could make it onto plates for the 5:30 supper shift.

Except for the fresh additions supplied by the garden, they followed a menu issued by the Bureau of Prisons in Raleigh. Joe was pleased with the generous yield of okra they'd harvested. Several bushels were piled high in plastic baskets. While the rest of the men headed to the showers, Joe hosed off the produce outside the back entrance to the dining hall. Dickie, a government employee in charge of the kitchen, came out to see him. Joe tossed Dickie a piece of okra. The kitchen boss squeezed it with his fingers.

"That would make my aunt Sally smile," Dickie said and nodded. "First harvest is always best. Isn't there something about that in the Bible?"

Joe's reputation as a man of faith wasn't limited to the prison population. He squinted his eyes for a moment.

"In Proverbs it says, 'Honor the LORD with your wealth, with the firstfruits of all your crops.' We'll honor the Lord by being thankful and eating as much as we can."

Dickie helped Joe carry the buckets into the kitchen.

"That's why you scratched green beans off the menu," one of the cooks said when he saw them.

"Are you complaining?" Dickie asked.

"No, sir," the man answered with a nod to Joe. "We'll be eating good in the neighborhood."

"Remember how I like it," Joe said.

The cook pointed to a pair of massive iron skillets hanging from hooks in the wall.

"Lightly dusted and fried crisp," he said.

Joe left the kitchen that had become his home after twenty years at LPCC. He knew every inch of the facility and many of the men and guards who lived and worked there. The leadership ability God placed in Joe before he was born didn't emerge until he was incarcerated, but it had risen to the surface in prison. He nodded in greeting to several men as he walked across the exercise yard to Unit C, the building where he stayed.

The long brick structure housed fifty men. They had a common shower and bathroom area, a large TV room, and bunk beds lined up in neat rows. The three guards assigned to the unit mostly stayed in an office surrounded by windows. They didn't carry weapons when in direct contact with the prisoners, but there were firearms in the office, and a dozen guards could descend on a unit within seconds if an alarm sounded. Joe passed by the TV room where men who'd returned from other work details were watching an afternoon game show. Both screens were tuned to the same channel. The guards controlled what the prisoners watched. No crime shows, movies about prison breaks, MMA fights, or films that featured gory scenes were allowed.

After taking a shower, Joe put on a pair of white pants with a narrow orange stripe down the side, white socks, and a white T-shirt. He had two bags for clothes: one dirty, the other clean. The dirty clothes were washed together every fifth day in a single load so they didn't get mixed up. Everyone dressed the same, but the men were allowed limited personal preferences in their choice of shoes. Joe's favorite pair were jogging shoes in the school colors of Cranfield High, where he'd been a member of the marching band during football season and played on the basketball team in winter. Joe still had a decent jump shot that he put on display from time to time on the basketball court at the south end of the exercise yard, but he'd lost his quick step toward the basket. He was tying the laces on his shoes when Deshaun came over to him.

"Any more ideas about what to do with my wife?" the young man asked.

"I was asking the Lord about it while we were finishing up the last two rows of okra."

"Hear anything?"

"It's percolating."

"What's that supposed to mean?" Deshaun asked in frustration. "I have to do something!"

Joe stood so that he could look directly into Deshaun's eyes. "I'm going to eat okra tonight, but after that I'm going to fast and pray for you and your wife for a few days. Can you hold off that long?"

"Yes," Deshaun replied in a subdued voice.

"Don't tell anyone outside the prayer group what I'm doing."

"I won't," Deshaun said. "But how are you going to be able to do your work in the garden? Won't you get tired? And where will you go during mealtimes?"

"I'll drink plenty of water," Joe replied with a slight smile. "And slip off to the chapel during mealtime. That's allowed by the guards."

Joe sat on his bunk and flipped through notes from his recent personal Bible study while he waited for the group study and prayer meeting to start. A slightly built and heavily tattooed young man in his twenties who was a recent arrival to LPCC and Unit C came over to him.

"Are you the guy in charge of the church meeting?" he asked Joe.

"If you mean the one that meets here, I lead it along with Ray Simpson. Chapel services are Sunday morning at ten o'clock. What's your name?"

"Dawson Crabtree, but people call me Squirrely. I got here last week."

Joe extended his hand. "I'm Joe. Would you rather be called Dawson?"

"No one calls me Dawson except my mama."

"I'll call you Dawson if you want me to."

The young man hesitated. "Yeah, that would be fine. I've been wanting to get a fresh start. Maybe that's one way to do it. Getting locked up has hit me hard."

"It hit me hard, too, and took me three years to make the change. Are you interested in hearing how that happened?"

Dawson glanced to the side. "Yeah, I guess so."

Chairs weren't allowed in the general area of the unit. Joe scooted over so Dawson could sit on the other end of the bunk.

"I'm serving a life sentence for double murder," Joe began. "I started out in Central Prison in Raleigh. My mother would always write and encourage me to go to church. There wasn't much else I could do to try to ease the pain I'd put her through, so I did. One Sunday morning the preacher in chapel was talking about Jesus being the Light of the World. I'd known darkness but not much light. The preacher said anyone who turned in faith to Jesus could walk in the light." Joe paused. "There were a couple hundred men in the meeting, but every word was directly for me. I went forward at the end, and a couple of men prayed with me. One of them was also in prison for murder. When he told me Jesus could forgive my sin, I cried like a little kid. When I left that room, I felt like I'd had a shower on the inside. That was the beginning."

Dawson was sitting with his arms resting on his legs and his hands folded in front of him. He looked down for a moment and then turned to Joe. "That's what I want."

"Let's get started."

Thirty minutes later Joe and Dawson walked into the room where they held the prayer meetings.

"Men, welcome Dawson Crabtree. Before we do anything else, there's something he'd like to tell you."

CHAPTER 3

Paige had a busy afternoon editing a lengthy proposal scheduled for submission in a couple of weeks. Sitting at her desk, she stopped typing and put her hand on her abdomen. She was experiencing a roller coaster of emotions. What if simultaneously with receiving news of a positive pregnancy test, Ryan was getting fired? She sent him a short text:

How's lunch? Everything okay?

Moments later, he replied with a photo of a white plate with a large piece of prime rib, broccoli, and mashed potatoes. Beneath the photo, he wrote:

Great. Hope you're not jealous.

She sent him a meme about a massive lobster. Paige preferred lobster or fish to beef. But it was hard to think about food, work, or anything else. She was pregnant! Ninety percent of her mind and emotions was positive, but the ten percent that wasn't had an inordinately loud voice. She thought about the tiny person living inside her. Paige had never bought into the belief that an unborn child was nothing more than a blob of tissue. As a middle school student, she'd watched a video in biology class about fetal development and what happened in a woman's uterus during pregnancy. Closing her business file, she started researching what she should do during the early days of pregnancy. Paige normally ate a healthy diet and couldn't think of anything in her regular lifestyle that might pose a risk to her baby.

She checked out available doctors in Cranfield. There were only two ob-gyn practices. Paige wasn't sure she could trust small-town medical providers or the local hospital. Driving to Charlotte was a possibility, but the time required to get there when she went into labor would be a concern.

There was another knock on the front door. That was a quick turnaround for the FedEx delivery woman. Sandy let out a sharp bark. Paige saw through one of the sidelights that it wasn't the driver.

"Are you Paige Clark?" asked a plump woman in her late forties or early fifties.

The woman was perspiring in the afternoon heat. Beads of sweat were running down the sides of her face. In her right hand she held a plastic bag with the name of the town printed on it.

"Yes," Paige replied.

"I'm Madge Norton, a volunteer with the Cranfield Welcome Wagon. We like to drop off a gift bag and a packet of information for new families who've recently moved to town."

"Come in where it's air-conditioned," Paige said, stepping aside.

"No, I wasn't trying to pop in unannounced."

"Please come in. Would you like a glass of water?"

"That sounds lovely," Madge sighed. "You're the last of five stops."

Paige led the way to the kitchen and motioned for Madge to have a seat.

"It's been several years since I was in this house," Madge said. "Did you and your husband buy it from the Vaughn family?"

"No, we're renting from Mr. Vaughn."

Sandy positioned her head close to Madge's knee and looked up with pleading eyes.

"Is it okay if I pet her?" Madge asked. "I heard her barking when I rang the bell."

"Yes, the barking is a warning. There's not an ounce of attack dog in her. Now that you're inside, she wants to be friends."

Madge rubbed Sandy's neck. The animal closed her eyes in appreciation.

"If I could find a dog with her disposition, my husband might let me bring one into the house," Madge said. "As of six months ago, Ralph and I are empty nesters."

Paige listened as the woman talked about her three children—two boys and a girl. The girl was in college and the boys had married and moved away from Cranfield.

"Do you have children?" Madge asked.

"Not yet," Paige responded. "But we want to."

"If you do, maybe they'll get your hair color. It's gorgeous. At my age, I get to pick any hair color I want, but I don't think I could do your look."

Madge shifted in her chair and glanced at a piece of paper in her hand. "My information sheet says your husband is a lawyer and works with Tom Clark. Are they related?"

Paige repeated what she had learned about second cousins once removed.

"I love genealogy," Madge replied, then launched into a long story about her family roots that branched out from Virginia to North Carolina, South Carolina, and Tennessee.

"Because we're spread out all over the place, we haven't had a family reunion in ten years."

"Every couple of years my husband's family gets together in Fayetteville."

Madge took a long drink of water. "I hope it works out for him at the law firm. Tom Clark is a character."

Paige was curious about what Madge meant, but she had a more pressing concern on her mind.

"Where were your children born?" she asked.

"Right here. I loved my obstetrician. Dr. Hester was young then, and he's still a fantastic doctor. He's the most popular ob-gyn in town."

"And the hospital is okay?"

"Better than okay. Of course it's been a long time since I was there, but women your age give it a good grade. It's set up to give tons of extra care to new moms and babies." Madge stopped and eyed Paige. "Are you pregnant?"

Paige blushed. "Since I'm new in town, I'm trying to find out what I can about doctors, dentists, that sort of thing."

"Makes sense. Would you like my contact information? I'd love to be available for anything you need."

"That would be nice."

Paige took out her phone, and the friendly woman shared the information. After finishing the glass of water, she stood.

"You've made my day," she said. "Before knocking on your door, I was thinking about quitting the Welcome Wagon, but I'm going to soldier on. Oh, and if you have any problem getting an appointment with Dr. Hester, let me know. I'm friends with one of his nurses and can get you in."

After Madge left, Paige called the doctor's office. The physician was accepting patients, and she scheduled an appointment.

———————

Normally, Ryan wasn't a big fan of cheesecake, but the rum-spiced version was different from anything he'd eaten before.

"This is good," Ryan said after a second bite. "But it was hard to turn down the chocolate pie at the other end of the dessert table."

"There's no restriction against multiple desserts," Charlie replied. "And when Tom left, the number of dessert portions available for the rest of the room went up."

It was true that Tom loved sweets. Ryan grinned.

"No need to confirm what I already know," Charlie continued. "Since you're not leaving until I do, tell me more about yourself."

Not sure where to begin, Ryan hesitated.

"Personal or professional?" he asked.

"Professional."

Ryan gave the client a thumbnail history of his academic career. He wasn't sure how to navigate his rocky start to practicing law.

"I worked for two firms, one in Raleigh, the other in Durham, before moving to Cranfield and joining Tom," he said.

"I don't blame you for deciding not to stay in the city," Charlie said. "Small-town life has benefits. You get to really know the place and the people. I bet Tom gave you a rundown on every lawyer in town. Who to trust, who's shady, who's smart, who's lazy. And which judge is better to have in the courtroom."

"I guess around here it's impossible to hide."

"That's one reason I like it. I rent residential as well as commercial real estate. The tenants in my houses almost always work out because I know who they are. The problem I was telling Tom about earlier comes up when I rent a commercial or industrial property to a company from someplace else."

They continued eating dessert.

"My wife and I are renting a house from Seth Vaughn," Ryan said.

"The two-bedroom cottage on Hamilton Street? The one with the tiny bathroom off the master bedroom?"

"Yeah."

"People didn't hang out in the bathrooms back then," Charlie said. "Nice place. I've tried to buy it from Seth several times, but it has sentimental value to him because that's the first place he and Lynn lived after they married."

Ryan finished his dessert.

"I'm full," he said, pushing away his plate. "But the prime rib was better than any dessert. I should probably grab a slice of cheesecake for Tom and get back to the office."

"First, if you don't mind, tell me about your father. It must have been tough on you, losing him when you were a teenager."

Ryan never voluntarily brought up the tragedy, especially with someone he'd just met. But he couldn't avoid a response without appearing rude. "Uh, my dad worked as a sales rep for a yarn manufacturing company. He died in a fishing accident."

"What happened?"

"Fell out of a small boat on a cold day."

"Were you with him?"

Ryan swallowed. "Yes. He stood up to untangle my fishing line. The boat wasn't very stable."

Ryan stopped. He didn't include the fact that he'd jerked his rod and angrily told his father to leave him alone. His father reached out to retrieve the rod. The sudden movement caused the boat to tip precariously to the side. His father lost his balance and tumbled into the frigid water. Wearing a thick coat and heavy boots, he immediately sank out of sight. Ryan stared at the water for a few seconds, then started screaming. He never saw his father again. The rescue crew that dredged the lake recovered his body the following day.

"I'm sorry," Charlie replied. "My father died three years ago from a heart attack. We weren't as close as I would have liked. He and my mother moved to the beach shortly after my sister died. Dad loved to play golf and had no interest in the family business or staying in Cranfield. Death is a part of life, but that doesn't make it easy to face."

They left the country club. Charlie drove a big black Mercedes. At a traffic light, the businessman rested his right hand on top of the steering wheel.

"There's something you should know," he said, staring straight ahead. "You'll find out eventually, and I'd rather you hear it from me. Tom represented the man who murdered my sister and her fiancé."

"He did?" Ryan asked in shock.

"Appointed by the judge, so from what I understand Tom didn't really have a choice. Guilt wasn't in question. The only real issue was the sentence. We didn't push the DA to seek the death penalty, and the killer got life in prison. I never blamed Tom for representing him. He was just doing his job. Later, when I got to know him, I started sending business his way instead of to one of the bigger firms. Tom gave me more personal service."

"He did mention you were his best client."

Charlie chuckled. "It's always nice to hear."

They pulled into the parking lot. Ryan opened the passenger door. "Thanks for the ride, Mr. Drummond."

"You're welcome. And it's Charlie. Around here, Mr. Drummond was my grandfather."

———

Paige accomplished less than half of what she'd wanted to during the afternoon. Editing often took more effort than writing original content. Her mind kept drifting off, forcing her to start over again. She thought about surprising Ryan with a fancy dinner before sharing the big news but knew she couldn't compete with prime rib. In the end, she ordered Chinese takeout from a small restaurant next door to a laundromat. Both Paige and Ryan liked the American version of Chinese cooking. He enjoyed spring rolls dipped in duck sauce, so Paige ordered extra. Shortly after the delivery driver dropped off the food, Sandy let out a sharp bark at the sound of Ryan's vehicle in the driveway. Paige had put on a nice outfit. Ryan kissed her and then scratched Sandy's head.

"Looks like we're going out to eat," he said.

"No, I ordered Chinese from that little place with the green-colored dragon by the front door. The food is in the oven staying warm."

"Is that why you got dressed up?" Ryan asked.

"No, I wanted to look nice for our dinner. Is that okay?"

"Yes, sorry."

"How was work?"

"I'll tell you while we eat."

"Anything bad?"

"No, no. Tom took me to lunch at the country club to meet the law firm's biggest client. He's a local guy who owns several businesses along with a bunch of land and commercial property."

While Ryan talked about a man named Charlie Drummond, Paige picked at her food. They had shrimp and scallops in a brown sauce. Ryan didn't slow down until he'd finished his third spring roll. He paused.

"What about your day?" he asked. "I shouldn't monopolize the conversation."

"Keep going. We'll get to me later."

"After Tom was called away for an emergency with a client, Charlie started asking me questions about my father and how he died."

"What did you say?" Paige raised her eyebrows.

"As little as possible. He then told me about his older sister, who was murdered about twenty-five years ago."

"That's horrible."

"Yeah, and driving back to the office, he dropped the news that Tom represented the murderer who was convicted and sent to prison. Apparently, Charlie didn't harbor any negative feelings toward Tom and later hired him to be his lawyer. I guess that's how it can work in a small town."

Paige didn't respond. It wasn't the sort of discussion she wanted to have prior to revealing her news. She ate more rice. A few kernels slipped off her chopsticks and fell to the floor. Sandy, who was sitting beside the chair, quickly scooped them up with her tongue.

"A woman from the Welcome Wagon stopped by after lunch," Paige said. "She came in for a few minutes. It's nice to meet someone who can recommend things like doctors and dentists."

"Yeah, I'm overdue for a dental appointment and promise not to put it off now that I'm on the insurance plan at the law firm. There is separate dental coverage with a very low deductible. We may want to switch you over—"

"Madge gave me a recommendation for a local ob-gyn," Paige cut in.

"Good," Ryan replied as he finished the last spring roll and started in on the shrimp and scallops.

"I thought I ought to set up an initial visit as soon as possible," Paige continued. "Especially since I'm pregnant."

Ryan dropped his chopsticks and sat up straighter in his chair. "When did you take a test? Are you sure?"

Paige held up two fingers. "Two tests, both positive."

Ryan's face revealed his shock. Paige waited. Ryan leaned forward and grabbed her hand.

"This is wonderful," he said.

"I'm glad you're excited. I wasn't sure it was a good time to start a family."

"Beyond excited," Ryan said, speaking rapidly. "I've been ready but kept it to myself. I've felt like such a professional failure that I'd started doubting myself in every area of my life and—"

Paige reached up and put her index finger to Ryan's lips. "We've gone through some rocky times, but you're a good husband, and I think you're going to be an even better father."

Ryan stood and pulled her up close for a kiss. He squeezed her tightly, then quickly released her.

"Sorry, I don't want to hurt you," he said.

Paige looked into his eyes. "I'm not fragile. I could still reach the top of a big mountain faster than you."

"This is a mountain we're going to climb together."

CHAPTER 4

The okra exceeded Joe's expectations. Several men stopped by the table to let him know how much they enjoyed it. He went back for a second helping. Savoring each morsel, he began to question his earlier decision to fast and pray for Deshaun's marriage. Maybe Joe could pray and eat. God wasn't impressed by human sacrifice. Jesus accomplished everything needed for full salvation on the cross.

"It'll be even better tomorrow," said Ray, who was sitting beside him at the table.

A short, wiry man with a fringe of graying hair, Ray was the same age as Joe and serving a long sentence as a repeat felony offender despite not being a violent man. It was the volume of Ray's offenses, rather than their ferocity, that convinced the judge in Buncombe County to impose a lengthy sentence. He and Joe had been together at LPCC for more than fifteen years and proved race was no barrier to close friendship.

"I may not be eating any," Joe muttered.

"What do you mean? Are you feeling poorly?"

"No, the Lord told me this afternoon it's time to fast and pray for Deshaun's marriage. His wife says she wants a divorce."

Ray shook his head. "That's a shame."

The two men ate in silence for a few moments.

"Did the Lord say anything about me fasting?" Ray asked. "When we fasted for three days last year, my stomach was hugging my spine so tight by the end of the third day, I thought it was going to come out my back side."

Joe managed a smile. "It worked, didn't it?" he said.

Joe glanced across at the next table, where a large inmate in his late thirties contentedly ate his supper. When Everett Robinson, a racist troublemaker, arrived at LPCC, there was a high likelihood he was going to either start a bad fight or join one. The men's Bible study and prayer group in Unit C was multiracial and began secretly praying and fasting for him. A week after the fast ended, Everett showed up at a meeting. By the end of the evening, he asked Jesus to forgive his sins. Later he stood and asked the Black men in the group to forgive him for his unreasoned hate. Ever since, he'd been a regular member of the Bible study. Everett didn't say much, but when he spoke, everyone paid attention.

"Yeah, fasting would do Everett some good," Ray said. "He's a big boy and has been packing on a few extra pounds."

They finished the meal with a dessert of canned peaches.

"This would be way better in a cobbler," Ray said. "While you're fasting for Deshaun's marriage, can you ask the Lord to move on Dickie's heart to order up cobbler? Once or twice a year isn't enough."

"With vanilla ice cream on top?"

"Even better."

Joe dropped his tray off at the window for the dishwashers and then walked alone to Unit C. With the sun going down, the air had cooled. It was still too early for crickets to start calling to one another. Pockets of men gathered in the exercise yard prior to breaking up for the night. Major disturbances in the exercise yard were rare. And when they occurred, the culprits were promptly placed in lockdown. Joe took two deep breaths. The decision to fast, though troubling to his stomach, had brought peace to his soul.

———————

Most evenings, Ryan watched TV to relax. He liked all kinds of sports. Paige wasn't a sports fan but would sit in the same room and read while he watched a game. It was baseball season, and Ryan was a lifelong fan of the Baltimore Orioles. He'd never lived in the Baltimore area, but his father grew up in a small town on the Chesapeake Bay and passed down his allegiance to his son. Tonight the Orioles were playing the Boston Red Sox at Fenway Park. By the end of the first inning, Boston was ahead 2–0.

"Do you think our son will play baseball?" Ryan asked from the sleek brown leather chair he'd bought when he landed his first job.

Paige looked up from her novel. "Or she'll enjoy softball."

"Only if it's fast-pitch. That's a legitimate sport. In college a girl on the school team bet me and a few of my buddies that she could strike us out."

"Did she?"

"Mostly," he said.

"What about you?"

"No, I got a hit."

"Did you use a tennis racket?"

"No," Ryan chuckled, "but I pretended I was returning the serve from the guy who played number one on our team."

Ryan kept glancing at Paige out of the corner of his eye. She was sitting on the couch with her legs curled up beneath her as she read.

"Do you have any strange cravings yet?" he asked.

Paige laid her book on the couch. "Of course not, but when I do, what are you going to do about it?"

"Fulfill them."

"No matter what it is?"

"Absolutely."

"That's not a big risk. You know I'm too practical to ask for something outrageous."

"Yes, but from what I understand, pregnancy changes a woman."

"That's going to be obvious as the weeks go by and my abdomen starts to expand. But we don't have to think about that right now."

"It's hard for me to think about anything else," Ryan said.

Paige patted the spot on the couch beside her. "Turn off the game, and we can talk about any aspect of having a baby you want to."

"How about I mute the sound and only turn on the volume if the Orioles do something good?"

"No!"

"I was kidding," Ryan said, turning off the TV.

He joined Paige on the couch. She placed her right hand in his.

"Did you read up about pregnancy this afternoon?" he asked.

"Yes, because it was too hard to concentrate on my editing work."

"What did you learn?"

Ryan listened as Paige rattled off a lot of information.

"There's also an app that tracks fetal development for fathers," she said. "It uses smaller, more easily understood words and descriptions."

Ryan handed her his phone. "Download it for me."

Paige did so and returned the phone to him.

"Why didn't you say something sooner?" Ryan asked.

"Too many false hopes, I guess. And there's been so much upheaval in our lives. Is that okay?"

"Yeah, I'm glad you confirmed it."

Paige returned to her book. Ryan held his phone and read about the three layers of the unborn child. The inner layer would become the lungs, stomach, and bladder. The middle layer the heart, blood vessels, muscles, and bones. The outer layer the brain, nervous system, eyes, skin, and nails. It was amazing that so much development already existed in a creature the size of a poppy seed.

"It's still in a yolk thing," he said.

"That's where she receives her nourishment until the placenta forms, attaches, and my body takes over."

"It's so amazing," Ryan said, then hesitated before asking, "When are you going to tell your mother?"

"Not yet."

Later Ryan lay awake on his back after Paige fell asleep. His enthusiasm about becoming a father was tempered by the thought that now, more than ever, he needed a stable job. Long before Paige became pregnant, they'd agreed she would continue to work as much as possible, but pregnancy, childbirth, and everything associated with it meant uncertainty and change. On the personal level he had a nagging fear that in spite of what Paige said at dinner, he wouldn't be a good father.

His relationship with his own father had been rocky long before the tragedy in the boat. Ryan did well in school and sports, but no matter what he accomplished, it never seemed to be enough to win Sam Clark's approval. There were always follow-up questions about whether he could have made a higher grade or performed better on the playing field. Eventually, Ryan quit caring about his father's opinion. But his resentment came out in bitterness and negativity, which triggered increased tension between them. The three-day fishing trip was an effort by his father to mend fences, and the night before the accident he made a half-hearted effort to apologize. Instead of responding in a positive way, thirteen-year-old Ryan used the moment of vulnerability to unload the full weight of how he felt. His father shut down, and they went to bed. They barely spoke the next day in the boat. At the funeral Ryan tried to bury his feelings in the ground with the casket containing his father's body. But dead voices aren't easily silenced. Both times Ryan lost his job he could imagine his father's reaction and shuddered. Paige knew the facts but not the depth of Ryan's inner turmoil.

The following morning, Ryan rolled over and threw his arm in Paige's direction. It landed empty on the sheet. He opened his eyes. Paige wasn't there or in the master bath. Getting out of bed, he went into the hallway. The bathroom light was on. Ryan stood quietly, listening for the telltale sign of Paige throwing up. The bathroom door opened. She came out and jumped back.

"What are you doing sneaking up on me like that?" she demanded.

"Uh, I was listening to make sure you're okay. I thought you might be throwing up."

"No, I'm starving. Just because I'm pregnant doesn't mean I'm going to suffer from morning sickness. Twenty to thirty percent of women don't have any stomach issues."

Ryan wanted to smooth things over. Normally, Paige would eat a light breakfast of yogurt, fruit, or granola, but they occasionally enjoyed a bigger breakfast.

"Would you like to go out?" he offered. "We could try that place on Baxter Street. I've only been there for lunch, but I know they're open early."

Paige frowned. "Just because I'm hungry doesn't mean I want a pile of grits with a pat of butter melting in the middle."

"I suspect it's margarine."

"That's even worse."

"When I looked at a breakfast menu the other day, I saw they have smoked sausage."

Paige hesitated.

"But would it be any good?" she asked. "And can I get rye toast?"

"Don't know, but let's try it. I'm getting hungrier by the second talking about it."

Paige stepped forward and hugged him. "Okay, maybe it will be a good start to a new day."

CHAPTER 5

Paige's agreement to go to breakfast was a way to push forward in a positive way with Ryan. She brushed her hair and put it in a ponytail. She was wearing exercise clothes but stopped when she saw Ryan wrapping a silk tie around his neck.

"Are you going to court today?" she asked.

"Only if Tom asks me to fill in for him at the last minute. That's happened four times in the past three weeks. I know he has a case on the motion calendar, because I prepared the response. I'd better be ready."

"It makes sense to anticipate, but it's exciting when you rush home, burst through the door, and change into a suit in ninety seconds."

"Were you timing me?" Ryan asked as he adjusted his red tie.

"Only the last two times when my phone was near enough that I could grab it and start the stopwatch."

Paige picked up her phone and moved her finger across the screen.

"I was wrong," she said after a few moments. "You were in and out of the house in one hundred ten seconds the last time. Before that, you did it in eighty-eight seconds. That's impressive, but overall you're not improving, which is concerning."

Ryan chuckled. "I can't wait to use my stopwatch to time your contractions when you go into labor."

Paige stood in front of the cramped closet she shared with Ryan. "You're all dressed up. What should I wear?"

"Don't change a thing."

"I guess this is acceptable for a pregnant woman."

Paige gave Sandy a quick pat on the head as they left the house. The dog would lie in a soft bed set up for her in the kitchen and stare at the door. A stranger could barge in and Sandy wouldn't twitch or growl because Paige wasn't around. When Paige returned home, the cream-colored animal would turn herself inside out in an excited greeting and instantly go on guard duty.

The drive to the restaurant took only seven minutes. The local definition of a traffic jam was waiting two times for one of the town's twelve traffic lights to turn green before a driver could proceed.

"It was the lace-up shoes," Ryan said as they slowed to a stop at the intersection immediately before Baxter Street.

"What are you talking about?"

"Why it took longer for me to get dressed. The eighty-two-second day I was wearing loafers. The other time, I put on my nice black shoes."

"Okay, but it was eighty-eight seconds. And that's generous because it took a moment or two for me to grab my phone and start the stopwatch."

The redbrick restaurant occupied the corner of two busy streets. The parking lot was filling up with a mixture of nice cars and construction vehicles.

"Breakfast is popular," Paige said.

"Especially for husbands taking their newly pregnant wives out to eat before launching into a busy day."

A hostess with gray hair pulled back in a tight bun and wearing wire-framed glasses perched on the end of her nose stood behind a greeting station. Her name tag identified her as Beulah.

"Two for breakfast," Ryan said.

The woman scratched an "X" on a plastic seating chart.

"Number eight," she announced with satisfaction. "Follow me."

Grabbing two menus, she took off at a fast pace without pausing to see if Paige and Ryan were following. They caught up with her at a table for two beneath a plate glass window. The menus were already on the table.

"Bonnie will be taking care of you," the hostess said and returned rapidly to her post.

"I bet she doesn't have a problem getting in her daily quota of steps," Ryan said.

Moments later, a woman with "Bonnie" on her name tag appeared with two plastic glasses of water. Paige looked at the woman's face and immediately glanced across the room at the hostess station. Beulah was picking up another stack of menus.

"Are you twins?" Paige asked, pointing toward the entrance of the restaurant.

Tilting her head to the side, the waitress said, "She's eight minutes older. Coffee?"

"Black for me," Paige replied.

"Cream and one sugar," Ryan said.

"You doctor it yourself," the waitress said as she pointed to a small wire container that held individual servings of sugar and creamer. "Ready to order?"

Like her sister, Bonnie seemed intent on moving everyone through life as quickly as possible.

"I'll have two fried eggs, hash browns, crisp bacon, and biscuits," Ryan said.

"One egg scrambled, smoked sausage, and rye toast with real butter," Paige said.

The waitress scribbled on a pad with a stubby pencil. "Got it."

The waitstaff dropped off orders and picked up plates of food at a high counter at the rear of the restaurant. A nearby table of men in construction clothes burst out in loud laughter.

"Do you think our waitress has given that explanation about her relationship with her sister before?" Paige asked.

"No more than ten thousand times."

Bonnie returned with their coffee in industrial-grade white cups. Paige took a tentative sip.

"This is good," she said to Ryan. "Doctors say 150 to 200 milligrams of caffeinated coffee a day is okay. That means this cup and maybe another half would max me out."

"You've done a lot of research in less than twenty-four hours."

Paige raised her cup. "Only focusing on the things that are important."

Breakfast arrived. The scrambled egg looked fine, and the toast was nicely browned, but the sausage was formed into a patty, not a link. Paige eyed it skeptically. She cut a small sliver and put it in her mouth. An explosion of flavor hit several savory and smoky notes.

"Wow," she said. "This is really good."

Ryan reached out with his fork. Paige knocked it away. "Order your own. I'm already eating for two."

The concern that crept to the edge of Ryan's mind about the responsibilities of fatherhood before he fell asleep retreated in the sunlight of a new day. And being at breakfast with Paige was a delight. He loved her humor and feistiness and appreciated how diligently she'd stuck with him during the ups and downs of the years since he'd graduated from law school.

Glancing past her right shoulder, he saw a man several tables away with his back to them lean over to pick up a napkin that had fallen to the floor. When he did, the man's face came into view. It was Charlie Drummond. Ryan hoped there would be a chance to introduce the client to Paige before leaving the restaurant. When Charlie moved his head to the side, Ryan saw who he was eating with. It was Wyatt Belk, the principal attorney in the largest firm in town. The dapper lawyer in his early sixties with neatly cut gray hair was wearing his signature bow tie.

The fact that a wealthy man like Charlie was spending time with the top lawyer in town shouldn't be unusual, but Ryan knew that Tom would be alarmed. There weren't a lot of big clients in a pond the size of Cranfield, and having one on the line was important to a law firm's stability. The poaching of clients was a constant problem, and Tom's personality didn't always promote stability.

"Don't look," Ryan said to Paige. "But three tables behind you is Charlie Drummond, the client I met yesterday at the country club. He's having breakfast with Wyatt Belk."

"If you see our waitress, please ask her to bring another piece of smoked sausage," Paige replied. "If you do, I promise to share it with you."

"Okay." Ryan raised his hand as Bonnie came into view. "Tom would be upset if he knew Charlie was spending time with another lawyer."

"It's a small town. A lot of people know each other."

"True, but Wyatt may be making a play for Charlie's business."

Bonnie arrived. Paige told her how much she was enjoying the sausage.

"That's my favorite item on the breakfast menu," the waitress said in a slower pace of voice. "It's one hundred percent local. I know the farmer who raises and butchers the hogs. He smokes the meat the same way my great-grandpa did. This is a good batch. I ate some for breakfast."

"You mean it's not always the same?" Paige asked.

"There can be differences, but it's always good."

Bonnie left.

"Do you think I should introduce you to Charlie even though he's with Wyatt Belk?" Ryan asked.

"You told me I didn't have to dress up."

"It's not that . . ." Ryan stopped and continued to stare past Paige.

She took a drink of coffee. "Do you believe meeting me will help keep this guy as a client or drive him away?"

"Oh, I wouldn't put that kind of importance on it."

"Then it's up to you if you feel comfortable or not."

Ryan stood and made his way to the other table. Wyatt saw him first. They'd only met briefly in court at a calendar call. Ryan wasn't sure the lawyer would remember him. He extended his hand.

"Mr. Belk, I'm sorry to interrupt," he said. "I'm Ryan Clark."

"Of course," Wyatt said, shaking his hand. "Good morning."

"I wanted to invite you and Mr. Drummond to meet my wife before you leave. We're having breakfast together."

Drummond smiled. "I told you yesterday—it's Charlie, and I meant it."

"Yes, sir."

"Sure," Wyatt responded. "Charlie and I are almost finished with our business."

Ryan returned to the table with a long face.

"What happened?" Paige asked when he sat down.

"They're going to come over when they finish their 'business.' That sounds like trouble for Tom."

Paige pressed her lips together tightly. "I refuse to let this ruin our time together. This is part of our pregnancy celebration."

"Of course it is," Ryan replied, his attention back on Paige. "And we've discovered a place where you can get good smoked sausage along with rye toast and real butter."

The wake-up call time at the prison was 5:30 a.m. There was no sleeping once the shrill siren sounded throughout the prison. Joe usually climbed out of bed a few minutes early. Around 6:00 a.m. the men filed out of Unit C and headed toward the dining hall. Bible in hand, Joe left the unit and, without fanfare, turned right. The chapel was across the exercise yard on the lower level of the administration building. He approached the guard on duty. The rotund man was well known to Joe.

"Is it okay if I spend some time in the chapel?" he asked.

"You'll be late for breakfast," the guard replied.

Joe held up his Bible. "Got some other business to tend to."

The guard moved aside and pressed a button that opened a locked door. The entrance to the chapel was down a hallway on the left. Except for the small wooden pulpit at the front of the room, it could have been used for any purpose. The ceiling was the same height as in the adjacent offices and administrative areas. Rows of plastic folding chairs were set up. On a typical Sunday morning, most of the chairs would be occupied.

Joe sat down in the front row, bowed his head, and closed his eyes. He had fifty minutes before the time to leave and get ready for work detail. He opened the book of Psalms and began to read. He was looking for a Scripture that would serve as an anchor for his prayers on behalf of Deshaun and Kiesha. A verse from Psalm 143 jumped off the page: "Let the morning bring me word of your unfailing love, for I have put my trust in you. Show me the way I should go, for to you I entrust my life." He read the verse several times. Intercession didn't always follow a person's agenda. Before responding to any petitions about Deshaun's marriage, the Lord wanted to minister to Joe.

CHAPTER 6

Ryan arrived at the office before Tom. He greeted Nancy, who was on a phone call. She held up her finger, signaling Ryan to wait.

"I'll give the message to Mr. Clark, but that case was closed a long time ago," Nancy said.

The receptionist ended the call.

"That was odd," she said. "A woman was calling about a criminal case Tom handled years ago."

"What did she want?"

"To talk to him about reopening it. Anyway, have you talked to the boss this morning?"

"No."

"He wants you to defend the motion to dismiss in the Highland Park case."

"I came prepared for court."

"You're a quick learner. Check with Sue. She's organizing the file for you."

Ryan didn't move.

"I saw Charlie Drummond having breakfast with Wyatt Belk

this morning," he said. "Should Tom be concerned about Wyatt trying to steal Charlie as a client?"

Nancy tapped a brightly painted fingernail against the glass top of her desk. "That's always a possibility. But the Drummond and Belk families have known each other forever. I've always thought one reason why Charlie hired Tom was because he didn't want the Belks to know all his business. But they might be involved in some deals together. Both of them have their fingers in a lot of pies."

"I hadn't thought about that possibility." Ryan paused. "Should I mention seeing them at the restaurant to Tom?"

"That's up to you."

Ryan headed toward Sue Ferrell's desk. Sue, a slim, dark-haired woman in her early forties, had two teenage children. An experienced legal assistant who'd been trained at a law firm in Raleigh, she started working for Tom after her husband left her for another woman. Sue returned to Cranfield where she had family support to help with her kids.

"Here you go," she said briskly as soon as Ryan appeared in front of her desk. "You did the research on the motion, so everything should be ready to go."

"Who's on the bench this morning?"

"Judge Whitmire. He's out of Wilmington."

"Good or bad?"

"Don't know anything about him."

Ryan's office was larger than his workspace at either of his previous firms. Part of that was due to the architecture of the house. The former bedroom had three windows that allowed in plenty of natural light and provided a pleasant view of the green grass in the side yard. Tom had given Ryan a large desk that the senior partner bought years before from a local lawyer who was retiring. Ryan had placed several framed photos taken by Paige during her mountain-climbing expeditions on the walls. But his favorite picture was from their wedding. It was in a small frame on the corner of his desk where he could easily see it.

Ryan reviewed the brief he'd filed in opposition to the motion to dismiss. He felt confident about their position. Most likely, the defense lawyer from the big Charlotte law firm had filed the motion as a way to generate billable time and learn a little bit more about the case prior to discovery.

It was a sunny morning for the three-block walk to the court-house. Ryan was already familiar with every detail of the route. There were multiple cracks in the aging sidewalk and two places where the roots of nearby trees caused the concrete to bulge upward. Retail shops and businesses around the courthouse square included restaurants, a jewelry store, a women's dress shop, several account-ing firms, and four law offices, including the impressive building that was home to the Belk and Banner firm.

The courthouse was a two-story white brick building built in the 1950s. The clerk's office, deed room, and district attorney's office were on the first floor, with the main courtroom and judge's chambers on the second floor. The courtroom was large enough to seat several hundred people and served as the gathering place for community events and meetings. Ryan didn't stop by the clerk's office. The file would have been sent to the judge's chambers prior to the hearing. He climbed the broad stone staircase. A single deputy at the top of the stairs used a hand wand to check for weapons. The judge was on the bench listening to arguments by two other attorneys. Several lawyers were seated on benches with their clients. Ryan didn't see the out-of-town female lawyer on the other side of his case.

"How do you expect me to make a decision without that information before me?" Judge Whitmire asked one of the lawyers.

Ryan listened as the lawyer tried to explain why the evidence wasn't available.

"That's a problem I'm not going to solve for you," the judge barked. "Case dismissed."

Ryan swallowed. He wasn't aware of anything lacking in his case. He sensed movement beside him and glanced to the side. It was his opponent. She sat down several feet away and nodded. A few seconds later she was joined by Wyatt Belk, who leaned over and shook Ryan's hand.

"Twice in one morning," Wyatt said with a smile. "We've been associated on this case, and I'll be arguing the motion in front of Judge Whitmire."

Fifteen minutes later, Judge Whitmire frowned at Ryan and said, "Case dismissed. Refile your lawsuit where the parties agreed it must be heard."

The client had neglected to provide critically important information to Tom that any lawsuit between the parties to the contract had to be filed in Mecklenburg County. It wasn't a disaster like the situation involving California law but was still an embarrassment. Tom and Ryan could refile the lawsuit in Charlotte or find a lawyer there who would. Ryan slowly made his way from the courtroom and into the hallway.

"Ryan!" a voice called behind him.

He turned around. It was Wyatt Belk. Still stinging from what had happened in the courtroom, Ryan pressed his lips together and waited.

"No intent on my part to sandbag you," the older lawyer said. "I didn't know about the amended agreement until Ms. Pinson showed it to me this morning. And she didn't receive it from the client's home office until last night. Normally, I would have given the lawyer on the other side a courtesy call."

"Okay," Ryan replied, not sure whether to believe Belk or not.

Ryan prepared to move on.

"There's another matter I'd like to mention to you if you have a moment. Could you come to my office for a few minutes? It has to do with Charlie Drummond."

"And you want to talk to me?"

"Yes, and you can pass the information along to Tom."

"I don't think I should be the intermediary—"

"Charlie suggested I mention this to you. That was one of the things we discussed at breakfast when you showed up with your lovely wife. It almost seemed providential."

After Ryan dropped her off at home, Paige let Sandy out into the backyard. Instead of running off, the dog stayed close to Paige's side and nuzzled her several times. There had been times when Paige suspected the animal had companion dog qualities. If someone who was upset or going through a difficult time came to the house, Sandy would invariably go directly to the person and hop up beside them on the couch. Since Paige and Ryan had moved to Cranfield, Sandy was Paige's best friend.

Paige missed the relationships she'd forged with other women in the Raleigh-Durham area, but she wasn't the best at maintaining relationships after moving to a new location. Other than following longtime friends on social media, she rarely kept up with women she'd known growing up in Colorado. Everybody seemed busy.

"I'm okay," Paige said to her pet. "You're probably getting a whiff of smoked sausage. You'd like it, but it's not going to be on your menu."

Inside the house, Paige turned on her computer and dove into the project she wanted to complete prior to an 11:00 a.m. meeting. The topic was how Paige's company could manage a high volume of telephone calls more efficiently than their competitors. The paper was wordy and filled with passive voice sentences. Communicating efficiency had to be done using active verbs. This was going to take a total rewrite. Two and a half hours later, Paige had turned ten pages into six and sent the file to the supervisor assigned to the project. The original author of the paper, a young man who'd attended a well-known university in the Midwest, might never see the rewrite. Paige's bosses showed no interest in training people to write better. Company policy was to dump a problem into Paige's lap and let her fix it. Ryan said that meant job security.

Paige brushed her hair and changed into a nice blouse before the online conference. She set a bottle of water beside her monitor. Drinking plenty of water was a high priority. While she waited, Paige checked on a couple of Colorado friends. Two of the women had recently given birth. Paige smiled at the photos. Having a child would be a reason to engage with others. Faces began to populate her computer monitor. Paige scribbled dates on a notepad in an effort to pinpoint when she might have become pregnant.

———

As Joe left the administration building, a husky white man about his same height and age approached. The man's head was shaved, but he sported a thick, grayish-blond mustache. He stopped and stared at Joe.

"Are you Joe Moore?" he asked.

"Yes."

"I'm Ned Walker. Are you from Blanton County?"

"I grew up there."

"I lived in Vicksboro," the man replied.

Vicksboro was an unincorporated jumble of small houses, trailers, and two or three stores about ten miles from Cranfield.

"I used to buy gas from a convenience store there," Joe said. "It was the cheapest in the area. How did you know I was here?"

"A buddy named Rick Getz told me about you and suggested I look you up."

"I don't remember him."

"He's from Vicksboro and knew you were at LPCC. I got here last month after being sent off for stealing a car that someone loaned to me."

The denial of guilt, along with attorney incompetency, was a common refrain from inmates.

"Sorry about that," Joe said.

"Yeah, my lawyer messed up my case big-time," the man added, ticking off several reasons. "What are you in for?"

"Murder."

"Whew," the man said and pursed his lips. "I guess you got a lot more than thirty-six months."

"Yes."

"I'm working in there," Ned explained and pointed to the administration building. "On a good day, they have me doing HVAC work. On a bad day, I'm cleaning the bathrooms."

"I've done bathroom duty in the past," Joe replied. "Hope it's a good day and you're not scrubbing toilets."

"Yeah, I'll see you around."

Joe paused. "What unit are you in?"

"G."

"There's a Bible study there. I'm not sure how often they meet, but you can ask Lonnie Mixon about it."

"Big Black guy? About six-five?"

"Yeah."

Joe made his way to the toolshed, where a guard handed out what they would need for the day's work. Each man was responsible for items checked out in his name. The prisoner wasn't disciplined if the implement broke, but he would be punished if he didn't return what he checked out.

"Anything yet?" Deshaun asked as they stood in line. "You didn't show up for breakfast."

"I went to the chapel. I'll let you know."

Deshaun leaned in closer. "I did what you asked. I called my brother last night and told him not to do anything. He agreed to hold off for now."

"Good."

The guard handed Joe a pair of pruning shears and a hoe. Joe signed his initials on the checkout sheet. The clippers were the most lethal item the men were allowed to use. The blades were sharp and great for harvesting fruit and vegetables. They could also be used as a deadly weapon. Only three pairs of shears were available. Deshaun received a hoe and a mattock.

"The thoughts in my head are running wild," Deshaun said as they turned away. "It's all I can think about."

Joe adjusted his straw hat. "Do you remember the teaching Ray gave a few weeks ago about taking every thought captive to the obedience of Christ?"

"Not really."

"Ray!" Joe called out. "Will you go over with Deshaun what you told us about the Lord taking charge of our thoughts?"

Ray, who was walking ahead of them, turned around. He, too, had a pair of shears in one hand and a hoe in the other.

"If I can remember it myself."

"He'll remember," Joe said to Deshaun. "Why don't the two of you start out hoeing the green beans. I noticed a bunch of weeds coming up at the south end of the bean patch."

"Deshaun, you take the lead," Ray said. "I'll follow along behind."

The first thing Joe did upon reaching the garden was check on what looked ripe and ready to harvest. They would deliver more okra to the kitchen. It was amazing how fast the pods grew once the plants started to flower. They wouldn't cut any in the morning. Better to give them a few more hours on the vine for maximum freshness. Harvesttime would be early afternoon. Joe sighed. Unless he had an unforeseen breakthrough during the day for Deshaun, okra wouldn't be on his evening menu. After giving the men their initial work assignments, he took a long drink of water and headed to the west side of the garden to check on a new addition this year, strawberries.

The men had missed the early season for strawberries and decided to put in a later crop in raised rows. The plants were producing a lot of flowers. Joe leaned over and began to pluck the tiny white and yellow blossoms. It was necessary to remove the early blossoms so the plants would grow bigger and ultimately produce larger, juicier fruit. Joe glanced across the garden and saw Ray and Deshaun working close to each other. He made it to the end of one row and started another. From the perspective of the strawberry plants, Joe's act of blossom picking might have seemed cruel. But for the long term, pruning was beneficial.

Joe had been pruned a lot over the past twenty-six years since his arrest on a steamy July night outside a rural nightclub in Blanton County. He'd finished the final set with the band and taken a third snort of methamphetamine. Each rush or flash he experienced after ingesting the drug crested higher. A harmonica player and backup singer, Joe vaguely remembered the crowd going wild when he launched into a final harmonica riff. He pressed the instrument against the microphone and his eyes closed as he soared where the blues music transported him. He took a fourth snort backstage to celebrate, even though the inevitable crash would make it impossible for him to show up for his regular job at a local warehouse the following Monday.

The events that followed near the stage door exit were a swirl of anger and blood. Meth had made Joe verbally volatile in the past and, on occasion, physically violent. That night he allegedly punched a member of the band, who threw him out the back door of the club and slammed it shut. For Joe, trying to sort out what took place after that had proved as impossible as unraveling a chaotic dream. Eventually, he abandoned any effort to do so. At trial he lowered his head and looked down while listening to the district attorney's opening statement, in which he told the jury that Joe robbed and killed the Drummond girl and her boyfriend before passing out in his car. He forced himself to look up when a detective named Norris Broome identified the bloody knife on which a forensic expert found Joe's fingerprints and the blood of both victims. Joe didn't recognize the knife and claimed it wasn't his, but Tom Clark warned against taking the stand to say so. The prosecutor would have used the opportunity to emphasize Joe's illegal drug use, violent behavior that night, and the presence of his fingerprints on the murder weapon. A denial without an alternate theory of who owned the knife and used it to kill the young couple would be futile. Finally, the horrific photographs of the victims made Joe sick to his stomach. Anyone who did that to another human being deserved life in prison, or worse.

Even after receiving God's forgiveness at Central Prison, Joe occasionally struggled with shame and regret. There would be seasons when old images took a long vacation. But then a memory with an accusation draped around its neck would parade across his consciousness. Today was one of those days. As he leaned over to remove a flower from a strawberry, Joe saw an enlarged photograph of the bloody knife lying on the gravel parking lot of the roadhouse. The district attorney placed the photograph on the railing in front of the jury, along with a picture of the dead couple, while he gave his closing argument.

Joe shook his head and reminded his accuser of the power of Jesus's sacrifice for sin on the cross. Joe needed to do what he'd suggested to Deshaun—bring his thoughts into obedience to Christ. He plucked a flower. Beneath it, he saw a small, perfectly formed strawberry. It was deep red and ripe. He'd not seen another like it all morning. He carefully removed the berry and held it close to his nose. It gave off a fragrance unique to strawberries. Joe casually popped the strawberry into his mouth and bit down. The flavor of the warm, juicy fruit was better than the fragrance. Joe couldn't recall a more delicious strawberry. And then he remembered that he was fasting. Joe stopped chewing and prepared to spit the fruit onto the ground. But then he heard a stern voice in his spirit.

Don't do it.

Joe stopped. The strawberry remained in his mouth. He slowly finished chewing and swallowed. The fruit remained delicious. Joe wasn't sure what had happened. Picking and eating the strawberry seemed the most natural thing in the world, a beautiful gift given as an antidote to a toxic memory. He looked across the garden at Deshaun and Ray. They stood beside each other with their heads bowed. Puzzled, Joe leaned over and continued plucking flowers from the strawberry plants.

CHAPTER 7

Ryan and Wyatt entered Belk and Banner through a large wooden door with the name of the firm etched on a brass nameplate. Wyatt held open the door for him. The reception area was nicer than at any of the law firms where Ryan had previously worked in Raleigh or Durham. The wood floor was covered with an ornate oriental carpet. The wood and leather furniture glistened. Several vases of fresh flowers sat on side tables.

"This rug is magnificent," Ryan said.

"My grandfather bought it many years ago during a trip to Iran. He even had a chance to meet the shah."

"It looks like it should be in a museum."

"Don't you think beauty should be enjoyed by as many people as possible?" Wyatt smiled. "That's why we decided to bring it to the law firm, not keep it at home."

An attractive young receptionist nodded to Ryan as he followed the older lawyer. Wyatt's office was enormous. It held a desk with two chairs in front of it and had an area set up like a parlor. Another vase of fresh flowers rested in the middle of a table surrounded by a small couch and three chairs. Wyatt sat in one of the parlor chairs and motioned for Ryan to sit across from him.

"Do you hold depositions in here?" Ryan asked, glancing around. "This is a nice setup."

"Occasionally, but most of the time in one of the conference rooms." The older lawyer leaned forward. "I don't want to take up too much of your time. Charlie said you're aware of the tragic circumstances of his sister's death many years ago."

"A little bit. He told me that she and her boyfriend were murdered."

"Martin Brock was best friends with one of my sons. Marty was a fun-loving young man, but it wasn't very smart for him to take Cherie to the club that night. It could be on the rough side. We all do stupid things when we're young, but—"

Wyatt stopped and shook his head before continuing. "Anyway, a relative of the man who killed them is in town for a few days and recently contacted our office, asking to speak with Scott Nelson, my law partner who specializes in criminal cases. Have you met Scott?"

The two times Ryan had appeared in court to represent a client in a misdemeanor criminal case, the six-foot-tall lawyer with broad shoulders and a booming voice was present on behalf of at least half the defendants on the docket.

"No, I've just seen him in criminal court for calendar calls."

"Scott wasn't in, so the receptionist transferred the call to me. I spoke to the young woman and explained that we wouldn't consider getting involved. There's no legal conflict of interest, but given my son's close relationship with Marty, it's not something I'd be comfortable with the firm handling. I mentioned the conversation to Charlie this morning and asked what he thought about referring the woman to Tom since he originally represented the defendant."

Ryan jerked his head back in surprise. "That would be awkward. Tom does a lot of work for Charlie."

"Charlie didn't see it that way. He gave me permission to pass along Tom's contact information to her."

"Why would he agree to that?"

"As the person who originally represented Joe Moore, Tom is in the best position to answer the woman's questions. Also, it would be better for him to handle the situation than to have someone else digging around in old mud."

Ryan felt extremely uncomfortable. He didn't like what was going on. Wyatt shouldn't have told anyone, especially Charlie Drummond, about the phone call, and the two of them had no business manipulating who the woman should talk to.

"Did she tell you why she wants to meet with a lawyer after so much time has passed?" he asked.

"No, but I assume it would be some type of habeas corpus action. I wanted to give you a heads-up in case she reaches out to you."

Ryan remembered the call Nancy received earlier that morning. "What's the woman's name?"

"Shana Parks. She's the murderer's niece and lives in Richmond. She was a child at the time of the trial."

———

Ryan left the ornate office. It was easy to understand why Tom or any other lawyer in town would be apprehensive about competing with Belk and Banner for business.

"Is Tom in?" he asked Nancy.

"No, he drove from home to a client meeting."

Ryan paused. "Was Shana Parks the name of the woman who called earlier this morning about an old criminal case?"

"Yes, it was," Nancy replied, raising her eyebrows.

"Wyatt Belk mentioned her to me. She's a relative of the man who killed Charlie Drummond's sister. She called Wyatt's firm seeking representation for the murderer."

"Well, I hope she hires Belk and Banner," Nancy replied curtly.

"Wyatt wants to pass her off to Tom."

"What?!" Nancy exploded.

"That was my reaction, only a bit more low-key," Ryan replied.

"The killer was a man named Joe Moore," Nancy said, shaking her head sadly. "He murdered Cherie Drummond and her boyfriend. It was a horrible crime. It took me a long time to accept that Cherie was really gone."

"You knew her?"

"I worked at the high school when she was a student. Cherie volunteered in the office during study hall her junior year, and I got to know her. She was full of life, one of the most popular girls in her class. Even after she graduated, she always made a point of taking time to chat when we ran into each other."

"What about her boyfriend?"

"He was good-looking, and they ran in the same social circles, but I've always thought he was a bad influence. There's no way he should have taken her to a place like that roadhouse on the east side of town."

"That's what Wyatt said. What did people think about Tom representing the defendant?"

"There were plenty of folks who didn't believe the killer deserved anything except the death penalty," Nancy said. "But I guess someone had to represent him."

Ryan thought for a moment. "I didn't feel comfortable about anything Wyatt told me, which tells me we should steer clear of this situation."

"I agree one hundred percent," Nancy said, nodding. "And I hope Joe Moore is locked up in a dark cell where he has to think every day about what he did."

———————

Paige made it through the online meeting without being asked a question. Even though she'd eaten a big breakfast, she was hungry. She opened the refrigerator door and stared at the contents. The front doorbell chimed. Sandy began to bark.

"I wish you'd learn that's not necessary," Paige said to the dog as she made her way to the door.

Sandy continued to woof. Two women about Paige's age were standing on the front step. Through the sidelight, Paige could see they were wearing nice outfits. Paige still had on a fancy top for the meeting, along with exercise shorts and flip-flops. There was no time to change. She cracked the door open.

"Are you Paige Ryan?" asked the taller of the two women, a slender blonde.

"Yes."

The shorter of the two women spoke. She had dark, curly hair. "I'm Vicki Lennox, and this is Candy Bynam. Madge Norton told us how much she enjoyed meeting you yesterday. We wanted to add our welcome and brought by a salad and a homemade cheesecake."

Candy was holding a salad bowl covered with clear wrap. Vicki had a cheesecake with blueberries on top. Sandy continued to bark.

"Come in," Paige said, stepping aside.

Candy hesitated. "The dog won't bite, will he?"

"No, she's just letting me know that you're here. She'll switch to welcoming mode in a second."

"I have a golden retriever named Beauty," Vicki said, confidently stepping forward. "She's way more obedient than my kids."

Vicki leaned over and patted Sandy on the head. Candy kept her distance. Paige led the way into the kitchen. She took the salad from Candy and placed it on the counter. The bowl contained lettuce, fruit, veggies, and different kinds of cheese.

"This looks delicious," Paige said.

"There's homemade dressing," Candy said. "It's a champagne vinaigrette."

"And this cheesecake is my grandma's recipe," Vicki added.

"I love cheesecake," Paige said. "And this salad is perfect. I just finished a long online meeting and was wondering what to eat for lunch."

"Madge said you're a writer," Candy said. "That sounds so exciting. What kind of writing do you do?"

Paige was used to the question and the deflated reaction when she explained her role. "I'm more editor than writer. I work for a big company. It's technical stuff, not creative."

"I'm still impressed," Candy replied. "I froze up every time I had to write a paper in school. I wasn't sure how to start, what to say, or how to finish."

"But you're a great storyteller," Vicki said. "You had me on the edge of my seat when you told us about your rafting trip in Colorado. I knew you survived because you were standing there in front of us, but I had no idea how you and Chris made it to shore after your raft flipped over."

"We're both good swimmers. But I think an angel rescued us."

"I'm from Colorado," Paige said. "Where were you rafting?"

"A place called Gore Canyon. With a name like that, we should have known better."

"You rafted Gore Canyon?" Paige asked in surprise. "That's a very challenging stretch of water."

"Oh, Candy and Chris are adrenaline junkies," Vicki said.

"Not so much anymore," Candy replied. "Having kids changed that."

Vicki turned to Paige. "Listen, we don't want to impose on your time. Enjoy the salad and cheesecake. And we'd love for you and your husband to visit our church. It's called Grace Fellowship. You've probably seen the building."

Growing up, Paige had attended church on rare occasions with friends. Ryan occasionally went to church as a child but totally stopped after his father's death. As a couple, they used Sunday as a day for recreation.

"It's not far from Cornelia's Kitchen," Candy continued. "Everyone knows where that is."

"Ryan and I ate breakfast there this morning," Paige said.

"Then you were almost there," Vicki said. "Bruce and I have three children. Candy has four."

Paige gave the slender blonde a startled look.

"Two of mine are stepchildren," Candy explained. "Chris's first wife passed away, and we have two of our own."

"You'd love our Sunday school group, and everyone would be excited to meet you," Vicki continued. "The class meets at nine thirty on Sunday morning. Our phone numbers and emails are on a slip of paper taped to the bottom of the salad bowl. I live a few streets over."

Candy touched Vicki on the arm. "We should go now."

"Thanks again," Paige said.

Vicki gave Sandy a final pat on the head.

"Nice to meet both of you," she said to Paige. "My five-year-old daughter would love your dog."

Paige accompanied the women to the door. After a pair of surprise visits in two days, she'd made a good start on making new friends in Cranfield.

———————

Joe and the other men gathered for their lunch break. Unfiltered by clouds, the sun had climbed into the sky. It was hot and felt nice to sit on the ground and have long drinks of cool water. Joe stretched his legs out in front of him. Deshaun, a sandwich in his hand, came over and sat beside him. Joe had enjoyed the solitary strawberry. A bologna sandwich on white bread didn't tempt him.

"How was your morning?" Joe asked Deshaun.

"That's what I wanted to talk to you about," the young man said. "Something has changed."

"What do you mean?"

Deshaun touched his chest. "When Ray and I prayed together, a heaviness, a darkness, left me. I didn't even know it was there until it was gone. Does that make any sense?"

"Yes."

"And now there's a peace in my heart," Deshaun continued. "It stayed with me the rest of the morning, even when I thought about Kiesha."

Joe looked across at Ray, who was watching them with a big smile on his face.

"Did you tell Ray about this?" Joe asked.

"Yeah, and there's a verse he had me memorize." Deshaun thought for a moment. "'Taste and see that the LORD is good.' It's in the book of Psalms."

"Psalm 34:8," Joe replied. "The goodness of the Lord has gotten inside you as if you'd eaten a delicious strawberry."

"Yeah," Deshaun agreed, then quickly continued, "Here's what I'm going to do. I'm going to tell Kiesha what happened. She'll probably doubt it's real, but I'm going to tell her anyway. She's been going to church. That's where she met the guy she's running around with. If I can find out the name of the preacher, maybe someone can contact him and ask him to set them straight. My aunt knows a bunch of pastors. That would be better than what my brother and cousin had in mind."

"I like that idea."

Deshaun grew quiet. He'd not touched his sandwich.

"Would you still pray?" he asked. "I really believe it will do some good."

His faith strong, Joe bowed his head and closed his eyes.

CHAPTER 8

Ryan sat in Tom's office and told him about the conversation with Wyatt Belk and what he'd seen at the restaurant early that morning. Tom listened without interrupting.

"Wyatt is always trying to get the Drummond business," Tom said when Ryan finished. "Charlie and I have talked about it several times over the years. He reassures me that he's satisfied with my representation and likes the fact that his work is always at the top of my pile."

"What about talking to Joe Moore's niece?"

"Do you know her name or anything about her?"

"Shana Parks. She lives in Richmond. That's all, except she was a child when Moore committed the murders."

"Alleged murders," Tom corrected.

"You think Moore was innocent?" Ryan asked in surprise.

"No, but it's a good habit to refer to a client charged with a crime in that way. Let's find out what we can about Ms. Parks. Did Wyatt say how long she's going to be in town?"

"I think he said a few days."

Tom turned to his computer keyboard and began typing. The law firm subscribed to a proprietary service that provided detailed background information about any person whose name was entered. After several minutes, Tom nodded. "Her mother is Joe Moore's older sister. Barbara Hawthorn. I remember her. She and Joe's mother were present for every hearing and the entire trial. They sat directly behind Joe and kept passing him notes."

"Have you heard from either of them since then?"

"The sister drove to Raleigh when we argued the appeal before the Supreme Court of North Carolina. After that didn't go our way, I didn't see her or the mother again but heard they moved away."

Tom leaned back in his chair. "I'm interested," he said.

"You're thinking about talking to this woman?" Ryan asked in surprise. "Don't you think that's risky? We don't handle that type of case, and things could get crossways with Charlie down the road."

"I like you challenging me," Tom replied with a grin. "Keep doing that."

"I wasn't trying to be disrespectful—" Ryan started.

"Then pay attention to what I just told you," Tom cut in. "You're young and smart enough to do the legal research needed to figure out if we can help. Leave Charlie to me. I'm going to call him now."

Tom put his phone on speaker and punched in the number.

"Do you want me to leave?" Ryan asked.

"No, I want you to listen. Charlie may have a question for you."

Ryan shifted in his chair. The phone rang several times. Ryan hoped the call would go to voicemail so he wouldn't be asked anything.

"Tom," Charlie said. "How are you doing?"

"Good, good. Do you want to shoot skeet the last Saturday of the month? Percy Burns has invited a group to his place on the river. Afterward there will be a cookout. It's also a fundraiser to support the local group home for delinquent boys."

"I already heard about it. Put my name on the list, along with my checkbook."

"Great. Listen, Wyatt Belk talked with my associate about a call that came into his office from one of Joe Moore's relatives. It seems Moore's family wants to talk to a local lawyer about trying to help him."

"Yeah, I suggested to Wyatt they should speak with you since you represented him."

Tom looked at Ryan and raised his eyebrows before saying, "I'm not sure I'm interested, especially given my loyalty to you as a current client."

"And I appreciate that. But don't let that keep you from finding out what's going on."

"I suspect it has to do with a request for a copy of his file or a complaint about how he's being treated. Some of these prisons are like hotels, but others can be rough."

While Tom talked, Ryan grabbed a legal pad from the front of his boss's desk and hurriedly scribbled, "You wouldn't be able to tell him anything about what they want." Tom glanced at the sheet and nodded.

Charlie spoke: "I think it would be better for someone local to respond than an outside agitator from Charlotte or Raleigh."

"Gotcha," Tom replied. "I'll give it some thought."

"I trust you to do the right thing. And don't forget to put me down for the skeet shoot."

"Will do."

The call ended.

"Tom, the way Wyatt and Charlie are approaching this makes me nervous," Ryan said. "Ethically, if you give someone advice—"

"What do the ethical rules say?"

75

Ryan wasn't exactly sure.

Without picking up a book or turning toward his computer monitor, Tom recited, "'A lawyer's advice has to be independent and free from inappropriate outside influence and cannot entail disclosure of confidential communication to a third party, which includes information shared while an attorney considers whether or not to represent a client.' That means Charlie and Wyatt can't be in the loop."

"Yes," Ryan said with relief.

"And I think it would be okay for me to hear what the niece has to say."

Ryan frowned.

"Within the rules," Tom continued. "Ms. Parks has come a long way and deserves a few minutes of our time."

"Okay," Ryan replied reluctantly. "Do you want me to call her?"

"No, I'll do it. Hopefully, she can come in today. Bring down the file from the attic. It's in some banker's boxes. Of course we can't release the records to anyone, including his niece, without the client's permission."

Paige ate a bowl of salad and a large piece of cheesecake. The blueberries were both tart and sweet. Afterward, because there were no more meetings on her calendar, she decided to take Sandy for a walk. As soon as Paige opened the drawer of the small cabinet in the foyer where she kept the leash, Sandy became excited. The dog trembled as Paige attached the leash. As soon as the leash was secure, Sandy bounded toward the front door.

"Not too fast," Paige said. "We're not going to jog. It's warm outside."

Paige had changed into a T-shirt that matched her shorts. Her flip-flops were sturdy and comfortable. When they reached the sidewalk, the dog turned right.

"We could go left instead," Paige said.

Sandy ignored her and trotted rapidly forward.

"But that wouldn't take us to the park."

They walked five blocks along Hamilton Street. The houses close to Ryan and Paige were mostly cottages built on small lots in the 1970s and '80s. Once they reached Washington Avenue, the houses occupied spacious lots and were much larger. This was the part of town where people with old money lived. Paige admired the flowers and landscaping. She'd taken a landscape design class as an elective in college.

There was no question about her favorite house. It was a Victorian residence with a long porch across the front and trellises covered with yellow climbing roses. The house was painted light blue, which provided a postcard backdrop for the azalea bushes and flowers. Two massive oak trees with first limbs at least twenty-five feet in the air framed the house instead of blocking the view of it. The land was surrounded by a low wrought-iron fence in a fleur-de-lis pattern. Paige reeled in Sandy and walked slowly. When she reached the driveway at the far end of the property, she saw a small brass sign that read "Drummond House, circa 1927." This must be where the man she'd met at breakfast lived. Parked in front of the detached two-car garage was a large white Mercedes sedan. An attractive woman with brunette hair came out of the house and onto the porch to water some hanging baskets. She saw Paige, smiled, and waved. Paige waved back.

"I like your dog!" the woman called out.

"Thanks!" Paige replied.

"What kind?"

"She's a Soft-Coated Wheaten Terrier."

The woman returned to the house. When she did, Paige caught a glimpse of fluffy white fur. It was a dog, not a cat, but Paige couldn't discern the breed.

At the end of Washington Avenue, Paige reached a large municipal playground that was more modern than expected for a small town like Cranfield. A sign beside the entrance gate announced the local benefactors who contributed to the project. Once again, the Drummond name appeared. It was a sunny day, and the playground was packed with mothers looking for a place where their children could burn off energy. Dogs weren't allowed inside the play area. Paige usually continued to a nearby grassy area where Sandy could sniff around and interact with other dogs. Afterward, they might stop at the playground to watch for a few minutes.

Today Paige didn't go to the grassy area but found a seat on a bench outside the fence so she could sit and watch the children. This was the first time she'd visited the playground since finding out she was pregnant, and she began imagining what it would be like to bring her little girl or boy to climb or slide or ride. The surface of the play yard was a spongy material that softened the impact of any falls. A toddler boy with blond, almost white, hair was pulling himself up on a piece of equipment. Based on baby pictures of Paige and Ryan, there was a good chance their child would start out with a similar hair color. The little fellow lost his grip and plopped down on his diaper. He looked over at his mother but didn't fuss. Instead, he worked to pull himself up again. Paige remained on the bench and watched the children for a long time. She also paid attention to different types of strollers and diaper bags and made notes in her phone. When she finally checked her email, she found several messages from work.

"I need to stop daydreaming so we can go home," she said to Sandy. "There's a lot to be done before you and I bring a baby to this playground."

———

Ryan climbed the steep stairs to the attic. The large and dusty space was filled with junk. Three bare bulbs provided light. There were stacks of books no longer relevant in the age of computer research, used furniture, discarded office equipment, five or six desktop computers, and at least fifty large cardboard boxes with case names scribbled on them in black marker. The boxes were in three different areas. Looking for *State v. Moore*, Ryan started searching. The sleeves of his white shirt became streaked with light brown dust. He sneezed violently and rubbed his itchy eyes. At last, when he repositioned a group of boxes in the third section, he found what he was looking for. Sitting next to each other were two dingy boxes with "Moore" written on the lids. He looked inside to confirm they contained documents related to a criminal case. Directly on top of a jumbled pile of papers was a folder marked "Sentencing Hearing." Ryan flipped it open and saw a document Tom had filed with the court, asking the judge not to impose a double life sentence for the murder convictions. The margins of the papers were slightly yellowed with age.

Hauling the boxes downstairs to his office, Ryan went to the kitchen and used a wet paper towel to wipe off the dust. The phone on Ryan's desk buzzed. He pressed the receive button. Nancy's voice came over the speaker.

"Shana Parks is here," she said in a clipped tone.

"Where's Tom?"

"Out of the office until four this afternoon at a deposition."

"I thought he was going to be here," Ryan replied irritably.

"Do you want me to reschedule an appointment for tomorrow?"

Ryan hesitated. He knew Tom would want him to find out what Ms. Parks was interested in talking about.

"No, I'll meet with her. Put her in the conference room and offer her coffee or water."

Ryan went to the bathroom and tried to remove as much evidence of his time in the attic as he could from his face, neck, and shirt. Straightening his tie, he grabbed his tablet and walked down the hall to the conference room. Seated across the table from the door was an attractive, well-dressed woman in her thirties. Ryan introduced himself.

"I'm Shana Parks," the woman replied with a puzzled look on her face. "Are you Mr. Clark? You can't be the lawyer who represented my uncle Joe."

"That was my boss, Tom Clark. He's out of the office, but we discussed the case earlier today."

Ryan sat down at the table.

"I know it's not typical for a person to drop in without an appointment, but I'm only in town today and tomorrow before I have to return home," Ms. Parks said.

"I located your uncle's file. It's in a couple of large boxes, but we can't release anything to you without his permission."

"I'm not here to pick up his records. At least not yet. Our family wants to hire someone to determine what can be done to get Uncle Joe out of prison."

"That would require a discussion with Mr. Clark."

"Understood. Would you like to talk now, or should I wait to discuss with him?"

Ryan powered up his tablet. "Go ahead," he said. "I'll fill him in."

"My mother, Barbara, is Joe's older sister. She and my father moved away from Blanton County shortly after the trial. I only met Uncle Joe a few times when I was a little girl and barely remember him. After he was arrested and convicted, my grandmother didn't want to stay in Cranfield and eventually moved to Richmond to be closer to my mother. My grandmother never believed my uncle killed anyone. Before she died last year, she made my mother promise to try to get him out of prison."

"Why did she believe he wasn't guilty of the crime?"

"It was completely out of character for him. He didn't graduate from college like my mother or always choose the best friends, but he got along well with people. He wasn't a violent person."

"I don't know the circumstances of the crime, but a jury found him guilty."

"That was before police in places like Cranfield had tools like DNA evidence to independently corroborate a person's connection to a crime."

"You're not a lawyer, are you?" Ryan asked.

"No, I'm a chemist who works for an agricultural products manufacturing company, but I did some research to find out what needs to be done. According to my mother, there was no DNA analysis of the blood or skin samples on the knife supposedly used in the killings. She sat through the trial."

"Like I said, I'm unfamiliar with the evidence, but my boss should be in the office later today. Will you be available to come back late this afternoon?"

"Yes. Tomorrow I'm driving to the prison. It would be good to tell my uncle we have an attorney willing to help."

"He doesn't know you're here?"

"My mother sent him a letter telling him about my grandmother's request. He responded that he didn't want us to waste our time and money. I hope to change his mind. It's very important for my mother to honor my grandmother's wishes. My father patented and sold an industrial process for use in the auto industry a few years ago. My parents can afford to hire an attorney."

The mention of ability to pay a fee convinced Ryan that Tom would be interested.

"Are you sure your uncle would want the lawyer who represented him at trial to help? He might not have been satisfied with the representation."

"That's one reason why I thought it might be better to hire Mr. Belk's firm, but when I called my mother a few minutes ago and told her I was coming here, she said Uncle Joe liked Mr. Clark and appreciated what he tried to do for him. But you're right—I'd want to ask my uncle. The passage of time can change things."

Ryan tapped the bottom edge of the tablet without hitting one of the keys. "Again, I'd need your uncle's consent before sharing any information with you or your parents."

"Of course."

"What's your phone number so I can text or call when Tom is available to meet?" Ryan asked.

He entered the information and escorted Ms. Parks to the reception area. He remained standing by Nancy's desk. Sue joined them.

"What was that about?" Sue asked.

Ryan told her.

"You know what I think," Nancy said bluntly. "And I'm not going to repeat it."

"It's a good thing the family has money," Sue said in a calmer tone of voice. "If the family is interested in post-conviction relief, the law firm I worked for in Raleigh handles that sort of thing. It can be more detective work than law-related."

"Maybe we can refer this woman to your old firm."

Nancy brightened up. "That's a great idea."

"Those types of cases are expensive," Sue continued. "It can take a lot of time to develop the evidence and produce a legal theory to argue. I wish I had access to the pleading and brief bank at my old firm."

"I definitely think we should refer her to them," Ryan said. "This is way over my head."

CHAPTER 9

Joe didn't eat lunch, but when he found another ripe strawberry in the middle of the afternoon, he didn't hesitate to eat it. He was also looking forward to another supper that included fresh fried okra. His stomach rumbled in anticipation. The fast for Deshaun's marriage was the shortest on record. Across the garden, Joe saw the young prisoner hoeing beans with a smile on his face.

A horn sounded from the guard tower nearest them, and the men assembled beneath the pine trees for the short walk back to the prison compound. Joe retrieved the pruning shears from the man who'd been using them. The men had filled several five-gallon plastic buckets with freshly cut okra.

"I know I shouldn't say this to you, but I'm looking forward to another plate of okra," Ray said to Joe as they started moving away from the garden.

"Me too."

"I thought you were fasting for Deshaun," Ray said in surprise.

"I did, but it's over."

Ray gave him a puzzled look. "I'm not going to criticize you, but that was quick. Deshaun and I had a good talk, but we don't know anything has changed between him and Kiesha."

"It's not always about seeing results. It's all about faith."

"What do you mean?"

Joe touched his chest. "Believing in here before circumstances or people change."

While they walked, Joe told Ray about eating the strawberries and his conversation with Deshaun. "And when he came over and said you'd asked him to memorize Psalm 34:8, I realized both Deshaun and I had tasted the goodness of God."

Ray shook his head from side to side. "Joe, sometimes you're so deep I have no idea what you're talking about."

They reached the kitchen and delivered the okra. A guard called out to Joe: "Moore! Over here!"

Joe walked across the exercise yard. It was the same guard who'd let him into the chapel early that morning. For a prisoner to be singled out usually wasn't a good sign. Prison officials didn't hand out achievement certificates to inmates.

"I didn't do anything in the chapel this morning except pray," Joe said in his defense.

"It's not about that. The warden's received a request from one of your relatives who wants to come tomorrow for a visit. The officer in charge needs to know if you want to see them."

"Who's the visitor?" Joe asked.

The man glanced at a slip of paper in his hand. "Shana Parks. Says she's your niece."

Joe remembered Shana as a vivacious, talkative girl of four or five with her hair in braids. He'd not seen a photograph of her as an adult and doubted that he'd recognize her. Before her family moved to Richmond, his sister visited Joe regularly. When she did, she always brought their mother, which was painful for Joe. Instead of his mother's presence making him feel better, the deep sadness in her eyes haunted him for weeks after she left. As her health declined due to uncontrolled diabetes, Myra Moore's visits slowed to a trickle, then finally stopped altogether. Barbara would send Joe a card on his birthday and make a deposit to his prison expense account at Christmas. Joe always sent Barbara a note on her birthday, but he'd not had a visitor in almost three years. In Joe's mind, the men he was confined with every day had become his family.

When their mother died the previous year, Barbara sent details about the funeral arrangements and a copy of the obituary. Joe sat on the edge of his bunk and read the obituary before putting it on top of a stack of letters his mother had sent him. He grieved, but the tank of sorrow over his loss of family had drained away years before. When his sister later wrote and mentioned their mother's desire to see Joe exonerated and released from prison, he'd immediately replied that wasn't worth pursuing. God's mercies were new every morning, but life's disappointments could be just as regular and didn't need extra opportunities.

Joe entered the warden's office. Elle Evert, the woman on duty, was a friendly person about Joe's age who called him "Mr. Moore." She'd been working at the prison for about six months.

"Good afternoon, Mr. Moore," said the blue-eyed woman with hair dyed a light brown.

"It has been," Joe replied. "We're about to harvest strawberries."

"I wasn't sure planting them this late in the year was going to work," Elle replied. "Bring me some, and I'll bring you back a piece of strawberry shortcake. Did you get the message about your niece coming for a visit?"

"Yes. She was a little girl when I was locked up. Did she say whether something has happened to my sister?"

"No."

Joe scratched his head. "Well, I guess it's okay if she wants to come."

"Tomorrow is the midweek family schedule, and visits only last an hour after you come in from work detail."

"Okay. Thanks."

"Don't forget about the strawberries."

Leaving the administration building, Joe continued to Unit C. When he stepped out of the shower with a towel wrapped around his waist, Deshaun quickly approached him with a piece of paper in his hand.

"You'll never believe this!" he said. "It's a letter from Kiesha that she sent before we started praying. Read it."

"I'm not sure I should read your personal—"

"I'm only giving you the first page."

Joe took the sheet from Deshaun. It was handwritten in a style that slanted to the left. The letters were packed close together.

"Is she left-handed?" he asked.

"Yes."

Joe's eyes got bigger as he read. Kiesha had decided that she didn't want a divorce and was committed to making the marriage work even though Deshaun was in prison. She'd been talking to a cousin named Lola whose husband was also incarcerated. Lola told her to read some Bible verses, which Kiesha took seriously. She even quoted a few of them in the letter.

"That's great news," Joe said, returning the sheet to Deshaun. "There's hope."

"Looks like we didn't have to pray."

"I don't know about that. Time doesn't exist the same way for the Lord. Even though he knew about our prayers before we prayed, that doesn't mean we weren't supposed to pray them."

"I'm just glad to hear from her. She's going to come for a visit tomorrow and bring the boys."

"Maybe I'll see them. I'm expecting a visitor too."

As soon as Tom returned to the office, Ryan told him about the meeting with Shana Parks. His boss perked up when he learned Moore's family was able to afford an attorney.

"Where's the file?" Tom asked. "Were you able to locate it in the attic?"

"Yes."

"Call Ms. Parks and ask her to come back around five o'clock. That will give me time to get up to speed."

Later Nancy had a frown on her face when Ryan came to the reception area to escort Shana Parks to the conference room. Tom greeted her graciously and demonstrated remarkable memory of the details of the case. He'd clearly done his homework. Ryan listened. When Tom finished, Ms. Parks was silent for a few moments.

"Given what you already know about the case, I can see how it makes sense to consider hiring your firm," she said. "Would there be a retainer?"

"Yes. Fifty thousand dollars that we'll bill against at an hourly rate, with a monthly accounting for you that includes a detailed summary of everything we've done."

"That's reasonable and less than what our attorney in Richmond said might be required."

"Excellent," Tom said. "Overhead is cheaper in this part of the world. Ryan, ask Sue to prepare an attorney-client contract to be signed by both Ms. Parks and Mr. Moore. We'll also need a representation letter that sets the amount of the deposit."

Ryan went to Sue's desk and told her what he needed.

"Do you think fifty thousand dollars is too much for a retainer?" Ryan asked. "Ms. Parks didn't seem to have a problem with it."

"That's on the low end. These can be expensive cases. Attorney fees can run to six figures. Few people associated with inmates have those kinds of resources."

"It seems Ms. Parks does. And she understands that she'll be billed monthly. She's going to meet with her uncle at the prison tomorrow."

"Give me ten minutes."

Ryan went into his office and checked his phone. There were no messages. He was responding to an email when Sue appeared in the doorway.

"Here you go," she said. "And I'll pass along the information for the lawyer I worked for in Raleigh who knows about these types of cases. He's not going to open up his brief bank to you, but I believe he's committed enough to the profession to share a few nuggets of wisdom with a young lawyer."

"I'll have to do some research before trying to ask him questions," Ryan responded.

He took the representation paperwork into the conference room and handed a copy to Tom and to Ms. Parks.

"This is standard language," Tom said to the young woman. "But take a minute to review it in case you have any questions."

Tom turned to Ryan. "What's on your calendar tomorrow?"

"I have an appointment in the morning at nine thirty. After that, I'm clear."

"Good. Ms. Parks would like you to be there when she meets with her uncle. The drive from here is only an hour and a half. She's leaving directly from the prison to drive home."

Ryan was glad Ms. Parks was reading the proposed contract of representation so she didn't see the expression on his face. He started to protest but clamped his mouth shut. There was nothing he could say that wouldn't threaten the potential client's confidence in the firm.

"I'm not able to go because of a previous commitment that can't be rescheduled," Tom continued to the new client, "but your uncle Joe has already spent a lot of time with me, and it will be good for him to make a connection with the other member of the team who's going to represent him."

"When was the last time you saw him?" Ryan asked Tom.

"During the appeal of the original conviction. I was able to keep him at the local jail while that was pending. The State allows it so the lawyer can easily communicate with the client about the issues in the case."

Ryan wondered how many times Tom had visited the Blanton County Jail to consult with Joe Moore about legal issues.

"I only have one question," Ms. Parks said when she finished. "Could you try to overturn my uncle's conviction without his consent?"

Tom spoke: "A lawyer can't completely ignore a client's wishes, but there's no prohibition against someone like yourself hiring an attorney to initiate post-conviction relief. Tell Joe why your family wants to honor his mother's final request, and Ryan can explain the legal process. Hopefully, that will convince him to let those who want to help him do so."

Ms. Parks nodded. "Okay. I'll let my mother know next steps and where to wire the money."

"What time do you plan on leaving Cranfield?" Ryan asked.

"Shortly after three. Visiting hours are from five to six."

"Okay."

Tom stood. "Ryan, wait for me in my office while I show Ms. Parks out."

The boxes from the attic were in Ryan's office. Several of the files were on the floor beside them.

"Good job convincing Ms. Parks to come back and see me this afternoon," Tom said when he entered the room. "She was going to hire someone while she was in town, and I'd rather it be us. But it's going to take some time to get Nancy on board. She ambushed me as soon as the client left."

"Yeah, I'm not surprised."

Tom clapped his hands together. "Did you take a post-conviction relief class in law school?"

"No."

Ryan mentioned Sue's offer to connect him with one of her former bosses.

"Excellent," Tom said, clearly pleased. "Schedule a phone call as soon as possible so you can get your head around what we need to file on behalf of Joe."

Ryan paused for a moment. "Ms. Parks wants us to get her uncle out of prison. Charlie Drummond isn't going to like that idea."

"Don't worry about Charlie."

"How can you be so confident?"

"While you were getting the paperwork together, I slipped out of the conference room and called Charlie to run it by him."

"That's unethical!" Ryan exploded.

"Calm down," Tom replied. "I didn't give Charlie any details or ask his permission, only that we'd be pursuing post-conviction relief. That will come out as a public record eventually if we file something in court."

"It's still not right," Ryan fumed.

"Charlie reminded me of our conversation when he first hired me to represent him. We discussed the Moore case then, and he told me it was in the past."

"If we represent Mr. Moore, it won't be in the past any longer."

Tom pressed his lips together tightly. Ryan was concerned he'd stepped out of bounds.

"I'm sorry," he said.

"Don't apologize. Remember what I told you this morning. Speak honestly and openly. And don't sell yourself short. You can investigate and do the research needed. I'll be here to help, especially when it comes to interviewing people who might have relevant information."

"Okay," Ryan sighed.

"This isn't a situation in which I'm looking for an excuse to fire you. I want you to succeed, and this will give you a chance to work on something significant without a lot of pressure."

"Why won't there be pressure? I'm feeling it right now."

Tom tilted his head to the side. "What do you think are the odds that we'll be able to convince a federal or state court judge to let Joe Moore out of prison?"

"I can't answer that without researching the law and the facts."

"Correct. And if we reach a dead end quickly, we'll refund the unused retainer to the client. Agreed?"

"Yes, sir."

Tom patted Ryan on the shoulder. "There's no harm in conducting a thorough investigation at your hourly rate to pursue it as far as possible. But results? I don't know much about post-conviction relief claims except they're almost never successful. And when they do succeed, the story ends up in the newspaper. Do your best. That's all I ask."

CHAPTER 10

Paige decided to surprise Ryan with a nice dinner. Knowing that he liked chicken only if it offered a significant kick of flavor, she tried a recipe for Jamaican chicken curry served over egg noodles. The aroma from the skillet drifted from the kitchen throughout the house. Paige turned down the heat on the stove and went into the living room to wait. Ryan was usually punctual and had arrived home later than 6:00 p.m. just once since they'd moved to Cranfield. It was an advantage of working for a relative in a small town. Fifteen minutes later, she stirred the chicken and began to wonder if she needed to add more coconut milk to keep it juicy. She sent Ryan a text:

Where are you? I'm hungry.

It was a minute before he replied:

Lost track of time. I'll be home soon.

When Ryan finally came through the door, Paige was concerned the noodles had turned into a congealed glob. She was sitting with her arms crossed over her chest in the living room.

"It smells great!" Ryan called out.

Paige waited until he joined her in the living room. "And it would have tasted great if you'd been here forty-five minutes ago."

Ryan winced. "What did you cook?"

"Jamaican curry chicken and noodles."

"I didn't know you were fixing something special."

"It would be nice to know that you're running late. I've gotten used to a regular routine."

"Me too, but today wasn't routine. I don't want to talk about it right now. Let's eat."

The noodles were overcooked, but the chicken was tender and full of flavor.

"This is fantastic," Ryan said after a couple of bites. "And I'm not saying that to get out of the doghouse."

"The noodles—"

"Are my fault," Ryan said. "They're way better than what my mother fixed on a good night."

Paige never had to worry about Ryan making a favorable comparison between her cooking and what his mother prepared. Nora Clark didn't like to cook and catered the Thanksgiving meal when it was her turn to host the family for the holiday.

"Tell me about your day," Ryan said.

Paige told him about her walk to the playground and described the Victorian house she admired so much.

"It's called the Drummond House," she said. "An attractive woman in her forties came out and asked about Sandy. Do you think it was your client's wife?"

"Possibly. The reason I'm late had to do with Charlie's sister, the one who was murdered."

"Why?"

Ryan lowered his fork to his plate. "The defendant's niece contacted Tom about trying to get her uncle out of prison. After she left the office, I had my hands deep in a box of old papers about the case. That's what I was doing when you sent your text. I'll be late getting home again tomorrow because I'm driving to Lower Piedmont Correctional Center to meet with the defendant and his niece. The family isn't even sure he wants us to represent him. My job is to convince him that it's a good idea."

"I didn't know Tom practiced criminal law."

"He hasn't in years and has no experience in post-conviction relief. He's going to assign primary responsibility for the case to me."

"Ryan, I don't have a good feeling—" Paige started then stopped.

Ryan took a drink of water. "The past few days, Tom has turned a corner in his attitude toward me. He's less negative and is encouraging me to speak my mind. This case is an opportunity for increased responsibility even though the chance of success is probably slim."

"But are you up for it?" Paige asked, then immediately regretted her words. "That's not fair. I believe in you."

Ryan ate another piece of chicken. "Don't apologize. I'm not sure I believe in myself. Sue Ferrell used to work for an attorney who handled post-conviction relief cases and thinks he might be willing to give me a few pointers. I'm scheduled to talk to him in the morning before I leave for the prison."

"It's hard for me to get excited about you getting involved in a case like this," Paige said. "Law school does something to a person's brain. It teaches you to separate the real world from the legal world."

"I'm not sure that's true," Ryan started but reconsidered. "Or maybe it's partly true."

Paige got up, leaned over, and kissed him on the cheek. "Whatever the truth, I'm always on your side."

———————————

Waking up early the following morning, Ryan couldn't go back to sleep. Not wanting to disturb Paige, he turned on his side and held his phone so that his body blocked light from the screen and began searching for information about post-conviction relief. He quickly found several articles that dealt specifically with North Carolina law. As he scrolled through the information, Ryan was glad he'd conducted preliminary research before talking to Sue's former boss. A federal habeas corpus action wasn't available for Joe Moore because it had to be filed within one year after a conviction. It would have been embarrassing if Ryan had asked the more experienced lawyer about habeas corpus. In North Carolina, the best way to challenge an old conviction was something called a motion for appropriate relief.

"What are you reading?" Paige's voice interrupted his research.

"I didn't know you were awake."

"I wasn't until I heard that noise in your throat you make when you're reading and thinking."

"What noise?"

Paige made a sound similar to a person clearing their throat but incorporating a subtle upward change in pitch at the end.

"I do make that sound," Ryan admitted, rolling onto his back.

"Marriage is a mirror."

"I'm researching the law applicable to the case I told you about at supper," he said.

"Find anything?"

"Yes, but I'm ready to take a break and make a pot of coffee."

"And bring a cup to me in bed?"

"Sure."

Ryan swung his legs over the edge of the bed.

"And let Sandy out into the backyard," Paige continued.

"Okay."

"And put her breakfast in her bowl," Paige added. "One scoop of the food in the purple bag in the pantry. It's new, and she loves it. Don't forget her daily vitamins."

Ryan went into the laundry room where Sandy spent the night. The dog gave him a puzzled look before starting to dash toward the bedroom.

"No you don't," Ryan said as he grabbed Sandy's collar. "Not until you go outside."

Attaching a leash, Ryan led the reluctant pet to the rear door and stayed on the brick pavers while the now-unleashed Sandy sniffed around the yard. It was a pleasant morning. Sandy trotted up to him with her nose in the air. She followed him into the kitchen, where he measured out the dog food, adding what he hoped was the proper dose of vitamins. Sandy ignored the food and ran toward the bedroom. Ryan didn't chase her. Instead, he prepared a pot of coffee. When he returned to the bedroom, Sandy was lying on the floor, and Paige was scratching the dog's head. Ryan handed Paige a cup of coffee and sat down beside her. Paige took a sip.

"You've not lost your touch," she said. "Did Sandy eat her food?"

"Nope."

"I understand," Paige said to the pet. "Love is more important than food."

"The evidence speaks for itself."

"Yes, and since you're in lawyer mode, I don't want to hold you up," Paige said. "I'll finish my coffee in the kitchen. That way Sandy will eat breakfast."

Ryan selected a sport coat, striped tie, and khaki pants. He hoped it was appropriate attire for a prison visit. In the kitchen, Sandy had eaten all the food in her metal bowl.

"Do I look like I'm about to go to jail?" he asked Paige.

"Or a fraternity mixer."

Ryan chuckled. "I'll call you on the way back from the prison."

———————

Joe was ready for the day with fifteen minutes to spare before the dining hall opened for breakfast. Taking one of his three harmonicas from a box beneath his bed, he sat on a short bench made from unfinished wooden planks screwed into stubby posts. He placed the instrument to his lips and started to play. Joe was friends with every note on the harmonica. He could play classic blues, jazz, and pop tunes, but he often improvised. He finished one song and tapped the harmonica against the palm of his hand. By this time, a group of men had assembled around him.

"Play the blues," one man requested.

"I love the blues," Joe responded, "but that's for the end of the day, not the beginning."

"We're in prison," the man replied grumpily. "It doesn't matter whether it's day or night."

Joe pointed to his heart. "I'm not in prison in here."

Joe then launched into his version of "Happy" by Pharrell Williams. Some of the men began to clap their hands. A small crowd of twenty-five had gathered by the time he finished. Next he played

"Ode to Joy" by Beethoven. Joe had developed a sublayer to the basic melody that made it sound like a jazz tune.

"Who wrote that?" a man asked. "It sounded kind of familiar."

"Guys named Pharrell and Ludwig," Joe replied. "Whether you've heard of them depends on where you hang out."

Joe stuck the harmonica in his pocket. He and Ray walked to the dining hall together.

"You going to take your harmonica to work?" Ray asked.

"Yeah."

"Any reason?"

"Sometimes I wake up glad to be alive. Music is a way for my soul to tell the world."

"Okay," Ray chuckled. "I get it. But I'm not sure the way you shot down Pete when he told you to play the blues was very smart. I've heard he's got a wicked temper."

"I wasn't trying to get him riled up, just telling the truth. Trials and sorrow are real, and the blues are a big part of my heart. But the way I play the blues is to show my heart who's boss."

They reached the dining hall, where Joe sought out Pete. "Hey, man, I wasn't trying to put you down when I refused to play the blues."

"Then what were you doing?" Pete replied gruffly. "It sounded that way to me. All I did was ask you to blow a tune. You've done that plenty of times."

"And I will again."

Pete moved away. Joe let him go. Not making enemies was an important social skill in prison. Even though LPCC didn't house habitually violent offenders, it was impossible to keep anger and hostility outside the fences. Joe picked up his tray and sat down beside Deshaun. The scrambled eggs were extra runny this morning.

"I had trouble sleeping last night," Deshaun said.

"Excited or worried?"

"Both."

"That makes sense. You might want to let Kiesha do most of the talking at first. I'm sure there's a lot bottled up inside that she wants to get out. Some of it might be negative. Don't let that be the only thing you hear. I've made that mistake. Listen to everything she says without letting your feelings get in a knot. Once she stops, it'll be your turn."

"If I don't say anything, she'll ask me what's wrong."

"And you respond by telling her what's right with you and that you want it to be right between the two of you."

Deshaun nodded. "I like that. She won't be expecting it."

"She's in for a surprise," Joe said and smiled. "I'll be in there praying for you."

Joe ate a bite of eggs then reached for a spoon.

"Who's coming to see you?" Deshaun asked.

"A niece who I haven't seen since she was a little girl. She lives in Richmond."

"Why is she coming?"

"I'm not sure. Her mother is my older sister. It may have something to do with her."

———

Joe spent the morning working in the long rows of okra. It was a miracle how fast the plants could produce. Today would yield the biggest harvest yet. Joe stopped a few minutes before lunch, drank two large cups of water, and took the harmonica from his pocket. He sat on his rock and began to play "Lil' David, Play on Yo' Harp." The notes traveled on a slight breeze toward the garden. When Joe was a little boy, most of the Black men his father's age in Cranfield would instantly recognize the tune. Joe was still playing when Deshaun and another, older inmate came over for their lunch break.

"Did you make that up?" Deshaun asked.

"No, that song has been around a long time."

"It's one of those slave songs," the other inmate grunted. "Those things ought to die."

Joe didn't want a repeat of the misunderstanding with Pete. Before he could say anything, Ray spoke up: "That's true. Anything that celebrates the evil in the past doesn't have a place in the present. But this song is about David in the Bible and how he played his harp and defeated his enemies. There's nothing oppressive about it. Play it again, Joe."

Joe started, and Ray joined in with a melody line in his baritone voice. All the rest of the men stood in a semicircle in front of them and listened. When they finished, the inmate who'd criticized the song spoke up.

"The words are okay if you're religious," he said. "But the music still sounds like a slave song."

"Not when it passes my lips," Ray responded.

"Now you're talking like Joe," Deshaun said with a chuckle. "You know, coming up with stuff to say that sounds like Jesus."

The men settled down to eat lunch. Ray joined Joe.

"Pray for me," Joe said to his friend. "I don't want to get prideful."

Ray was chewing a bite of a ham-and-cheese sandwich. "Because Deshaun says you talk like Jesus?"

"Yes, brother. That's a heavy burden for these shoulders to carry. At least you're going to bear it with me."

Ray chuckled and shook his head. "At least I know you're kidding."

They ate in silence for a few moments.

"Seriously, I want to say the right things when I meet my niece later this afternoon," Joe said. "It always seems harder to do that with family."

"I know what you mean," Ray agreed. "When I try to talk with my oldest son about anything important, the words never seem to make it past my teeth."

———

Ryan's phone conference with Mitchell Norman, the lawyer at Sue's former firm, was set for 9:30 a.m. Shortly before the time set for the call, he went to Sue's desk.

"Any last-second tips before I talk to Mr. Norman?" he asked.

"Ask questions. Don't try to tell him what you know. That really irritates him."

"Okay. I was going to fill him in on my preliminary research into the law."

Sue shook her head. "Off-limits."

"What if I don't know the answer to his questions?"

"Just tell the truth. Don't try to justify your ignorance." Sue lifted her hand and placed it over her mouth. "Sorry, I shouldn't have phrased it like that."

"No, it's okay. You're inside his brain right now."

"That's a big space. Mitch is the most brilliant lawyer I've ever worked for. He doesn't have a huge ego, just impatience with anyone wasting his time."

"I don't see how I can avoid coming across as a person who's wasting his time."

"Tell him that you want his input early in the process so you can avoid mistakes. He'll appreciate that approach."

Ryan nodded. "Okay."

Ryan was sitting at his desk trying to avoid getting nervous when Nancy buzzed him at precisely 9:30 a.m. Mr. Norman was on the line.

"Good morning," Ryan began. "Thanks for taking the time to talk to me."

"You're welcome. Give me the elevator synopsis of your client's case."

Ryan was glad that he'd already typed out a brief summary. "Convicted by a jury of two counts of murder and sentenced to two concurrent life sentences. Client was under the influence of methamphetamine at the time of the crime. No known prior relationship between the defendant and the two victims, a young man and woman in their twenties. They were killed outside a nightclub where the defendant had been performing as a musician earlier in the evening. Murder weapon was a knife. The defendant's fingerprints were on the knife. He was found in a nearby car covered in blood with a large amount of cash in his pocket. No confession. The defendant has been incarcerated for over twenty-six years. Verdict was affirmed on appeal. No MARs have been filed." Ryan stopped.

Norman cleared his throat. "Any basis for a claim of ineffective assistance by trial counsel?"

"Tom Clark, my boss at this firm, was the defendant's appointed trial counsel. Ineffective assistance of counsel can't be considered this long after conviction and the initial appeal period."

"Correct. Glad you've figured that out. Since it's a capital case, do you have evidence now available that was unknown or unavailable at the time of trial and could not have been discovered by due diligence?"

Ryan felt like he'd returned to law school and was being quizzed by one of the professors.

"Not yet," he said.

"Any recanted testimony?"

"Not that I'm aware of."

"Good."

"Why is that good?" he asked.

"Because if you had that sort of evidence, the clock would have been ticking, and the MAR would have to be filed within a reasonable time of discovery. That can be a pitfall because it's up to a judge's discretion to determine what is reasonable. You've read General Statutes 15A-1411–1420?"

"Yes."

"And the cases interpreting the statute?"

"Some of them."

"There's not as much case law as you might think. Some of it was decided under the previous procedures for post-conviction relief, so it has dubious precedential value. I'll send over my summary of what I think is important."

"That would be great." Ryan felt like heaving a big sigh of relief.

"If you uncover something and want to run it past me for an opinion of whether or not it meets the statutory criteria, give me a call." Mitch paused. "And pass along my regards to Sue. She's a gem. I'm sorry her divorce forced the move to Blanton County, but you're lucky to have her."

"Yes, we are." Ryan hesitated. He had to ask the question on the top of his legal pad. "Is there a chance you might be interested in representing Mr. Moore? I have no experience—"

"Would you believe there was a first time that I investigated and filed an MAR?"

"Yes."

"My offer to help was sincere."

"Yes, sir. Thanks."

The call ended. Ryan had remained calm throughout the conversation. He returned to Sue's desk. Before he could speak, Tom appeared.

"Got a fire to put out," Tom said to Sue. "Pull the Samuelson file and bring it into my office."

CHAPTER 11

Paige was partway through the first item on her to-do list when her phone rang. It was the obstetrician's office.

"Are you available to come in at ten thirty this morning?" a woman asked. "Dr. Hester has an opening and you're at the top of the list for a fill-in if there's a cancellation."

Paige didn't have a conference call until early afternoon. "I'll take it."

"Arrive fifteen minutes early to complete a health history, and make sure you bring your insurance information."

The call ended. Paige took a deep breath. This was going to make the pregnancy official. She leaned over and scratched Sandy's head before resuming work on her editing project. A half hour later, Paige finished. She stretched and drank a glass of water. Going to the en suite bath in their bedroom, she noticed some bleeding but quickly reminded herself that based on her research, implantation bleeding was positive.

The doctors in Blanton County were clustered around the local hospital. There were three physicians' names on the sign in front of Dr. Hester's office. Paige knew from the experience of friends in Raleigh that she'd likely see all the doctors associated with the practice and whoever was on call would deliver her baby. She found an open parking space near the door. Inside, five women at various stages of pregnancy sat in the waiting room. Paige received a clipboard from the receptionist and selected a chair close to a woman with a massively extended abdomen. An empty chair sat between them.

"First visit?" the woman asked Paige.

"Yes."

"Twins," the woman said with a weak smile as she rested her hand on her babies. "If they don't come in a few days, the doctor is going to induce labor."

Paige was awestruck. "I hope it goes well. Do you know the genders?"

"Boys, and they've been fighting with each other every day for the past six months."

The door to the doctor's suite opened and a nurse appeared. "Ms. Clifford?"

The woman put both hands on the arms of the chair and hoisted herself to her feet. The size of her abdomen was even more pronounced when she was standing.

The maternal side of Paige's family had a history of twins. She finished the paperwork and returned it to the receptionist. Moments later, a nurse called her name.

The visit included everything Paige had read about. After being weighed, stuck with needles, and questioned in more detail, she was left in an examination room for several minutes. The door opened, and a short man in his fifties with black hair, dark eyes, and black glasses entered. A nurse accompanied him. The obstetrician was holding a tablet in his hand.

"I'm Dr. Hester," the man said in a kind voice. "Congratulations. You're pregnant."

"Thanks."

"Tell me a bit more about the spotting you've experienced. It started this morning?"

The doctor listened and then turned to the nurse. "Based on the uncertainty as to when she became pregnant, let's go ahead and perform an ultrasound."

"Today?" Paige asked in surprise.

"Yes. If you're truly seven weeks pregnant, it's not too early to do so, especially with the history of twins in your family."

Paige swallowed. After sitting next to Ms. Clifford, she already felt ten pounds heavier.

"Better to know than wonder," she managed.

During the ultrasound, the technician didn't give any indication about what she was observing.

"Dr. Hester will discuss the findings," she replied when Paige asked her.

Paige returned to the same examination room for a longer wait before the doctor appeared.

"No sign of twins," Dr. Hester said as he entered. "There's one baby. And you're six to seven weeks pregnant. There was a cardiac pulse even though the heart isn't fully formed. The crown-to-rump length is fine. We're going to watch the placement of the placenta, but it's too early to diagnose a problem. We'll schedule an extra ultrasound in six weeks or so to make sure everything is progressing as it should."

"What sort of problem?"

"The position of the placenta relative to the cervix. Like I said, it's too soon to diagnose a problem, but as a precaution we want to keep an eye on the situation."

Paige tried to keep fear out of her voice. "If there's a problem, what might that mean?" she persisted.

Dr. Hester removed his glasses. "There's nothing I recommend you change about your lifestyle except what's normal for a woman your age with a first-time pregnancy. That's all included in the packet of information you'll receive before you leave today. Start taking a prenatal vitamin and schedule a return appointment."

"Okay."

"You're in great health," the doctor said with a smile. "I saw in your history that you listed mountain climbing as a hobby."

"In the past, not so much recently. Compared to Colorado, there aren't any mountains around here."

"Pregnancy is a different type of mountain, and you're well prepared for the journey."

The doctor left Paige with the nurse.

"Did you see the sonogram?" Paige asked. "Should I be worried?"

"Dr. Hester is the expert," the woman replied reassuringly. "He sees things other physicians might overlook. Trust him to take care of you."

Because both Deshaun and Joe expected visitors, they left the work detail a few minutes early.

"Put on your Sunday-best clothes," Joe said to Deshaun as they walked across the yard toward Unit C after turning in their tools.

"I can't joke about the prison uniforms," Deshaun replied. "It's always tough to handle the look in Kiesha's eyes when she sees me like this. It's not just the fence around the outside that makes it impossible to pretend we're sitting down for a normal talk."

Joe shrugged. "It's been a long time since I thought about what I might look like to a person from the outside world."

Joe showered and changed into a clean uniform, then waited for the younger inmate. The same guard who'd let Joe into the building to pray was on duty. He buzzed them through. There were twelve to fifteen prisoners standing along the wall in the hallway. He looked into the warden's office. Elle was on duty.

"Hope you have a good visit!" she called out.

The door to the visitation area remained closed. Joe looked up as Ned Walker came down the hallway.

"Good morning," Joe said to the man from Blanton County. "Why the delay?"

"One of the visitors was caught with contraband, so they're searching everyone and won't let them in until they finish."

"What kind of contraband?" Joe asked.

"Don't know. Who are you seeing?"

"My niece. What are you doing today?"

"I'm on my way to the cleaning closet to get the mop bucket." Ned frowned.

"Did you connect with Lonnie Mixon?"

"Not yet."

Ned moved on. Joe and Deshaun waited another ten minutes before the door to the visitation area finally opened and a guard appeared.

"Joseph Moore!" he called out.

Joe slowly raised his hand above his head.

"Come up here," the guard ordered. "You're not going in."

Joe moved past the other inmates. He couldn't imagine his niece being the one caught with some kind of contraband. And if so, he had nothing to do with it. Once he reached the guard, the man stepped into the hallway.

"Follow me," he said.

With a puzzled glance back at Deshaun, Joe walked down the hallway. They reached a corner and turned left.

"You'll be in consultation room A with the lawyer and your relative," the guard said.

"Lawyer?" Joe asked in surprise. "I don't have a lawyer."

"There's a lawyer here to see you. Otherwise, you wouldn't be meeting in one of the interview rooms. Do you want to cancel the visit?"

Joe hesitated. "No, I'll go ahead."

Joe opened the heavy door and went inside.

"Hi, Uncle Joe," a young woman said as she stood up. "I'm Shana."

Joe blinked his eyes and stared. Seeing Shana was like looking through a window at his sister. His emotions flooded to the surface.

"You're formed from the same batch of dough as your mama," he managed.

Shana smiled. "I hear that a lot. She sends her love."

Joe couldn't take his eyes off his niece. She turned to a young man seated beside her. "This is Ryan Clark, a lawyer I asked to come with me today. He's from Cranfield."

"Clark?" Joe asked.

"Tom Clark is my second cousin."

"That's a name I haven't thought about in a long time."

Joe was more interested in Shana than finding out why the lawyer was with her. They sat down.

"Tell me about the family," he said. "Is everybody healthy?"

"Yes."

As Shana talked, Joe fought back tears. Without frequent contact, the bonds of kinship could stretch so thin that they became invisible. Shana's news about his family touched him deeply. Barbara and her husband had recently moved into a new home. It was strange to picture his sister living in a big house in a fancy neighborhood on the outskirts of Richmond. But in another way, it made sense. Barbara had always been the obedient child who made the choices necessary to get ahead in life.

"How's her walk with the Lord?" Joe asked when Shana paused.

"She told me you'd ask that," Shana replied with a smile. "Mama sings in the choir at the church and works with the hospitality ministry."

"Do you go with them?"

"Every once in a while. I've been traveling a lot with my job, and my husband and I grab every minute we can to be together. He has an IT job." Shana stopped and cleared her throat. "Uncle Joe, I asked Mr. Clark to be here because Granny made Mama promise to try to get you out of prison. This meeting is the first step—"

"And you can stop going down that road before you lift your foot," Joe said, holding up his right hand. "Your mother wrote me about this, and I told her to drop it. It's been too long. No one is going to let a guilty man like me go free. There may be a time way off in the future when the parole board considers my case, but I'm not holding my breath until that day."

The lawyer spoke: "There's something called a motion for appropriate relief. It's a legal request filed in court, arguing that an inmate be released early. Your family would like our firm to see if there are grounds to file a motion. Because Tom represented you, we have all the old records and are going to analyze everything with fresh eyes.

There have also been developments in forensic analysis that may be relevant to your situation. We'll work on that and try to uncover other evidence that could support the motion."

Joe leaned forward. "Mr. Clark," he started.

"Please, call me Ryan."

"Okay, Ryan. I'm familiar with an MAR. I've seen lots of men put their hopes in one of those things, only to end up disappointed and more bitter because they're still locked up. You can toss out fancy words like 'forensic analysis,' but they don't mean a thing. I heard the evidence at my trial. I know what I did, and I don't want my family wasting a bunch of money."

"I read Tom's notes from his initial interview with you," the lawyer said, clearing his throat. "You told him you didn't remember what happened outside the nightclub."

Joe closed his eyes for a moment. "How soon was that interview after I was arrested?"

"Two days. Right after he was appointed by the judge to represent you."

"I'm sure that's what I said and probably believed it at the time. But I was coming off a methamphetamine binge and thought I could tell the sun to rise in the west and it would obey me. When I heard the evidence at trial, I realized that I'd killed those young people in a drug-crazed rage." Joe shook his head. "I've repented and asked God to forgive me. But the State of North Carolina works on a different system. Filing an MAR won't bring back the Drummond girl or the Brock boy. That's what I really wish I could do."

Joe stopped. His mouth was suddenly dry. He licked his lips. No good would come from digging up the bones of the past. The young lawyer shifted in his chair.

"This is something we want to do, even if you don't," Shana said in a soft voice. "Granny was just as stubborn as you are. She made Mama promise. Show him the contract."

The lawyer took a folded sheet of paper from the inside pocket of his jacket and placed it in the middle of the table. "This is an attorney-client agreement for our firm to represent you in an effort to obtain an early release from prison. There's a deposit that we will bill against as the work is performed."

Joe didn't touch the sheet of paper. "How much did you ask my family to put down as a deposit?"

"Fifty thousand dollars."

"The answer is no!" Joe said, his voice getting louder. "Is that clear?"

The lawyer quickly picked up the contract.

"Please, Uncle Joe," Shana pleaded. "Give us a chance to help."

Joe looked at Shana and spoke in a softer tone of voice. "Don't be mad at me, but I'm not budging on this. Seeing your beautiful face is all I care about and makes me wish we could keep in touch. I know that's impossible given the distance, but I can hope—"

"I'm going to write," Shana replied firmly. "And I'll tell Mama she needs to schedule a trip to see you. Daddy only works part-time now and has a lot of flexibility."

"Wonderful. Tell her I look forward to seeing her."

CHAPTER 12

Ryan and Shana left the consultation room. A guard escorted them to the reception area where visitors entered and exited the building. They had to wait several minutes before someone opened the door. Outside, the sun had crept lower in the sky and hovered in the spindly limbs of nearby pine trees. Ryan felt a profound sense of relief. In his heart, he believed Joe Moore had made the right decision.

"That didn't go well," Shana said sadly. "I don't think it's feasible for us to hire your firm if Uncle Joe is so stubbornly against it."

Ryan agreed but had to be cautious in his response. Tom had expected him to close the deal with Joe Moore.

"It was a difficult conversation," he said.

Shana sighed. "I don't know what I'm going to tell my mother. Except that I think she should visit. I wasn't prepared for my feelings when I saw Uncle Joe. I've always been told he was a smart man who made bad choices when he was younger. Thinking about him being locked up all these years when he's obviously not a threat to anyone hurts my heart. If he were free, he could be doing something worthwhile and fulfilling with his life. Why do you think he was so quick to reject an attempt to get him out?"

"You heard him," Ryan said. "Maybe the money. And I can't blame him for not wanting to relive what happened years ago."

"I guess so."

"Did you know your uncle was so religious?"

"Yes."

They started walking slowly to the parking lot.

"Mr. Clark?" a female voice called out.

Ryan turned around at the sound of his name. A female guard was standing in the doorway they'd just exited through.

"Yes."

"Mr. Moore wants to see you again."

"Me?" Ryan asked, touching his chest.

"Yes. Just you."

He looked at Shana.

"Go ahead," she said. "I'll wait in my car."

Ryan joined the female guard, who took a walkie-talkie from her belt and spoke into it: "Calvin, I have the attorney. Bring Moore back to attorney consultation room A."

"Ten-four," a voice crackled in response.

Puzzled, Ryan retraced his steps with the guard. Joe Moore was sitting at the same table. He gave Ryan a look that was hard to interpret.

"Thanks for coming back," Joe said.

"Sure, what can I do for you?"

"Let me see that contract," Joe replied.

Ryan took it from his pocket and handed it to the prisoner, who took a couple of minutes to read it.

"Any questions?" Ryan asked.

"I'm going to consider it."

"Why did you change your mind?"

"I didn't have much choice. The Lord told me to do it."

"The Lord?"

Joe pointed upward. "He did."

"Can you explain?"

"Yes, but I'm not sure you'll understand. After I left the meeting with you and Shana, I was walking across the exercise yard, and the Lord told me I'd made a mistake turning you down without praying about it."

Joe was right. Ryan had no frame of reference for someone who claimed to talk to God.

"Like you said earlier, the chances of a successful MAR are small," Ryan said. "But if you hire us, I promise not to waste any time and fairly bill your family for the work I do."

"I appreciate that. And whatever happens, I'm already free in the place that counts the most."

"I assume you're talking about your mind."

"And my spirit." Joe paused and stared at Ryan for a few moments. "You seem like an honest young man. Did Tom Clark send you down here to sign me up because he didn't want to do it? Who's going to do the work?"

"I'm here because Tom had another commitment. I've only been at the firm a few months. Tom is busy with other clients, and he delegates quite a bit of the work to me."

"So my family is going to pay for your education."

"Mr. Moore—"

"No need," Joe cut in. "This whole thing has caught me off guard."

Ryan paused for a moment before asking, "How satisfied were you with Tom's representation in the initial case?"

Joe shrugged. "One of the most common things you hear in prison is that a guy is locked up because his lawyer messed up the case. Tom Clark was probably about your age when the judge told him he had to represent me. I could claim he did a bad job, but you heard me earlier. I knew I was going down. When the jury foreman read the verdict, it wasn't a shock to me. Not long after I was locked up, I talked with a woman attorney from a public defender outfit. She looked over the case and said I didn't have grounds to file a habeas corpus claim for ineffective assistance of counsel. Tom seemed to fly by the seat of his pants, but I think he did the best he could with the experience he had. I don't hold a grudge against him."

Ryan was impressed with Joe, whose analysis of Tom was on point.

"Give me your card," Joe continued.

Glad he'd stuck some cards in his pocket, Ryan handed one to Joe, who turned it over in his fingers.

"I know my family wants to do this," he said. "But like I said, I need to pray and seek the Lord's will. How does that sound to you?"

"Whatever you think is best."

"What do you do when you have to make an important decision?"

It was Ryan's turn to be caught off guard. "Uh, I might make a list of the pros and cons to consider, then debate them in my mind or talk it over with someone I trust."

"Does the longer list usually win?"

"Not necessarily."

"I probably won't make a list," Joe replied. "But I'm definitely going to talk it over with someone I trust."

"Okay."

The prisoner stood. "You'll hear from me soon," Joe said.

After returning from the doctor's office, Paige managed to complete only one project on her schedule. She took two long breaks and sat on the couch with Sandy beside her. As she scrolled through articles about the placenta, Paige stroked the dog's back. Sandy loved the attention and eventually took a nap. The articles about placenta previa, placenta abruption, and placenta accreta didn't do anything to relieve Paige's anxiety. The issue could be serious, with the possibility of miscarriage, fetal growth restriction, birth defects in the baby, or stillbirth. One of the toughest things was the need to wait before determining a diagnosis. Paige never liked delays. It was one reason she was a successful editor. She didn't need a deadline for motivation. Her phone vibrated. It was Sara, her boss. Paige had let four previous calls from other people at the company go to voicemail. She needed to accept this one.

"Hello," she said.

"Are you okay?" Sara asked.

The question startled Paige. "Why are you asking?"

"You didn't log in for the meeting we finished five minutes ago. One of the reasons Bud Carrier joined at the end was to put a face to your name. I know it wasn't scheduled until a few hours ago, but you didn't indicate a conflict."

"Oh no," Paige replied. "I must have been at the doctor. I'm behind on my emails and didn't see the invite."

"Are you sick?"

Paige paused. "No, I just found out I'm pregnant. This was my initial visit with the obstetrician."

"Is this good news? You don't sound excited."

"Yes, I am happy about it," Paige answered, making herself sound positive. "Ryan and I are ready for a child."

"Then congratulations! If you suffer from morning sickness, you have my sympathy. I had a terrible time with my first child. Much less with the second."

"No, that's been okay so far. And I don't think it's going to interfere with my workload."

"Don't promise what you can't deliver," Sara said, then chuckled. "Sorry about the pun. 'Deliver' is going to have a whole new meaning for you in eight or nine months."

"I'm sure it will," Paige replied. "Should I reach out to Mr. Carrier and apologize?"

"No, I'll send him an email."

"Okay."

"Don't forget the conference call about the Oklahoma bid in the morning."

"It's on my calendar, and I finished the edit on the written submission from the technical team. I'll send it to you as soon as we hang up."

"Great."

The call ended. Paige gave Sandy a final vigorous scratch. "I can't spend the next six weeks worrying."

———————

Paige was putting her salad bowl in the dishwasher when Ryan arrived.

"You're earlier than you thought you'd be," she said.

"There's almost no traffic on the roads."

"Are you hungry?"

"No, I ate in the car."

"How did the meeting go?"

Ryan sat in a kitchen chair and told her about the trip to the prison. Paige tried to act interested, but all she could think about was the best way to share the news from her visit to the doctor's office.

"Except for the high fences, the prison looks like a military camp. Joe Moore is an interesting man. Nothing like you'd imagine a convicted murderer might be. He comes across as very smart and religious. He didn't hire us yet because he has to pray about it first."

"That's odd," Paige responded. "It seems like he'd be glad his family wants to try to get him out of jail."

"He knows the chances of success for a case like this are small. He also described Tom as flying by the seat of his pants when he represented him years ago. Tom knows a lot more about the law now than he did then, but he still has that tendency."

Ryan also told her about his conversation with a lawyer named Mitch Norman.

"How was your day?" he finally asked.

"I didn't accomplish much this morning," Paige responded slowly. "The doctor's office called and offered me an earlier appointment. I took it."

Ryan leaned forward. "How did it go?"

Paige managed to smile. "Mostly good. They did an ultrasound, and I'm about seven weeks along."

"Wow! Seven weeks?"

"Yes. There's concern about the position of the placenta. It's too early to diagnose anything, but I'll have another ultrasound in six weeks."

"What sort of concern? Why didn't you call me?"

Paige's lower lip trembled and tears suddenly streamed down her face.

"There may not be anything wrong," she managed. "But I'm scared there might be. I wanted to wait to talk about it until we were together."

Paige grabbed a tissue from a box on her desk. She wiped her eyes. "It's all unknown—"

Ryan reached over and touched her lips with his index finger. "I'm here now," he said. "And we're in this together. That's what I know for sure."

CHAPTER 13

B y the time Joe made it to the dining hall, all the okra was gone. A server wearing an apron dropped a scoop of instant mashed potatoes onto Joe's plate, added a clump of macaroni and cheese that had already begun to harden, and topped it off with a piece of gray-colored meat that Joe knew wouldn't pass his lips.

"Wait a minute!" a voice called out from behind the serving line.

It was Dickie. He motioned for the server to give him Joe's plate. The supervisor went into the kitchen and returned with an extra plate piled high with okra cooked the way Joe liked it. He handed both plates to Joe.

"One of the boys said you'd be late because you had a visitor, so I saved some okra for you," Dickie said.

"Thanks," Joe replied gratefully.

He took his two plates of food and sat beside Ray, who was almost finished eating.

"You must be hungry," Ray said.

Joe told him what Dickie had done for him. Ray nodded his head in approval.

"How was the visit?" Ray asked.

"Not what I expected. I enjoyed seeing my niece, but the main reason she came was to bring along a young lawyer who works for the man who represented me when I was convicted. My family wants to hire their law firm to file a motion for appropriate relief."

"On what grounds?"

"They don't have any, but my sister insists on paying for it. Claims it was one of my mother's dying wishes, which is probably true, but I don't see how wasting money honors her memory."

"Hmm," Ray grunted.

The okra was still warm and crispy. Mixing a bite of okra with the mashed potatoes made the latter dish edible. Even in prison, comfort food could live up to its name.

Deshaun entered the dining hall. There was no way to tell from the expression on the young man's face whether the visit with his wife had gone well or badly.

"I wonder how it went with Kiesha," Joe said. "They put me in a private interview room with my niece and the lawyer, so I didn't see how they were getting along."

Joe swallowed another bite, then took out the contract of employment and showed it to Ray.

"I wish someone in my family was willing to pay a bunch of money to try to get me out," Ray said. "But I understand you not wanting them to get ripped off. I wouldn't want the lawyer who represented me within ten miles of my case now. I found out later he'd lost eleven straight jury trials. I was number twelve."

"You never told me that before."

"It's embarrassing because I picked him. The judge didn't appoint him. I convinced my grandfather to borrow the money from a credit union to pay the attorney's fee. That was fifteen thousand dollars flushed down the toilet."

"That's what I want to avoid, but I promised the young lawyer I'd pray about it."

"You did?" Ray asked in surprise.

Joe told his friend how the Lord prompted him to go back and talk to Ryan Clark.

"Maybe that was the Lord," Ray replied doubtfully. "Or it could have been the devil."

"Why do you say that?"

"Talking to a lawyer can be like speaking with the devil. The evil one wants you to get all balled up and thinking about the wrong stuff. God wants you focused on advancing the kingdom. I think we're on the verge of a revival. There's a hunger in the men that fried okra can't satisfy."

As soon as Ray spoke, Joe knew what he said was true. He, too, was hopeful about the future of their ministry.

"I think you're one hundred percent correct," Joe said.

Deshaun joined them.

"What happened to you?" he asked as he sat down. "They dragged you down the hallway. Were you in trouble?"

"Never mind that. What about you and Kiesha?"

A smile spread across Deshaun's face. "We spoke our minds and listened to each other. I did what you said and let her go first. She felt bad about stepping out with that other guy and told me it convinced her that she still had feelings for me. She's already dropped the divorce. It was hard, but I forgave her. She started crying. Then I apologized again for what I've put her and the boys through. This time it wasn't about me feeling sorry for myself. I think she could tell the difference."

Deshaun turned to Ray. "And I told her what we talked about the other day in the garden about getting my life turned around while I'm locked up. She believes it's possible but wants to see that it's real."

"That's true for all of us," Ray said.

———————

Later that evening, Joe took his harmonica to the bench outside Unit C. It was never totally dark at the prison. Floodlights illuminated the entire perimeter inside the fence, and bulbs at the four corners of every unit stayed on all night. But the lights didn't silence every cricket, and some could be heard chirping from shadowy corners. Joe raised the harmonica to his lips and began playing the blues.

Joe knew a lot of famous tunes by heart. And he'd listened to recordings by some of the greats of the past. But he didn't need to walk in another man's shoes. His own soul was fertile ground for sounds that went deep. Tonight, thoughts of his family provided the emotions. He was both sad and thankful. He improvised a tune that captured the sorrow of separation that could never be overcome but also expressed hope that couldn't be extinguished. One man cracked open the door and heard Joe playing. Quickly, about fifteen others came outside to listen. Pete wasn't one of them. Joe finished and lowered the instrument from his lips.

"That was some powerful stuff," one man said, shaking his head. "It sounds crazy, but I heard myself in that tune."

"That's the way it's supposed to work," Joe replied.

"More," another man said.

Joe thought for a moment. He couldn't remember what he'd played twenty-six years earlier on the night of the murders, but he knew it was raucous and rebellious. That style no longer had a home in his heart. Now he only wanted to echo his regret. He raised the harmonica to his lips and began with a high, desperate note. That's what he wished he'd done. If only he had cried out for help. One note followed another until he dove into the lowest octave the instrument provided. When he finished, the men stood in silence. Nobody moved.

"Boys, that's what it sounds like when darkness takes over your soul. The good news is, God doesn't want any of us to stay there. If anyone wants prayer, I'll hang around and pray with you until the guards order me inside."

Ryan held Paige while they lay in bed until her breathing became regular. He carefully rolled over and tried to wrap his head around the depth of her fear. He'd remained surprisingly calm, which seemed to help her. Before they went to sleep, he quickly researched placement of the placenta. The chance of a serious medical issue seemed remote. But Ryan had been married long enough to realize Paige needed his presence, not his analysis.

When he awoke in the morning, Paige wasn't there. Ryan went into the kitchen and found her drinking a cup of coffee and spreading cream cheese on a bagel. Sandy was curled up at her feet.

"Good morning," Paige said. "First thing on my list for today is to apologize to you. I was a mess last night and dumped all of it on you."

"That's okay."

"Not really, but that's what I expected you to say. Anyway, when I let Sandy out this morning and saw the sun, I knew I couldn't live in the dark place where I went last night. If I did, I'd have a nervous breakdown."

Ryan poured a cup of coffee and sat at the table beside her. "What can I do to help?"

"You did pretty well last night."

Ryan took a sip of coffee and made a negative face. "This coffee is terrible."

"It's decaf. I should have warned you. I guess we need to buy another coffeepot. I'll do it today."

———

At the law office, Ryan spent an hour replying to emails and phone calls from the previous afternoon. He was almost finished when Tom entered.

"How was prison?" his boss asked.

"Not what I expected. The men live in barracks and work at jobs either inside or outside the facility. I don't know what Joe Moore was like when you represented him, but he's smart and deeply religious."

"The religious part is new, but I remember him being intelligent. He'd been to college."

Ryan summarized the two visits.

"He's going to hire us," Tom replied when he finished. "Otherwise, he wouldn't have asked to meet with you a second time. Good job."

"If he does, can we agree that neither one of us will communicate anything about the case to Charlie Drummond?"

Tom stared sternly at Ryan for a few moments, then gave him a wry smile. "I thought about that after our conversation the other day, and you're right. Charlie's business and the work we do for Moore have to be kept totally separate. Speaking of Charlie, I need you to research a question I received yesterday from him. I'll forward his email. Communicate with him directly."

Ryan read the email but had additional questions. He called Charlie.

"Good morning," Charlie said. "Did Tom tell you about the spat I'm having with the bank?"

"Just a little bit. Would you send over the paperwork?"

"Yes, I'll ask my assistant to do so. I can't believe James Sheppard at the bank is giving me a tough time about this."

"Okay, I'll look over the documents as soon as possible and get back to you."

"Good," Charlie said and then paused. "Tom told me you drove to the prison yesterday to meet with Joe Moore."

Ryan pressed his lips together. "Yes."

Charlie was silent for a moment. "Okay. Get me an answer as soon as you can about the dispute with the bank."

CHAPTER 14

Joe spent a restless night with disturbing dreams. While walking to the dining hall with Ray, he told his friend about his troubled night and a dream in which he kept losing his way.

"Do you think it means anything?" Joe asked.

"My guess is it was stirred up by what happened yesterday and trying to figure out the right decision to make about letting your family hire a lawyer."

Joe nodded. "Yeah, you're probably right."

"I prayed for you last night and tried to put myself in your shoes. I felt like the Lord showed me a few things."

They continued walking. Joe glanced over at Ray.

"Are you going to tell me?" he asked.

"No."

Joe chuckled. "You're giving me a dose of my own medicine. That's the way I try to get the younger guys to hear from God for themselves. Then I come along to confirm or challenge."

"What's true for them is true for us."

Joe used a hoe to weed the rows of bush beans. The leafy plants were covered with one- to two-inch pods. The prisoners would let the beans reach about five or six inches before picking them. Harvested too early, the beans would lack substance. Too late, and they tended to be tough. The cooks let the beans simmer in large pots of salted water along with pieces of fatty pork.

In the open sunlight, the negative reaction Joe had initially felt the previous day about meeting with the lawyer wasn't as strong. And there was no denying the clear direction from the Lord to speak a second time with Ryan Clark. But Joe remained unsure what to do. During their lunch break, Joe watched Deshaun smile and laugh with the other men. He silently prayed that the positive direction in the young man's life and marriage would continue. Ray brought his sandwich over and sat beside Joe.

"What was going on?" Joe asked his friend. "You worked past break time."

"I wanted to complete the row," Ray replied, then motioned toward Deshaun. "He's in a better state of mind."

"If the Son sets you free, you're free indeed," Joe said, referring to John 8:36. "That's one of the verses my mother gave me the day I was sentenced. I still have the slip of paper in a box beneath my bunk."

"You've never told me that," Ray replied.

Joe shrugged. "Seeing my niece stirred up a lot of memories."

Ray took a bite of his sandwich. "How many men did you end up praying with last night?"

Joe silently counted. "Eight. You were right about the increased hunger. They were looking for help from on high."

"In my anguish I cried to the Lord, and he answered by setting me free," Ray replied.

"Where's that?"

"That's my version of Psalm 118:5. It's a new verse I stumbled across last night."

"You should share that at the next meeting."

"Planning on it," Ray said, taking a long swallow of water. "Verses like that can also speak to practical stuff."

Joe was silent for a moment.

"Based on that verse, do you think I should let the lawyer file an MAR to set me free from this place?" he asked.

"Is that what I said?"

"I'm leaning in that direction myself."

"Why?"

Joe took off his hat and scratched the top of his balding head. "Nothing I can put my finger on exactly. I'm biding my time and trying to make a difference for God's kingdom in this place. But I have to consider what my family wants to do and God's purposes for the young lawyer who came to see me."

"The lawyer?" Ray asked in surprise.

"It's strange, but I found myself wanting to get to know him. Kind of like when I first laid eyes on Deshaun. I knew there would be a connection between us even before he showed up for Bible study."

"Do you think the attorney is a Christian?"

"Don't have a clue," Joe said and slowly shook his head. "He listened when I talked about the Lord but didn't give any sign that he agreed. All he wanted me to do was sign the paper authorizing his firm to represent me."

"Maybe you can help him, but don't forget that we're surrounded by a group of men who are ready to bear as much fruit as the green bean plants."

The positive front Paige gave Ryan collapsed as soon as the door closed behind him. She hated to deceive him, but she couldn't bear the thought of forcing him to face the anxiety that continued to bombard her mind from every direction. She knew Ryan struggled some with worry, but she'd never experienced anything like this in her life. In an effort to calm her racing thoughts, she forced herself to read several longer, more scholarly articles about problems related to the location of the placenta during pregnancy. She wasn't sure if more knowledge would lessen her anxiety or not. The articles had no impact. She took a final drink of coffee. She couldn't delay working any longer without having to call in and use a sick day.

Ryan sent her a text:

Still doing better?

Paige bit her lower lip.

About the same.

Ryan answered:

Any bleeding?

As she texted her response, she felt herself become teary-eyed:

Yes.

Ryan immediately replied:

Sorry. I believe you and the baby will be okay.

Paige knew Ryan intended his answer to reassure her, but it didn't. There was no way he could know anything about her future health or that of their baby. Gritting her teeth, she went to her desk, turned on her laptop, and forced herself to work for three hours before taking a break. While in the backyard with Sandy, she looked over the fence and saw someone walking down the sidewalk with a dog. It was Vicki Lennox, wearing shorts and a T-shirt.

"Hey!" Paige called out.

Vicki looked in her direction and waved.

"Do you want a drink of water?" Paige asked.

Vicki walked over to the fence. Her dog was overweight and had a ring of gray fur around its muzzle. Sandy peered through the fence and yelped. She pranced back and forth on her back legs.

"I'm okay, but Beauty is panting," Vicki said.

"I'll bring a bowl of water to the front porch."

Paige found a clean bowl, filled it with water, and dropped in a handful of ice chips. Leaving Sandy in the house, Paige set the bowl in front of the dog, who began rapidly lapping up the water.

"How did you know she loves ice in her water?" Vicki said. "It's one of the ways I spoil her."

"I'm glad she likes it."

Vicki patted her dog's back. "Candy and I enjoyed our visit with you the other day."

"Yes, I'm so glad you came by. The food was delicious."

"How are you doing?"

"What do you mean?"

"Oh, I may be off base, but I have the feeling something is troubling you. I'm not trying to be nosy—"

Paige realized how desperately she needed to talk to another woman.

"I'm pregnant," she said. "I had my first visit with Dr. Hester yesterday."

"Oh, good," Vicki said, her eyes lighting up. "He's the best. He delivered all three of my kids. Madge went to him too. Are you having morning sickness?"

Paige didn't want to reveal details. "Not really," she said. "But I'm worried whether everything is okay."

"Being pregnant for the first time can be scary even when it shouldn't be. I actually enjoyed my third pregnancy but still told my husband no more kids after Annie was born. Bruce knew better than to argue with me." Vicki extended her hand far out in front of her stomach. "I gave new meaning to the term 'great with child.'"

"Did you ever have any complications?"

"Early in my second pregnancy, I was at risk for a miscarriage, but everything turned out okay. I spent a month flat on my back in bed. You'd think that would be great, but I had a three-year-old who couldn't understand why I couldn't play with him all day and wanted to turn my bed into a trampoline. Thankfully, my mother was between jobs. She drove over from Birmingham and stayed with us for six weeks. Bruce liked having her around because she's a great cook. He must have gained eight or nine pounds." Vicki stopped. "Sorry, once I start talking, I can be like a runaway freight train. You probably need to get back to work."

"No, it's fine. I'm glad I saw you."

Beauty lifted her face from the water bowl. She'd lapped up a surprisingly large amount.

"She was thirsty," Paige said.

"According to the vet, she's prediabetic, which scares me to death. Taking her for walks is part of her treatment."

"Maybe we can walk together sometime," Paige said. "I like to take Sandy to the park and playground at the end of Washington Avenue."

"That's a long way," Vicki said. "Beauty wouldn't be able to do that."

"We can come up with something shorter."

"That sounds good."

Vicki stopped. "Seriously, if I can ever be of help to you, don't hesitate to reach out. People say that all the time, but I do mean it."

"Thanks."

Paige watched as Vicki and Beauty continued down the sidewalk. Something about the way Vicki spoke comforted and calmed Paige. Inside the house, she turned on her laptop and got back to work.

Ryan had to give Charlie Drummond bad news about the equipment lease. Surprisingly, the client took the news well.

"Thanks for getting back to me so quickly," Charlie said. "Even if I don't like the answer, you explained it well, and I'm patient. Perhaps I'll be repaid eventually."

At 4:30 p.m. Nancy buzzed Ryan's phone. "Joe Moore is calling."

"I'll take it," Ryan quickly responded.

He took a deep breath and picked up the receiver. "Hello, Mr. Moore."

"I only have a few minutes," Joe said. "I signed the agreement for you to represent me and put it in an envelope that will go out in the mail tomorrow morning. Will you let Shana know?"

"Yes."

"And send me copies of each invoice for attorney fees."

"Will do, along with a detailed explanation of what I've done."

"Probably not a good idea. My mail comes directly to me, but I don't have a place to keep things secure and private. When will I see you again?"

"Not until I have something important to discuss with you. I'm not going to make a trip just to charge your family for my travel."

"Good. What are you going to do first?"

"Go over the trial transcript and the investigative file and see if anything stands out. Any suggestions on where I should focus?"

"I doubt I can be of much help," Joe said slowly. "A lot of what happened back then is a blur to me. But I'll be praying for you and ask you to do the same for me. There's a verse I wanted to pass along to you. Would you like to hear it?"

"Uh, sure."

"Psalm 34:4 says, 'I sought the LORD, and he answered me; he delivered me from all my fears.' Hope that's helpful for you."

"Thanks."

"Time's up. I have to go."

The call ended. Ryan phoned Shana Parks. She didn't answer, so he left a message. He went to Tom's office. His boss was leaning back in his chair with his feet propped up on the desk. He was on the phone but motioned for Ryan to enter and sit down.

"Right, right," Tom said. "Hey, call me tomorrow. Someone just stepped into my office with an urgent need."

Tom lowered the receiver. "Thanks for rescuing me," he said. "Betty Lou Swanson is a sweet lady who pays her bill by return mail, but she always has one more question. Tell me something urgent so I'm not a liar."

"I had to give Charlie Drummond bad news about the piece of equipment he financed. His claim is second in line to the bank's."

"How did he take it?"

"Good."

"Not surprised. Charlie is one of those rich guys who doesn't stress out about a dollar here and a dollar there."

"There's a lot more than a dollar at risk."

"That's what I mean. He knows if he doesn't do well on one deal, there's another one coming along that will be profitable."

"And I just got off the phone with Joe Moore. He's going to hire us."

"Excellent. Did you let his niece know that we're on the case?"

"Left her a message." Ryan paused. "I assume you want me to start by going through the information in the boxes from the attic."

"Yes."

"What am I looking for?"

"You heard what I said to Ms. Parks the other day. Keep that in mind as you read the transcript of the trial and my brief to the North Carolina Supreme Court."

Ryan was already partway through the transcript but hadn't read the brief.

"Use the Moore case as a time-filler," Tom continued. "Work on it when you have a lull in other projects. It's always good to have something like that on your docket."

"Okay."

Tom was silent for a moment.

"Do you feel up for this?" he asked.

"Not really."

"You'll rise to the occasion. What's happened in the past isn't going to define your future as a lawyer."

Tom's final comment ringing in his ears, Ryan returned to his office. He'd never received anything close to such a strong word of encouragement.

Later, before leaving for the day, he removed the lid from one of the boxes that contained the Moore case and found a folder labeled "Appeal." It wasn't very thick. He flipped through it and decided to take it home to read later.

CHAPTER 15

Joe handed the envelope containing the representation agreement to Elle. She looked at the addressee.

"This will go out today," she said.

"Thanks, and I'm going to bring you a bucket of fresh strawberries tomorrow. There should be some really good ones on the plants in the morning."

Elle smiled. "Yummy."

In the hallway, Joe passed Ned Walker, whose face was streaked black, his hands dirty.

"Where have you been?" Joe asked.

"Up to my neck in the vent fans for the dining hall. Everything we've eaten for the past two weeks is crammed up my nose. I had to get approval from the warden's office to order the necessary parts. How about you?"

"Talking on the phone to my lawyer," Joe replied.

"What's going on?"

"He may file an MAR."

"What's that?"

"Motion for appropriate relief. It's a way to seek post-conviction release from prison."

"Even for somebody that's in here with a murder conviction on his rap sheet?"

"Two murder convictions, and yeah, it's a long shot."

Ned wiped his forehead with the back of his hand and expanded the largest streak of black. "My lawyer never told me about that. Who's representing you?"

"The Clark law firm in Cranfield."

"I've heard of Tom Clark," Ned said with a nod. "I tried to hire him on my case, but he was going to charge too much money. Wish I could have gotten him involved. I ended up with a public defender."

"Did you go to trial?"

"Yeah, no way I was going to plead guilty to something I didn't do. The DA offered me eighteen months to serve, followed by probation, but I turned it down. Jury stayed out thirty minutes."

"Clark was my appointed lawyer. He was young and didn't have much to work with."

"Maybe things will go better the second time around."

"We'll see."

"Gotta clean up before supper," Ned said. "Stay away from the meat loaf tonight. I saw what they're mixing into it."

Joe continued to Unit C. Something seemed familiar about Ned Walker. Their paths could have crossed in Blanton County, but Joe didn't know in what way.

That evening at supper, Joe was sitting with Ray and saw Ned enter the dining hall. Joe pointed him out. "It seems like I've met him before, but I can't remember when or where."

"I've never paid attention to him," Ray replied. "But men are coming and going all the time. How many people live in Blanton County? Five thousand?"

"Back then at least fifteen thousand. I'm not sure about now."

"How did your conversation with the lawyer go?"

"Okay, I guess. You can't say much in the time they give you."

"What's he going to do?"

"Read the trial transcript and the investigative file. Better him than me. That would be depressing."

Joe took a bite of meat loaf, then remembered what Ned said about it. It tasted okay, but he wanted a second opinion. He glanced at Ray's plate. Only a small amount remained.

"What did you think about the meat loaf?"

"It's not like my mother's, but it's been so long since I had hers that I can tolerate something less."

Joe raised a forkful to his lips. "Yeah, it's not bad."

Paige took a seafood casserole from the oven. She'd splurged at a local market that sold fresh fish. Cranfield was only three hours from the coast, but that didn't mean the items resting on ice in the run-down building were actually fresh. She decided the shrimp and snapper were safe bets and combined them with a vegetable mix. She finished it off with a mixture of cheeses that now bubbled. The door opened.

"That smells good," Ryan said. "Is it pizza?"

When Ryan came into the kitchen to greet her, Paige threw her arms around him for a tight hug followed by a long kiss.

"Thanks," Ryan said when she released him. "What did I do to deserve that?"

"Loved me well last night when I was a wreck."

"How are you tonight?"

Paige stepped back. "Worried crazy but didn't want to say anything because I know you have to focus on your work."

Ryan embraced her again. This time she couldn't hold back the tears and rested her face against his chest. It felt good to cry. He gently stroked her back until she calmed down.

"I want to be strong," Paige sniffled.

"You were there for me when I got fired. This is way more important than a job. I don't want you to pretend that you're okay when you're not."

While they ate, Paige told him about her conversation with Vicki Lennox.

"I didn't tell her specifically what I'm going through, and I felt sorry for her sweet dog. She isn't going to be around much longer."

"Do you think you'll go for a walk with Vicki sometime? Sounds like her dog would slow you down."

"I need a friend more than I do the exercise."

Ryan had placed a folder on the kitchen counter.

"What's that?" Paige asked when she got up to refill her glass with water.

"Appeal paperwork in the Moore case. He's going to hire us. I thought I might look over the documents after supper," Ryan said, then added, "But if you need me to do something else, just let me—"

"It's okay."

After supper they settled on the couch in the living room. Ryan glanced through the folder before turning on a baseball game. Paige was curled up on the couch with her novel. Slipping into a common routine helped a bit. Forty-five minutes later, she finished the last page. Ryan had tossed the folder on the coffee table in front of the couch. Paige touched the folder with her toe.

"Would it be okay if I read this?" she asked.

"What?" Ryan replied, not taking his eyes off the screen. "This batter avoided a strikeout with the bases loaded by fouling off six straight pitches."

"About the murder case. Unless it's confidential."

"Go ahead." Ryan glanced down. "The brief filed by Tom and the decision by the Court are public record. The confidential stuff is at the office."

Paige took out Tom's brief. It was twenty-three pages long. She bypassed the legal jargon at the beginning and turned to the Statement of Facts. Tom's prose was remarkably crisp and clear. At least early in his career, the lawyer was a decent writer. She read Tom's version of what happened on a July night more than twenty-five years earlier.

Joe Moore had finished the night performing as a musician in a band and was seen going outside through a door at the back of a nightclub. Fifteen minutes later the police arrived and identified the bodies of Cherie Drummond and Marty Brock. A bloody knife lay on the ground beside them. Both Cherie and Marty died from multiple stab wounds. Twenty feet away from the bodies, Joe Moore was semiconscious in his car. Cherie's and Marty's blood was found on Joe's clothing, and his fingerprints were on the handle of the knife. A thick roll of one-hundred-dollar bills was in the front pocket of Joe's jeans.

Officers arrested Joe and took him to jail. When questioned the following morning, Joe denied remembering anything from the previous night. At that point, he was charged with murder. Subsequent analysis of his blood revealed the presence of methamphetamine. There were no eyewitnesses to the crime. Paige stopped. Ryan was leaning back on the couch.

"There weren't any eyewitnesses to the murder," Paige said. "And Joe Moore claims he didn't remember anything."

"Yeah, it was all circumstantial evidence." Ryan looked over at her before continuing, "But it was overwhelming, especially the blood and the fingerprints on the knife. Joe was so drugged up, it's possible he didn't remember what happened."

"If he was barely conscious at the time of his arrest, how did he kill two people?"

Ryan's eyebrows rose. "Tom would have wanted you on the jury. Have you read anything except the Statement of Facts in Tom's brief?"

"Not yet."

"Read the facts in the state supreme court's opinion."

Paige found the opinion by Judge Brinson. It painted a different picture.

Ryan turned off the game to avoid further pain after watching the Orioles blow a four-run lead in the eighth inning. If they staged a miraculous comeback, he could read about it on his phone before going to bed. Paige was curled up at the end of the couch with her tablet in her hand. Sandy was sound asleep on the floor. The dog's legs were twitching back and forth. Ryan pointed to her.

"What's she dreaming about?" he asked.

"Being part of the wolf pack chasing down a caribou," Paige replied with a yawn. "I wasn't sure I would be able to stay up with you."

"You could have gone to bed."

Paige tapped the folder containing the appeal paperwork in the Moore case that was on the end table next to where she sat.

"Which facts are true?" she asked. "Tom's version or what the judge said about Joe Moore taking multiple snorts of methamphetamine and then getting into a fight with someone before he stormed out of the nightclub?"

"He ingested a crazy amount of the drug. A blood test doesn't lie. But another witness says the fight was more a verbal altercation with a member of the band who wouldn't give him another line to snort. But Tom couldn't disprove that Joe had crossed over to the violent side of a prolonged meth trip. The prosecutor claimed that Joe robbed Cherie Drummond and Marty Brock so he could buy more drugs. In the process, he killed both of them."

"What was the couple doing in a place like that?"

"They'd come to see the show. The parking lot was full, and they'd parked at the rear of the building. Marty was driving a Corvette, which sent the message that he had a lot of money."

Paige was silent for a moment. "Tom claimed the prosecutor didn't have any evidence that the knife belonged to Joe," she said.

"That's true, but the DA proved it was the murder weapon, and it had Joe's fingerprints on it. Ownership wasn't really an issue at that point. Who used it and what they did with it was all that mattered."

"That makes sense."

Ryan waited. Paige didn't continue.

"Do you have doubts about Joe's guilt?" he asked. "The jury didn't stay out very long before returning a guilty verdict."

"What do you think?"

"There are small holes in the government's case. Maybe I can make them bigger. If there was prosecutorial misconduct or wrongly withheld evidence that should have been disclosed and considered, we may be able to get him out."

"That sounds like lawyer talk to me."

"It is."

Ryan yawned. "One other thing happened when I talked with Moore this afternoon. He quoted a Bible verse, something to do with God not wanting people to worry. It was from the book of Psalms."

"Why did he quote a Bible verse?"

"I'm not sure. I guess he thought I needed it."

Paige thought for a moment. "Maybe I'm the one who needs to hear it."

———

The following morning, Ryan had a busy schedule but stayed home for a few extra minutes to be with Paige. He could tell she'd not slept well. Arriving at the office, he ignored Tom's instruction to work on the Moore case only when he had a gap in his schedule. He went into the break room and poured a large cup of coffee. Nancy joined him.

"Tom says we're representing Joe Moore," she said.

"Yes," Ryan replied, then braced for the receptionist's response.

"I'll try to have a professional attitude," Nancy continued stiffly. "But it's going to be hard, so don't get upset if I fail."

"Understood."

Ryan went to his office and began to remove everything from the boxes he'd brought down from the attic. The individual files weren't in chronological order. He then hauled in an empty metal cabinet and put the files in four drawers. He began with the initial interview notes and concluded with the appeal file he'd taken home the previous evening. From now on, the Moore case was as new and relevant as anything he'd discussed with Charlie Drummond. He stopped by Sue's desk.

"Joe Moore hired me," he said.

"Congratulations."

He told her what he'd done with the files.

"It makes sense to get them out of boxes," she replied. "But that's just busywork."

"Yes," Ryan admitted. "Mitchell Norman gave me some great advice during our phone conversation. But do you have any idea what he would focus on first?"

"Mitch would imagine it was a new case and try not to be influenced by what already happened. He'd ask me to locate as many witnesses as possible so he could conduct his own interviews."

"Even in a case that's over twenty-five years old?"

"I don't remember one that went back that far," Sue admitted. "And he'd try to gain access to the physical evidence if it still existed."

"I'd already thought about that, especially the knife linked to the murders. I want to have it retested. A forensic expert from Raleigh testified the blood of both victims was on the blade, and another witness identified Moore's fingerprints on the handle. But there was no DNA testing to see if anyone else may have touched it."

"There's probably other physical evidence worth a fresh look. Mitch always spent time focusing on the medical and autopsy information. In one case, he was able to prove an older man most likely died from a brain aneurysm and not a blow to the head from when he fell after his wife pushed him during an argument."

"I'll look into it, but there's not much chance for a different cause of death. The victims were stabbed multiple times."

"Do you know what Mitch would say to you right now?"

Sue wrinkled her nose and narrowed her eyes to slits. "If you think you know everything without investigating, you're either clairvoyant or arrogant. Which is it?"

Ryan chuckled. "You sound just like him. Did he know you could imitate him?"

"No way. I kept that to myself and a few of the staff."

CHAPTER 16

The men at the prison worked six days a week. Saturday evening had a festive feel. Dickie often planned a nicer meal for supper, one that featured a legitimate dessert, not something scooped from a can onto the plates. Tonight it was pineapple upside-down cake prepared in long rectangular aluminum pans.

"Can I have a corner piece?" Ray asked as they made their way down the serving line. "I like the crispy edges."

The man serving the dessert looked at Ray and rolled his eyes. The next pieces of cake to be removed from the pan were all in the middle. The man paused for a second, then turned around to a pan on a metal table behind him. He took out a corner piece and put it on Ray's plate.

"Thank you, sir!" Ray beamed.

"Do you know him?" Joe asked as he accepted a middle piece of the cake that was saturated with pineapple juice.

"We played Ping-Pong last Sunday, and I let him win."

"Did he know that?"

"No, but I could tell he needed a victory more than I did."

Joe and Ray joined other men from Unit C. The meat for the meal was fried fish with Cajun seasoning.

"The fish is good," Joe said after his first bite. "This wasn't frozen in a box."

"You're right," a man across the table replied. "I heard they trucked in several cases of whiting from down east. Be on the lookout for a stray bone."

"Like this?" Ray pulled a small fish bone from his mouth and held it up. "I could save this and use it for a toothpick."

Out of the corner of his eye, Joe saw Ned Walker sit down at the end of their table. This was unusual. The men normally gravitated toward the same table. Ned struck up a conversation with Everett Robinson. They were too far away for Joe to overhear, but at one point he noticed both men looked in his direction. Joe cleaned his plate. The dessert was soggy but tasty. Ray was still nibbling his cake.

"What's wrong with the corner piece?" Joe asked. "That's what you wanted."

"It's delicious," Ray replied. "I'm trying to make it last."

Joe chuckled. He wiped his mouth with a thin paper napkin.

"Have any of you heard who's speaking at the church service in the morning?" Joe asked in a voice loud enough for several men to hear.

"I was in the administration building this morning," one man replied. "It's an outside guy who used to be in a motorcycle gang."

"That means he'll share his testimony," Ray said.

On his way to Unit C after supper, Joe saw Everett walking ahead of him. He came alongside the large man.

"I saw you eating supper with Ned Walker," Joe said. "How do you know him?"

"He came over to me when I was lifting weights in the yard after I got off work. You wouldn't know it by looking at him, but he was a powerlifter before he injured his back in a motorcycle accident. He's going to show me a picture of what he used to look like."

"He's from Blanton County, where I grew up."

"Yeah, he says the two of you are about the same age, but it's hard to tell with him because he shaves his head."

"The speaker planned for the church service used to be in a motorcycle gang," Joe said. "What do you think about inviting Ned to come?"

"Sure, I'll catch up with him at breakfast. He promised to bring some pictures in the morning to show me."

Saturday evening, Paige and Ryan took Sandy for a walk after supper. It had been a warm day. As the sun dipped below the trees, an evening breeze dispelled the heat. Several times during the walk, Paige had Sandy's leash in one hand and held Ryan's hand with the other. The word "placenta" wasn't mentioned. They encountered multiple people out for a stroll and a few dogs for Sandy to meet. They reached the Drummond House on Hamilton Street and stopped in front of a wrought-iron gate. The flowering bushes were in full display along with hanging baskets near the front door.

"Should we knock and see if anyone is home?" Ryan asked.

"That would be rude since what I really want is a full tour and can't expect that on an unannounced visit. Also, I don't see any lights on except in a room on the second floor."

"That's Charlie's car," Ryan said and pointed to a black Mercedes parked next to a matching white one. "He gave me a ride back to the office the other day after lunch at the country club."

"Maybe we should get matching cars," Paige said. "They wouldn't have to be Mercedes."

"Good. What colors would they be?"

Paige was quiet for a moment. "Mine would be green to make me feel like I'm in Colorado. Yours would be white."

"Why white?"

"Because you don't care what color car you drive."

"That's true," Ryan admitted.

It was the first attempt at humor Ryan had heard from Paige in days. The front door to the house opened, and a blond-haired woman wearing a plain dress and apron stepped outside with a watering can in her hand. She didn't look in their direction.

"That's not the woman I saw the other day," Paige said.

"Maybe a maid?"

"Yeah, although I didn't know people still had maids."

"If you're as rich as Charlie Drummond, you can have a maid."

They continued walking.

"If we get matching cars, you're going to have to start wearing a dress and an apron around the house, especially when you water the flowers in hanging baskets."

"We don't have any hanging baskets, and I don't own an apron."

Returning home, they sat in plastic Adirondack chairs in the backyard as the shadows lengthened. Sandy trotted along the fence line sniffing out interesting smells.

"Isn't there a baseball game on TV?" Paige asked.

"Maybe, but how can it compete with this? I mean, sitting here on a nice evening with you and Sandy."

Paige reached over and patted him on the arm. "Thank you. I've had an up-and-down day," she said. "This afternoon was better."

"I'm glad."

They sat in silence as the first stars began to appear.

"Do you want to go to church in the morning?" Paige asked.

"Where did that come from?" Ryan wondered.

Paige told him what she'd learned about the church from Vicki and Candy. "I liked them, and in a town like Cranfield, church is one of the main ways to meet people."

Ryan grunted. "Joe Moore quotes the Bible to me, and now you want to go to church."

"We don't have to—"

"No, we'll give it a try."

———————

The following morning, Ryan stood in front of his narrow section of the closet.

"Should I wear a coat and tie?" he called out to Paige, who was down the hall in the kitchen.

A few seconds later she appeared with a bagel in her hand. "It's always better to be overdressed than underdressed," she replied.

"Yeah, but I don't want to stand out as a newbie."

"We are newbies. Should I call one of the ladies I met and ask what their husbands wear to church?"

"Yes."

"Are you serious?"

"No," Ryan grumbled.

Paige picked up her phone from the nightstand. "I'll check the church website for photos of the service."

While he waited, Ryan rubbed his chin. He often skipped shaving on the weekends. Paige didn't mind. She liked the rugged look, but he probably couldn't avoid the razor this morning.

"Not a tie in sight," Paige said. "And there are as many men in blue jeans as khakis."

"Should I shave?" he asked.

Paige stroked his face. "Absolutely not. They're going to have to accept or reject us for who we are."

Ryan put on a nice pair of light gray pants and a polo shirt. Paige selected a casual dress. Growing up, Ryan attended a church where all the men wore a suit and tie. No one looked particularly happy about it.

"We need to be there by nine thirty to make it to the class Vicki and Candy attend," Paige said.

"Do you know what they're teaching in this so-called class?"

"Not a clue, but I downloaded a Bible app on your phone while you were in the shower."

Ryan chuckled. "You're enjoying this, aren't you?"

"Maybe a little. I feel good about it."

"Then I'm glad we're going. Did you download the app on your phone?"

"Of course. I wouldn't want to be a hypocrite."

When they arrived, the parking lot was filling up. Inside at an information desk, two older women were on duty. Paige mentioned Vicki and Candy.

"That's the New Life Class," one of the women said as she nodded and pointed behind her. "They meet in the big room at the end of the hall."

Ryan and Paige made their way through a crowd of people. After passing several rooms, they came to a sign on the wall that identified the New Life Class. A couple at the door greeted them and handed them blank name tags. Ryan let Paige print his name. Her handwriting was much more legible than his.

"Paige!" a female voice called out.

Moments later, Ryan and Paige were surrounded by people greeting them and shaking hands. They sat beside the woman named Candy and her husband, Chris. Paige asked Chris about a rafting trip in Colorado. Ryan glanced around the room. He wondered if any lawyers attended the church. Connecting with this many people could be good for business. Tom and his wife attended an older church a block from the courthouse, but Tom hadn't invited Ryan and Paige. A couple stepped to the front of the room.

Two and a half hours later, Ryan and Paige left the sanctuary and exited through the same door they'd entered earlier. They'd attended both the class and the service that followed.

"I kept looking for Madge Norton but didn't see her," Paige said. "She must have been out of town. But everyone was friendly and welcoming."

"There were more names fired at me than I could remember."

"What did you think?"

"That's a big question. There were a lot of different things going on. You go first."

"I like Candy and Chris. You and he could be friends."

"Possibly. Thanks for not suggesting we play tennis."

"You're going to do that with the tall guy you talked to before the church service started."

"Yes, Danny Milton. I met him the other day at the country club. He works in the DA's office and played tennis in college. We're going to set up a time to hit it around. That could be fun."

They got into the car.

"Vicki's husband seemed nice, even if he was an introvert," Paige said. "They complement each other."

"Like you and me."

"Exactly."

Paige was quiet as they left the parking lot. "Seriously, the class surprised me," she said after a moment. "I've read biblical references in literature, but I was clueless when they started talking about all that stuff in the Old Testament. It was like a college class on metaphors. Did you know anything about the tabernacle and the symbolism of the different items in it?"

"No."

Paige glanced over at him. "But the best thing to me was the prayer time at the end of the class," she confided.

"Really?" Ryan asked in surprise. "That was the most uncomfortable part of the morning. It was very awkward when we had to break up into little groups and were expected to pray out loud."

"We didn't have to say anything. Chris and Candy and the other couple prayed." Paige paused. "And Candy prayed so beautifully for all the pregnant women in the class. It almost made me cry."

"I can certainly see how that would mean something for you," Ryan admitted as he stopped for a red light. "I had trouble staying focused during the sermon."

"I could tell you were zoning out. The speaker wasn't very good, but the main minister was out of town. He'll be back next week. Maybe we should give him a chance."

"I'll pretend to be a judge and take that under advisement."

CHAPTER 17

J oe sat in his usual seat toward the front in the prison chapel. Ray was outside looking at the motorcycles the visiting group rode into the facility. The roar of the engines as they came through the front gate drew a large crowd. The motorcycles were choppers with loads of custom features. Joe saw Ray talking to Ned Walker.

The service followed the usual pattern. There were three songs followed by a prayer from the chaplain. The speaker for the morning was a man in his mid-fifties who'd spent two years in an Arizona prison for a drug offense. The room grew quiet when he described an incident in which his life was in danger. The speaker pulled down the collar on his shirt and revealed a scar left by a knife wound intended to kill him. Seeing the scar, Joe shifted uncomfortably in his seat.

"While I was flat on my back in the hospital, I realized that I wasn't in control of my life and was ready to listen to what the prison chaplain had to say to me about Jesus Christ."

When the man gave an altar call at the end of his message, a number of men stepped forward. Joe didn't see Ned. A moment later, a young man from Unit C came over to Joe. His name was Ronnie.

"Would you pray for me even though I don't come to the Bible study?" Ronnie asked.

"Of course. What's going on?"

Joe listened. Every man was different, but all shared a common need for forgiveness and God's love. When Joe prayed, he sensed the Lord's direction in the words and Scriptures that came to mind. Ronnie opened his eyes and nodded in agreement.

"Thanks," he said.

"Do you have anything you want to tell the Lord?" Joe asked.

"You want me to pray?"

"Think of it as talking to God. You don't even have to close your eyes if you don't want to."

Ronnie stared at Joe. After taking a deep breath, he managed several halting words. But then the sentences began to flow. Finally, the young man stopped.

"Where did that come from?" he asked.

Joe pointed to the young man's heart. "From in there."

Ronnie scratched his chin where he'd grown a scruffy goatee. "I feel like I've had a shower on the inside. I'm going to start coming to the Bible study. You know, more and more men are talking about it."

"Good to hear. I think you'll like it."

Fifteen minutes later, Joe and Ray were walking together to the dining hall.

"What's wrong with Ronnie?" Ray asked.

"Getting right with God."

They entered the eating area. A long line snaked along one wall.

"They're late opening up," Ray said. "I hope it's because they're cooking something good for Sunday dinner that isn't ready yet."

A man near them yelled, "What's the holdup? I'm hungry!"

The door to the serving line opened, and the men began to file in.

"Where did you get off to?" Joe asked Ray as they took a step forward. "You left as soon as the preacher gave the altar call."

"I went after your neighbor. I'd been praying for him during the service. I caught up with him outside at the motorcycles. He left early. I believe he was under conviction."

"Why do you think that?"

"Just the way he acted. Kind of jumpy and nervous."

"Did you talk to him?"

"Talked instead of listening, which was my fault. I launched into preaching to him without asking what was going on. When I stopped to catch my breath, he asked if you believed the same way as me. I told him yes."

"Then he wanted to know whether I'd ever been afraid of you because of why you're locked up."

"Afraid of me?" Joe asked.

Ray closed his right hand into a fist and flexed his bicep that had once been formidable but had shrunk with age. "I know; I'd crush you with one punch if you ever made me mad. Anyway, I said you'd never been in a fight all the years I've known you. Maybe now he'll come around and you can get to know him. I'm sure the Lord is working on his heart."

———

Monday morning, Ryan had an email in his inbox from Mitch Norman. It contained a summary of the appellate decisions but also a multipage investigative checklist linked to relevant statutes and case law. Ryan printed it off and laid it on Sue's desk.

"Have you seen this before?" he asked.

The assistant glanced at it. "Yes, I typed the first draft of this for Mitch. He's expanded it since then."

"Along with the advice he gave me on the phone, this is really going to help me."

"That's Mitch for you. He probably couldn't stand the thought of you making a mistake due to inexperience."

"I still wish I could associate him on the case."

Sue shook her head. "He'd take over."

"And I could watch and learn."

Ryan returned to his office. A few minutes later, Tom buzzed him: "Come to my office."

Ryan grabbed a legal pad and headed down the hall. Tom was sitting behind his desk in a short-sleeved shirt with the collar open.

"How busy are you?" he asked.

"I could take on something if you need me to."

His boss ran his fingers through his thinning hair. "It may be more than that. I had an appointment with my internist last week for a routine physical. He saw something on my EKG that concerned him, and he set me up with a cardiologist who's scheduled a heart catheterization later this morning. My blood pressure hasn't been responding to the medication even after an increase in the dosage. He thinks I may have a blockage or be at risk for a stroke. As you know, heart trouble runs in our family. It kills way more people than cancer."

Ryan was unaware of that tendency. "Should you go home and take it easy until the test?"

"No, let's huddle up with Sue and identify the matters that require immediate attention in case I have to be out for a few days. If I'm lying on a table at the doctor's office worrying about what's going on here, it won't be good for my health."

"Of course."

Tom paused. "I hate this because I felt that we were just starting to hit our stride working together. You're doing a fantastic job, way better than anyone else who's worked with me before. I think you're going to be an excellent lawyer."

Ryan sat up straighter in the chair. "I'm willing to do anything to help."

———————

Paige placed her cell phone beside her computer. An hour later, her phone vibrated. It was Vicki.

"We hope you and Ryan enjoyed the church. Everyone was excited about meeting you," Vicki said.

Paige realized that she and Ryan had probably been the topic of multiple conversations. "It was nice."

"Come back next Sunday so you can hear Pastor Mike. Pastor Neal is more of a shepherd than a Bible teacher."

Paige wasn't sure exactly what Vicki meant and didn't want to ask the necessary questions to find out. She took a deep breath. "When the leaders of the class asked if anyone had a prayer request, I wasn't sure if that only applied to members of the church."

"No, no, we pray all the time for people who live in other parts of the country or even different parts of the world."

"Okay." Paige took a deep breath. "I would appreciate prayer but don't want to make a big deal out of it or have it go onto a list."

"I understand. It can be between us."

Paige knew she was committed to disclosure. "It would be fine if you tell Candy, and I may say something to Madge Norton, who was so nice to me the first day we met. But I don't feel comfortable with anyone else. Not yet."

"What's going on?"

Paige told Vicki about the appointment with Dr. Hester. She had to stop twice when tears filled her eyes. Vicki listened well. Paige was relieved to unburden her heart to another woman.

"I'm so sorry you're going through this," Vicki replied. "Bringing a baby into the world is a challenge. Anyone who claims otherwise is projecting a fake persona on social media. Candy and I will certainly be praying for you. How is your husband responding to the uncertainty?"

Vicki's question made tears flow from Paige's eyes and down her cheeks. She was glad Vicki couldn't see her face.

"Great," she managed. "He's been so tender and supportive."

"That makes a world of difference. It took a crash course in Husband Training 101 for Bruce to climb out of his shell and be there for me when it came to pregnancy and kids. But once he understood, he's been a big help."

"Ryan has been a natural."

"Keep us up to date on your health. Is your offer to go for a walk with our dogs still on the table? Mornings are best for me when the kids are in school."

"Yes."

They set a day and time. After the call ended, Paige rested her head on the back of her chair and closed her eyes. She wondered what it would look and sound like when Candy and Vicki prayed for her. Did they fold their hands? Would they get down on their knees? She hadn't seen any kneeling or hand-folding during the church service. Sandy was lying on the floor beside her. Paige reached down and stroked the dog's fur. Sandy rolled over so Paige could scratch her stomach.

"You always get what you want by looking at me with your soulful brown eyes," she said to the dog. "It's tougher for humans."

CHAPTER 18

Joe finished breakfast and was walking back to Unit C to get ready for work duty. An inmate he knew jogged up to him. "I was at the administration building, and there's a FedEx packet for you. You may want to pick it up before your work detail."

It was Joe's turn to jog to the administration building. The guard let him inside when he told him why he was there. Joe went to the mail room. A low counter separated the workers from the inmates.

"I'm Joe Moore," he said to a woman he didn't recognize. "Do I have a FedEx package?"

"Envelope," the woman replied, reaching behind her.

She handed him the envelope that had been slit open for inspection. Standing in front of the counter, Joe reached inside. It contained photographs of his sister and her family, as well as a letter from Barbara: "Shana so enjoyed seeing you. She'd heard Mama and I say that you're a good man, but it made a difference for her to spend a few minutes with you herself."

Joe stopped reading and took the packet into the hallway. He started over reading the letter. Barbara ended by telling him that she loved him and would make a trip to see him before the end of summer. Joe hurried to Unit C and stowed the envelope on top of the other letters he'd received and saved. He then joined the garden workers who were lined up to check out tools and garden implements.

"I thought you might have gone to the infirmary," Ray said to him. "The sausage this morning had a weird taste. It may have been old."

"No, I'm fine."

Joe told him about the FedEx packet and the photos.

"I'd like to see your family," Ray said. "Does your sister look like a female version of you?"

"No," Joe chuckled. "She takes after my mother. I favor my dad."

"Good for her."

The men received their tools and made their way to the garden. It was an overcast day, and the clouds shielded the men from the worst heat of the sun. While he worked, Joe thought about what he would write to Barbara. During their lunch break, he sat beside Deshaun. The young man peeled a banana that was past ripe and took a couple of big bites.

"I got a letter from Kiesha," Deshaun said when he stopped chewing. "I was worried she might have changed her mind after the visit last week, but she still wants to make the marriage work. She's bringing the boys for a visit in a few weeks."

"That's good. My sister who lives in Richmond is going to come see me this summer."

Deshaun finished the banana. "I heard your family hired a lawyer to try to get you out," he said.

"Who told you that?" Joe asked in surprise. "I haven't mentioned that to anyone except Ray."

"I heard it in the dining hall," Deshaun replied. "Some other guys were talking, and I overheard your name."

Joe then remembered saying something to Ned Walker.

"Do you think anything will come of it?" Deshaun continued.

"No," Joe answered.

The men brought in a first harvest of lima beans. Joe and Deshaun delivered the white plastic buckets to Dickie at the rear door of the kitchen.

"There's only enough for each man to have a small serving on his plate," Joe said. "Do you want to hold off until we harvest more tomorrow?"

Dickie picked up a pod and broke it open. "These are babies," he said, holding up a bean. "Those are the best. When they get big and fat, the beans can turn mushy. I'll butter them up and serve them tonight."

Before going to Unit C, Joe stopped by the administration building and delivered the promised strawberries to Elle. She took one from the top, popped it into her mouth, and closed her eyes. "This is heaven," she said.

"Strawberries will be even better there," Joe replied with a smile.

"But until then, this will do just fine. I'll do my part. Check back tomorrow afternoon."

After taking a shower, Joe sat on his bunk and retrieved the FedEx envelope. Studying one of the photos of Shana, he could see a hint of his father in her eyes. He started to return the envelope to the chest when he noticed something odd. Joe always kept his study Bible in the bottom right-hand corner of the box. This afternoon it was in the bottom left-hand corner. He lifted a few more items. One of his harmonicas was also in a different location. He quickly inspected the entire contents of the box. He didn't store anything of value beneath his bunk. Petty theft was a common occurrence. To his relief, nothing was missing.

He glanced around the room. During the workday, all the units were locked for security reasons, and no one was allowed inside. That way the guards didn't have to constantly patrol the sleeping areas. A man named Bobby who'd occupied a bunk across from Joe for over six years returned from the showers. He also had a storage box beneath his bunk.

"Hey," Joe said to him. "Check your box to see if anyone has been snooping around in your stuff."

Bobby, a heavyset Black man who was a few years younger than Joe, pulled his box from beneath his cot.

"If they did, I hope they throw my socks in the laundry," Bobby replied.

He lifted the lid and peered inside. "It looks the same to me," he said. "Has someone been in your stuff?"

"Yeah, but I don't see anything missing."

"Someone might steal one of your harmonicas," Bobby said. "But if they tried to sell it or play it themselves, someone would be onto them. Everyone knows you're the harmonica man. What else do you have worth taking?"

"Nothing," Joe replied. "If someone stole a Bible, I'd hope they would read it."

It was late in the afternoon, and Ryan hadn't heard anything from Tom or his wife, Karen. He went to Nancy's desk.

"Shouldn't Tom have let us know by now?" he asked the receptionist.

"Yes, and I'm worried. He's always calling to check on things when he's not here. This place is always on his mind." Nancy lowered her voice. "I think Tom has a touch of ADHD."

It was a part of his boss's makeup that Ryan hadn't identified, but it made sense. Nancy took an incoming call. "Yes," the receptionist said, then listened.

Ryan turned to leave, but Nancy raised her finger to delay him.

"When will he be able to have visitors?" she asked.

"Oh," Nancy said as her eyebrows rose. "Tell him not to worry about the office. We'll take care of everything."

She slowly lowered the receiver and looked up at Ryan. "That was Karen. Tom had a heart attack before they performed the catheterization. He's in ICU at the hospital. The doctors are trying to stabilize him so they can send him to the Sanger Clinic in Charlotte for further evaluation and treatment."

"It's like he had a premonition something was seriously wrong," Ryan said, shaking his head. "How bad was the heart attack?"

"Karen said something about the kind that involves a partially blocked artery but can still cause permanent damage."

Ryan returned to his office. He called Paige to tell her the news, then stared at his framed law school diploma and the certificate of admission to the North Carolina Bar on a nearby wall. Ryan could feel panic start to rise up within him. He had four years' experience in unstable work environments. He tried to focus on Tom's recent encouraging words, but they weren't much to hang on to. Then he remembered what Joe Moore said to him about God and fear at the end of their last conversation. Grabbing his phone, he entered a few key words and the verse popped into view: "I sought the LORD, and he answered me; he delivered me from all my fears." Ryan didn't pray, but he hoped the verse might be true for him. He summoned Sue and Nancy to the conference room.

Ryan avoided sitting in Tom's usual chair at the head of the table. Sue and Nancy sat across from him. An hour later, they ended the meeting.

"See you in the morning," he said. "If I hear anything else about Tom, I'll send you a text."

Sue stayed behind after Nancy left. "I know you're not asking for feedback, but that was good," she said. "Nancy isn't going anywhere, but I have a family to support and wondered if I should start looking for another job. My ex-husband is way behind on child support, but I'd rather stay and see if you can make this work until Tom gets back, but if things go poorly—" She stopped.

"I don't want to go there in my mind," Ryan replied. "And thanks for your willingness to give this a chance."

On his way home, Ryan received a text from Karen letting him know that Tom was in an ambulance on his way to Charlotte.

Paige had finished a light supper when Ryan walked through the door. She put her plate in the dishwasher.

"I thought you'd be working late," she said.

Ryan sat down in a kitchen chair. "We did what we could today, and I was too emotionally drained to attempt anything else." Running his fingers through his hair, he added, "Karen just sent me a text letting me know that Tom is on his way to the hospital in Charlotte."

"Hopefully, we'll get good news soon."

"Yes."

"Are you hungry? I ate a salad."

"Actually, I'm starving. I skipped lunch. What do we have?"

Paige told him about the leftover options in the refrigerator. "I'll pop the lasagna in the microwave. It's one of those dishes that can taste better on the second or third day."

"And you can talk to me about your day."

"There's not much to tell," Paige replied. "I participated in a couple of online meetings that lasted an hour each and didn't say a single word. But that was a good thing because no one had any questions about the work I did beforehand. After we finished, Sara texted and mentioned that she's going to lobby the big bosses to hire more editors."

"The English professors of the world appreciate your efforts."

Paige was silent for a moment. "I know you've been focused on Tom, and for good reason. But I called Vicki Lennox and told her about my concerns with the placenta placement for the baby. I thought she and Candy Bynam could be praying for me. I specifically asked them not to put it on the list they publicize at the church."

Ryan brought his plate of warmed-up lasagna to the table. "I thought you'd want to keep this kind of personal information private."

"Maybe it's time to ask for all the help we can get."

Ryan's cell phone vibrated. "It's from the prison where Joe Moore is locked up," he said.

Paige watched Ryan's face as he listened to the caller. His eyes widened.

"He had a heart attack and is on his way to the hospital in Charlotte," Ryan said, then continued to listen.

"I'm sure he would appreciate that."

He lowered the phone onto the table. "That was Joe Moore. He had some kind of sense that something might be wrong with Tom and was calling to check on him. He convinced someone at the prison to let him make a phone call even though it's not normal procedure."

"A premonition?"

"He didn't use that word. He had heartburn after supper and somehow connected it to Tom. He's going to be praying for him."

Not sure what to make of the call from the prisoner, Paige left the table and stepped over to the refrigerator to refill her water glass. She took a drink.

"Do you think I should say anything to Tom or Karen about the phone call from Moore?" Ryan asked.

"That's up to you."

Ryan finished the lasagna, then took a smaller serving of leftover Chinese takeout from the fridge and put it in the microwave.

"That's over a week old," Paige said. "I should have thrown it out."

"I don't want to waste it."

"Heat it extra hot."

"Will that help?"

"It can't hurt."

After Ryan finished eating, they sat on the couch in the living room. Paige was beginning a new book. Ryan turned on the TV. Sandy lay between them. Paige suddenly felt a sharp pain in her abdomen. She placed her hand on the spot that hurt. Another pain followed. Going into the bathroom, she was worried the bleeding might be worse. To her relief, no blood appeared. She returned to the couch but didn't say anything to Ryan. A few seconds later, during a commercial break, Ryan turned to her.

"Should I ask Joe Moore to pray for you?" he asked.

"He doesn't know anything about me," Paige said.

"You barely know Vicki and Candy. And he seems serious about this sort of thing."

"What would you tell him?"

Ryan paused for a moment. "I could mention that you're pregnant and there are health concerns for the baby."

"I guess it would be okay," Paige replied slowly. "It would be weird if he experienced some kind of stomach pain that he associated with pregnancy."

Paige returned to her reader. To her relief, the pain in her abdomen lessened. An hour later, she took Sandy outside for the final time before putting the dog in the laundry room for the night.

"I'm not sure I'll mention anything to Moore," Ryan said, turning off the TV. "My focus needs to be on his case, not trying to develop some kind of personal relationship with him."

CHAPTER 19

The Bible study and prayer meeting ended in Unit C. It was the largest gathering Joe could remember. The men filed out of the room. The pain in Joe's chest had stopped as soon as he called the young lawyer. During the meeting, he requested prayer for someone he knew from his hometown who'd suffered a heart attack. He didn't reveal that it was Tom Clark. Joe didn't pray, but several other men did.

"Glad you could make it," Joe said to Bobby, who'd not participated in the group in months.

"I needed it," the large man replied without explaining why. "If I hadn't come, I would have wasted the time laying up in my bunk or listening to trash talk on the exercise yard."

Ray came over to Joe. "Except for the prayer request, you were quiet tonight."

"I didn't have anything to add to the discussion."

"You always have something to add to the discussion."

"Are you saying I run my mouth too much?" Joe chuckled. "We're trying to raise these other guys up to do their part. That happened tonight."

"True. Who's the person who suffered the heart attack?"

Joe told Ray about his heartburn and the phone call to Ryan Clark. His friend's eyes widened.

"That's crazy," Ray said, raising one hand to cup his chin. "I wondered why you left the dining hall in such a hurry. One of the other guys at the table thought you were sick. Has anything like that ever happened to you before? And how did you connect heartburn to your lawyer? I would have gotten an antacid pill from the pharmacy."

"Never before. Right after it hit me, I had a thought that I couldn't get out of my mind about the lawyer."

"What did your young lawyer say?"

"Not much."

"Maybe he'll try to get you transferred to a prison with a mental ward," Ray said.

"That's not funny."

"Sorry. And I can't criticize you, because it turned out you were right."

Later that night, Bobby began to snore. Joe's bunkmate generated a distinct noise that made it possible to identify the source of the low rumble. Soon the room was filled with the sound of human bullfrogs. If Joe concentrated on taking slow, regular breaths, he could usually tune out the distractions and fall asleep. Before doing so, he offered up a final prayer for Tom Clark. The story in Scripture about the Roman centurion who told Jesus he didn't have to come to the soldier's house to heal his servant came to mind. Long-distance prayer could work.

Paige woke up twice during the night with abdominal pain accompanied by bleeding. Going into the kitchen, she drank half a glass of water. Sandy, who was on her bed in the laundry room next to the kitchen, whimpered. The dog knew something bad was going on. Sandy rubbed against Paige's leg. Paige went to the living room and lay down on the couch. Sandy joined her and nestled against her leg. Paige's breathing slowed, and in a few minutes she fell asleep.

———

A slender ray of morning sunlight touched Paige's face and woke her. Sandy was still lying beside her. Paige took Sandy outside. Moments later, the dog trotted over, licked Paige's right foot, and wagged her tail.

"Thank you for that sweet 'Good morning,'" Paige said. "And thank you for being there for me last night. I'm glad you don't have any worries."

Paige went inside and fixed Sandy's breakfast. A text from Candy came through:

> Praying for you, my new friend. Also heard about
> Tom Clark.

Candy had copied Vicki with the text. While Paige read it, Vicki added a "praying hands" emoji to it. Paige placed the phone on the kitchen table and measured out coffee beans for the grinder. It wasn't surprising that the news about Tom's heart attack had spread rapidly through Cranfield. The coffee was dripping into the pot when Ryan appeared and rubbed his eyes.

"Is that decaf?" he asked.

"No, I decided I needed a cup of regular today."

"Great," he replied, then met Paige's eyes. "Or is there a bad reason for that?"

Paige told him about her troubled night.

"I don't think I lost the baby, but I was worried," she said. "The uncertainty while I wait to see the doctor again is hard."

Ryan stepped closer and wrapped his arms around her. She leaned into him and sighed.

"I wish you'd have let me know," he said.

"Maybe I should have, but Sandy earned a week's worth of dog treats."

"How?"

Paige told him. The coffee maker signaled the end of the brewing process. They sat at the kitchen table. Paige picked up her phone and handed it to Ryan.

"Here's the text I received from Candy Bynam."

"Word gets out," Ryan said. "I wonder when I'll hear from Karen. Tom should be settled in at the hospital in Charlotte."

"When you find out, should I let Candy know?"

"Not till I get the okay from Karen. Are you going to let anyone know about last night?"

"No."

While Ryan was spreading cream cheese on his bagel, Paige received another text from Candy.

"You don't have to talk to Karen," she said to Ryan. "According to Candy, the cardiologist in Charlotte couldn't correct the blockages with stents. Tom is scheduled for open-heart surgery this morning at ten o'clock."

Paige pressed her lips together for a moment. "Do you think we should pray for Tom?"

Ryan, who was about to take a bite from his bagel, instead lowered it to a small plate. "I guess so," he said.

"You do it."

Paige watched as Ryan folded his hands in front of him and closed his eyes. She closed her eyes too. Ryan spoke slowly and deliberately: "God, we pray for Tom that he will have a successful surgery and won't die. Amen."

They both opened their eyes.

"How was that?" Ryan asked.

"Fine."

"Is there something you want to add?"

As soon as Ryan asked the question, Paige felt tears well up in her eyes. She reached for a paper napkin from the holder in the center of the table. Then she took a deep breath and closed her eyes. A tear escaped and ran down her cheek. She took another deep breath, then began to pray.

"God, the reason we're praying for Tom is because we hope it will do some good."

Paige's words were halting at first, but as she continued, ideas for things to say popped into her head. Her own worries retreated. She felt a deep, unexpected concern for Tom Clark. He wasn't just Ryan's boss and a distant relative, but a man in desperate need of help. Paige found herself sincerely asking God to give that help. She prayed much longer than she thought possible. Her tears ended, and she concluded with a request for Ryan.

"And help Ryan do a better job at the office than he believes possible. Give him the ability to provide good advice to clients who will go along with what he says. May he and the staff communicate well and work smoothly together. Amen."

Paige opened her eyes. Ryan was staring at her with his mouth slightly open.

"Where did you learn to do that?" he asked. "You sounded like some kind of expert prayer person."

"I don't know. Maybe I was influenced by what we heard the other day at church. It was almost like writing a memo."

"A memo?"

"It's the best description I can come up with. Sometimes the words just flow."

Paige shut her eyes tightly. "Let me add one more thing," she said. "God, please position our baby in the right place."

Ryan reached out and took her hand in his. "Yes," he said.

Ryan left the table to take a shower and dress for work. Paige stayed in the kitchen. She, too, was surprised by her prayer. Talking to God felt as natural as speaking with a friend who cared. Paige laid her hand on her abdomen and prayed again for her baby.

Even though Ryan arrived early at the office, Nancy was already there.

"Did you get the update about Tom?"

"That he's having surgery this morning at ten o'clock."

"No." Nancy shook her head. "They can't do the surgery. He tested positive for COVID."

"What? Where was he exposed?"

"Maybe a friend of Karen's who came over for dinner the other night. She has it."

"How long will he have to wait for surgery?"

"Karen said something about the risk of blood clots being greater until he's clear of infection."

After the prayers by both Joe Moore and Paige, Ryan felt deflated. "I'll be in my office if you hear anything else."

Ryan didn't do anything for several minutes. He considered giving Paige an update but decided to wait until he had more information. Pulling a file from the stack on the front corner of his desk, he started to work. Shortly before lunch, he received a call from Danny Milton.

"Hey," Danny said. "I wanted to follow up and get a date on the calendar to play tennis. Any chance you could sneak away from the office around four o'clock tomorrow and meet me at the country club?"

Ryan told him what was going on with Tom.

"I'm sorry to hear that," Danny said. "I'll let the folks at the DA's office know. Maybe you and I can get together in a few weeks."

Ryan started to agree, then changed his mind. "Actually, it might be good for me to get a break for an hour or so tomorrow. It's going to be intense around here. Maybe just for one set."

"Unless the first set is over quick because I constantly charge the net for a kill shot."

Ryan smiled. "Tomorrow at four," he said.

"But if you have to cancel, let me know. I'll understand."

Ryan ate an apple at his desk. It felt uncomfortable being the one to make final decisions on recommended actions to clients, but he had no other option. Around three o'clock, Nancy buzzed him.

"Shana Parks is on line two. Do you want to take it?"

"Yes."

Ryan pressed the button to receive the call.

"I asked for Mr. Clark, and the receptionist directed me to you," Shana said.

"Tom had a heart attack yesterday and is in Charlotte for treatment," Ryan explained.

"Oh, I'm so sorry to hear that, but we have a question about the invoice for the initial discussions at the office and the trip to the prison. It was my understanding we'd be billed at the first of the month."

Ryan hadn't seen a bill, and they hadn't discussed it in the meeting with Tom before he left for the heart catheterization. Apparently, Tom had accelerated the payment process due to the cash-flow problem at the office.

"And he deducted the amount from the retainer without giving us five days to respond. Or at least that's the way I read the contract of employment with your law firm."

Ryan had seen that provision in the documents. He now wondered if Tom wasn't thinking straight because of his heart issues.

"You're right. I'm sorry about that. Did you have any issues with the amount?"

"We were overcharged by almost two hours for the time we spent at the prison. You and I were together the whole time."

"Let me pull that and correct it," Ryan replied. "And I'll make sure the proper procedure is followed in the future."

"Okay. What else have you done on the case?"

"I've talked to your uncle on the phone, and I'm going to visit the scene of the crime later today. I also have a meeting set up with a lawyer at the district attorney's office."

"Sounds good." Shana was silent for a moment. "Will you be able to manage the case without oversight by Mr. Clark if he's out of the office for an extended period of time?"

"Absolutely."

The call ended. Ryan printed out his time entries for the Moore case and went to Nancy's desk.

"Tom usually doesn't make mistakes like that," she said, shaking her head. "But you deserve every penny for the work you do on—"

"Nancy, please pull up the bill?"

Nancy sniffed as she printed out a hard copy of the invoice and handed it to Ryan. He glanced over it and compared it to what he'd entered in his records.

"Reduce the time at the prison by two hours and also issue a credit for an hour Tom allocated for research. Email the change to Shana Parks."

"If Tom asks about it later—"

"I'll explain."

"Okay."

Ryan checked his watch. "I'm going to scout out the nightclub where the murders took place."

"There's not going to be much to see. The building has been abandoned and boarded up for years."

CHAPTER 20

Joe inspected the long rows of strawberry plants. The past two days had witnessed an explosion of berries. He called together the men on the work crew.

"This afternoon we're going to harvest strawberries. Manny, jog over to the kitchen and let Dickie know we'll be bringing him several gallons of fruit, in case they want to put strawberry shortcake on the menu."

"With whipped cream," another man added.

"What are the odds of that happening?" a third man asked. "I bet my dessert it will be dry cake and fruit tonight."

"You're on," Manny replied.

"Only if you promise not to tell Dickie about the bet," the man said.

Manny frowned.

"Both of you run over to the kitchen," Joe said. "That way you can keep an eye on each other. And ask for more ice water. It's going to be scorching hot this afternoon."

Joe had spent the morning weeding and harvesting the strawberry plants. He ate several warm berries, but none tasted as good as that first one of the season had. After his lunch siesta, he lay on his side and rested on his elbow.

Ray came over to him. "You were snoring so loud, I moved closer to the fence to get out of earshot."

"I snorted once. It woke me up. That only happens when I lie on my back."

Ray picked up a long piece of grass, rolled it between his fingers, and put the stem in the corner of his mouth. "Another guy who snores told me someone went through your personal stuff. How did you figure it out?"

Joe told him.

"Nobody keeps anything valuable under their bunk," Ray replied. "Valuables have to be locked up in the administration building."

"What do you have locked up?" Joe asked.

"Nothing. Same as you."

Ray took the grass from his mouth. "I have a suspect," he said.

"Who?" Joe asked.

"Ned, that guy from your hometown."

"Why him?"

"His job working on the heating and cooling systems gives him access to the buildings when the rest of us are on work detail. And he's been interested in finding out about you. Remember how he asked me the other day if I'd ever been afraid of you?"

"Yes."

"He's checking you out. Maybe he wanted to find out exactly what you have under your bunk."

"He's welcome to read my prayer journals and the notebook I use for Bible study."

"Is there anything in there you wouldn't want anyone else to see or know about?"

Joe thought for a moment. "Praise the Lord. I have nothing to hide."

"That's a good testimony, brother."

The two men were silent.

"Should I say something to Ned?" Joe asked.

"What would you say? Without proof, you can't accuse him of going through your stuff. And starting a conversation like that in prison can go in several directions, none of them good."

"Yeah, you're right."

Ray pointed his finger at Joe. "You should spend time trying to get to know him. I've felt a burden from the Lord for his soul. Maybe we could talk to him together."

Joe nodded reluctantly. "All right, but only if you take the lead."

At quitting time, the work crew left the field with multiple buckets overflowing with okra and strawberries. Joe and Ray delivered everything to the loading dock for the kitchen. Dickie came out and sampled a strawberry.

"They're still a little tart," he said. "If we wait a day or so, they'll be sweeter. I'm stewing tomatoes and onions to mix in with the okra."

"Sounds good," Joe replied. "What's for dessert?"

"Applesauce."

"Applesauce?" Ray snorted. "That's not dessert."

"It's poured on top of sheet cake that turned out dry as corn bread. I'm also dropping a cherry on top."

"I hope the applesauce dessert doesn't start a riot," Ray said.

Dickie put his hands on his hips and frowned.

"Only kidding," Ray continued.

"What he should have said is that the stewed okra will be like dessert," Joe added.

"Yeah, that's what I was thinking."

Later, while standing in line, Joe spotted Ned Walker across the room. He was sitting at a table surrounded by men from Unit G. Joe nudged Ray and pointed him out. "No chance of talking to him during supper."

"Maybe afterward," Ray replied. "Sometimes he hangs out in the exercise yard near the basketball courts."

———

There wasn't a sign on the highway for the former nightclub. The GPS directed Ryan to leave the main road heading east out of town and turn onto a long unpaved drive. He passed a cluster of run-down houses. The road veered to the left and ended in a dirt-and-gravel parking lot with scraggly grass growing in it. Several light poles with broken fixtures on top were scattered around the lot. The club was still standing, but barely. It was a long, low wooden structure that at one time had been painted bright red and orange. Large sections of the roof were missing shingles. Beside a rusty double metal door, he could still make out the words "Eastside Music Barn."

Ryan parked directly in front of the door. He'd not seen a "No Trespassing" sign. Getting out of the car, he walked over to the building and turned the knob on the door. To his surprise, it wasn't locked. When he tried to open it, though, he heard the clank of a metal chain. The door cracked open only three inches. The interior was streaked with sunlight from the holes in the roof. It was an empty space. The investigative file mentioned a rear door. Ryan walked the length of the building outside. To his right was an open field. In the middle of the field was a dilapidated mobile home resting on cement blocks. An old truck and the shell of a car were parked in front of the mobile home. A large brown dog emerged from beneath the trailer and began to bark. Ryan started to return to his car but then realized the dog was tied by a rope to a post in the ground.

At the back of the building, he saw an old propane tank, a refrigerator with the door removed, and a pile of miscellaneous pieces of metal. In the eave above his head was a huge exhaust fan. Ryan turned the corner and saw the rear door. At one time it had been painted lime green. Above the door hung a crooked light fixture for a single bulb. Scrubby grass grew all the way up to the structure. Ryan tried to turn the knob for the door. It wouldn't budge. It was either locked or rusted shut. He stood with his back to the building and tried to imagine what everything would have looked like on a Saturday night more than twenty-five years earlier with the exhaust fan whirling and the music and the crowd noise making the walls vibrate. He inspected the ground and wondered where in the grass the young couple's blood was spilled. Time and nature had removed any evidence from the scene. He decided to give the doorknob a final try. This time he grabbed the knob with both hands. He felt it move slightly.

"What are you doin' here?" a male voice behind him demanded.

Ryan spun around and faced a tall, heavyset man who was wearing blue overalls and no shirt. A rope in his right hand was connected to a brown dog. The dog was bigger up close. A low rumble emerged from its throat.

"I'm Ryan Clark. A lawyer investigating a case."

The man squinted his eyes and opened his mouth. Only a few yellow teeth remained. "Who gave you permission to be here?"

"No one. I didn't see any signs. But I'm leaving. Sorry to bother you."

The man released a few feet of rope. The dog lunged forward and blocked Ryan's path. The rumble became a menacing growl.

"What kind of case?" the man demanded.

"A murder that happened here years ago."

The man removed an oily-looking cap and wiped sweat from his brow before returning it to his head. He was older than Ryan initially thought. His wispy hair was gray and white.

"Involving the harmonica player?"

"Joe Moore. I don't know if he plays the harmonica or not."

The man nodded. "Oh, he played a mean harmonica. Why is that case coming up again after all these years?"

"I can't say. I've just started my investigation."

The man eyed him for a moment. "Come over to the house," he said.

"Thanks, but I need to be going."

"Not till we talk."

"Really—"

The man reached into the pocket of his overalls and took out a pistol. Ryan swallowed. Only once in college, when he and a few buddies were stupid enough to buy bootleg liquor at two o'clock in the morning in downtown Greenville, South Carolina, had he been in a situation in which a gun appeared.

"Listen," Ryan said, holding his hands out in front of him. "I'm not here to cause you any trouble."

"Maybe. But now that you're here, we're going to talk."

"Put the gun away first," Ryan said in a voice he hoped sounded more authoritative than he felt.

"No problem." The man returned the pistol to his pocket. "I'm like Rex here. I just wanted to get your attention."

As Ryan walked beside the man toward the mobile home, he calculated the odds of running to safety. He doubted the man would actually shoot at him if he sprinted toward his car. But outrunning Rex would be impossible. Ryan looked down at the animal's imposing jaw and noticed drops of drool escaping the dog's mouth. They reached the trailer. Breathing heavily, the man ascended the three wooden steps to the door.

"The place is a mess," he said in a normal tone of voice. "I wasn't expecting company."

Ryan stayed at the bottom of the steps. "Let's talk out here."

"No," the man replied. "I need to sit down."

Ryan reluctantly climbed the steps. Inside was a long single room that contained the living area to the left and the kitchen to the right. A brown vinyl couch and matching chair furnished the living area. He could see dishes piled up in the kitchen sink, and a stale odor hung in the air. The man unhooked the rope from Rex's neck. The dog ignored Ryan and trotted over to a maroon dog bed with bits of stuffing sticking out.

"Take your pick," the man said, pointing to the couch and chair.

Ryan sat on the edge of the couch and noticed a small old-fashioned TV on a stand beside a narrow window. The man lowered himself into the chair. Ryan took a business card from his wallet and handed it to him.

"I'm Ryan Clark. I work with Tom Clark."

"Heard of him," the man grunted as he looked at the card, then tossed it on the floor beside the chair. "Can't recall if it was good or bad. My name is Vesper Garrison. Most folks call me Doc."

"Do you own the property where the old nightclub sits?"

"Nah; if I did, I would sell and move. The Drummonds have owned a bunch of land around here for a long time."

"Including the nightclub?"

"I reckon. All they care about is me coming up with the rent money for my lot. This trailer is falling down around me. When it's gone, I'm not sure where I'll find a place to live."

The older man took off his cap and rubbed his hand across his head and down the back of his neck. Ryan wondered if the Drummond ownership went all the way back to the time of the murder. He could check the real estate records at the courthouse.

"So you're a lawyer," Doc continued. "Is it true that after enough time passes, they can't lock you up for what you've done?"

"That's true for some crimes."

"What about cooking meth?"

"I don't know. I'm not a criminal defense lawyer."

Doc's eyes narrowed. "I thought you claimed to be working for the harmonica player sent off for murder."

"I am, but this type of case is different." Ryan stopped and took out his phone. "Let me check on that question for you. No charge."

A minute later, Ryan logged off a website.

"Manufacturing methamphetamine is a felony, and there's no statute of limitations for felonies in North Carolina," he said. "That means a person can be charged at any time even if the crime occurred a long time ago."

"That don't seem right," Doc grunted. "It's been at least twenty years."

Ryan stood. "I'm sorry that's not the answer you wanted. If you have any other questions, you have my card and can call me—"

"The harmonica player didn't kill those folks," Doc said.

CHAPTER 21

Joe and Ray didn't see Ned Walker in the exercise yard after supper. That night, Joe dreamed about fishing in his favorite pond in Blanton County. The dream was so vivid that he could feel the breeze that caused the water to ripple in the afternoon sunlight. He was intently watching as a fish nudged his line with its nose when the morning siren woke him up. Joe rolled over in bed. Bobby was already standing beside his bed. Joe told him about the dream.

"I wish I could have seen that fish take the bait," Joe said.

"I like to dream about fish," the large man replied. "But in my best dreams, they're on a dinner plate with a side of hush puppies and French fries."

Joe was late for breakfast. The dining hall was crowded, and there wasn't an empty seat at the table where the men from Unit C usually sat. Joe stood at the end of the serving line with his tray and looked over the room. He didn't see Ned Walker either. There were scrambled eggs and two sausage links on Joe's plate.

The sausage links were green at one end. He turned away from the serving line and walked directly to the large opening where the men dropped off their trays and plates when they finished eating. Joe shoved his tray across to one of the workers. The man looked at Joe's plate.

"What's wrong?" he asked. "Are you sick?"

"Not hungry," Joe replied.

The man picked up one of the sausages. "Are you worried about this? It's just the dye they use to identify the case of meat. Yours were on the end and got sprayed. It won't hurt you."

Joe held up his hands. "I'm done."

He walked across the exercise yard toward Unit C to retrieve a pack of crackers from beneath his bunk. It was a cloudy morning and darker clouds at the edge of the skyline held the possibility of rain. It had been ten days since any rain had fallen, and the garden needed the water. If a shower came, the work crew would leave the garden and return to the toolshed to perform maintenance. Joe would welcome a day doing maintenance. As he entered Unit C, he was almost knocked down by someone rushing out. It was Ned.

"Sorry," Ned quickly said as he reached out to steady Joe. "I was in a hurry."

Joe grabbed his arm. "What's the hurry? And what were you doing in Unit C?"

Ned roughly shrugged off Joe's grip.

"My shift started early today," he replied, brushing his hand down his sleeve. "The AC in the guardroom is acting up, and I need to install a new switch for the condenser so the men on duty don't start roasting by this afternoon."

"Were you working over here yesterday?"

"Yeah, that's when I got the service call. What's your problem?"

In his younger days, Joe could tell when he was about to get into a fight. It didn't happen often, but an anticipation of violence would rise up on the inside. When it surfaced, he'd launch an attack. It had been a long time since he'd had that feeling. A quick blow from Joe's right hand would land on the side of Ned's head before he could react. Joe clenched his fist and then opened it.

"Nothing," he managed. "You startled me."

"Okay," Ned said, relaxing. "I don't want trouble with anyone. Especially someone who's from Blanton County."

"Can you tell me why you've been asking around about me?"

"Curious, I guess. You don't remember me, but my cousins and I were in the crowd several times when you and your band were playing a gig. You could rock the harmonica like nobody's business."

"Where did you hear us?"

"The Triple Door, Davis's Lounge, Eastside Music Barn."

Joe nodded. "That just about covers it."

Ned licked his lips and glanced down at the ground for a moment. "I want to ask you something, if it's okay."

"Go ahead."

"Would you be willing to give me a lesson or two on the harmonica? One of the guys I talked to said you still play."

Joe eyed Ned. The fellow inmate seemed sincere.

"Tell you what. I'll give you a lesson if you promise to go to the Bible study in Unit G," Joe said.

"Deal," Ned said, holding out his hand so Joe could shake it. "But with my job, they can call me out anytime day or night if there's a maintenance problem that needs fixing. No overtime." Ned laughed at his own joke.

"We're a captive labor force," Joe replied.

Ned laughed again and slapped Joe on the shoulder. "I like that," he said. "I always say it's better to laugh than curse."

"I'd agree with that."

"Let me know when you're ready to give me a lesson," Ned said.

"Do you have a harmonica?"

"I can get one. My relatives are good about sending me anything I ask for, and the warden's office will approve me having it. I'm in good with them."

Ned reached into the top pocket of his uniform and took out a photograph.

"Here are some of my people," he said. "I was going to show them to Everett Robinson. This was taken years ago."

In the photos, Ned, with a full head of curly hair, was standing next to two other men. None of the men were wearing shirts. They all looked like serious weight lifters. The man directly next to Ned was especially well muscled.

"That's my brother, Larry," Ned said. "Next to him is our cousin Frank."

"Everett told me you were a bodybuilder."

"Not me," Ned chuckled. "But Larry was stout."

"I can see that."

Ned returned the photo to his pocket. "It's sad. Larry has cancer. He's skinny as a rail now."

Paige was sitting with her legs propped up on the couch. The rolling pain across her abdomen returned. She gritted her teeth while she waited for it to subside. She'd suffered several similar episodes since eating a light lunch of salad and fruit. This was the worst and longest pain yet. She groaned. Sandy, who was lying across the room on a dog bed, padded over to comfort her.

She sent Ryan a third text asking him to give her a call. Unless he was in court or in a deposition, it wasn't like him not to promptly reply. Ryan hadn't said anything about having to go to the courthouse or taking a deposition before leaving that morning, but Paige knew with Tom in the hospital anything might come up at work. Desperate, she reached for her phone and called Dr. Hester's office. The woman who answered listened then asked her to hold. Pop music from the 1980s played in the background. During the long wait, the pain subsided. A different woman came on the line.

"This is Patty Jenkins, one of the nurses. Dr. Hester is at the hospital with a patient in labor. If you're able, we'd like you to come into the office for an exam. Are you able to drive?"

Paige thought about calling Vicki or Candy and asking one of them to take her but dismissed the idea.

"I believe I can make it," she said.

"Just tell the receptionist to notify me as soon as you're here."

Paige was both relieved and worried, especially by the urgency in the nurse's voice. She was barely seated in the waiting area before the door opened and a slender, petite woman in her forties with brown hair entered.

"Ms. Clark, I'm Patty. Come with me."

The nurse took her vital signs and entered information in a tablet. "Any bleeding associated with the cramping?" she asked.

"At least half the time."

"Your chart has you down for another ultrasound in a few weeks, but we're going to run one today to check the baby's health."

As she waited for a technician, Paige thought about her prayers earlier in the day. Maybe it was time for another attempt. She took a deep breath and tried to form words in her mind. A moment later, the technician arrived and escorted her to the ultrasound examination room. Lying on the examination table, Paige watched the woman's eyes for clues as the ultrasound wand moved back and forth.

"All done," the technician announced. "I'll let the nurse know."

"How's the baby?" Paige asked.

"Looks good," the woman replied matter-of-factly.

Paige breathed a sigh of relief. When she returned to the examination room, Patty was waiting for her with the tablet in her hands.

"I'm glad you came in," the nurse said, holding up the device. "There has been a positive change in the position of the baby. Unless Dr. Hester recommends otherwise, it may not be necessary to schedule another ultrasound until time for your regularly scheduled one."

Paige felt tears of relief rush into her eyes. "Why the cramping and bleeding?" she managed.

"Part of the attachment process. Your baby has taken a circuitous route to get to the place where he or she needs to be."

The nurse showed Paige images from the scan and explained what they meant. Even though her eyes were bleary, Paige absorbed every detail.

"The bleeding should taper off," the nurse continued. "If it doesn't or changes significantly in the next few days, please call again."

"So everything looks normal?"

"Yes."

Paige needed more reassurance. "Will Dr. Hester review the sonogram?"

"Yes."

"And let me know what he thinks?"

"I'll make sure he's aware that you want a follow-up call or text."

On her way home, Paige tried again to reach Ryan. When he

didn't respond, she called her mother with the news of her pregnancy. A quick word of congratulations was followed by a question about the stability of Ryan's job.

"It's fine," Paige replied.

"I hope so," her mother responded. "I don't want him getting fired again, leaving you as the only means of support for a baby. How far along are you?"

"Maybe seven weeks."

"Seven weeks! Why didn't you call sooner?"

"Just wanted to make sure everything was okay."

"Let me know as soon as you know whether it's a boy or a girl."

"Do you have a preference?"

"I enjoy your sister's boys, so that would be good, but I think you'd do well with a girl."

———————

Ryan shifted on the sofa in the living room of Doc Garrison's mobile home.

"Why would you say that Joe Moore didn't kill that young couple?" he asked.

Doc squinted his eyes and scratched the side of his face. "There's a fellow, I'm not saying his name, who sold Joe some high-quality meth that night and saw him take a big hit. After that, Joe was stumbling around in no shape to murder anyone with a knife unless they were already knocked out and lying on the ground."

Ryan thought for a moment. "Did this man sell meth to Joe on other occasions?"

"Oh yeah. Many times. Joe claimed it made him play his harmonica like a rock star."

"How can this man be sure what he's describing happened the night of the murders?"

Doc looked directly into Ryan's eyes. "A person don't forget when two dead bodies later show up on his doorstep."

"Are you saying the bodies were in front of this trailer?" Ryan asked sharply.

"No, no. But you saw how close this place is to the club. The rear door of the club was like the front door of a store. People knew where to shop for all kinds of pills and other stuff to help them have a good time. After the deal with Joe, this fellow was gone for a few minutes to stock up. When he came back, there was a crowd of people at the rear of the club. Someone yelled out that the Drummond girl and her boyfriend were cut to pieces."

"Did you see a bloody knife or any blood on Joe?"

Doc held up his hands. "I didn't see anything at all that night. I was in my trailer watching a ball game on TV. And that's what I'd say if anyone put me under oath at the courthouse."

"Where was Joe when the crowd gathered?" Ryan asked.

"Passed out in his car."

"What else did the man you're talking about see that night?" Ryan asked.

"Once the sirens started blaring and the blue lights showed up, he hid out and didn't come around until the next morning after the cops cleared out. There was that yellow tape all around the rear of the club."

"Did anyone with the sheriff's department ever interview this man?"

"Nope." Doc shook his head. "Which suited him fine."

"How about Joe's lawyer?"

"No."

"Why not keep quiet now?"

Doc was silent for a moment. The older man's eyes held a faraway look. "Some things that happen in life can be pushed away, and after a while they give up coming around. But that's not true about everything. The idea of a man rotting in prison for something he didn't do eats away at you."

"But this man isn't willing to come forward to help because he could still be charged with a felony for the manufacture and distribution of methamphetamine. Is that true?"

"And other things that don't need to be brought up after all these years."

Ryan leaned against the back of the sofa. "I'm not sure what to do with this story. How does it help Joe Moore?"

"It helps his lawyer."

"How?"

"To know that Joe's innocent. Isn't that important?"

"Yeah," Ryan admitted, then paused. "If the DA agrees not to prosecute this man for past crimes, would he be willing to tell what he knows in court under oath?"

Doc didn't immediately answer. He pulled a tissue from a misshapen box beside his chair and loudly blew his nose. He dropped the tissue on top of Ryan's business card.

"This fellow doesn't know much about the law and if what a DA says can be trusted or not."

"It would be in writing," Ryan said.

"Signed by a judge?"

"I'm not sure how that would work."

Doc shook his head. "This place may look bad to you," the older man said. "But it beats a jail cell. And someone has to take care of Rex."

CHAPTER 22

Paige was pulling into the driveway of the house when Ryan called. She turned off the engine.

"Sorry," Ryan began. "I left my phone behind when I was out of the car and didn't see your texts or know you'd called. Is everything okay?"

"Yes!" Paige exclaimed. "Better than okay."

The news spilled out of Paige. Twice she had to back up and fill in the blanks.

"I'm jumping all over the place," she said.

"I wish you could see the smile on my face."

"Any chance you can come home early so we can celebrate? I know that's asking a lot, but—"

"Would you like me to take you out to eat?" Ryan asked.

Paige didn't hesitate. "Yes, and surprise me."

"I'm working on something special."

Inside the house, Paige vigorously rubbed the sides of Sandy's face when the dog greeted her. The extra interaction caused the animal to jump from side to side.

"I know," Paige said. "I'm excited too."

In the backyard, Sandy ran rapidly back and forth. Paige's phone vibrated. It was the doctor's office.

"This is Mark Hester. I saw that you came in today, and I've reviewed the sonogram."

"Is the baby in the right location?" Paige quickly asked.

"Much closer to normal. I may want to schedule an extra ultrasound, especially if you continue to cramp and bleed."

"The cramping hasn't happened since I left the office. Do you think it could have been related to stress?"

"Possibly."

"And today's results were positive, right?"

"Very positive."

The call ended. Paige was able to work steadily the rest of the afternoon.

It was 6:15 p.m. when she leaned back in her chair and realized she'd not had a single cramping episode. She was in the kitchen pouring a fresh glass of water when Sandy barked sharply and Ryan entered. Paige left the glass on the counter and gave him an extra-long hug.

"Sorry I'm late. Do you still want to go out to eat? I think a celebration is in order."

"Yes, I'm starving."

"How about a steak?"

"Yes, but where? We didn't like the steak house we tried when we first moved to town."

"There's a place on Palmer Street that Nancy mentioned. It's a catering business, but one night a month they're open to the public. Usually, it takes several months to get a reservation, but I called and they had a cancellation."

Ryan was wearing a tie.

"Should I change clothes?" Paige asked.

"Probably—just don't take too long."

Paige rolled her eyes. "Do I have a reputation for needing a lot of time to get ready?"

Paige changed into a casual dress and sandals. She took a minute to arrange her hair. Ryan was sitting in the living room with his phone in his hands.

"How do I look?" she asked.

"Great. Let's go."

Ryan opened the car door for Paige. She stopped and eyed him curiously.

"What's really going on?" she asked.

"Nothing. We're going to eat a nice meal."

Paige settled in and waited for Ryan. "Where were you when I couldn't reach you?" she asked as he backed the car out of the driveway.

"Working on Joe Moore's case. Major development. I'm going back to the prison day after tomorrow."

"Good or bad?"

"Potentially very good. I met a man who claims there's no way Joe committed the murders. He confirmed what you wondered after you read the file: that Joe was too drugged up to have stabbed anyone to death."

Paige was silent for a moment. "Could we talk about something else?"

"Absolutely," Ryan replied, glancing over at her. "While you were changing clothes, I also called the catering company to find out more about the menu. It's not steak. They're preparing beef Wellington for everyone tonight. Have you ever tried it?"

"No."

"Neither have I, but it sounds like a perfect dish for a celebration."

Ryan and Paige arrived at a nicely renovated older house on Palmer Street. A small white sign in the well-groomed front yard announced "McKnight Catering—Special Events and Weddings." There were four cars in the driveway. All of the vehicles were expensive.

"How much is this going to cost?" Paige asked when Ryan parked beside a shiny Tesla.

"It's too late to back out," he replied. "I had to provide my credit card in advance to secure the reservation. We can treat this as my birthday present."

"Your birthday isn't for six months, and I was planning on buying you an electric lawn mower."

They rang the chime. The door was opened by a tall, stately Black woman, fortyish, wearing a long dress.

"I'm Celeste McKnight," the woman said. "My husband and I own the house and business. Come in."

They followed their hostess into a large formal dining room where a table was set for fourteen. Several other couples were already talking and drinking wine. Ryan hadn't previously met any of the other guests, but he recognized two names because of local businesses. Half the diners had driven in from out of town. A man who owned the largest insurance agency in the area shook his hand.

"I heard about Tom's heart attack. How's he doing?"

As Ryan talked, he saw that Paige was in conversation with a woman at the other end of the room. Three more couples arrived. Ms. McKnight rang a little silver bell to announce the start of dinner. There were assigned seats with name cards. Ryan was next to the woman Paige had talked to previously. Jessica Gurley was an attractive middle-aged woman with dark hair.

"Your wife tells me you're a lawyer," Jessica said. "Our older son is thinking about law school."

"It's a great education," Ryan said, giving his stock answer to the question. "You really learn how to think analytically about anything."

"That's what I had to do every day in my last job," the woman replied.

"What were you doing?"

"Forensic accounting for banks and investment companies. I was with a consulting group that would be brought in for an independent review when a problem came up."

"Why did you move to Cranfield?"

"It's temporary. My parents are here and need help as they deal with some health issues. I needed a break, and my husband, Jack, can work remotely from anywhere. Our kids are out of the house."

"Did you grow up in Cranfield?"

"Only for high school."

"Did you happen to know Cherie Drummond or Marty Brock?"

Jessica gave him a startled look. "Marty and I were classmates and dated two or three times during my senior year. And of course I knew Cherie. Everyone did. What a terrible tragedy. Why are you asking about them after all these years?"

Ryan regretted bringing up the subject. "Sorry, it has to do with an investigation I'm conducting."

"Into the murders?"

"Yes, but I can't go into any details."

A cloud crossed Jessica's face, and she turned toward her husband. The soup arrived. The main ingredient was creamed asparagus. Ryan tasted it and leaned over to Paige.

"I don't like asparagus, but this is great."

"Yes, and I heard what you said to Jessica and saw her reaction," Paige whispered.

"It was a mistake."

The soup was followed by an arugula salad with shaved slivers of Parmesan cheese on top. The conversations reached across the table and to the side, but Jessica Gurley continued to give Ryan the cold shoulder. He tried to push past the awkwardness and enjoy the food. Paige entered into an animated conversation with the wife of the insurance broker. The woman and Paige both attended Rice University. Encounters with alums of the selective private school were rare. The beef Wellington arrived on two large platters. The side dish for dinner was roasted fingerling potatoes with rosemary. Several people at the table took out their phones to take a photo of the main course. Ryan took a bite that included a mushroom. It was spectacular.

"This is a good birthday present," Ryan said to Paige. "Way better than an electric lawn mower."

"And you're sharing it with me," she said with a smile.

Out of the corner of his eye, Ryan could tell Jessica Gurley was also savoring the beef Wellington.

"This is as delicious as any I've ever eaten," she said to him. "And I've ordered it at top restaurants in New York and Chicago."

"First time for me," Ryan replied.

"Sorry for my reaction a few minutes ago when you brought up Marty and Cherie," Jessica continued. "I wasn't living here at the time of their deaths, but it was a horrible shock. I'm sure you're just doing your job. If my son is ever in your position, I hope people would be polite to him."

"I'm the one who should apologize," Ryan quickly replied. "I shouldn't have brought it up at an event like this."

The meal was better after clearing the air with his tablemate. When Paige paused in her conversation, he leaned over to let her know.

"Did you know beef Wellington is Gordon Ramsay's favorite dish?" she asked.

"The guy who dumps food prepared by other chefs in a garbage can?"

"Only if it isn't edible."

Dessert was an apple crumble and custard. Ryan was full but didn't slow down. He also ate the last bites of Paige's portion.

"Can't let anything go to waste," he told her.

When the table was cleared, the group applauded the McKnights and the two workers who assisted them.

"I'm ready to go home, put on my nightgown, and relax," Paige said to him when they stood.

Jessica Gurley leaned closer to Ryan.

"I do have a question for you about Marty if you can answer it," she said. "Are you trying to determine if Marty mistreated Cherie?"

"I haven't asked anyone that directly, but one person mentioned that he was a negative influence in Cherie's life."

"Based on my experience with Marty, I agree. That's one reason I reacted as I did. Marty had a mean streak. It brought up a bad memory."

"Sorry."

"But it was a long time ago. And he's gone."

During the drive home, Ryan told Paige what Jessica Gurley shared with him.

"Marty must have done something really bad for her to remember it after all these years," Paige replied. "But I don't see how it makes any difference to what you're doing."

"Unless it leads to something else."

"Like what?"

Ryan stopped for a red light. "I'm not sure. But I believe I need to find out more about him."

CHAPTER 23

Joe and Ray ate supper with Deshaun, who'd received another letter from Kiesha.

"She's having more trouble with the boys as they get older," Deshaun said. "She kept saying over and over that there needs to be a man in the house to help her out with them. By the time I get out, our older son will almost be a teenager."

"Is there a relative in your family who could spend time with the boys?" Joe asked.

Deshaun shook his head sadly. "My dad's not the answer. He works hard but starts drinking as soon as he gets home in the afternoon. And the liquor makes him mean. My brother wouldn't do it."

Joe knew this about Deshaun's past, along with the tragic fact that the young man's father punched his children when drunk.

"Any of your cousins?" Ray asked.

Deshaun was silent for a moment. "My cousin Rodney would be a possibility. He coaches his kids' sports teams, but he has four boys of his own. Trying to fit in two more would be asking a lot."

"Does he live in the same town?"

"On the east side. Kiesha is on the west side. His boys go to a different school."

"It's worth a try," Ray said.

"Yeah." Deshaun shrugged. "But first I'd have to apologize to Rodney. Before I got into the trouble that got me locked up in here, he spent a night in jail because he was hanging out with me, and I was arrested for possession of some pills. Rodney didn't know the stuff was on me or that I was going to sell it. He thought we were just going to shoot some hoops, not do a drug buy."

"Get right with Rodney even if he can't help Kiesha," Joe said.

"I know. I was thinking about him the other day."

Deshaun picked up his tray and headed across the dining hall.

"Another idea would be if there's a man in Kiesha's church who would take an interest in the boys," Ray said.

"I thought about that, but she just got untangled from a man in the church. Temptation doesn't stop at the door to the house of God."

"True," Ray replied, then pointed across the dining hall. "There's your harmonica student."

Ned Walker had arrived late for the mealtime. He saw them, headed in their direction, and sat in the chair vacated by Deshaun.

"Wasn't sure I was going to make it," Ned said. "Whoever did the electrical wiring for this facility didn't know what they were doing. This place is a death trap. If I hadn't fixed a short in the light switch for the showers in Unit B, someone could have gotten electrocuted if they flipped it on while standing in a puddle of water."

"Did you fix the problems in Unit C?" Joe asked.

"Yeah."

Joe glanced at Ray and signaled for him to say something.

"You shooting any hoops after supper?" Ray asked.

"No, I'm tired. All I'm going to do is watch a little TV and go to sleep." Ned turned to look at Joe. "And show up for the Bible study if I want harmonica lessons."

"Is your harmonica on the way?" Joe asked.

"Should be here in a couple of days. I told my aunt the brand you recommended. She'd do anything for me."

"Does she live in Blanton County?" Joe asked.

"All her life, but you don't know her. She keeps to herself."

"Is she in the Vicksboro area?" Joe asked.

"No. Will I have to trim my mustache to play the harmonica?"

The facial hair on Ned's upper lip was impressive and dipped down over his mouth.

"We won't know until you give it a try, but I doubt it," Joe replied.

Ned twisted one end of his mustache. "Good. It's taken me a long time to get this to the place I want it. And now there aren't any ladies to appreciate it." He laughed.

After the meal, Joe and Ray left the dining hall together.

"What did you make of that?" Joe asked Ray.

"I thought the chicken was okay, but the mashed potatoes were so runny you needed a spoon to eat them."

"I mean Ned Walker, the way he talks about stuff."

"That's just his way, I guess." Ray shrugged.

"If I'd asked his aunt's name, I don't think he would have told me."

"There are a thousand reasons why someone in here wants to keep his life outside off-limits. How are you going to feel when I show up at your nursing home and tell the lady at the front desk that I want to visit my old friend from prison days?"

Paige pulled the cotton sheet up to her chin. Since becoming pregnant she'd turned down the thermostat on the air conditioner. Being cool was a high priority.

"I'm going to get a blanket from the closet," Ryan said.

"Are you going to be okay with a higher electric bill?"

Ryan spread out the blanket and then rolled onto his side so that he faced her. "You work. And this house is your office. The last thing I'm going to complain about is you adjusting the temperature. If this blanket isn't enough, I can put on wool socks."

"Do you own any wool socks?"

"No, but I can buy some from the money you earn."

Paige smiled. She reached out and touched him on the shoulder.

"Thanks for praying for me this morning," she said. "I thought about it when I was scared and driving to the doctor's office."

"I didn't say anything. You're the one who's become an instant expert in prayer."

"But it was our prayer, and it was answered."

Ryan held her hand and kissed it. "For whatever reason, I'm glad our little boy is moving into his temporary home."

"And that she stays there until it's time for us to meet her," Paige replied.

Ryan was asleep within minutes of resting his head on the pillow and closing his eyes. How he could turn off his brain in a split second and lose consciousness was a mystery to Paige. Because the day had been so eventful, she went over the highlights in her mind. The greatest news was the healthy status of the baby inside her. She placed her right hand on her abdomen and silently prayed for the unborn child. Once again, thoughts seemed to flow out of her. The thought of a sweet little voice, whether male or female, calling her "Mommy" brought joy to her heart. Ryan snorted.

"It will be okay if 'Daddy' is her first word," Paige whispered softly. "I'd love that too."

Paige woke early in the morning. Slipping out of bed, she went to the bathroom and then took Sandy into the backyard. Paige hadn't felt any cramping or abdominal pain in the night. And there wasn't any sign of bleeding when she was in the bathroom.

"Is that really behind me?" she asked out loud.

"I am," a male voice replied.

Paige jumped and spun around.

"Why did you sneak up on me like that?" she demanded.

"I didn't sneak up on you," Ryan replied, holding up his hands in front of him. "I knew you'd be out here with Sandy and wanted to know if you want hot tea or decaf coffee. Were you talking to God?"

"No, myself."

"How long has that been going on?" Ryan asked with a grin.

"Decaf," Paige said, ignoring the question. "With extra cream."

After Ryan went inside, Sandy came over and Paige scratched the dog's head.

"Why didn't you bark when he came into the yard?" she asked. "You're supposed to let me know when anyone enters my space."

Sandy licked Paige's hand.

"I forgive you."

Ryan threw his tennis gear in the trunk of his car and left the house without eating breakfast. At the office he asked Nancy if there was any update on Tom's status.

"Nothing new," the receptionist replied. "Karen sent a text last night that because of COVID, she's not allowed into the room, but he can receive texts and emails on his phone."

Ryan spent twenty minutes composing an email to Tom. He didn't go into any details about his work on the Moore case other than to mention the number of hours he'd been able to bill and his upcoming trip to the prison to meet again with the client. He included a lot of specific information about regular clients. He was about to press send when he decided he had something he wanted to add:

> And I want to thank you for your trust and confidence in me to keep things together while you're out of the office. What you said to me before you left meant a lot, especially after my struggles as a young lawyer. It's the kind of thing I wish I'd heard from my father but never did.

Ryan reread the paragraph, then deleted the final sentence. He didn't want to put pressure on Tom, especially now, to be a surrogate parent.

After sending the report to Tom, Ryan spent the rest of the morning phoning clients who had questions and sending emails to others, updating them on their cases. By noon he was hungry. He stopped off at Sue's desk on his way out the door.

"I was able to do some digging into Vesper Garrison's background," she said. "In his younger days he didn't miss a chance to get in a fight. Multiple arrests for disorderly conduct along with a pair of DUIs. No felonies and no drug arrests. Looks like he's avoided prosecution for anything serious. Oh, and he was part of a large group arrested at a cockfighting event many years ago. No conviction on that one either. It was probably the sheriff's department wanting to let them know that sort of event wasn't welcome in Blanton County."

"Anything else?"

"In one case, there was a letter to the sheriff's department from Mr. Drummond asking for leniency. I thought that was strange."

"Charlie Drummond is his landlord." Ryan paused. "I need to corroborate Garrison's presence at the nightclub property on the night of the murders. Standing alone, his testimony, even if he's willing to give it, lacks credibility."

"That's an understatement," Sue replied.

"Next step is to see what Joe Moore tells me about him."

After a quick lunch, Ryan found a reply from Tom in his inbox. In a lengthy email, his boss included a number of helpful suggestions for some of the cases Ryan mentioned. He concluded by stating, *I'm glad you listened to what I told you the other day. I meant every word.*

At a little before four that afternoon, Ryan left for the country club. The security guard at the gate let him enter when he told him he was playing tennis with Danny Milton.

"Good luck!" the older man said as he waved Ryan through. "You're going to need it!"

Ryan changed clothes in the locker room. Everyone else was preparing for a round of golf. Ryan recognized one of the men who'd been at the dinner the previous night. The middle-aged man came over to shake Ryan's hand.

"I'm going to walk my round," the man said. "I need to burn a few of the calories I took in last night."

"It was a great meal. Have you been there before?"

"No, the McKnights just started offering those dinners last year, but I'm going to make another reservation soon. They've come a long way from the days when they owned a meat-and-three place. Who's your tennis partner?"

"Danny Milton."

The man leaned in closer. "Don't play for money, even if he gives you what sounds like great odds. He's one way during warm-ups but totally different when it gets serious. I'm a decent player but lost a hundred dollars to him even though he gave me three points per game."

Ryan smiled. "I'll be careful."

There was no sign of Danny on the courts. Ryan warmed up against a practice wall.

"Sorry I'm late," Danny said, placing a tennis bag that contained three rackets on the edge of the court. "There have been big changes at work over the past twenty-four hours. I wasn't sure I'd be able to make it."

"We could have rescheduled."

"No, I need this. It will be a good way for me to burn off stress."

"And I need to get rid of some calories," Ryan said, echoing what he'd heard in the locker room. "I ate a lot of rich food last night."

They warmed up by volleying back and forth. Danny hit with power, but Ryan had no problem running down and returning the much taller man's shots.

"Okay," Danny said when they stopped for a drink of water. "This is going to be fun even though I can tell you're going to drive me nuts. Two sets?"

"Depends on how long it takes. I want to be able to walk when I get out of bed in the morning."

"Do you want a friendly wager to make it interesting?"

"Only if you give me three points a game."

Danny laughed. "You've done your homework. I have a reputation as a low-level hustler, but I never keep my winnings. They go straight to a charity of the loser's choosing. Let's play for the enjoyment of the game. You serve first."

Ryan hadn't yet revealed anything about his serve. He unleashed one with a high bouncing spin that Danny barely touched with the end of his racket.

Danny laughed. "That's nasty."

Ryan followed with a hard, fast serve down the middle that Danny didn't touch at all and qualified as an ace.

"That's as good as I have," Ryan said as he bounced the ball against the court and prepared for his third serve of the game.

"All designed to keep me off balance."

Ryan won the first game, then faced Danny's serve. As promised, Danny played a serve-and-volley game. Because of his long arms, it was challenging to get the ball past him at the net. He won the second game. Each man held serve, and the set was decided by a tiebreaker that Ryan won after a long volley that saw him running all over the court. They took a break to towel off and drink water.

"Don't tell anyone you beat me," Danny said. "I have a reputation to uphold in Blanton County."

"Why would I do that?"

"I suspect it's not your style. Are you good for another set?"

"Yes."

Danny got ahead in the second set when Ryan began to tire and slow down. But then Ryan broke Danny's serve and they again went to a tiebreaker. This time Danny won. They sat beside each other on a bench at the edge of the court.

"That was the most fun I've had on these courts since I moved to Cranfield," Danny said, wiping his face with a towel. "I want to contribute a hundred dollars to a charity of your choice."

"You don't have to do that," Ryan replied.

"But I want to."

"Oh, how about the church?"

"Whatever you say."

Danny took a long drink of water.

"You're going to hear the news soon," the assistant DA said. "Steve Fain is resigning to take a job with the attorney general's office in Raleigh. I'm going to be the interim district attorney until elections are held in November."

"Will you run for the job?" Ryan asked.

"That's what I'm trying to figure out. I always viewed this as a stepping stone to a job with a private firm. Now I have to consider if I want to hang around and be in charge of the office."

"Any opponents likely to surface?"

"Scott Nelson at the Belk firm. They'd like to have their man in the position." Danny tapped his racket against his left hand. "With Wyatt Belk's backing, he'll be hard to beat. But I may give it a try anyway. Talk it over with Tom when you can and let me know if your firm would be willing to support me."

"With Tom being out of the office, my caseload is crazy."

Danny took another drink of water. "That's a lot of responsibility to drop on your plate all at once. Any criminal cases? Maybe I could help you get them handled efficiently."

Ryan cleared his throat. "There's one matter. I may be filing an MAR in an old murder case that Tom handled over twenty years ago. It would be great if I could obtain access to the State's file without having to jump through a bunch of hoops. Just the information we know the judge would eventually allow anyway."

"Send me the details, and I'll look into it."

CHAPTER 24

Walking to the toolshed, Joe thought about the Bible study and prayer meeting the previous evening. The Spirit of God truly was stirring among the men. There had never been a meeting like it the whole time Joe had been in prison. Prayer for one topic led to prayer about another. Everett stood and, with tears streaming down his cheeks, confessed a stubborn sin and asked Jesus to set him free. The meeting lasted until one of the guards came into the room and told them it was time for lights-out. Several men said they wanted to share at the next meeting.

Ray stood beside Joe as they waited in line to return their tools.

"I've been thinking about the prayer meeting all day," Ray said. "Should we ask permission to hold another one tonight? There's a lot of unfinished business. Why should we have to wait a week?"

"That's exactly what I've been thinking," Joe said.

Before going to Unit C to shower, Joe and Ray walked across the exercise yard. All prisoner gatherings had to be approved in advance and placed on a calendar. Usually that required a one- to two-week process. The prison chaplain handled requests by Christian groups. The guard let them into the building, and they went to the administration office.

"How was the strawberry shortcake I made for you?" Elle asked when they appeared.

Joe looked sheepishly at Ray.

"It was so good I ate all of it myself before returning to my unit," he said.

"And likely thanked the Lord for every bite," Ray added.

"I'm sorry—" Joe started.

"Bring me another pail of berries and I'll bring you a whole cake," Elle said with a smile.

"If she does, will you share?" Ray asked.

"Yeah."

"I was going to send a message to you," Elle said to Joe. "Your lawyer called and requested an in-person meeting with you tomorrow afternoon after you get off work."

"Okay, I'll be here. We'd like to speak with Chaplain Jim."

"He's out for the day at a seminar in Raleigh."

Joe glanced at Ray.

"Could we speak with the warden?" Ray asked.

"What about?"

"We'd like to hold an extra Bible study and prayer meeting in Unit C," Joe answered. "The Lord was really moving last night, and we want to keep the momentum going."

"Let me check," Elle said, picking up the phone.

Joe and Ray sat on gray plastic chairs while Elle talked on the phone.

"Warden Gunton said for you to wait until Chaplain Jim returns, then fill out the form requesting an additional meeting."

She pushed a piece of paper across her desk.

"Could we talk to the warden directly?" Joe asked. "This is a good thing that's going on."

Elle lowered her voice. "I already asked that. The warden shut me down and said the form is what you have to do. You know how it is. Any meeting by a group of eight or more men requires prior authorization."

"Thanks for trying," Joe said.

"Don't forget the strawberries."

Joe and Ray left.

"I think Elle has a crush on you," Ray said as soon as they were outside.

"I wish I could think about that sort of thing, but you know I can't," Joe replied. "And what good is it going to do her?"

"I don't know, but the desserts she's baking are going to be good for you and your friends."

They walked across the exercise yard.

"What do you think your lawyer wants to talk about?" Ray asked.

"Nothing as important as what we want to do," Joe answered.

They took a few more steps.

"There's no rule against two or three guys standing around talking and praying," Ray said.

"Or five or six," Joe added. "So long as we don't have eight. Let's see if we can make that happen."

"Should we let the guards at the unit know?"

"No, we won't make a big deal out of it."

A group of men approached, including Ned Walker.

"Ned!" Joe called out.

Ned came over to them.

"Did you know your lawyer is coming to see you tomorrow?" Ned asked. "I was in the warden's office earlier and heard about it."

"Yes," Joe replied.

"And my harmonica arrived in the mail this morning. I had to get special permission from the warden to have it because the metal parts could be disassembled and turned into a weapon. Who'd think about doing that?"

"I couldn't have one when I first got here," Joe said. "And I have to show my harmonicas to the guards every time there's an inspection."

"How many do you have?"

"Three. They're in different keys, which is something we'll go over. Can you come over to Unit C after dinner for a first lesson?"

"Yeah, I can use the excuse that I need to check on the air-conditioning unit for the guardroom."

"See you later," Joe said.

Ned moved on.

"What are you up to?" Ray asked Joe as they continued walking.

"I'd like Ned to hear testimonies from other men. The harmonica lesson is an excuse to get him to a meeting."

———————

Ryan had a quick cup of coffee with Paige before leaving to visit Joe Moore. As he passed the Cranfield city limits sign on his way to LPCC, his phone vibrated. It was Charlie Drummond.

"Good afternoon," Ryan said.

"I called the office, and the receptionist told me you were driving out of town to see a client. Is this a good time to talk?"

"Yes, I have an hour-and-a-half drive."

"We won't take that long. How's Tom doing? I heard they had to halt treatment while he gets over COVID."

"Still true, but he feels well enough to read and respond to daily memos I'm sending about our cases."

"Good. I also saw that you visited the former Eastside Music Barn a couple of days ago."

Ryan hesitated before answering.

"That's true," he said slowly.

"There are surveillance cameras on the property, and the company that manages it included footage of you pulling into the parking lot, getting out, and trying to enter through the front door."

"Sorry. I didn't see any 'No Trespassing' signs."

"That will be corrected. Someone must have taken them down. Not that I have a problem with you being there. What were you looking for? Maybe I can help you."

"Just checking the scene of the crime so I have a picture in my mind when I read about the night of the murders."

"Let me know if you want to look around inside the building. There's not much to see. We stripped out everything of value."

Ryan hoped Charlie wouldn't ask him any questions that might require him to mention the encounter with Doc Garrison.

"Why have you held on to the property all these years?" he asked.

"I didn't want any other business to go in there. To me, it's like a graveyard. I probably should have torn it down."

"I understand. I doubt I'll want to go inside, but if I change my mind, I'll let you know."

"Okay. And keep me updated about Tom's status. I'm rooting for him."

"Will do. Thanks."

"Oh, one other thing," Charlie said. "Did you hear the news about Danny Milton running for district attorney?"

"Yes, he told me after we played tennis yesterday afternoon."

"Danny is a decent man, but he's going to have opposition in the race, most likely from Scott Nelson at the Belk law firm. Have you met Scott? He's an excellent lawyer who grew up about twenty miles from Cranfield."

"I've not met him, but I'm sure Tom knows him."

"I'm leaning Scott's way. It's better to have a person in that position with solid local contacts. It's a legal job but also a political position."

"I can see that," Ryan replied without saying more.

"I'll be in touch with you and Tom, especially if I'm part of any effort to host a fundraiser for Scott's campaign. Elections aren't won without money."

The call ended. Dipping his toe into Blanton County politics might be riskier for Ryan than he'd thought. He wondered if he could support Danny while Tom backed Scott. Glad he didn't have to sort it out immediately, he stayed on the phone most of the drive. He fielded one call after another forwarded by Nancy. In between conversations, Ryan made recorded notes on his phone about things he needed to do. The responsibility on his shoulders hadn't doubled. It had quadrupled.

Joe came in from the garden with the largest harvest yet of strawberries. Holding back a choice pailful for Elle, he stopped by the kitchen to deliver the fresh fruit to Dickie. The dining hall supervisor picked a fat strawberry from one of the white buckets and put it in his mouth.

"That's what a strawberry is supposed to taste like," he said, reaching for another. "You can't get ones like this at the grocery store. I'm going to take some home for my wife."

"What's on the menu for us?" Joe asked.

"Strawberry cornmeal cobbler," Dickie replied. "I've been saving the ingredients for the perfect day."

"Never heard of it," Joe said doubtfully.

"Trust me. The men will love it."

Joe showered and made his way to the administration building. He put the strawberries on Elle's desk. She put one in her mouth, chewed, and smiled.

"Did I say these strawberries taste like heaven?"

"Yes."

"Well, the first batch was good, but these are better. There's enough here to make a strawberry shortcake and a strawberry pie."

"That would be awesome."

"It's the Christian thing for me to do," Elle said, putting the pail beneath her desk. "I mentioned your request for another Bible study to Chaplain Jim when he came in this morning. He's going to consider it."

"Okay, thank you."

Joe sat down to wait. Elle answered a phone call but glanced over at him while she talked. Joe thought about what Ray had mentioned about her. Joe liked the administrative assistant, but he really couldn't allow himself to think of anything beyond being friendly toward her. That part of his life had been shut down permanently. Cracking open the door would only lead to frustration and distraction. Maybe she was being kind to him as a prisoner as part of the overflow of her faith. The walkie-talkie on the corner of Elle's desk squawked. She picked it up.

"Moore's lawyer is in consultation room A," a male voice said.

"I'll send him down."

Ryan Clark was sitting on the far side of the small table. He stood when Joe entered.

"How are you?" the lawyer asked as they both sat down.

"Pretty good. How's Tom doing? Were the doctors able to find out what was wrong with his heart?"

"He's going to need bypass surgery, but they put it on hold because he has COVID."

"I'll keep praying for him."

"I'm sure he'll appreciate that." Ryan cleared his throat. "I wasn't planning on coming back so soon, but there's been a development in your case that I wanted to discuss with you. Do you remember a man named Vesper Garrison? He goes by the nickname 'Doc' and lives in a trailer near the Eastside Music Barn."

Joe hadn't thought about the drug dealer in years. It wouldn't have surprised him if the large man who walked around with thick wads of cash in his pockets had shown up in prison.

"I know Doc but haven't heard from him since I was locked up. I wasn't sure if he was alive or dead."

"He's alive. I met with him when I drove to the club to inspect the scene of the crime. Let me tell you what he said about your condition on the night the young couple died."

Joe was shocked at what he heard.

"Is what Doc told me consistent with what you remember?" Ryan asked.

"I can't say," Joe managed, shaking his head. "I know we played a gig at the club, but my next memory is waking up in a jail cell."

"Did Doc sell you any methamphetamine that night?"

"Do we really need to go over this?"

"Yes."

Joe shrugged. "It's possible. I had several sources. The bartender at the club kept a stash of meth under the counter and would provide a hit to band members with the cost taken from our pay to perform."

"What was the bartender's name?"

"Kenny," Joe replied. "He acted like a manager for the whole operation. His last name isn't coming to me right now."

Joe watched as Ryan made a notation on a legal pad that he'd brought with him.

"If you locate Kenny, be careful," Joe continued. "He wouldn't hesitate to pull out a knife and use it if someone crossed him or didn't pay a drug debt. Of course he's a lot older now, but that's no guarantee that he's less violent."

Ryan told Joe about Doc waving a gun in his face.

"Yeah," Joe said, nodding. "That was a common move for those guys. Doc was more bark than bite. Kenny was mean. I wish I could remember his last name. He lived in an old white farmhouse about a mile from the club. I can see it in my mind."

"That's okay. Did you own a gun?" Ryan asked.

"Nothing except a rifle I used for squirrel and rabbit hunting. I stayed away from handguns. They're nothing but trouble."

"And the knife used in the murders didn't belong to you, correct?"

"I'd never seen that knife until they brought it into court in a plastic bag. But according to the government expert, my fingerprints were all over it. There were times when I was high and went off on people, but I wasn't much of a fighter. There's no such thing as winning a fight. Everyone is a loser."

Ryan leaned back in his chair. "Doc isn't willing to go on the record yet because he's concerned about facing a drug charge, but what he told me is consistent with how mentally impaired you must have been that night."

"Like I said, meth will do strange things to you," Joe said.

"Do you think it might help jog your memory if you read some of the information in the investigative file? I talked with the current DA. He may give me voluntary access to their records."

Joe shook his head. "Having this conversation with you is hard enough. Reading that old stuff isn't something I'd want to do," he admitted, then paused. "And who would believe Doc Garrison? Is he going to remember details that happened on a Saturday night over twenty-five years ago when he was probably half-lit too? I'm not sure why he even talked to you."

"I think it had to do with guilt. He's sorry that he didn't come forward before to help clear you from the murder charge."

Ryan's comment stopped Joe. Confession of long-held sin was at the heart of what had been taking place in Unit C over the past forty-eight hours.

"I'd like Doc to get set free," Joe said thoughtfully. "You have my permission to tell him that I don't hold anything against him and want him to make his peace with the Lord."

"I'm not sure how that is going to—"

"It should be from me," Joe said, speaking rapidly. "I'll write out something you can deliver to him. There's been a lot of water under the bridge since Doc knew me. I'm not the same man, and he doesn't have to be the same either. Can I borrow your legal pad?"

"You want to do it now?" Ryan asked in surprise.

"Yeah, unless you're in a hurry. I won't take long because I know this is costing my family money."

Ryan glanced at his watch. "I'll go off the clock."

Words for the drug dealer poured from Joe's heart onto the page. He included a summary of his testimony and tried to make everything easy for Doc to understand. Joe quoted snippets of several Bible verses from memory without giving the reference and concluded with a prayer that he encouraged Doc to pray out loud. He used the front and back of the page, then ripped it out.

"Here you go," Joe said, sliding the paper across the table to Ryan. "That didn't take too long."

"Eighteen minutes."

"Longer than I thought."

Ryan folded the sheet of paper in half.

"You should read it before you give it to him," Joe said. "In case he has any questions."

"Not my area of expertise," Ryan replied.

"That needs to change, don't you think?"

Ryan opened his mouth but then shut it.

"And it would be good if you printed out the verses so Doc doesn't have to go to the trouble of looking them up in the Bible."

"Okay."

"Thanks for coming," Joe said before going silent for a moment. "By the way, what's your wife's name?"

"Paige."

"You can let her read what I wrote Doc if you like."

"I'll see if she's interested."

Joe had a lightness in his step as he crossed the exercise yard, heading toward the dining hall. The depression that weighed down his spirit when they talked about the night of the murders retreated before the opportunity to share the gospel with Doc Garrison. He remembered something his mother had written him years before about God's Word being a sword that cuts through whatever binds a person.

CHAPTER 25

Paige received a text from Ryan letting her know that he'd not be home from the prison in time for supper. She ate a salad and then took Sandy out for an early evening walk. The sun was below the trees and a gentle breeze was rustling the leaves. Instead of following one of her usual routes, Paige turned south at an intersection not far from the house. After six blocks, the houses were much smaller and the yards less well maintained. Large trees crowded close to the street. The sidewalk stopped. If she continued, Paige would have to walk on the edge of the road. With all the trees it was much darker than where she and Ryan lived. Paige's heart started beating faster. When she turned around, she almost ran into a tall man with a baseball cap pulled down low over his eyes.

"Excuse me," she said as she moved to go past him.

"Let me see that dog," the man said.

Before Paige could say anything, he grabbed the leash and pulled Sandy close to him.

"No!" Paige cried out.

Sandy barked sharply and resisted the pull of the leash. The man focused his attention on the dog. A car horn honked, which startled Paige and caused the man to drop the leash and move quickly away. A large black car came alongside her. The driver lowered the window. It was Charlie Drummond.

"Are you okay?" Charlie asked.

"I am now," Paige replied gratefully.

"I'm Charlie Drummond. We met the other day at breakfast."

"I remember. Thanks so much for stopping. I'm not sure what that man wanted, but I was scared."

"Could I give you a ride home?"

"That would be great. I never walk this way and didn't realize it was a bad neighborhood."

"It's not the best. Will your dog be fine riding in the rear seat?"

"Yes."

Charlie opened the rear door. Sandy hopped in. Paige walked around the vehicle to the passenger side. With a final look in the direction the man had gone, she got in. Immediately, she felt herself begin to shake.

"I'm so glad you showed up," she said, rubbing her hands together. "That was scary."

"I own several rental houses in the neighborhood and was checking on one that's being renovated. What did that guy say to you?"

"Just that he wanted to see my dog. I think he was following me."

"If it's the man I'm thinking about, he has mental problems, but I've never heard about him threatening someone. Let me make a phone call to report this to the police."

"That's not necessary," Paige said, but Charlie pulled to the curb and hit a few buttons on the screen beneath the dashboard for a speaker call.

"Blanton County Sheriff's Department," a female voice answered.

"This is Charlie Drummond. Is Detective Alcott available?"

"Just a minute, I'll check."

A male voice with a slow Southern drawl came on the line. "Mr. Drummond, what can I do for you?"

Charlie told the detective where they were and what happened to Paige.

"I didn't get a good look at him, but I think it may have been one of the Polk boys," Charlie said.

"Based on what you're telling me, that's probably right," the detective replied. "Davey has a mental disability. I'm not sure exactly what it is, but he's harmless. Recently, he lost his dog. It was hit by a car on the same street where you are now. He came down to the station wanting to file charges against the driver. I explained to Davey that it was an accident and nothing could be done about it."

Paige spoke: "This is Paige Clark. Do you know what kind of dog he had?"

"No idea. He showed me a picture, but I don't remember any details."

"Which is unusual for Detective Alcott," Charlie said. "He's the best officer in Blanton County and remembers every detail of what he sees and hears."

"Thanks, Mr. Drummond," the detective said with a laugh.

The call ended. Charlie pulled away from the curb.

"That makes me feel better," Paige said. "But now I feel sorry for the man who lost his dog. Maybe Sandy reminded him of his pet."

"Would you like to help him get another animal?"

"Yes," Paige replied, turning slightly in the seat.

"I'll look into it," Charlie said. "I have a renter who lives next door to the Polk family."

"If there's any cost, I'd like to pay—"

"That won't be necessary," Charlie said. "I appreciate the help Ryan is giving me. He's stepped into big shoes with Tom having such a serious health issue."

"He's working a lot of hours and had to go out of town today to visit a client who's in prison."

As soon as Paige spoke the words, she regretted even obliquely bringing up the tragic history linking Charlie Drummond and Joe Moore. He didn't respond.

"You're living in the house owned by Seth Vaughn?" Charlie asked.

"Yes."

After another turn, they reached the house.

"Sandy and I both thank you again," Paige said.

"Glad I showed up," Charlie replied. "You and Ryan should come over for dinner sometime. You could bring Sandy. We have a bichon who's never met a stranger, either human or canine."

———————

Even though it was late, Ryan stopped by the office instead of driving directly home. He quickly realized his mistake. There were multiple matters requiring immediate attention that Nancy hadn't forwarded to him. Over an hour passed before he finally left. The hamburger he'd eaten earlier during the drive was long gone, and his stomach growled as he pushed open the front door. He heard Sandy bark from the living room. Paige was lying on the couch with a pillow. She stretched her arms over her head.

"Sorry, I tried to wait up but dozed off," she said.

Paige moved her feet, and Ryan sat at the end of the couch and told her what he could about his day.

"I saw Charlie Drummond today," Paige said. "He rescued Sandy and me, but it turned out not to be as scary as I first thought."

Ryan listened with concern as Paige talked about the encounter.

"I should have told you not to head in that direction," he said.

"No harm." Paige sat up on the couch. "I let it slip that you were out of town meeting with a client in prison. Charlie didn't ask any questions, but I was worried he might guess who you were visiting."

"I talked to him on the phone earlier today without telling him. I have to keep reminding myself that he didn't shut down the firm representing Joe Moore when the possibility first came up."

"The last thing Charlie mentioned was having us over for dinner."

"I'd like that, but I need to eat before that happens. Do we have any deli meat in the fridge?"

Paige brewed tea while Ryan made a sandwich. His phone was on the kitchen counter. It vibrated, and the caller ID appeared.

"That's Charlie Drummond," he said as he picked up the phone and placed it on speaker mode so Paige could listen.

"Hope it's not too late to call," Charlie said.

"No, and this gives me a chance to thank you for helping Paige today."

"Glad I happened to be driving by. I mentioned inviting the two of you over for dinner to my wife, and we wondered if Friday evening next week would work for you."

Ryan looked at Paige, who vigorously nodded her head.

"That would be great. What would you like us to bring?"

"That sweet dog of yours so Captain can meet her. Seven o'clock?"

"Yes, that sounds great."

They sat at the kitchen table while Ryan ate.

"What's that paper in your shirt pocket?" Paige asked.

"I forgot about that," Ryan said, taking it out. "It's a note Joe Moore wants me to give to the man I interviewed the other day. Joe suggested that you read it too."

"Why me?"

"No idea."

Ryan slid the paper across the table to Paige, who unfolded it. While reading, she didn't touch her drink. She turned it over, finished, and looked up.

"I'm going to get my phone so I can look up the Bible verses he recommends."

"Oh, and I'm supposed to print them off before I deliver it."

"I'll do it," Paige volunteered.

Ryan finished supper. Paige returned.

"What does the editor think?" he asked.

Paige sat down. "I read what he wrote, not to see what I thought about it, but to figure out what it says about me."

Curious, Ryan reached out for the letter. Paige pushed his hand away. "You had all afternoon to read this and can wait a few more minutes until I'm done. I want to read it one more time."

Paige left again. Ryan went to the refrigerator and fixed himself a bowl of ice cream with bits of toffee candy embedded in it.

"The man who wrote this doesn't need to be in prison," Paige said when she returned and sat across from him.

Ryan raised his eyebrows. "You think that even though you know what they say he did to that young couple?"

"It's not about what he did then but who he is now. This gives me a real reason to support what you're doing for him."

"You didn't support me before?"

"Yes, but not like I am now."

It was an angle on the case Ryan hadn't considered. "The motion I'm working on has nothing to do with whether Joe is rehabilitated, only whether he was properly convicted."

"I understand. But what's going on with him as a person is bigger than your motion."

Ryan shook his head. "Now you're sounding like Joe."

Harmonicas in their hands, Joe and Ned Walker sat beside each other on a bench in front of Unit C. Joe shooed away spectators. Ned tried to mimic Joe's wail of an upper register chord on his shiny new harmonica. The notes came out as a jumbled squeak, and he quickly pulled the instrument away from his lips.

"You don't need to tell me. That was bad."

"The main reason is that you're trying too hard." Joe tapped his heart. "The sound begins in here, not in your mouth."

"I'm not sure how to make that happen."

"Pretend you're talking to someone you care about, but they want you to shut down the conversation. What you have to say is very important to you, and the only way you can convince the person to listen is by playing a note on the harmonica that softens their resistance. Can you come up with that sort of situation? Maybe someone in your family or a close friend."

Ned stared at Joe for a few seconds. "That would be my brother, Larry, the one with cancer."

Ned shut his eyes and, beginning with lower notes, slowly moved up the instrument to the higher range. The volume and tone ebbed and flowed. He ended with a single high note, which he held for at least ten seconds. Ned opened his eyes and looked at Joe.

236

"I don't have to tell you," Joe said. "That was much better."

True to his commitment, Ned stayed after the lesson, but instead of joining a Bible study, he went to the guardroom and took the thermostat off the wall. The small prayer groups began to form. Finally, Ned came out and walked over to Joe. The group of men with Joe stopped talking.

"There was a problem with the thermostat," Ned said. "It was almost like someone had put a governor on it to keep it from cooling past a certain point."

"Join us now."

"I don't have long," Ned replied, looking down at this watch. "I have to be in my unit in fifteen minutes."

"Then let's make the most of the time you have."

One of the new men in the group spoke.

"There's something I need to get off my chest," he said. "If I don't, I think I'm going to bust open."

"Now's the time," another man said. "What does it say, Joe? If we confess our sins, he is faithful and just to forgive us our sins and to cleanse us from all unrighteousness."

"That's right."

The first man began. The prisoner wasn't just sorry he got caught selling stolen car tires. He started listing wrongs he'd committed against other people. Joe listened with amazement. There was no explanation for this type of spontaneous behavior by an inmate except the influence of the Holy Spirit. Within a few minutes, the man was praying while leaning against the end of a cot, wiping away tears. Everyone else bowed their heads.

When he finished, Joe opened his eyes. Ned Walker was gone.

"You did your part," Joe said to the man who'd prayed. "Trust God to do his part."

"That's better than a hot shower after a hard day's work," the man said.

Joe looked across the room at Deshaun's group. As soon as they broke up, Deshaun came over to Joe.

"We're not going to be able to keep what's going on a secret," Deshaun said, his eyes shining with a light brighter than Joe had witnessed in the young man's countenance before. "People all over the prison are going to be talking about what's going on in here."

Joe listened as the account of the meeting poured out of Deshaun.

"I'm seeing what God can do for someone else, not just for me," Deshaun said. "And I'm getting to be part of it. You know how tough C.J. Bell is. I saw God reach down to touch him. It wasn't my imagination. Not that I saw God, but you know what I mean. And then C.J. broke. You've got to let him share his testimony at the next Bible study."

"Will do."

"What about Ned Walker?"

"He stood at the edge of the group but then left without saying anything. If there were any angels flying around his head, he beat them off."

"I think we need to focus on those who're hungry for what God has to offer them," Deshaun responded.

"You sound like a preacher."

"Maybe I am"—Deshaun grinned—"or have been for at least the past few minutes, standing beside my bunk."

Later Joe lay in his bunk and silently thanked the Lord for the mercy and grace being poured out on Unit C. What was happening with Deshaun was also encouraging. Joe had seen a lot of lives transformed in prison. The extent of change wrought by Jesus was one of the great unknown facts about men behind bars. The media didn't report it. The only accurate records were kept in heaven. The names of several other men in Unit C came to mind for prayer. Joe included Ned Walker. The Spirit could turn Ned's indifference into zeal in an instant. As his eyes grew heavy, Joe offered up a quick request for several other people, including Tom and Ryan Clark. Just before he lost consciousness, he added a request that God would also touch Ryan's wife but couldn't remember whether her name was Pam, Patsy, or something else.

CHAPTER 26

Ryan fell asleep as fast as usual. Paige continued to think about what Joe Moore had written to Doc Garrison. She reached for her phone to pull up the photos she'd taken of what the inmate wrote. Joe described the change in his life once he arrived in prison and how good it was to live without the influence of drugs, alcohol, or bad company. The concept of a personal journey to become closer to God through religion wasn't totally foreign to Paige, and it was understandable that Joe Moore would try to find a way out from the place his choices in life took him. But the verses Joe recommended about confessing sin would apply to anyone, including her. Being a drug user convicted of murder wasn't a prerequisite for a changed life.

One section toward the end particularly captured her attention: "To really know God, he has to be living inside you. That's when everything changes, and it becomes possible to experience forgiveness, freedom, and life as God wants it to be." The idea of God being *inside* a person was completely new to Paige. Before becoming pregnant, she wouldn't have had a point of reference for the idea. Now she did. The parallel with her pregnancy touched her deeply.

Joe recommended that Doc Garrison read 1 John 5:11–12: "And this is the testimony: God has given us eternal life, and this life is in his Son. Whoever has the Son has life; whoever does not have the Son of God does not have life." Lying in bed, Paige read the passage several times. The multiple uses of the word "life" jumped out at her. Who wouldn't want to live life in the way God intended it to be? Paige silently prayed the prayer Joe had written and asked God to give her eternal life through Jesus Christ. When she finished, she felt a burden she didn't know existed lift from her soul.

"What was that?" she whispered softly.

Paige intuitively knew. It was the departure of those things that had blocked her from knowing God—the weight of trying to be in control of her own life. Paige lay as still as she could. She wanted to let whatever was happening continue. The sensation she felt wasn't euphoria but peace. After several minutes she relaxed, snuggled under the covers, and fell asleep.

In the morning, Paige immediately thought about what she'd prayed the previous night. The sense of peace remained. She slipped out of bed and let Sandy into the backyard. It was still cool outside, but she could tell the day would be warm. While brewing coffee, she sat at the kitchen table and reread Joe's letter along with the list of Bible verses she'd printed off the night before. She was still at the table when Ryan appeared and rubbed his bleary eyes.

"There's regular coffee in the white pot," she said.

"Thanks. What are you doing?"

"Reading what Joe Moore wrote and the Bible verses I printed out."

"That really got your attention, didn't it?"

Ryan stood at the counter, poured a cup of coffee, and joined her. Paige looked up.

"There's more," she said. "I realized that knowing God is like getting pregnant. Listen to this."

She read what Joe wrote about God living inside a person and 1 John 5:11–12. She stopped and waited for Ryan to respond. He took a sip of coffee before saying anything.

"Yeah, I can see the analogy."

"No." Paige shook her head emphatically. "It's not an analogy. It's a reality. Before I went to sleep, I prayed the prayer Joe suggested and something happened inside me."

Paige described the lifting of the burden from her soul and the deep sense of peace that followed. She hoped what she said was clear, but as the words came out of her mouth, she doubted herself.

"Does that make sense?" she asked as she finished.

"I think so," Ryan responded slowly. "We'll talk more about it later. What do you want to do this weekend?"

"Stay home and relax?" Paige asked.

"Yeah, I need a couple of days without any responsibilities."

Arriving at the office on Monday, Ryan put the letter and information for Doc Garrison on the credenza behind his desk. Later in the morning, Nancy buzzed his phone.

"Danny Milton is on the phone," she said.

"I'll take it."

"Any sore muscles after the other day?" Danny asked when Ryan answered.

"No, I felt fine."

"That doesn't make me feel better. I was stiff when I got out of bed. I'll chalk it up to you being six years younger than I am."

"I think it's eight years."

Danny laughed. "Either way, both of us were a long way from attending law school when Joe Moore was convicted of murder. I retrieved his investigative file and requested the items in storage. I suspect most of it is discoverable. I'll be willing to grant you access with supervision."

"What do you have?"

"Standard police reports, mostly handwritten and barely legible. This was before some of the detectives knew how to type, and the main detective used some kind of personal shorthand that only he could translate. We have the murder weapon recovered at the scene, photos of the deceased couple, coroner's report, and results of blood and fingerprint testing."

"Witness interviews?"

"Yes, but some of those are in this code I mentioned. I didn't compare their names to those of the people who actually testified at the trial. I've not had time to look at the transcript."

"Understood."

"And no DNA testing. This investigation occurred before that was used in Blanton County."

Ryan looked at his calendar. He wanted to take advantage of Danny's offer as soon as possible.

"When could I come over?" he asked.

"That's up to you. Everything is in the secure evidence locker at our office."

"I know you're busy, but would five o'clock this afternoon work?"

Danny was silent for a moment.

"Yes, I'll be here," he said.

"See you then."

As soon as the call ended, Ryan went to Sue's desk.

"That's unusual," the assistant said. "Mitch usually had to go to war and obtain a court order to get that level of access to the investigation file and physical evidence. The acting DA is either super-confident there's nothing there to help you, or he doesn't care if you uncover something."

"Maybe Danny is being cooperative because he wants Tom and me to support him when he runs for office next year."

"Are you going to?"

He told Sue about the conversation with Charlie Drummond and Scott Nelson's likely candidacy for district attorney.

"I'll vote for Danny," Sue replied.

Ryan paused for a moment. "Do you think I should call Mitch Norman for advice before I review the file?"

"You could, but this sounds like more of an inventory to see what's there. Once you know what's available, Mitch may have ideas. Is the DA going to give you copies of the illegible interview notes?"

"I didn't ask, but I will."

"If he turns those over and you can decipher them, that could be important. There are always nuggets in the interviews that the defense lawyer didn't know about at trial."

Ryan returned to his office and worked through lunch. By mid-afternoon he was hungry and found a slightly overripe banana in the break room. He took it to the reception area. Nancy was the employee who usually brought fruit to the office.

"Is this available for purchase?" he asked.

"It's free," she said. "But thanks for asking. Tom never does."

"Any word from Karen? Tom didn't respond to the status email I sent him this morning."

"He's about the same. At least he's stable."

Ryan took a phone call that lasted longer than expected, and it was after 5:00 p.m. when he left for the courthouse. The DA's office was on the main floor across the hall from the clerk of court. Ryan had never been inside. The few minor criminal cases he'd handled were processed over the phone or quickly in the courtroom. He opened a door with opaque white glass in the upper half, on which the name of the former DA was stenciled in black. An older woman with short gray hair was sitting at a desk with her purse in front of her.

"We're closed," she announced curtly.

"Danny Milton is expecting me. I'm Ryan Clark."

The woman frowned as she picked up the phone and pressed a button.

"He's on a call," she announced as she lowered the receiver.

She proceeded to pick up her purse and move toward the door.

"Should I wait here?" Ryan asked.

"Whatever you like. I'm locking the door, so you won't be able to get back in if you leave."

Ryan sat on a dark wooden chair. He took out his phone and sent Danny a text letting him know that he'd arrived. Five minutes later the door opened and the tall tennis player emerged.

"The receptionist left and locked the door," Ryan said.

"Yeah," Danny said and rolled his eyes. "With Steve moving to Raleigh, I gave her a two-week notice of termination about an hour ago. She's worked for the county over thirty years. Past DAs have tolerated her sour attitude because of her institutional knowledge, but I'm going to make a change."

They entered a short hallway. Danny occupied a small office on the right.

"I won't move into the DA's big office until next week," he said. "Have you ever had to terminate an employee?"

Ryan didn't want to mention that he'd been on the receiving end of the process. "No."

"Firing Edith may not be the smartest move politically. She has tons of personal connections, but it needed to be done. I'll get the Moore file."

While he waited, Ryan glanced around. There were a couple of tennis photos on Danny's desk. In one picture the prosecutor, dressed in white with a racket in hand, was standing behind the service line at Wimbledon in England. Danny returned holding three boxes in his long arms. He placed them on the front of his desk.

"When did you compete at Wimbledon?" Ryan asked, pointing at the picture. "Taking a set from you the other day just went up a notch on my list of accomplishments."

"Don't change your world ranking," Danny chuckled. "That was staged as a joke. I knew someone who gave me access during a practice session."

Danny unstacked the boxes. He removed the lid from one of them.

"This contains the physical evidence," he said. "There's more than I mentioned over the phone. It also includes the clothes worn by the victims."

Ryan peered into the box.

"May I take things out?" he asked.

"Yes, but don't open any of the bags."

The first large clear plastic bag Ryan removed was marked "Martin Brock." He could see a pair of dark jeans, a yellow short-sleeved shirt, and sports socks but no shoes. The shirt was extensively discolored with dark stains.

"I assume that's blood," Ryan said, holding up the bag.

"Most likely."

"I don't recall the clothes being admitted into evidence at the trial."

"Like I mentioned earlier, I've not read the transcript."

A second bag was marked "Cheryl Drummond." It contained a yellow dress and a pair of formerly white sandals. The dress was similar in color to the shirt. The couple may have coordinated their wardrobe for the evening. The dress was also covered in dark stains. He took out the bag containing the murder weapon. It was smaller than he'd imagined. The blade wasn't more than three inches long. The handle was made of metal, perhaps stainless steel. He held it up. He couldn't see any sign of blood. The handle had a small button on it.

"No blood on the knife?" he asked.

"No longer visible. Over time it wouldn't adhere to the handle."

"What kind of knife is it?"

"Spring-operated switchblade. I've seen knives like this one in other cases. The blade comes out directly from within the handle. It's called an OTF, or 'out the front,' model. It's illegal in North Carolina to have one in your possession unless you're at home."

"If I want to get DNA tests on the knife or the clothes, would you oppose it?" Ryan asked.

"No, because you'd eventually obtain approval from a judge." Danny added, "What about agreeing to a lab?"

"You'd do that?"

"Eliminates competing experts. If the outcome favors the State, then it's tougher for the defendant to disprove. In the alternative, if it leans your way, it's hard for me to argue exclusion from consideration by the Court."

"This wouldn't be performed by a State-employed expert?"

"No, an independent lab. I can provide you a short list of those who will follow necessary protocols to guarantee the integrity of the testing."

When Ryan reached the bottom of the box, he found several plastic containers. Inside were the photographs from the crime scene. Ryan had seen photographs from serious automobile accidents but nothing like this. He tried to make himself study the photos but kept looking away.

"This is horrible," he managed.

"It's never gotten easy for me either," Danny said. "Some of the worst images are of people killed in a fire. And drownings can be a lot grislier than people imagine."

Ryan had never seen a photo of his father after he drowned. The casket was closed for the funeral. He suddenly wanted to run out of the DA's office. He forced himself to stand still and take a deep breath.

"Are you going to request copies of the photos?" Danny continued. "This was before local law enforcement used digital cameras, so I'll have to find out if the negatives exist."

"No," Ryan answered, shaking his head. "I don't need them."

Danny pointed to another box. "That contains the investigative notes, witness interviews, and trial documents. You can have copies of most everything. Deciphering it will be another problem."

"Is the detective who used the personal shorthand system still around?"

"Norris Broome. He's retired but still lives here."

"Do you know him?"

"Yes, he was with the sheriff's department when I first arrived in town. He was a tough but fair detective. Made a lot of money in some kind of side business and bought a big farm on the east side of the county."

"Do you think he'll talk to me?"

Danny shrugged. "That's not for me to decide. Just because I'm giving you access to information doesn't mean we're not going to oppose an MAR."

"Of course, and I appreciate what you're doing. Let me know when I can pick up copies."

"Will do."

Ryan walked slowly back to the office. It was going to be impossible to erase what he'd seen from his mind.

CHAPTER 27

Joe woke up refreshed. He was looking forward to picking strawberries, okra, and green beans. The okra plants needed particular attention since ongoing production required constant harvesting. On his way to the dining hall for breakfast, a guard came up to him.

"Moore," the burly man said gruffly. "Come with me."

Joe knew not to ask if he was in trouble. Even if the guard was aware, he wouldn't say anything. They entered the administration building and went to the waiting area for the warden's office. The guard left.

"Good morning," Elle said.

"Good morning. Am I in some kind of trouble?"

"I don't think so. The warden wants to see you as soon as Chaplain Jim arrives." Elle lowered her voice. "The strawberry shortcake and strawberry pie are in the break room refrigerator with a note on them warning anyone not to touch them. Do you want to come back after work and pick them up?"

Joe perked up. "That would be great. Then I can take them to the dining hall for our table. Thanks so much."

"I have something else," Elle replied with a sly smile. "When was the last time you had a bagel with cream cheese?"

"Uh, there weren't any bagel shops in Blanton County when I was growing up."

Elle reached beneath the desk and took out a white bag.

"Cinnamon raisin?" she said. "They were made fresh this morning, and I have extras. There's also cream cheese in the bag."

Joe hadn't eaten a bagel in years. The surge in their popularity in the rural South had taken place since he was locked up, and he'd never eaten anything except a plain one.

"Do I have time?" he asked.

"Yes, the chaplain is in some kind of meeting for a few minutes."

Joe scooted his chair closer to the desk. Elle handed him a bagel that was already sliced in two. Joe spread cream cheese on it and took a bite. He closed his eyes.

"Oh, this is good," he said.

"Yeah, it's from a new place in Fayetteville. Their coffee is good too."

Joe continued to eat the bagel. The fragrance and taste of cinnamon brought back memories of his mother making frosted cinnamon rolls for breakfast. He told Elle.

"That's sweet," she said with a smile. "My mama cooked something like that. She passed away around the first of the year. I miss her, but she's with Jesus. And when there's not much to do, I've had a lot of time to pray on this job. The warden says you're a leader among the Christians in the prison."

"I try to set a good example."

The door opened, and Chaplain Jim entered the waiting area. He looked startled to see Joe eating the bagel.

"Would you like a bagel?" Elle asked the chaplain.

"Uh, no thanks. Let the warden know I'm here for our meeting."

Joe stuffed the last bite in his mouth.

"Can I swallow this first?" he asked the chaplain, but his mouth was so full that the words were garbled.

Elle waited a few seconds, picked up the phone, then nodded to the chaplain.

"He'll see you now."

Joe followed the chaplain into a large, spartanly decorated office. Warden Gunton was six feet tall with square shoulders, a large head topped with gray hair, and a booming voice. He'd served twenty years as an MP in the Army before starting to work with the North Carolina Department of Corrections. Joe swallowed the last bit of bagel.

"Have a seat," the warden said in a friendly voice. "Good to see you, Moore. How are things going in the garden?"

Joe gave him an update.

"Excellent."

"Thanks for your support."

The warden held up a brown envelope in his right hand. "I received notice yesterday of your transfer to another facility."

Joe's mouth dropped open. "Where?"

"A new camp on the coast. Sounds like a real country club. It opened last year. Most of the inmates are white-collar prisoners. Minimum security. No need to be looking over your shoulder because somebody has a grudge against you. Liberal visitation with family members. They even have a swimming pool and air-conditioned gym. I'm surprised a man with your record was selected, but someone in Raleigh must have read in your file what the preacher and I have written about you."

Joe looked at the two men in surprise. He had no idea anything like that had occurred.

"You've done a lot of good here," the chaplain said. "It deserves to be acknowledged, either now or when you come up for parole."

"Parole for me is so far off—"

"We're not here to go into that," the warden said. "And I don't normally get involved in this sort of thing, but Chaplain Jim thinks you might want to stay here. If that's true, I can pull some strings to rescind the transfer."

Joe tried to absorb what he was hearing. He'd assumed that he would remain at LPCC until he was an old man and then be sent to a facility designed to care for elderly prisoners.

"Can I have some time to think and pray about it?" he asked.

"Twenty-four hours," the warden responded. "I can't promise to prevent it. But I'm willing to try. To be honest, I'd much rather have you sleeping in one of our beds than whoever they send to fill your spot."

Joe cleared his throat. "While I'm here, I was wondering if you would approve our request for additional Bible study and prayer meetings in Unit C. God is moving among the men in a good way. Even if I'm not here, Raymond Simpson can provide leadership."

"According to the reports I read from the guards on duty, you're already doing it without permission," the warden responded.

"We've kept it small—" Joe started.

The warden held up his hand to stop him before turning to the chaplain. "Jim, prepare the paperwork, and I'll sign it."

Joe and the chaplain returned to the waiting area.

"Thank you for what you've done," Joe said.

"If I was pastoring a church on the outside, I'd want you on my leadership team."

"Here," Elle said to Joe, holding out the bag of bagels. "Take them. And don't forget to come back later."

Joe caught up with Ray outside Unit C.

"When you missed breakfast, I grabbed you a sandwich and a bag of chips," Ray said. "Why did they drag you off to the administration building?"

"To give me these bagels," Joe replied.

He took one out and gave it to Ray, who bit into it. "This is amazing."

Joe told Ray what had happened. Ray's face became serious. "I'd hate to see you go but wouldn't blame you. There was a bad fight in Unit F last night that sent three men to the hospital."

"Anybody we know?" Joe asked.

"Yeah, Randall Doster."

"Randy wouldn't get into a fight! He's older than we are."

"By two years. He didn't start the fight, but he was in the wrong place and got caught up in it. They say he may lose the sight in one of his eyes."

Forgetting about bagels and cream cheese, Joe somberly walked to the toolshed. He thought about Randall. He thought about himself.

Paige had a busy morning at work that included two virtual meetings followed by a last-minute editing job for a bid with a noon deadline. She barely finished in time. Her afternoon schedule was light. Hungry, she went into the kitchen. Nothing in the fridge looked appetizing. Picking up her phone, she sent a joint text to Vicki and Candy on the slim chance either of them was available for lunch. Both of them quickly responded that they were already planning to meet and would love to have her join them at a new restaurant downtown.

———————

Paige pulled into the parking lot of an old house a couple of blocks from the courthouse square. It was also in a neighborhood adjacent to the McKnights' catering business. The house was painted a bright yellow with white rocking chairs on the long front porch. A sign out front read "Pass the Thyme." The name of the restaurant was surrounded by painted flowers.

Inside, a mature woman in a patterned dress greeted her. "Welcome. Are you dining alone?"

"No, I'm meeting two friends." Paige looked past the hostess but didn't see Vicki or Candy at any of the tables in the dining area. "But I don't see them."

"Oh, I bet they're on the veranda. Follow me."

Paige followed the woman past an exclusively female crowd seated at delicate wooden tables with wicker chairs. The veranda was a screened-in porch behind the dining room. Large fans overhead circulated the air. Vicki and Candy waved her over.

"So glad you could join us," Candy said. "This is the second time I've eaten here this week. This is exactly what we need in Cranfield. Something to balance out the barbecue joints."

"It's pricey," Vicki said as she inspected the menu.

"But it's worth it," Candy said.

Vicki lowered the menu and looked at Paige. "How are you feeling?"

"Much better," Paige said, smiling. "I had another ultrasound, and the baby is moving into a good position."

"That's an answer to prayer," Vicki said.

A waitress arrived. Paige hadn't decided what to order. She hesitated.

"Try the wedge salad if you like that sort of thing," Candy suggested. "It's more than just a piece of lettuce on a plate. And I love the chicken piccata. The lunch portion is perfect as a first course."

"No need to convince me," Paige replied, handing her menu to the waitress. "I'll order both of those."

Paige looked around. The ambience was nice, and she hoped the food was as good as Candy claimed.

"Ryan and I ate dinner the other night at a place near here on Palmer Street," she said. "The couple run a catering business—"

"You ate at the McKnights' place?" Candy asked, her eyes wide. "I've wanted to go there for months!"

Paige told them about the experience. When their food arrived on rectangular white plates, Vicki offered a quick prayer of blessing.

"Finding out that I'm pregnant and eating at the McKnights' isn't the only excitement in my life," Paige said.

"What's going on?" Candy asked.

"I prayed last night and I believe God heard me."

Vicki and Candy were about to take bites of food. Both women stopped and lowered their forks.

"I'm not going to eat another bite until you tell us more," Vicki said.

"No," Paige protested. "Your food will get cold."

"Okay, but don't leave out any details," Candy replied.

Slowly at first, but with increasing confidence, Paige told them what happened.

"After I prayed, peace covered me like a blanket," she said. "I know feelings can vanish in an instant, but this was different. It's just as true sitting here with the two of you as it was last night."

"I have goose bumps," Vicki said, rubbing her arms. "Paige needs to share this in the Sunday school class."

"Don't push her. And don't talk as if she isn't sitting here with us."

"Sorry, I didn't mean to come across like that," Vicki said.

"Go back to the beginning," Candy said. "What started all this?"

Paige knew she had to mention Joe Moore's letter. "Last night Ryan brought home a letter one of his clients wrote."

In between finishing her wedge salad and the chicken, Paige told the two women what was written on the paper.

"So this client wanted Ryan to share the letter with another man?" Vicki asked. "Why couldn't he do it himself?"

"He's in jail."

"Letters from prison," Vicki said, her eyes wide. "Just like the apostle Paul."

"Maybe Vicki is right," Candy said. "You should share this in Sunday school. I can think of five or six people I'd want to invite to come hear you."

"I don't know," Paige replied doubtfully.

"Is there more?" Vicki asked. "I believe this is going to get even better."

Paige finished by taking out her phone and reading 1 John 5:11–12. Vicki pointed up at the sky.

"This is one of the most incredible things I've heard in years," she said. "You say everything clearly and beautifully. I guess it's because you're a professional writer and know how to express yourself so well."

"That's it!" Candy clapped her hands. "Paige can write out her testimony so people can read it."

"Now you're the one talking like she's not here," Vicki replied.

"You know what I mean," Candy shot back. "Women will especially identify with your story."

"Ryan didn't really understand me when I told him and compared what happened to my pregnancy," Paige said. "Maybe that's why."

"Men ought to get it," Vicki said. "And they'd better get used to identifying as the bride of Christ."

"The bride of Christ?" Paige asked.

"It's in the Bible," Candy said quickly. "I don't want to embarrass myself, but it's either a metaphor or an analogy. I always got those two confused in school."

"It's not a metaphor or an analogy," Vicki responded. "It's a truth."

Paige listened to the two women debate back and forth.

"We're way off track," Candy said, holding up her right hand. "Here we are arguing after being blessed by Paige's beautiful experience."

"Yes." Vicki reached out and touched Paige on the shoulder. "I'm so honored that you've shared this with us."

"It's what happened," Paige replied matter-of-factly. "And I thought the two of you would be interested."

Candy insisted on paying for Paige's lunch as part of the celebration. They agreed to meet at the restaurant again the following week.

"Would you consider writing out what you told us?" Candy asked.

"I think that would be a good exercise for me. You know how easy it is to forget something over time, even if it feels intense in the moment."

Vicki nodded. "Exactly. My wedding was like that. Most of it is a total blur now."

Driving home, Paige thought about the response of the two women to her story. Their unrestrained enthusiasm was both encouraging and puzzling. Wanting to immediately publicize it caught her off guard. But the suggestion to write it out made sense. Some of the religious lingo used by Vicki and Candy made Paige realize that the church and the Bible were like law or medicine—there was a specialized language that would take time to learn.

CHAPTER 28

It was the middle of the afternoon. Ryan sat behind his desk and stared at his computer monitor. The deeper he delved into the Moore case, the more difficult it became to treat what happened with professional detachment. There was a knock on his door.

"Come in," he said.

Nancy entered with a solemn look on her face.

"I just received a text from Karen," she said. "Tom has taken a turn for the worse. His heart is beating irregularly, and they've put him in the ICU to stabilize him. I asked whether this meant they might perform surgery even if Tom isn't cleared from COVID. Karen didn't respond."

Ryan took a deep breath and exhaled.

"Up to now, I've thought trying to keep things together here was temporary," he said.

"I still hope you're right."

After Nancy left, Ryan turned to his credenza and saw the letter Joe had written Doc Garrison. He didn't want to drive over to Doc's house without phoning first. An unsupervised encounter with Rex off leash should be avoided. The phone rang several times before the answering machine came on, and Ryan left a message.

Tired and emotionally drained, Ryan was ready to call it a day. But before doing so, he decided to try to reach Joe Moore. He phoned the administrative office for the prison.

"The men are back from work detail," the woman who answered said. "I'll radio a guard to see if he can find Mr. Moore and send him over. Would you like to hold?"

"Yes."

Ryan was puzzled by the woman referring to Joe as "Mr. Moore" instead of the "inmate" or "prisoner." He placed the phone receiver in the cradle on speaker mode. Ten minutes later the woman came back on the line.

"A guard is bringing Mr. Moore to the administration building. He should be here in a few minutes."

"Thanks."

Another ten minutes passed. Ryan flipped through another file that would require his attention in the morning.

"This is Joe," the now-familiar voice said. "Were you able to give the sheet of paper I wrote to Doc Garrison?"

"No, but my wife printed out the Bible verses, and I have everything ready to go. I called Doc, and he didn't answer."

"Unless he's changed, Doc doesn't trust phones. He always claimed they were bugged by the police."

"Okay, I'll go see him, but let me get to the reasons for my call. The acting DA allowed me to review the investigative file in your case. There are witness statements from people who didn't testify at the trial. If anything is exculpatory, and the former DA didn't reveal it to Tom, that raises an issue we can argue." Ryan stopped. "Do you know what I mean by exculpatory?"

"Evidence tending to prove I wasn't guilty."

"Exactly. Once I organize the statements, I'll have them typed up so you can read them. There will be a delay because one of the detectives used some kind of personal shorthand that no one else can read."

"Is it Detective Broome?"

"Yes."

"He talked to me before I had a lawyer but didn't spend much time questioning me about what happened. He said he already knew enough to prove the case."

"Broome is retired, but I'm going to see if he'll talk to me." Ryan paused. "Also, the DA and I are going to agree on an expert to perform DNA testing on the knife."

"Okay."

"I reviewed the photos from the scene."

Joe didn't respond to that last statement.

"I know you've been praying for Tom," Ryan continued. "They couldn't perform open-heart surgery because he has COVID, and this morning he took a turn for the worse. He's in ICU."

"Sorry to hear that, but I'm not going to stop asking the Lord to touch and restore him."

Ryan prepared to end the conversation but then remembered one more thing.

"My wife read what you wrote to Doc several times. It made a big impression on her."

"How so?"

"I'm not exactly sure," Ryan replied. "But she doesn't think you need to be locked up in prison."

"Tell her in the ways that count, I'm freer than a lot of folks walking around on the outside."

———

Joe left the administration building and made his way to the dining hall. Ray had saved him a seat at the table where several men from Unit C were eating.

"Your lawyer sure calls you a lot," Ray said. "What did he want?"

"To tell me stuff that I already know about the investigation into my case. The DA is opening up his file."

Ray raised his eyebrows. "For a DA to do that without putting up a fight is unusual."

"Yeah, but it's depressing to have to think about it again. They're going to agree on an expert to perform DNA testing. That's never been done in my case."

Joe felt a tap on his shoulder and glanced up. It was Ned.

"Can I have a lesson tonight?" he asked.

"Will you be working on the thermostat in the guardroom?"

"No, I have another excuse to be away from my unit."

"What's that?" Joe asked.

Ned reached into his pocket, pulled out a sheet of paper, and handed it to Joe. It was a note from Chaplain Jim authorizing Ned to meet with Joe in Unit C.

"How did you get this?" Joe asked, handing the paper back to Ned.

"I asked the chaplain for it."

"You've been talking to the chaplain?" Ray asked.

"Yeah, and I told him about spending time with Joe. He's all for it."

"Okay," Joe replied. "Bring your harmonica at 6:15. We'll have thirty minutes before the Bible study and prayer meetings start."

"Got it."

Ned moved on. Ray shook his head.

"You're getting more powerful around here than Warden Gunton," Ray said. "I need to think about what you can do for me. A box of thirty-six Snickers bars would be a good start. Make them the extra-large size."

"Denied. Not good for your teeth."

"I'd share."

"Nope."

They finished their meal and returned to Unit C. Several men came up to Joe and Ray to tell them what God was doing in their lives. None had previously attended the Unit C prayer meeting. When there was a break, Joe turned to Ray.

"Men are talking to each other about the Lord during the day, not just at chapel time or in a Bible study."

Ray nodded. Another man came up to them with a praise report. Joe saw Ned enter through the main door. Going to his bunk, Joe retrieved one of the harmonicas from the box beneath his bed. When he returned, Ned was talking to an inmate named Max.

"I never thought Max would turn religious," Ned said when he and Joe were side by side on the bench. "I knew him from the prison where I was locked up before coming here. Nobody messed with him. He wants me to join his group tonight."

"Are you going to do it?"

"Yeah, I don't think turning him down would be a good idea."

Joe picked up his harmonica. "Listen to these five notes, and we'll see how long it takes you to find them."

Progress was slow, but Ned was determined to keep trying. When they finished, Ned started to walk away.

"What about your promise to Max?" Joe asked. "That's part of our deal too."

"I'm not feeling so hot."

"Ask someone to pray for you to get better. There's a lot of faith in that building."

Ned hesitated and then turned toward Unit C. "I guess it won't hurt to stay for a little while."

After the different meetings broke up, Max came up to Joe and Ray. The muscular young white man with full tattoo sleeves was carrying a massive Bible under his right arm.

"Look at this," he said, holding up the book. "Chaplain Jim gave it to me. It's not like the free ones they give away. This one has stuff written on each page explaining the verses. I've been reading it every chance I get."

Joe took the study Bible and opened it. On the front page was the name of a church group that had donated it to the prison.

"You'll learn a lot from this," Joe said. "How did the meeting go tonight?"

"Everett led it, so there wasn't any messing around."

"Did Ned Walker say anything?"

"No, but at least he was there." Max added, "When Everett talked about asking God to forgive us for our secret sins, I thought about Ned."

"Why Ned?"

Max glanced over his shoulder. "He shouldn't even be in a medium-security facility like this one, at least not this soon after what he did. When we were in Central Prison in Raleigh, he cut a guy with a shank in the exercise yard. Someone else got blamed for it."

"Are you sure about this?" Ray asked in alarm.

"Yeah, I was no more than five feet away when it happened. The guy Ned stabbed was a big troublemaker everyone avoided. I kept to myself at Central. I'm not sure what Ned had against him."

"Did the guy know that Ned stabbed him?"

"No, he didn't see it coming."

"How did Ned get away with it?" Ray asked. "There had to be cameras and other people around."

"There were, but we were all bunched together waiting to get into the dining hall. Ned cut him and then slipped the shank into another man's back pocket. Everyone had to drop to the ground, and the guards rushed in. They took the guy who was bleeding to the infirmary. The guy with the knife in his pocket threw it on the ground. A guard saw him, and they hauled him off to a punishment cell."

"Did you tell anyone about what you saw?" Joe asked.

"You know it's better to keep your mouth shut. Now I'm wondering if I made a mistake. You know, did I sin by keeping quiet? But who would believe me, and what difference would it make? If Ned found out, I'd have to worry about him coming after me here. I can handle myself, but anybody can get hurt if someone sneaks up on them." Max looked down. "You won't say anything, will you?"

"No," both Joe and Ray replied.

Max moved on. Ray shook his head.

"It's hard to know who to believe in here, but I'd go with Max over Ned," Ray said.

———

The negative news about Tom had put a damper on Paige and Ryan's conversation as they ate supper.

"Today I wondered what would happen if Tom died or isn't ever able to return to work," Ryan said.

"You've been able to manage things so far."

"I guess the experience I gained with the other two firms partially prepared me. Whatever happens, I'm going to have to manage the practice longer than I thought. It helps that Sue and Nancy know what they're doing."

"You know what you're doing too."

They ate in silence for a few minutes.

"The last thing I did before leaving the office was call Joe Moore," Ryan said. "I had news about his case but also wanted to let him know about Tom. He's shown some personal interest in him since the first time I visited the prison."

"What did Joe say?"

"That he's going to keep praying for Tom to get better."

"Joe Moore has a totally different agenda in life than I expected."

"Yeah, spreading religion at the prison is what he lives for. Oh, I mentioned you reading the letter he wrote to Doc Garrison, and Joe told me to tell you that he's freer in jail than a lot of people living on the outside."

Paige ate a bite of pasta and chewed thoughtfully.

"I ate lunch today with Vicki and Candy. I told them about Joe's letter without mentioning his name and the impact it had on me." Paige looked in Ryan's eyes. "That letter was one of the most important things I've ever read. Vicki and Candy were ready to turn me into some kind of church celebrity."

"Why?"

"What I said made a lot of sense to them."

Ryan was silent for a moment.

"Maybe you should write Joe and let him know," he said. "I can easily get it to him."

Later that evening they were sitting on the couch. Ryan was watching a baseball game on TV while Paige was composing a letter to Joe on her laptop. Sandy lay between them. Paige looked at Ryan's silhouette. The past few weeks had been both positive and difficult.

"I feel like we're closer together than we have been in a long time," she said.

Ryan turned off the TV and faced her. "Because you're pregnant?"

"There's more to it than that. It's as if I'm anticipating our closeness in the future but partially experiencing it now."

"That's deep," Ryan replied with a smile. "But whatever the reason, I'm glad. Anything else?"

Paige thought for a moment. She didn't want to bring up what had come to her mind.

"That's it," she said.

Ryan returned to the ball game. Paige shut down her laptop. She'd finish the letter to Joe Moore later. She sat in silence for a few minutes. She'd learned about the death of Ryan's father on their third date. The way he talked about the incident came across like a story he'd told so many times that he could repeat it verbatim. He'd not shown any emotion. At the time, Paige began to tear up but quickly squelched any display of feelings. She could tell that wasn't the response Ryan wanted. In fact, he didn't want any response at all. The drowning was a fact of life. It happened and couldn't be changed. What was there to discuss?

"Now that you're going to be a father, do you think you need to work through the loss of your dad?" she asked.

Ryan's head spun away from the TV and toward her.

"Where did that come from?" he asked.

Paige touched her heart. "Here."

Ryan again turned off the TV and placed the remote on a side table.

"I thought about him the other night after you went to sleep," he said. "And wondered if I'd be at least a decent father. I'd understand if you have questions about that."

"No, no, remember what I told you the other night," Paige quickly responded. "I think you'll be a great dad."

Ryan took a deep breath.

"I'm not putting pressure on you, but I want to be close enough to help you," Paige continued. "We'll talk when you're ready."

Later that night in bed, Paige was in turmoil. She'd opened a painful wound without any remedy to offer. To her relief, Ryan was asleep, his breathing regular. Paige allowed herself to do what she'd not done on their third date. She let the tears that formed in her eyes roll down her cheeks.

———

The following morning, Ryan was relieved when Paige didn't bring up their conversation from the previous evening. Around 11:00 a.m., he left the office and drove to Doc Garrison's trailer. Instead of parking in the gravel area for the former Eastside Music Barn, he drove around the edge of the parking lot onto the dirt driveway that led directly to Doc's dwelling. He hoped the surveillance cameras for the former nightclub didn't record his presence this time.

There was no visible sign of Doc or Rex. Ryan let the car roll to a stop and waited. Better to let Doc emerge than surprise him by knocking on the door. A minute passed without any sign of life. Ryan lowered the car window and tapped the car horn twice. He heard a deep-throated woof respond from inside the trailer. The front door still didn't open. Getting out, Ryan walked up the three steps and knocked. He waited and knocked again.

No response. At this point, he was committed to finding out if Doc was home. He didn't want to make another wasted trip. He banged loudly on the door with the side of his fist. A few seconds later it cracked open. It was chained from the inside. Ryan could barely see Doc's face peering through the crack.

"What do you want?" the old man demanded. "I'm not feeling well today."

"I have something to give you from Joe Moore. He wants you to read this." Ryan slipped the sheets of paper through the crack in the door. Doc let them fall to the floor.

"I don't have anything to say," Doc replied. "Forget what I told you the other day. It wasn't true. Now get, before I open the door and sic Rex on you."

Ryan opened his mouth to argue but realized it was pointless. "If you want to send a message to Joe after you read what he sent, let me know, and I'll be glad to deliver it."

The door slammed shut. Ryan backed down the steps and left. Mystified by the dramatic change in Doc's attitude, he drove slowly away from the trailer. Glancing over at the former nightclub, he noticed at least three surveillance cameras, one at each end of the building and one over the door. He couldn't remember how many there had been when he'd come the first time.

Reaching the main highway, he didn't turn in the direction of town. Instead, he checked his phone where he'd entered the address for former detective Norris Broome. It was only three miles away.

CHAPTER 29

Joe had trouble falling asleep. Insomnia wasn't usually a problem for him. Thoughts about Ned Walker's dishonesty kept him awake. A prisoner telling lies wasn't unusual, but something about Ned deeply troubled him. Joe mentioned it to Ray during breakfast.

"Why don't you ask your lawyer to look into him," Ray suggested. "He could run a background check."

Joe nodded. "I hadn't thought about that."

"I'm smarter than I look."

"I'm not sure about that," Joe said, glancing over at his friend.

It was a hot day. The men took an extra water break midmorning and circled up in the shade for a few minutes' rest.

"North Carolina heat is different from what we had in Arizona," said a prisoner who'd been on the garden crew for only a week.

"It's the high humidity," another man replied. "That means the amount of moisture that's in the air."

"You don't have to explain humidity to me."

"It saps you," Ray said. "But I'd rather be in the garden than clearing right-of-way with a sling blade and a bush axe."

"That's right," several men echoed.

Deshaun, who was sitting close to Joe, leaned over.

"I saw you talking to Max last night after the meetings," he said.

"Yes."

"We joined together because a couple of my guys didn't show up. I'm not sure it's my place to say this, but I'm not sure Max is ready to be a leader."

Max had been serious about his faith longer than Deshaun.

"Why?" Joe asked.

"He says stuff that he claims is true when I know it's not."

"What sort of stuff?"

"About his life. I know you want us to share testimonies about what God is doing. Max claimed something happened a couple of weeks ago when he prayed for a guy that's in Unit A that I know isn't true. It was someone else who actually did the praying. Max just stood there and listened."

"Since you saw everything, maybe you should bring it up with Max."

"I don't want to set him off," Deshaun said, shaking his head. "He has a nasty temper. Maybe it's under control now, but I don't want to test him and find out."

"I'll ask Ray to hang out with his group and see what he thinks."

While they were hoeing a row of okra, Joe told Ray what Deshaun told him.

"I think it should be you," Ray replied. "Max looks up to you more than anyone else. That also makes sense if Ned shows up again. It might help you get a better read on him."

"Part of me wants to end the harmonica lessons and forget about Ned."

"That's your call," Ray said.

Joe struck a stubborn weed with an extra-hard blow. When he did, the adjacent okra plant fell over. He leaned over and tried to get the okra plant to stand upright, but the damage was done. It flopped over again.

"No hope for that plant," Ray said. "Going after the weed did more damage than good."

Joe stood up and leaned on his hoe. He stared at the fallen plant for a moment.

"Remember the parable about the wheat and the tares growing in the same field?" he asked. "Jesus said to let both plants shoot up alone and not try to cull out the weeds until the angels sort it out in the end. That's what I need to do with Ned Walker."

"I'm not following you. What does that mean for you and Ned Walker?"

"Maybe I'm not supposed to try to figure out what's going on with Ned. Even if he's a tare now, with my help he could become a stalk of wheat."

The men worked in silence for a few moments.

"I'd still ask my lawyer to check him out," Ray said.

Groggy after Ryan left for the office, Paige was glad she had a light morning at work. She perked up around 10:30 a.m. and finished an edit for a proposal that wasn't going to be submitted for another week. It felt good to finish something that far ahead of the deadline.

Staring at a blank screen on her laptop, Paige remembered the request from Vicki and Candy that she write out what she'd told them over lunch. Not sure what to title it, she ran through several options in her mind before settling on "God and Me." Temporarily satisfied, she didn't know where to start. She typed: "The first time I prayed, I asked God to take care of my unborn baby." Paige stopped. The sentence came across as bland. She needed something else as a lead-in. She deleted the sentence and typed: "God answered my prayer before I knew he was listening." It was long but sounded like something she'd want to know more about.

It was 1:30 p.m. when Paige finished the first draft. She'd worked through lunch. Sandy, who was dutifully lying at her feet, whined.

"I need to let you out," she said to the dog.

Sandy jumped to her feet and padded over to the back door. It was a hot day, so Paige remained in the shade close to the house. Inside, the dog buried her nose in her water bowl while Paige drank a big glass of water. Returning to her computer, Paige saved the document but didn't send it to Vicki and Candy. She'd revisit what she'd written tomorrow with fresh eyes to spot errors or rough spots.

———

Ryan reached the entrance for Norris Broome's house, a rambling single-story ranch dwelling that looked like it had been built in the 1980s or '90s. A top-of-the-line white pickup truck was parked in the pebbled concrete driveway with an expensive SUV next to it. The house and large yard were neatly maintained. Next to the residence was an open pasture with black Angus cattle standing together under the shade of a solitary tree. As he approached the house, Ryan expected one or more dogs to come bounding out to either greet or warn him. None appeared. Ryan walked up three steps to the front porch and rang the doorbell. While he waited, he continued to glance around for the approach of a dog. He rang the bell again. He peered through the glass sidelight and didn't see anyone. Taking out a business card, he wrote a message asking the former detective to call him and slipped it between the glass storm door and the wooden entrance door.

As he descended the steps, Ryan heard a noise to his right. A large figure wearing a hood over his head came striding around the corner. Ryan took a few quick steps toward his car. The figure held up his hand and made a fist.

"Stop!"

Ryan froze. The man, who then removed the covering over his head, had a bushy mustache and salt-and-pepper hair cut military-style. He was sweating profusely and pulled a white rag from the pocket of his pants to wipe his face.

"I'm Ryan Clark. Are you Norris Broome?"

"Yes."

Broome came close enough for Ryan to see that the former detective had startling blue eyes.

"I'm a lawyer who works with Tom Clark," Ryan continued.

The detective eyed him. "What do you want?"

"To talk to you about an old case. But I don't want to interrupt what you're doing and can come back another day."

"I'm ready for a break. I've been making sure my hives don't overheat, but I'm overheated myself. Let's go to the back porch. Would you like tea or water?"

"Tea would be great."

Ryan followed Broome around the corner of the house to a screened-in porch with two large ceiling fans.

Broome switched on the fans. "Have a seat."

The porch was shaded and the fans vigorously stirred the air. Broome returned and handed Ryan a large glass filled with ice cubes and tea. Ryan took a sip. It wasn't too sweet.

"Thanks," he said.

Broome sat down in a wicker chair with floral cushions that matched the one Ryan sat in.

"How many hives do you have?" Ryan asked.

"Four right now, but I've had as many as twelve. CCD has wiped out a bunch."

"What's CCD?"

"Colony collapse disorder. It's a huge problem in the bee world."

Broome took a sip of tea.

"But that doesn't have anything to do with Joe Moore, does it?" the detective asked.

Ryan's eyes widened. "How did you know that's who I wanted to talk to you about?"

"You were smart enough to pass the bar exam. Tell me."

Ryan thought for a moment. "Danny Milton told you that I may file an MAR in his case."

"And that you wanted to talk to me about an investigation I headed up over twenty-five years ago. I remember the highlights. No one who's seen the photos from the murder scene will ever forget them."

"That's true."

"The DA says he's going to give you copies of my interview notes and gave me the okay to translate my shorthand if I want to. Can you give me a good reason why I would want to take the time and go through the trouble to help you?"

Ryan considered mentioning the possibility that a judge might require it. Hoping there might be an easier way to get what he needed, he stalled by asking a question.

"How many murder cases did you investigate during your career?"

"What is it you lawyers say? That's a nonresponsive answer to my question."

A couple of bees landed on the screen near Ryan.

"How do you get bees to do something without making them mad?" Ryan asked.

Broome stared at him for a second, then burst out laughing. Ryan was relieved the former detective found the question funny.

"That's good," Broome replied, continuing to chuckle. "I use smoke to make them think there's a forest fire in the area and then approach them with gentle movements that don't signal a threat."

"I'm not going to blow any deceptive smoke in your direction or threaten you. Not that I think you'd be intimidated by a young lawyer like me." Broome smiled.

"I like your honesty," the detective replied. "I'll take a look at the interviews and dictate the interpretation for a secretary to type, then review what's produced for accuracy."

"Thanks."

"And I'll pick up the copies from the DA's office," Broome continued. "I need to swing by there on another matter."

Broome took a drink of tea and wiped his face with the rag. "I investigated a lot of cases in which the accused was intoxicated or high on drugs when the crime was committed. Then, when you meet the defendant sober and straight, you wonder how they could have done such a terrible thing. That's the way it was with Joe Moore. He came from a good family. Polite and well-spoken. I think he even went to college for a while."

"And he's a model inmate, very religious since he's been in prison."

"That religion stuff doesn't move the meter with me," Broome said. "Especially in jail. I've seen too many prisoners haul a Bible into court in an effort to lighten the indictment. It never works."

"I think Joe is for real. He genuinely cares about other people."

"Whatever," Broome replied, standing up.

"Thanks again for agreeing to help," Ryan said.

"Six," Broome said.

"Six what?"

"You asked a few minutes ago. Six murder cases in thirty-four years of active duty."

They retraced their steps around the side of the house and stopped beside Ryan's car. Broome continued talking.

"Everything about the investigation was neat and tidy. There wasn't much for me to do except put the knife in a bag, confirm the sources of the blood on Moore's clothes, connect the cash in Moore's possession to Marty Brock, and develop the photos from the scene."

"Did you ever consider the possibility Joe might have been so messed up on drugs that he was incapable of the crime? From what I read in the transcript of the trial, the first deputies to arrive on the scene found him passed out in his car."

"I wasn't present for the arrest, but I don't recall him being that far gone."

"Okay . . ."

Broome stared at him for a few seconds. "And to be clear, I believe Moore was guilty. I'll cooperate with you to a degree because I still consider myself a professional, but I'm not interested in seeing my good work undone."

CHAPTER 30

Following an extra-warm day in the garden, Joe was sweating as he stood in the administration building and placed a call to Ryan Clark's office. Elle brought him a glass of cold water.

"I returned a few minutes ago from talking to Norris Broome," Ryan said when he came on the line. "He's going to cooperate, so I can review his investigative notes."

"I'm not calling about my case," Joe replied. "Would you run a background check on a prisoner from Blanton County named Ned Walker?"

"What's going on with him?"

"He's been here a few months and started asking a bunch of questions about me. He claims he heard our band years ago."

"I'm not making the connection. What's the problem?"

Joe took a deep breath. "Will you just do it? Ned is in for car theft, or so he claims. I want to help him find the Lord."

Ryan didn't immediately respond.

"Are you there?" Joe asked.

"Yes, I'm making a note. Did you say Ted Walker?"

"No, it's Ned. I'm not sure if that's short for something else.

He's about my age. White guy about six feet tall. He has family in Vicksboro, a little community on the east side of the county."

"I'll see what I can find out." Ryan hesitated before continuing, "What do you remember about your interaction with Broome? He said you were polite and well-educated, not a typical criminal. You didn't fit within his stereotype."

"I'm not sure how that's important," Joe responded. "My memory is fuzzy on the first time I met with Broome. The second meeting was when he told me that he didn't really need to talk to me because he had all the proof needed to convict. Other than that, I don't remember what he asked me."

"I'll let you know what turns up in the investigative file. I'll have access to more information because the legal standard of disclosure is different for post-conviction relief."

"Okay," Joe said, then sighed. "I may have been polite when Broome talked to me, but meth can really mess up a person's mind. After hearing and seeing the evidence, I was convinced I killed that couple even though I didn't remember doing it. The only way I've been able to move on with life is my belief that the sacrifice of Jesus cleanses us from the most horrible sins. Even so, there's still some guilt wrapped around my soul."

"That's understandable. And I say that from personal experience."

"Why is that?"

"My father died in a drowning accident when I was a teenager, and I've always blamed myself."

"Have you asked God to forgive you?"

"No, God wasn't in the boat with us. My father is the only one who can forgive me, and he's not here to do it. Anyway, I tried to pass along your note to Doc Garrison. He acted like we'd never talked about you before."

"Did you talk to him in person or on the phone?"

"In person. I was standing on the stoop in front of his trailer. Doc practically slammed the door in my face."

"That's the devil," Joe muttered under his breath.

"What did you say?"

"Thanks for trying," Joe said. "Maybe you'll get another chance."

"I slipped the letter through the door before I left, but I didn't see him pick it up."

"Okay, that's fine."

"But it had a big impact on my wife." Ryan described Paige's reaction to the letter.

"That's the Lord's way," Joe replied. "I'll be praying for your wife. She sounds like a good woman."

"The best."

The call ended. Joe walked slowly across the exercise yard to the dining hall. The news about Doc Garrison didn't surprise Joe. The drug dealer could be one way this week and change dramatically the next. Ray had saved Joe a seat at the table where they usually sat.

"I did what you suggested and asked my lawyer to run a background check on Ned," Joe said. "He'll follow through. He's been good about keeping in touch with me."

Ray pointed his fork across the dining hall. "Ned found me when I was in the line and told me to let you know he won't be coming this evening to play the harmonica. He didn't give a reason."

Joe stuck his fork in his macaroni and cheese. The two men ate in silence for a few moments.

"I know what you've always said about your case," Ray said, "but have you ever considered that you might not be guilty? You don't remember exactly what happened. I think you should ask the Lord to show you the truth."

"I'm not sure that's allowed."

"Why not?"

"I'm not sure I could trust what came into my head."

"Then I'll do it for you."

Joe gave Ray a slight smile. "You're biased. I'm not sure I can trust what might come into your head."

"It's worth a try. Whether I hear innocent or guilty, you're in this place or another like it until you're an old man and the State of North Carolina lets you out to die. The difference would be how you feel about yourself. For as long as I've known you, there's been a cloud of sadness over your soul. I've prayed for you to have peace, but if you're really innocent of murder . . ." Ray stopped.

"What?" Joe asked.

"That would change your whole way of thinking."

"Your imagination is out of control," Joe said.

"Not if it's sanctified."

Paige waited until after she and Ryan had eaten supper to mention that she'd written about her encounter with God.

"Do you want to read it?" she asked.

"Only if you're ready for my editorial critique."

"Give me your best shot. I dish it out to others and have to be willing to receive it myself. I have a thick skin."

"You do?"

"Not really, but I'll pretend. Will you clean the table and put the dishes in the washer while I take Sandy to the backyard? Then I'll let you take a look."

When Paige returned, they went into the living room. She opened the file on her laptop and handed it to Ryan.

"If you don't like anything, tell me. Every genuine writer welcomes feedback that will make what's written better."

"Paige, I'm not going to critique your writing. It would be like you analyzing my cross-examination of a witness."

"Just read it."

Paige watched Ryan's face, which remained inscrutable. He took a deep breath and exhaled.

"I'm going to read it again," he said.

Paige started to speak, but Ryan held up his right index finger. "Don't break my concentration."

Paige crossed her arms. This time she waited impatiently while he took even longer to reach the end of the document.

"Done," he said, returning the laptop to her.

"What do you think?"

Ryan looked into her eyes. "That I need to read it several more times so I can begin to understand what's going on inside your head. That's important to me, to us."

Relief washed over Paige. "I've started on some kind of spiritual journey and don't want to take it alone, especially without you," she said.

"Maybe it's so private that it should be off-limits to me."

"Didn't you hear what I just said? I want us to be together on this journey."

"And I'm not opposed to that. But this isn't something I can make up. One of the big takeaways from what you wrote is the fact that God reached out and touched you even when you weren't sure it could happen."

"I wrote it that way to help point the way for others."

"Which is another example of how unselfish you are."

Paige felt her emotions quickly rise up inside.

"Don't worry about me," Ryan continued. "I've got a lot on my plate right now, and there's only so much I can eat."

"I've seen you eat a lot." Paige managed a smile. "Promise you'll let me know if I start bothering you with this or it becomes bad for our relationship."

"Forward what you wrote. I really do want to read it again."

"Okay. Should I let Vicki and Candy share it with other people? I'm happier watching words appear on a monitor than speaking to a live person."

"Sure."

Ryan leaned back on the couch. "It wasn't all good news today about what Joe Moore wrote on that sheet of paper. When I tried to deliver it to Doc Garrison, he acted as if we'd never discussed Joe or his case."

"Why?" Paige asked in surprise.

"No idea, except that he's a very unstable person after all the years of chemical abuse he's afflicted on his body."

"Or has some kind of mental illness. I wish you could believe what he told you the other day."

"Actually, I do believe him," Ryan said, then raised one shoulder. "Or about seventy-five percent of me believes him."

Ryan listened for sounds of Paige in the kitchen brewing coffee but heard nothing. Getting out of bed, he found her in the backyard sitting in a chair as Sandy sniffed around on the grass.

"Usually, you don't loiter out here in the morning," he said.

"Nothing feels usual. I'm pregnant, which is altering my normal biorhythms, and I have all these new thoughts and feelings bouncing around inside me. I decided to take time to relax out here and greet the day more slowly."

"That's fine, but I don't have that luxury."

Paige started to get up from the chair. "Do you want me to fix breakfast for you while you shower and shave?"

"No," Ryan said as he held out his hand. "All I want is a cup of coffee and I'll be on my way."

When Ryan was ready to leave, Paige was still sitting in the backyard. He leaned over and lightly kissed her. She reached up and put her hand behind his neck and brought him in again.

"In the middle of your busy day, do you think you can remember that?" she asked.

Ryan grinned. "Yes. That won't be difficult."

The smile remained on his face during the drive to the office. Once there, he checked in with Nancy.

"Updated news about Tom," she said. "According to Karen, he's cleared for surgery on Friday. He still has COVID symptoms, but the risk of delay is too great."

When Sue arrived a few minutes later, Ryan told her about Joe's request for a background check on Ned Walker.

"Should this go to the top of my list?" she asked. "I have a lot to do that's time sensitive."

"No," Ryan quickly replied. "It's not urgent."

Ryan had a busy morning. He met with a prospective client. It was a small case but made him feel good about bringing in new business. He wished he could pass along the news to Tom.

Shortly before lunch, Nancy buzzed him. "Wyatt Belk is calling."

"I'll take it."

"What's the latest on Tom?" Wyatt asked.

"Scheduled for heart bypass surgery on Friday."

"That's good to hear. Our thoughts are with him. I guess it's both busy and lonely for you over there."

"That's accurate," Ryan replied succinctly.

"I know it's short notice, but do you have time for a quick lunch?"

"Today?"

"Yes. We could meet at Cornelia's Kitchen. The service is fast."

Ryan checked his calendar. He had an early afternoon appointment with an existing client who had demanded a meeting.

"I need to be back to the office by 1:15, which probably won't work—"

"That won't be a problem. See you in ten minutes."

Wyatt hung up before Ryan could respond.

CHAPTER 31

Driving to the restaurant, Ryan suspected the purpose of the meeting was to solicit his support for Scott Nelson's candidacy for district attorney. Beulah, who'd been working when he had breakfast with Paige, was on duty. She spoke before he said anything.

"Follow me," she said. "Mr. Belk is waiting for you."

Ryan had the strange feeling that his life was following a script not influenced by him. Wyatt was on his cell phone and motioned for him to have a seat. He ended the call and reached out to shake Ryan's hand.

"Thanks for joining me on short notice," the older lawyer said. "I recommend the lunch special. The stuffed peppers are one of the best items they serve. I pair it with the mashed potatoes and stewed squash."

Ryan, who had the menu in his hand, placed it on the table. "That sounds good to me."

Bonnie, the hostess's twin, took their order and left.

"I'll get to the point," Wyatt said. "You and I both hope Tom gets through this heart scare, but if he's not able to come back strong, I'd be interested in talking with you about joining our firm. And if Tom has to retire due to health reasons, there could be financial arrangements made to purchase his practice. Of course that would have to be decided by him or his legal representative. But regardless of Tom's capability, I wanted to mention this to you before someone else did. What's his wife's name? Carol?"

Ryan was caught completely off guard.

"Uh, Karen," he managed.

Wyatt quickly continued, "I was talking to Charlie Drummond at this exact table yesterday, and he brought up the possibility. He's been very impressed with your work."

"That's good to hear."

Wyatt leaned in closer. "In fact, I think Charlie's loyalties are shifting in your favor. Hearing that really impressed me, especially given the short time you've been working with Tom."

Ryan suddenly lost his appetite. He realized the reason for the lunch was to steal Charlie Drummond as a client from Tom. Wyatt saw someone he knew and waved across the room. The waitress brought their food.

"See how fast they are?" Wyatt said. "I almost always order the daily special. It's good and quick. That's the way I like to make decisions. Good and quick."

Ryan forced himself to eat. Wyatt engaged in small talk and gossip about the legal community in Cranfield. Ryan barely listened.

"How are things going in the case for the man convicted of killing Marty Brock and Cherie Drummond?" Wyatt asked. "Have you met with the killer?"

"Yes, several times."

"What's he like after all these years? Moore, right?"

"Yes. Decent guy. Model prisoner. Very religious."

Wyatt took a drink of tea. "I've always thought long prison sentences could become counterproductive from a societal standpoint. It's unlikely a man like Moore is an ongoing threat to the public, and the cost to taxpayers of keeping him locked up is a poor use of resources. But that point of view would never gain traction with the legislature in Raleigh. It would be politically impossible to sell. Hard-line law-and-order rhetoric appeals to voters."

"Regarding Moore, I would agree with you."

"One of my younger partners, Scott Nelson, is going to run for district attorney. I've had this conversation about long prison sentences with him, and off the record, I know he'll be more sympathetic than the current administration at evaluating each case on its own merits. You might want to keep that in mind."

"I will."

To Ryan's relief, Wyatt didn't follow up on the topic of the DA race. The older lawyer ordered a piece of coconut cream pie. Ryan passed.

"I should get back to the office," Ryan said.

"Of course. I appreciate you taking the time to meet with me on short notice. Glad I could give you food for thought about the future."

Ryan made it back in time to prepare for the meeting with the client. Before he could learn more details about the problem, however, the client terminated the firm's representation and demanded his file.

"Are you sure we can't work this out?" Ryan asked.

"No," the man replied curtly. "I've already made arrangements for new representation and don't want to hold that up."

"Okay," Ryan replied. "Let me get you a flash drive of everything in the file."

Ryan went to Sue's desk and told her what had happened.

"That'll only take a minute," the assistant said as she pulled up the client's records. "Oh, I checked out Ned Walker. His full name is Nathaniel Daniel Walker. Not my first name choice for a baby boy. Anyway, he has a long rap sheet of minor offenses, mostly for fighting, disorderly conduct, petty drug possession, and DUI, until the most recent conviction for stealing a car. He was drunk then too. The car theft was what sent him to prison. Part of the reason may be that he stole an expensive BMW, a two-seater convertible that sells for over a hundred thousand. Another interesting bit of data was that except for the car theft charge, he's never gotten into trouble alone. All the arrest records show him being part of a group that was picked up by the police at the same time. He has a brother named Larry and several other relatives who've been arrested along with him. Do you want me to run them down too?"

"No, you have plenty to do."

Sue handed Ryan the flash drive.

"That's everything," she said. "At least he didn't demand a refund of fees already billed and paid."

"Yeah."

Ryan returned to the conference room.

"One more thing," the man said. "I want a refund of the attorney fee paid last month in its entirety. The total is three thousand eight hundred sixty-five dollars. You didn't do anything."

Ryan hadn't performed the work on the file but doubted correcting that fact would make a difference. He hesitated.

"I will issue a check for five hundred dollars but nothing more," he said. "The attorney fee was for work performed consistent with the representation contract you signed with Tom."

The man glared at Ryan. "You'll hear from my new attorney, and I'm going to file a grievance with the state bar association!"

Ryan stood by the door as the man brushed past him but waited a few moments before going to Nancy's desk. Ryan told her to issue the five-hundred-dollar refund check and mail it to the now-former client.

"Do you think he'll file a grievance?" she asked.

"He seemed hot."

"Tom has a form letter he uses when that happens. If it comes up, I'll forward it to you."

"This is common?" Ryan asked in surprise.

"Enough that Tom created a form. Nothing ever comes from the complaints."

Ryan returned to his office. Thirty minutes later Sue appeared. She had a sheet of paper in her hand.

"I did some more digging on Nathaniel Daniel Walker," she said. "The date of one of his earliest arrests caught my eye, and I looked into the details. He was at the Eastside club on the night of the Brock-Drummond murders."

Ryan sat back in his chair. "What did he do that got him in trouble?"

"Possession of drugs. Methamphetamine. Five men were arrested and taken to jail. Not surprisingly, two of them were named Walker."

"The sheriff's department must have searched everybody in the club as part of their investigation into the murders and caught some other lawbreakers," Ryan said.

"That makes sense. I think I should check out the other men arrested that night. Oh, I think I figured out why he goes by Ned."

"Why?"

"Nathaniel Daniel, N.D., Ned."

"Brilliant."

Joe and the rest of the men scaled back the pace of their work due to the heat. It was the hottest week of the summer, and without rain the garden was in danger of drying up. The men gathered under the shade for their noontime meal.

"Preacher, it's time for you to pray for rain," a man named Clyde said to Joe. "If the Lord doesn't open the heavens, the strawberries are going to shrivel up and the beans aren't going to ripen. The only thing that might make it is the okra."

Joe didn't like being called Preacher or being told what he had to do for God. But under the circumstances, he didn't issue a correction.

"What if we have to fast and pray?" Ray replied. "Who's in for that kind of action?"

The men shifted and looked at one another. In addition to Joe and Ray, a few raised their hands, including Deshaun.

"Before we decide, let's pray about it this afternoon and evening and see what the Lord says," Joe said.

"I know what the Almighty is saying to me," Clyde replied, rubbing his ample belly.

"Whether it's a fast or a diet, you need to be the first one to raise your hand," another man said.

"Are you ready to back that up—" Clyde began to retort.

"Cool it, both of you," Ray said.

Joe knew it wasn't necessary to ask God whether he wanted to send rain. He closed his eyes and raised his hands to the sky.

"Lord, send the rain. Amen."

"That's it?" Clyde asked in surprise.

"You're welcome to add anything you like," Joe said.

"No, no." Clyde held up both hands in front of him. "I'm more likely to make God mad than convince him to do something."

"That's not how prayer works," Deshaun said, touching his chest.

Deshaun and Clyde began talking. Joe looked over at Ray, who nodded and grinned.

"In the meantime, let's harvest as many strawberries as we can this afternoon," Joe called out. "I'll go over to the dining hall and let Dickie know what's coming. Maybe we can have strawberries two different ways for supper."

While the rest of the men finished their lunch break, Joe walked to the dining hall and told the manager what they were going to do.

"How about strawberry cake topped with fresh fruit and a strawberry and cucumber salad?" Dickie asked.

"And whipped cream on the cake."

"You guys are always pushing for whipped cream."

"Any chance?" Joe asked.

Dickie set his jaw. "Okay, but only if you promise not to bring it up again until Christmas dinner."

"Done," Joe quickly agreed.

Leaving the rear entrance of the dining hall, Joe turned a corner and almost ran into Ned Walker, who was carrying a piece of thin metal pipe beneath his right arm. Joe jumped back. The edge of the pipe grazed his arm.

"Look out!" Ned exclaimed. "I could have sliced you open with that."

Joe looked down at his arm. A thin line of red blood appeared. He wiped it away with his hand.

"You got me, but it was only a nick."

"I'm on my way to replace a piece of ductwork in the dining hall. That place has enough problems to keep me busy three days a week.

Once I finish with this, there's another issue with one of the coolers in the kitchen."

"Sounds like you won't be cleaning bathrooms anytime soon," Joe replied, clearing his throat. "Any chance you could come to Unit C this evening to play harmonica and hang around for a Bible study?"

Ned hesitated. "Maybe," he said, "but only if I'm not in a group with Max. He and I don't get along."

"That's not a problem. You'll be with me."

"Okay, count me in," Ned said brightly. "I've been practicing my harmonica."

Joe returned to the garden and told the men what to expect for supper. Around 3:00 p.m. a few clouds appeared in the western sky. Thirty minutes later, the clouds had grown larger and darker. Ray, who was working near Joe, came over to him.

"I'm smelling rain," Ray said, touching the side of his nose.

Joe looked up at the sky. "At least we're going to get a break from the heat."

By 4:15 p.m. it didn't take a meteorologist to predict that a thunderstorm was on the way. When there was a distant flash of lightning, Joe called the men together.

"Let's take it in early," he said.

"Does this mean we're not going to fast and pray?" Clyde asked.

"I didn't see you raise your hand to volunteer," Joe replied.

Moments later, big drops started splattering the dusty ground.

"Run for it!" Deshaun said, taking off.

Joe and Ray fell behind the younger men. They were quickly soaked. Joe stopped running and started walking. Ray glanced over his shoulder and slowed down.

"Are you okay?" Ray yelled over the sound of the rain.

"I'm already soaked and want to enjoy this."

The two men stood at the corner of the exercise area. A bolt of lightning streaked down and struck a clump of pine trees just outside the fence line. It sounded like a rifle shot. Both Joe and Ray took off running faster than either of them thought possible. Inside Unit C one of the guards on duty came over to Joe.

"Got a call for you to report to the administration building," the man said.

"Did you hear that lightning strike?" Joe asked. "That was close. I want to stay here until this storm blows over."

"You'll be fine. Lightning never strikes twice in the same place."

Joe tilted his head to the side. "I think you'd better go with me to make sure I don't try to escape in the middle of the storm."

"Oh, I can't leave my duty station," the guard replied.

Joe rubbed his head dry with a towel. His clothes were still soaked. Outside, the torrential rain stopped as suddenly as it started. The ground was wet and steamy. Joe made his way through the mud to the administration building.

"Shoes off," the guard on duty said when Joe approached. "Leave them here."

Joe's damp socks left prints on the floor as he made his way to the office. Elle was working.

"Did you get caught out in the storm?" she asked.

"Yes. What's up?"

"Your lawyer wants you to call him. You can use consultation room A."

Joe went to the room where he'd first met with Shana and Ryan.

"I found out something interesting about Ned Walker and wanted to let you know," Ryan said when he answered Joe's call.

Joe listened as the lawyer told him what he'd uncovered about Ned Walker's whereabouts on the night of the murders.

"You're sure it was him?" Joe asked. "And you say there were other men named Walker present that night?"

"Yes, a brother named Larry. Maybe some other relatives. My assistant double-checked the arrest records. The birthdays match for Ned. I assume they were arrested because they were questioning a bunch of people who were at the club and included those in possession of illegal drugs."

"Ned claims he heard our band play a few times but never brought up being at the Eastside club that night. I have no idea why he'd keep that a secret. I'm going to ask him about it when I see him tonight. I'm giving him harmonica lessons."

"Harmonica lessons?"

"Yes, it's a way to get him to attend a Bible study."

The call ended. Joe stepped out of the conference room. As he made his way down the hallway, Elle approached.

"Big news," she said in an excited voice. "The warden says your request to stay at LPCC was granted. You're not going to be transferred."

"Thanks," Joe said.

"It would be different not having you around," Elle continued. "And not in a good way."

CHAPTER 32

Paige took a break from work and phoned Vicki between conference calls. "Do you have a minute to talk?"

"Only because I'm such a good multitasker. I'm fixing spaghetti for supper while supervising my first grader's homework and keeping an eye on the baby to make sure he doesn't crawl into the fireplace. I'm not sure where my five-year-old daughter is, but if she's quiet, that's usually a good sign."

"I've finished the paper you and Candy suggested I write about what God is doing in my life, and I wanted to send it over for you to read. I've never done anything like this and want to make sure it's within the genre."

"I haven't heard the word 'genre' since college. Send it over."

"I want honest feedback."

"Sure, but this sort of thing is so personal you can't pigeonhole it. Are you going to send it to Candy too?"

"Yes."

"The spaghetti sauce is going to have to simmer longer than normal."

"Hold off until the kids are in bed," Paige said. "I don't need a quick response."

"It's not about getting back to you. I want to read it for me."

After Paige sent the file to both women, her phone vibrated. It was Ryan. She suspected he was going to let her know he'd be delayed.

"Tom has taken a turn for the worse and is back in ICU," Ryan said. "They wanted to do his heart surgery on Friday, but that's up in the air. Karen just called Nancy with the news."

Paige frowned.

"That's not what I expected to hear," she said.

"There's more, but I'll tell you later. I'm going to work for another hour or so."

After the call, Paige sat on the couch for a moment before going into the kitchen to fix a snack to hold her hunger at bay until Ryan came home. A loud crash from the area of the front door startled her. Sandy leaped off the couch and started barking furiously. Paige walked rapidly into the foyer. One of the sidelights beside the door was shattered. Half of a red brick lay on the parquet floor. Paige looked out the open space where the window had been but didn't see anyone or anything. Her heart pounding, she picked up the brick and turned it over. When she did, she heard the sound of a firecracker in the distance, followed by a ping as something struck the corner of an aluminum picture frame behind her and made a hole in the wall. Paige screamed, dropped the brick, and lay face down on the floor.

Ryan called 911 as he raced home. From the street he could see the shattered sidelight. He ran up the sidewalk, unlocked the front door, and burst into the house. He saw the hole in the wall near the picture frame. Paige was sitting on the couch with her knees under her chin and hugging her legs. Ryan sat beside her and wrapped his left arm around her shoulders. Paige wasn't crying, but he could feel her body shaking.

"I'm sorry," he said after a few moments passed.

"I'm okay now," Paige replied, but the trembling in her voice belied her words. "Did you see the hole in the wall?"

"Yes. It's from a bullet."

Paige shivered more violently. Ryan squeezed her tighter.

"Where's the brick?" he asked.

"In the trash. I cleaned up the glass with a broom."

"Someone should be here soon from the sheriff's department."

"Why would someone want to do that?" Paige asked, her voice unsteady. "And will they come back?"

Ryan went into the kitchen and used a paper towel to retrieve the brick from the trash can. It was a dusky red with jagged edges where it had been broken in two. He placed it on the kitchen counter. When he returned to the living room, Paige hadn't moved.

"What are we going to do?" she asked, anxiously looking into his face.

"I was thinking about that on the way home," Ryan said, speaking rapidly. "We'll get permission from Mr. Vaughn to have a first-rate alarm system installed with multiple cameras inside and out. I'll buy a gun and get trained in how to use it. Maybe two guns so that—"

"I'm not sure I want to do that," Paige interrupted.

"We'll talk about it later."

Ryan ran his fingers through his hair. He couldn't sit still.

"I'm going out to wait for the deputy," he said. "Hopefully, he'll be here soon."

"No!" Paige blurted, sitting up straighter. "Stay here with me!"

Ryan remained beside her and fidgeted. "Maybe somebody else on the street with security cameras captured an image of the person or persons who tossed the brick and fired the shot," he said.

There was a sharp rap on the front door.

"Blanton County Sheriff's Department!" a female voice called out.

Ryan went into the foyer. A young woman with blond hair stood on the porch. Lights flashing, her car was parked in front of the house. The officer's name badge read "Lauren Jackson."

"I'm Deputy Jackson," she said.

"Ryan Clark. My wife, Paige, is in the living room."

"We've not met in person," the deputy said. "But I know who you are."

"I learned something new from my lawyer," Joe said to Ray as soon as they were both seated in the dining hall. "He got back to me about Ned."

"Already?" Ray asked in surprise. "Are you this young attorney's only client? What did he find out?"

Joe told him what Ryan had discovered concerning Ned's whereabouts on the night of the murders.

Ray nodded. "That explains why Ned has been so curious about you and worried about your temper."

"It does? Tell me, because I don't see it."

"It's easy. If Ned was there the night two people were cut to pieces, he'd be afraid of the man convicted of the killings."

"But what if Max is right and Ned stabbed a guy at Central Prison in Raleigh?" Joe kept his voice low. "Maybe Ned knows something about what happened that night."

"Whoa," Ray replied. "You think Ned may have committed the murders instead of you?"

"Two weeks ago, I would have told you no way. Now I'm not sure about anything."

The two men sat in silence for a few moments. Joe finished the salad on his plate.

"Did you tell your lawyer what Max said about Ned?" Ray asked.

"No."

"Why not?"

"His news caught me by surprise. I told him I'd talk to Ned."

"I'm not sure that's smart, especially if what Max claims is true."

"Yeah," Joe replied with a sigh. "I'm not sure what to do."

———

The deputy entered the living room and introduced herself to Paige. Sandy was barking as ferociously as she could.

"She's noisy but harmless," Paige said to the young woman, who appeared to be in her mid- to late twenties.

The deputy reached out and let Sandy sniff the back of her hand. The dog let out a final woof and then plopped down on the floor.

"Please, call me Lauren," the deputy said. "Do you have a piece of wood to cover the broken glass until it can be replaced?"

"There's a piece of scrap in the shed where we keep the lawn mower," Ryan replied.

"I'll send someone over tomorrow to remove the bullet from the wall. Hopefully, we'll be able to determine the caliber of the gun. Do you have the brick you mentioned in your call?"

Ryan left the room.

"My husband and I were in the Sunday school class when you visited Grace Fellowship," Lauren said to Paige.

"I don't remember, but it was our first time."

Ryan returned with the brick and handed it to the deputy. The officer turned it over in her hand. Seeing it made Paige shudder.

"It's not the sort of thing that's likely to produce fingerprints," Lauren said, "but I'd like to take it to the station so it can be documented with the incident report."

The term "incident report" sounded too mundane to Paige.

"Did either of you see anything?"

In a halting voice, Paige told her what happened. The deputy entered information on a tablet.

"The bullet came within two or three feet of my head," Paige said. "I'm terrified!"

"I completely understand," the officer replied in a sympathetic tone of voice. "For the next few days, I'll be glad to park my car in front of the house when I'm not on duty. That should serve as a deterrent."

"You'd do that?" Paige asked in surprise.

"Yes, my husband and I live on the next block. Sheriff Tipton encourages us to take our patrol cars home to increase the visibility of law enforcement in the community."

"That would be nice," Paige said. "But what if it's raining?"

"I own an umbrella. And I'll give you my cell phone number in case you ever need to call. Day or night. I can be here in less than two minutes."

Both the presence of the car and knowing that the officer lived so close helped ease Paige's anxiety.

"That makes me feel better," she said.

"Good. I'll submit my report and ask around the office in case anyone has an idea about why this happened. It could be a case of extreme vandalism or gang activity."

"Gang activity?" Ryan asked.

"It's hard to believe, but a gang has sprung up in Blanton County. They have initiation requirements that put other people's property and lives at risk."

"Have they done anything like this?" Paige asked.

"They used pistols to shoot up the side of a barn. A horse inside was wounded but survived."

The officer closed the cover on her tablet.

"Thanks for coming," Ryan said.

"You're welcome. Will I see you on Sunday?"

"Yes," Paige replied.

After the deputy left, Ryan went to the tiny shed in the backyard and returned with a narrow piece of plywood and nailed it in place. There was still a small one-inch opening at the top.

"Tomorrow morning, I'm going to begin the search for a security company," he said. "I bet Nancy can provide a recommendation."

"Okay."

"Are you too upset to eat supper?" Ryan asked. "If you are, I completely understand—"

"I'm not hungry, but I'd like to get away from the house for a while. That's what I really need."

Walking to the car, Ryan kept glancing around. He noticed that Paige was doing the same thing. Before he started the car, Paige's phone vibrated.

"It's Vicki," she said.

Paige pressed the receive button and placed the call on speaker.

"Are you okay?" Vicki asked. "I saw a sheriff's department car sitting in front of your house."

Paige told her what had happened.

"That's terrible!"

"Lauren Jackson is the one who came to investigate."

"Oh, she's great," Vicki replied. "When she speaks to the kids at school, they all love her."

"We have no idea why it happened."

"Oh, I do."

Ryan looked at Paige and raised his eyebrows.

"Go ahead. You're on speaker so Ryan can listen."

"The devil is upset about what God is doing in your life and your willingness to write out your testimony to share with others. He's behind the attack and used someone under his control to carry it out."

Ryan shook his head.

"We hadn't considered that possibility," Paige managed.

"That immediately came to my mind. You can usually know that you're doing something right because of the spiritual opposition you face."

"Maybe we can talk about this later. Right now, Ryan and I are on the way to dinner. I had to get out of the house."

"I won't keep you and will be praying for protection from other attacks. Is it okay if I mention this to Candy?"

Paige looked at Ryan, who shrugged.

"Yes, but I'd rather it not be brought up in the Sunday school class."

"Okay. Have a nice dinner."

The call ended.

"What did you make of that?" Paige asked Ryan.

"I have no idea. But I'm doubtful there's a security system on the market that claims to protect against the devil."

Listening to Vicki Lennox, Ryan wasn't sure he ever wanted to return to the church. They reached an Italian restaurant located in a small retail center along with a laundromat, a shoe repair store, and a dry cleaner. Portofino's had a sign in the shape of the Roman Colosseum. The hostess escorted them to a booth.

A waiter arrived and told them about the dinner specials. Ryan selected a pasta dish with mussels. Paige ordered a side salad. While they waited for their food, the door to the restaurant opened, and Ryan saw Norris Broome enter. The former detective glanced around the interior of the restaurant and then started walking toward their booth.

"Here comes the detective I talked to the other day about Joe Moore," Ryan said.

Broome reached their table. Ryan introduced him to Paige.

"I hate to interrupt your dinner," Broome said. "But I heard what happened at your house on the law enforcement scanner. Occasionally, I still listen in on calls. I'm so sorry about this."

"How did you find us here?" Ryan asked.

"Deputy Jackson followed you. She received permission from her boss to keep an eye on you for the rest of the evening. Would you mind telling me what happened?"

Ryan looked over at Paige, who nodded her head.

"Sit down," Ryan said as he moved to the other side of the booth next to Paige.

Broome listened without interrupting.

"This is odd," he said as he rubbed his chin. "Someone tossed a brick through a window at my house yesterday evening while I was at the grocery store."

Ryan felt the blood drain from his face. Paige reached for his hand beneath the table.

"Did you file a report with the sheriff's department?" Ryan asked.

"Not yet. There wasn't any evidence of a gunshot, and I dismissed it as vandalism or harassment from someone I locked up years ago. The security cameras on my property didn't pick up any activity, so whoever threw the brick was careful. The alarm sounded when the glass shattered, and I rushed home."

"What do you think about Deputy Jackson's suggestion it might be gang-related?"

"Certainly possible."

Paige released Ryan's hand. He glanced over and saw that her face was extremely pale.

"Are you okay?" he asked her.

"No. It feels like it's a hundred degrees in here, and the room is spinning."

"She's about to faint!" Broome said. "Lie down on the bench."

The words had barely left the former detective's lips when Paige slumped onto the table. Ryan lifted her head and positioned her body so that she rested against his chest. He dipped a napkin into one of the glasses of ice water on the table and held it to her forehead. Paige's eyes fluttered open.

"Should I call an ambulance?" Ryan asked.

"No," Paige mumbled. "I'm better."

"Be still until it passes," Broome said.

A few seconds later, Paige opened her eyes again and licked her lips.

"I really am better," she said, trying to sit up straight again.

"Take it slow and easy," Broome said.

"Thank you," Paige said to him. "I apologize—"

"When did you last eat?" Broome asked.

"Breakfast, and that wasn't much. I worked through lunch."

"And she's pregnant," Ryan added. "Why did you skip lunch?"

"Too much to do," Paige said with a wave of her hand.

Ryan held a glass of water to Paige's lips, and she took a drink. The waiter returned with their food.

"Are you able to eat?" Ryan asked.

"I think so," Paige said. "It's just so much coming at me at once."

"I'll talk to Deputy Jackson," Broome said. "Her car is at the end of the parking lot. I'm sure one of the detectives will be in touch soon. In the meantime, I'm going to do some checking on my own."

Broome left. Paige took a bite of food and closed her eyes as she chewed.

"Are you feeling faint again?" Ryan asked.

"No, I'm not dizzy. This is really good, and I need to eat. I'm glad Detective Broome is going to investigate what happened," Paige said. "He seems like a decent man."

"Former detective."

"He sounded more like a current detective to me," Paige replied.

"Yeah, he did."

———

Joe waited as Ned make his way across the exercise yard toward Unit C. Ned looked up at the sky as he approached the bench.

"Looks like the rain clouds are gone," he said as he sat down. "That was a big shower this afternoon."

As chief gardener, Joe usually enjoyed talking about the weather. Tonight it didn't interest him.

"And thanks to you guys for the strawberries," Ned continued. "That strawberry cucumber salad reminded me of what one of my aunts used to fix when the family came over to her house."

"Where did your aunt live?" Joe asked.

"Not in Vicksboro. Her place was in Hoke County where my father's folks lived."

"And who are some of your other relatives in Blanton County?"

"Most of them are scattered now."

"But they were still in the area when you came to hear my band play?"

"A few."

Ned took his harmonica from the front pocket of his pants.

"Listen to this," he said. "I'm not saying I'm proud, especially when I listen to you, but I think it's pretty good."

Ned raised the instrument to his lips and played a riff of several measures that caused Joe to nod his head and tap his foot.

"That's nice," he said. "Play it again."

Joe listened closely, and when Ned finished, he continued the theme by adding some improvisation of his own. Several men stopped to listen.

"More," one man said.

"I'm just a beginner," Ned protested. "This is a lesson."

"Play your part again," Joe said. "And when I take it up, see if you can find a line beneath what I'm playing."

"I can't do that."

"You can try."

Ned shook his head.

"Okay, we'll go at it this way," Joe said. "You play your line, and I'll come alongside you."

Ned started off, and Joe quickly joined him. It reminded Joe of some of the jam sessions of his youth. Ned had talent. They went back and forth. Ned stumbled a few times, but Joe picked up the slack. They both ended on a high note.

The fifteen or sixteen men standing in front of the bench clapped. Ned had a big smile on his face.

"Nice job," Joe said.

The men moved on. Joe slapped his harmonica against his hand to dislodge any extra saliva.

"Ned, you've not been telling me the truth."

Ned shifted on the bench. "What do you mean?"

"That wasn't a beginner's riff. You've played the harmonica before."

"I played for a while many years ago but forgot what I learned. I guess some of it is coming back."

"Anything else coming back?"

"Like what?" Ned asked.

"I don't know. Old memories you've kept in the dark."

"No. And that's the way I want to keep it."

Joe hesitated. He didn't see a way past Ned's defenses, at least not yet.

"I need to prepare a few things before the meeting," he said.

"No problem. I'll check the thermostat in the guardroom to make sure everything is operating as it should."

Joe went to his bunk and took out his Bible and notebook. He'd enjoyed making music with Ned. It brought back memories from his time with his band. Joe knew Ned was being evasive, but where the truth lay remained a mystery. It was hard for Joe to seriously consider the possibility that the man sharing the bench with him might have had a hand in the murders for which Joe had served more than two and a half decades. Ray appeared beside the bunk.

"That was some serious music," Ray said.

"Yeah, Ned admitted that he used to play the harmonica years ago. He's not a beginner."

"Did he admit anything else?"

"I cracked open the window for him to say something about the past, but he slammed it shut."

Joe patted his Bible with his hand.

"What are you going to talk about in your group tonight?" he asked.

"The book of Job," Ray replied. "The Lord showed me a lot of men in here who claim they're sitting on the ash heap of injustice and wrongful punishment when it's time to get up and get honest with God."

"I like that," Joe said with a slow nod.

"You're welcome to borrow what I said and claim it as your own."

"I might do that," Joe said. "I'm also going to use that freedom prayer you came up with a few months ago."

Ray reached into the front pocket of his uniform and pulled out an index card.

"This one?" he asked.

"Isn't that something? Both of us had the same prayer on our hearts for tonight. That's the Lord."

"Yep. I have one for every man," Ray said.

Joe was silent for a moment. "Sitting there with Ned, I realized my mind needs to be focused on what's in front of me, not running back to the past. In a few minutes, I'm going to lead a Bible study and prayer meeting with a group of men who need God. That's where my head has to be."

"Sounds good, but watch your back."

Joe led the group of six men without being bothered by Ned's presence. He shared what he'd heard from Ray. Several of the men nodded in agreement. Ned seemed to listen but didn't contribute until the very end.

"Tell us how to pray about this," Ned said.

"That's my final point," Joe replied, taking out a few index cards identical to the one Ray was carrying. "Ray Simpson, who taught me a lot about this subject, wrote out a prayer we can repeat. God knows our every thought, but I like to say the prayer out loud so I can hear it myself. This isn't for show. Keep your eyes open because we're going to read it slowly."

Joe passed out the cards. "Take a minute or two to read this so you can decide if you agree with it. Then, those who want to pray it can do so together."

Joe waited until they'd finished reading the cards.

"Any questions?" he asked.

"Let's do it," one man said.

Joe began the prayer. There was no hesitation by Ned, who continued to the end. Something about the sound of Ned's voice stirred Joe's heart.

"In Jesus' name, amen," the men said.

"Take this with you," Joe said. "Like I told you, I've prayed it many times."

The group broke up. Ned didn't stay to talk to Joe or anyone else. Joe found Ray and told him what had happened.

"Do you think he meant it?" Ray asked.

"We don't know what's in another man's heart."

"Yeah, but we can have an opinion."

Joe hesitated for a moment. "I think Ned was sincere."

"Then there should be fruit to prove it."

CHAPTER 33

While Paige ate, she could tell Ryan was carefully watching her.

"Don't worry," she said. "If I feel faint again, I'll let you know."

"Has that ever happened to you before?"

"Only when I was ten and had an emergency appendectomy. After the surgery, a mean nurse made me stand up before I felt able, and I crumpled to the floor."

"I'd like to sue her," Ryan replied.

"I think the statute of limitations has run out."

"I still want to sue her."

Paige took a drink of water. Ryan dipped the final piece of bread into a mixture of olive oil and balsamic vinegar.

"I hate being scared," she said but quickly added, "Even though I know you'd do anything you could to protect me."

———

To her surprise, Paige slept soundly. When she awoke, Ryan wasn't in bed. She found him in the living room drinking a cup of coffee. He'd already let Sandy out and fixed the dog's breakfast.

"I didn't hear you get up," she said.

"Yesterday was a huge emotional drain, and you needed to recharge."

"What about you?"

"My mind was in gear until after midnight."

"What were you thinking about?"

"Everything."

Paige leaned over and kissed the top of his head.

"Don't wear out your brain," she said.

Paige went into the kitchen. Ryan had moved a mirror so that it covered the bullet hole in the wall. Through the window over the sink, Paige could see Lauren Jackson's patrol car parked in front of the house. After pouring a cup of coffee, she returned to the couch. Sandy jumped up to snuggle next to her.

"I sent Nancy a text asking about a security service," Ryan said. "She gave me the names of two companies. Did you see Deputy Jackson's car?"

"Yes. That makes me feel better. Do you think we'll hear from a detective today?"

"We should. If you're not contacted by this afternoon, let me know."

While Ryan showered and dressed for work, Paige remained on the couch with her coffee and her dog.

"Keep in touch throughout the day," Ryan said as he kissed her goodbye.

"Multiple times, if that's okay."

"Absolutely."

"Oh, and I'll forward the letter I'd like you to pass along to Joe Moore. I finished it yesterday. You're welcome to read it."

"As his lawyer, I have to."

After Ryan left, Paige opened the Bible app on her phone and entered a search for verses that had to do with protection from evil.

As soon as he arrived at the office, Ryan told Nancy and Sue what had happened the previous evening. Both women gasped when he mentioned the bullet whizzing by Paige's head.

"Poor thing," Nancy said, wringing her hands. "I'm going to lock the door to the office unless you have an appointment on the calendar. I don't want someone barging in here with a gun."

Ryan held up his hand. "What if we have a delivery or a client drops in for some reason?"

"They can knock or ring the bell."

"I don't think that's necessary."

"Type a sign and put it on the door," Sue added.

Ryan surrendered. "Okay, but just temporarily."

Nancy pulled open one of the side drawers to her desk and took out a handgun.

"And I have this if needed."

"Do you have a permit for that?" Ryan asked in surprise.

"Yes, along with a concealed carry license."

"Does Tom know about it?"

"Yes. He has one in his office too."

"What about you?" he asked Sue.

The assistant nodded. Unaware that he'd been working in such a heavily armed environment, Ryan went into his office. Over the next few hours, he made his way steadily through his to-do list. One item jotted at the bottom was the name Ned Walker. Shortly before noon, he went to Sue's desk and told her about his conversation with Joe Moore.

"Joe wanted to talk to Walker, but I think I should interview him at the prison," Ryan said.

"That might work, but it's probably a waste of time unless you can come up with a reason why Walker would want to talk to you."

Ryan left the office for a quick lunch. He locked the front door behind him. Nancy had taped a sign to the door stating the office was open and to knock for entry. When he returned from lunch, he found the receptionist crying with a tissue in her hand.

"Karen called a few minutes ago," the receptionist said. "They're not sure Tom is going to make it another twenty-four hours."

Ryan sat down in one of the reception room chairs close to Nancy's desk.

"His heart stopped twice," Nancy continued through sniffles. "They were able to get it started, but it's weak and his blood pressure is in the danger zone."

"Is there anything Karen wants us to do?"

"I'm not sure. She's really torn up. Even with all that's happened, I believe she had hope. Until now."

Ryan felt like he had to do something.

"I should go to the hospital," he said resolutely. "I know Tom is in the ICU, but I could try to see Karen."

"No, she specifically said she doesn't want any visitors. Her sister came in from Nashville to be with her. They've always been close."

In his office, Ryan called Paige to give her an update on Tom.

"Would it be okay if I ask Vicki and Candy to pray for him?" she asked.

"Sure," Ryan answered. "And maybe I should let Joe Moore know."

"I agree," Paige responded immediately.

"Okay. Any news from the sheriff's department?"

"A detective is coming by at three o'clock."

Ryan checked his calendar. He had an appointment with a client that had already been postponed once.

"Do you want me to be there?" Ryan asked.

"No, I'll let him in so he can do his job. I just want the bullet out of the house. I'll let you know what he says. Also, the handyman who's going to fix the sidelight has an opening in his schedule later this afternoon and is going to try to come today."

"Good."

"I called and set an appointment with one of the salespeople for a security company early tomorrow morning," Paige said. "Can you be here when he comes? He's supposed to get here between eight and eight thirty."

"Yes. You've been busy."

———

Late in the afternoon, Nancy buzzed Ryan's phone. "Someone from the DA's office brought over a box of information for you from the Moore case. Where do you want me to put it?"

Ryan had offered to pick up the copies, but this would save him a trip. "I'll get it. It may be heavy."

Ryan brought the box into his office and lifted the lid. It wasn't just filled with papers. Whoever copied the records organized everything in folders. He pulled the one marked "Norris Broome" and flipped through the information. It was indecipherable. Picking up the phone, Ryan called the former detective.

"Let me give you my email," Broome said. "You can scan and send everything to me. That will save you a trip."

"Thanks," Ryan said appreciatively.

He gave the witness statements to Sue to scan and send. Returning to his office, he called the prison to set up a phone call with Joe.

"The men in his crew should be returning from work. I'll radio one of the guards to let Mr. Moore know."

The guard at the toolshed called out to Joe.

"Your lawyer wants to talk to you," the man said. "Head over to the administration building."

Joe and Ray were standing beside each other.

"I'm not believing this," Ray said with a shake of his head. "If I didn't know better, I'd think your attorney is going to adopt you. He's keeping closer tabs on you than if you lived across the street."

"He's young enough to be my son."

"What do you think it is this time?"

Joe shrugged. "No idea."

"If I had to guess, I'd think it has to do with Ned."

The men continued toward the main compound and crossed the exercise yard.

"I'm going to take a quick shower," Joe said. "I must have sweat a gallon today."

"Yeah, it was the hottest day of the year for sure."

The cool shower felt good, but it remained so hot outside that Joe was perspiring again by the time he reached the administration building. Thankfully, it was the coolest place in the prison. Elle was on duty.

"Good afternoon, Mr. Moore," she said. "Are you here to talk with your lawyer?"

"Yes."

"I'll contact his office and transfer the call to consultation room B when it comes in. It's the only room available today."

Joe went into the hallway. There wasn't a guard in sight. Inside the consultation room, he sat down in a plastic chair. The two consultation rooms were identical. A phone sat in the middle of the table before him. Beside it was a small scrap of paper with writing on it. Joe picked up the scrap of paper, intending to toss it into a small trash can in the corner. He stopped to read it. A single short sentence was written in crude, blocky letters:

MOORE TELL YOUR LAWYER TO DROP THE
CASE OR BOTH OF YOU ARE DEAD MEN.

All prisoners lived with the possibility of an assault or threat. Joe had always resisted the impulse to give way to fear or paranoia. The phone rang.

"I'm forwarding the call from your lawyer," Elle said.

Still holding the note in his fingers, Joe picked up the receiver.

"There are a couple of things I want to mention to you," Ryan said quickly. "First, Tom's health has seriously deteriorated. The doctors want to do the heart surgery on Friday, but they're not sure he's going to last that long."

Joe turned the note over face down on the table.

"Let's pray," he said.

Without waiting for permission from the lawyer, Joe started praying. He gave voice to the words and impressions God planted in his mind. There were Scriptures sprinkled in with his own thoughts. As he prayed, Joe had an image in his mind of what Tom Clark looked like the last time he'd seen him. The attorney might be feeble and failing now, but in Joe's mind, he was healthy and vigorous, and that was the way Joe prayed the lawyer would be. He didn't say "Amen" until he was sure there was nothing left to pray.

"I've never heard anyone pray like that," Ryan said.

"Prison is a good place to learn."

Joe knew he had to tell the lawyer about the threat. He held the piece of paper lightly between his fingers.

"There's something else," Joe said. "Someone left a note in this room before I came in to take your phone call."

Joe read what was written on the scrap of paper. There was no immediate response from the lawyer.

"Are you still there?" he asked.

"Yes," Ryan replied in a subdued tone of voice. "And I need to let you know what happened at my house last night."

Joe was shocked by what he heard.

"And it wasn't just my house," Ryan said. "Someone tossed a brick through a window at Norris Broome's house. No shots were fired."

"The detective? Why?"

"Perhaps because he's been willing to talk to me about your case."

Joe's mind was spinning. He was less concerned for his own safety than that of the people who weren't in the prison. All Joe had to do was put out the word within LPCC that he'd been threatened, and scores of men would be watching his back.

"Are there surveillance cameras in the hallway outside the consultation room?" Ryan asked.

"Yes, there are cameras everywhere. There's a control room in this building where all the video feeds are transmitted. I saw that when I used to work on the janitorial crew before we started planting a garden."

"Show the note to the warden and ask him to check into it. He certainly seems to be on your side."

"Okay, but I'm more worried about you and your wife."

"We're taking steps to increase security at our home."

"None of that is going to stop someone who is determined to harm you," Joe said. "Maybe you should stop the investigation. I can't risk having an even worse attack against you or your wife on my conscience."

"The sheriff's department is looking into it, and a deputy who lives in our neighborhood is keeping an eye out for us."

"Is that a guarantee of safety?" Joe asked in a stronger voice. "Trying to get me out of here isn't worth putting you or anyone else in danger!"

"You really want me to drop your case?" Ryan asked. "Shouldn't we think about it for a few days?"

"No! Every day increases the risk. I want you to contact my niece and explain what I want to do. She and my sister will understand."

"What about Ned Walker? Did you talk to him?"

"Yes, and I didn't learn anything."

Ryan was silent for a moment. "Ask the warden to review the surveillance videos for the area near the phone consultation room and see who turns up."

"It doesn't sound like you're dropping the case," Joe said.

"I don't want to do anything stupid, but we may be closer to a breakthrough than we realize."

"You're young and believe you're going to live forever."

"I believe Doc Garrison is connected to this," Ryan replied. "Not that he threw the brick or fired a shot, but he's talked to someone who feels threatened. Even though he's no longer a detective,

Norris Broome might be able to talk to Doc and uncover valuable information."

"You can keep talking, but nothing you've said changes my mind."

"Will you at least ask the warden to check the surveillance videos?"

"Yes," Joe sighed. "Are you going to talk to Shana?"

"What am I supposed to tell her?"

"I don't want my family to know about the threat on my life. Tell her that the more I've thought about it, the more convinced I am that I don't want to file an MAR. You tried to talk me out of it, but I wouldn't budge."

At the sound of a knock on the consultation room door, Joe's heart skipped a beat.

"Hold on," Joe said to Ryan. "I have to see who's at the door."

In the hall stood Elle from the warden's office. "Mr. Moore, you're past the time allowed for phone calls. Please tell your lawyer the conversation needs to end."

"Will do, thanks."

Joe relayed the message.

"Time's up," he said. "I have to go now."

"Let me know what the surveillance shows."

"And please contact my niece."

Joe returned to the warden's office.

"I'm sorry to interrupt," Elle said apologetically.

"That's fine. Is there a chance Warden Gunton could see me for a few minutes? It's important."

CHAPTER 34

Adetective from the sheriff's department took photos and removed the bullet from the wall. Paige wasn't interested in seeing the bullet, but he insisted on showing it to her. He held the smashed piece of metal between his fingers.

"The bullet nicked the metal picture frame, but the wood is fairly soft, so it compressed in a uniform way. We'll have it analyzed in Raleigh to determine the caliber and type of weapon."

Paige knew the shape of the bullet would be a forever memory. "Okay, thanks for coming."

"I'll let you know the results of the testing. You can go ahead and have the damage to the wall repaired."

Several hours later, a team of two workmen finished repairing the broken sidelight beside the front door and patching the wall.

"I kept a flake of paint and will try to match it as close as possible," the foreman said. "Would it be okay if we come back on Friday?"

"Yes, just call first."

After the men left, Paige's phone vibrated. It was a text from Ryan letting her know that Tom might be stable enough to undergo surgery, but now more likely on Monday rather than

Friday. It was nice to receive good news about someone in a worse situation than she faced. Moments later, Candy called. Paige had let her and Vicki know about Tom's worsening condition.

"I'm sorry to hear about Ryan's boss," Candy said. "He's already on the prayer list at the church. And Vicki told me what happened at your house. That's horrible. You don't think about things like that in your neighborhood. Do you have any idea why?"

"No, but it really shook me up."

"Would it be helpful if I came over for a while? You wouldn't have to entertain me. I'd just sit in another room while you worked. It's strange, but I always feel safer if another person is in the house, even if it's one of the kids."

"That's kind, but no thanks. I have Sandy. She may not be a guard dog, but she's a great watchdog."

"Okay, but I'm serious about my offer. Also, your sweet testimony about what the Lord is doing in your life made me cry."

"I didn't mean for it to be sad."

"Not that kind of tears. They were filled with joy. I was impressed with you before, but now I'm sure you're going to be famous some-day for the way you write."

"That's a big leap—"

"I had a dream about you last night. You were sitting at the table for a book-signing event with a huge stack of books in front of you. I couldn't see the title, but your name on the cover was clear as day."

"Writing a book hasn't been one of my goals in life."

"Maybe it should be. Oh, and the cover of the book was mostly yellow. I remember that part. Anyway, you should pray about it. It's easy for me to have a dream. You'd have to do the hard work, which will be tougher once the baby comes."

Paige didn't need something else on her list of things to do. Writing the next great American novel wasn't a dream she held.

"Are you and Ryan going to be there on Sunday?"

"Yes."

"Great! We didn't want to pass out your testimony unless you were going to be there. Vicki is going to print out forty copies."

"Okay."

"And don't forget my offer to come over."

————————

Thirty minutes after the phone call to the prison, Ryan had been unable to do anything but worry about what he'd learned from Joe Moore. He needed to call Shana Parks but couldn't make himself dial the number. Nancy knocked on the doorframe of his office. She had a tissue in her hand. It was clear that she'd been crying. Ryan braced himself for more bad news.

"Did Tom die?" he asked.

"No." Nancy shook her head. "Karen said he's rallying. His blood pressure is up, and the doctor says the worst effects of COVID are likely behind him."

"When did this happen?"

"I just got off the phone with her. It had to be this afternoon. I'm so used to getting the worst news when someone is close to death that this is a shock, in a good way."

"I know what you think about Joe Moore, but that's about the time he prayed for Tom during a phone call to the prison."

Nancy's eyes widened. "I know God hears everything, but I've never thought about a man like him who's in prison doing something like that."

Ryan glanced at the clock on his computer monitor. It was after four o'clock. "I'm leaving early," he said.

"Go ahead. I'm staying to get the firm financial records up to date."

"See you tomorrow."

"Okay," Nancy said, then turned back to Ryan. "And I'm going to take down the sign and unlock the front door tomorrow. I over-reacted earlier."

"No," Ryan replied slowly. "Let's keep the door locked and the sign in place for a few more days."

After Nancy left, Ryan leaned back in his chair and rubbed his temples with his fingers. He wasn't sure what to tell Paige about the possible explanation for the attack on their home. He'd never kept a major secret from her during their entire marriage. Driving home, he tried to imagine her reaction. Most likely, she'd agree with Joe that Ryan should drop the case, which really should be the client's choice.

"What are you doing home so early?" Paige asked when he entered the house.

Ryan stepped closer and wrapped his arms around her. The thought of any harm coming to her was more than he could bear.

"Couldn't stand another second being away from you," he said.

Paige gave him a quick kiss. Ryan inspected the repairs to the sidelight and the wall.

"It almost looks normal except for the place that needs paint," he said.

"But it's going to take a while to not think about it every time I come into the foyer."

They sat at the kitchen table. Ryan told Paige about Tom's health status.

"I had a call with Joe Moore earlier today. He prayed a remarkable prayer for Tom."

"That doesn't surprise me."

"And I sent your letter to him in an envelope from the law firm."

"What did you think about it?"

"It was beautiful and heartfelt. He will be encouraged."

Paige smiled. "Good."

Ryan cleared his throat. "I also talked to Joe about his case. He wants me to stop the investigation. I didn't call his niece yet to let her know, but he made it perfectly clear."

"Why now?" Paige asked in surprise.

"A combination of things," Ryan answered vaguely. "A big part of it is that he's content with his life in prison. That sounds crazy, but he gets the chance to help a lot of men."

"Didn't you say that his family could hire you to represent him even if he didn't agree?"

"Yes, but now that I know him, I believe he should make that decision."

Ryan's phone rang. It was Charlie Drummond.

"I know this is short notice, but could you and your wife join us for dinner tonight?" Charlie asked. "Something has come up, and we won't be available on Friday."

"Hold on and let me check."

Ryan muted the call and asked Paige.

"I guess so," she said. "I hadn't thought about what we'd eat here. If they're willing to change the day to make it happen, so should we."

Ryan left the phone on speaker and told Charlie.

"That's perfect. Don't forget to bring your dog."

"Sure. See you soon."

Ryan ended the call.

While Paige got ready for dinner, Ryan sat on the couch in the living room checking his phone for new messages. She soon appeared, wearing a nice dress and with her hair styled in an attractive updo.

"You look fabulous," Ryan told her.

"I thought this might be a fancy meal."

Ryan stood. "I'm going to put on a suit and tie. If I'm overdressed, I can pretend I came from the office."

They parked behind one of the Drummonds' two Mercedes. Paige attached Sandy's leash before they got out of the car.

"I'm so excited about seeing the inside of the house," Paige said. "I hope Monica offers me a tour."

When they rang the doorbell, they heard the sound of a small dog excitedly barking. Sandy growled deep in her throat. Ryan glanced at Paige.

"It'll be fine," she said.

———

Joe listened while Warden Gunton contacted the guard who was monitoring the surveillance cameras for the prison and gave him a time frame for the search. Hanging up, he picked up the slip of paper on the desk in front of him.

"I'll keep this note in a secure place," he said to Joe.

"Yes, sir."

"And I may place you in protective custody until we sort this out."

Joe hadn't yet considered that possibility. The small, segregated area of the facility was usually reserved for inmates who'd committed a serious disciplinary infraction at the prison. They weren't allowed to work, eat, or socialize with the general prison population.

"I'd hate to go there now, especially with the good things that are happening with the Bible study and prayer meetings."

"I appreciate that, but I'll decide where you'll be housed after I receive the report from the review of the video. There's a camera at the end of the hall. It should reveal who entered any of the consultation rooms today."

The warden leaned back in his chair.

"Any idea who may have left the note?" he asked.

Joe hesitated. "I'd hate to falsely accuse someone. Could we just wait to see who shows up?"

The warden shook his head. "Moore, you're a different kind of man."

As he walked across the exercise yard to the dining hall, Joe tried to decide whether to say anything to Ray. He made his way to the table where Ray was sitting surrounded by men from Unit C. One of them moved to the side so a chair could be squeezed in for Joe.

"Joe's lawyer can't go a day without a chat," Ray announced in a loud voice. "I think they're having a Bible study."

"My lawyer should read his Bible, but I doubt he has a copy," one of the other men said. "Which commandment is it that says it's wrong to lie?"

"Nine," Ray replied.

"He needs to get that tattooed on his right arm so he has to look at it every day. My attorney claimed he and the DA played golf every Saturday morning and could get me a good deal because of their friendship. Next thing I know, I'm buried in this place deeper than a golf ball in a nasty rough."

"Brody, you're full of it," another man replied. "Your sentence is within the guidelines for the crime. We went over that months ago."

"I should have pleaded to a lesser included offense and gotten probation."

While the men continued to talk back and forth, Ray leaned close to Joe.

"What's really going on with the lawyer?" he asked.

Joe told him about Tom Clark but not the threatening note.

"I prayed from the depths of my heart," Joe said. "If Tom Clark doesn't make it, it's not because I didn't ask."

"Your lawyer is listening to you talk about the things of the Lord as much as Deshaun does."

"Maybe, but Deshaun is a better student."

Joe didn't see Ned in the dining hall. As he and Ray were leaving, one of the guards near the door called him over.

"Moore, the warden wants to see you."

"Are you getting popular with Warden Gunton too?" Ray asked, his eyes wide.

"If I'm not back by the time the prayer meetings are supposed to start, don't wait."

As he made his way across the exercise yard toward the administration building, a familiar face exited. It was Ned. He didn't look worried or upset.

"I'm not going to make it tonight!" Ned called out. "Got a service call for Unit F. This summer heat is causing one of the units to overload and shut off."

"We're meeting every night, so I hope you can make it tomorrow," Joe said. "Bring your harmonica, and we can jam earlier."

Ned patted the back pocket of his uniform. "I've been carrying it with me all day in case I have some downtime to play it."

"Where have you been working?"

"All over the place. See you later."

The evening administrative clerk, a man, motioned for Joe to go into the warden's office. Warden Gunton was facing a computer monitor.

"Come over and take a look," he said when Joe entered. "The supervisor pulled and edited the footage for the whole day."

Joe stood beside the warden. He'd never been so close to the man in charge of the prison. Normally, such proximity wouldn't be allowed.

"Five people went into consultation room B, including you," the warden continued. "I checked the log-in records, and three of you had phone calls set up with attorneys."

Joe watched as brief clips showed a figure coming around a corner, taking three or four steps to the room, and opening the door. The camera recorded a fish-eye-type image from a considerable distance down the hall. Joe watched two of the recordings. The images were hard to make out. He couldn't see enough to identify the person. The recording would then jump to when the person exited the room. The same identification problem continued.

"From the distance and angle of the camera, you can't really see anyone's face unless they look to the side away from the door when they enter or exit," Joe said.

"Correct. We may need to fix that. The camera was originally set up because we're more interested in anyone heading down the hall toward these offices. Here's the next one."

Even without a clear view of the next man's face, Joe recognized him.

"That's Phil Fletchall," he said. "I can tell from his hair."

"Right. He had an appointment to speak with his attorney."

The next figure was wearing a black ski mask pulled down over his face. When he opened the door, you could see that he was wearing gloves. The man left within ten seconds. He never looked at the camera.

"The next person is you," the warden said.

Joe watched himself appear in the frame. As with the others, the camera never clearly captured his face.

"I'll back it up to the guy before you," the warden said. "I've watched it at least ten times."

It was impossible to tell if the man was Black or white, young or old.

"What about other cameras in the area?" Joe asked. "Or on other halls?"

"I already ordered a search for anyone wearing a black toboggan. I mean, it was over ninety degrees this afternoon. No other camera picked up a person wearing either a stocking hat or gloves."

Joe shook his head. "He knew what he was doing."

"It appears that way, which increases my level of concern for your safety. Sit down."

Joe sat in one of the chairs facing the warden's desk. "I'm going to file a report with Raleigh tomorrow. In the meantime, I'm going to leave you in the general prison population."

"You are?" Joe asked in surprise.

"Yeah, a threatening note isn't enough to jerk you out of circulation."

"Thank you. I know how to look out for—" Joe started.

Warden Gunton raised his hand. "I'm not going to put you in protective custody, but do you want to reconsider the transfer to another facility? It's only been a few days, and there may still be a spot for you."

"No, sir. I'd prefer to be here."

"That's what I thought you'd say. I've told the guards assigned to Unit C to keep an eye on you. Even though your work crew doesn't normally have anyone assigned to it, I'm going to send a guard along until further notice. That's all for now."

CHAPTER 35

Charlie Drummond opened the door. Paige half expected him to be wearing a British smoking jacket, but he had on a golf shirt and khakis. A fluffy white dog at Charlie's feet jumped back and forth as he barked. Sandy remained slightly behind Paige.

"Captain is as excited to see you as I am," Charlie said with a smile. "Come in. Monica and Nataliya are in the kitchen."

Sandy stepped forward and sniffed noses with the perky bichon. They entered a foyer with a high ceiling. A grandfather clock stood to the right and a staircase in front of them. They turned to the left into a parlor that featured a bay window and was furnished with an ornate couch and two side chairs.

"Have a seat," Charlie said. "This is the most Victorian room in the house. We even use gas lamps instead of electric lights."

"I've been curious about the inside of the house," Paige said.

"There will be a tour, either before or after dinner," Charlie said. "How's Tom doing? Is he still scheduled for surgery on Friday?"

"If not Friday, then Monday," Ryan answered. "He's rallied over the past twenty-four hours."

"Great. If it's not too much trouble, please keep me in the loop. Excuse me for a moment while I get a bottle of wine."

Charlie left. Ryan sat on the couch.

"Hold Sandy's leash," Paige said to Ryan. "I don't want to take the chance of her knocking something over."

Freed from her connection to Sandy, Paige continued to inspect the room.

"It's quaint," she said. "Can you believe they don't have any electric lights in here?"

"Would you like to take the electric lights out of our bedroom? We could use candles."

Charlie returned with the wine and poured three glasses. He raised his glass.

"To an entertaining evening," he said.

Paige pointed to some photos on a side table. "Your family?"

Charlie picked up the largest one, in which everyone was dressed in nineteenth-century clothes. "This is my parents with me and my sister. We had a vintage photo taken once when we were on vacation. It seemed to fit with the room."

He handed the photo to Paige.

"How old were you?" she asked.

"Twelve, and Cherie was fourteen."

Paige stared at the picture.

"It's been a long time," Charlie said. "I heard about the incident with the brick thrown through a window at your house. I'm sorry that happened."

"It wasn't just a brick," Ryan replied. "There was also a gunshot that came close to Paige's head."

"No!" Charlie exclaimed. "Thank God you're okay."

"Yes," Paige said solemnly, nodding. "How did you know about the brick?"

"Someone at my office follows the sheriff department calls and mentioned it to me. I suspected vandalism, but a bullet—" Charlie stopped.

"It's under investigation," Ryan said.

Charlie turned to Paige. "Do you feel safe?"

"Most of the time."

"Well, I'd like to increase that sense of security," Charlie said resolutely. "If you're willing to accept an offer, I'd like to assign one of the security guards who works for my company to check on you for at least a few weeks. He supervises the crew that monitors my buildings and is a former officer with the sheriff's office. I'd want you to meet him, of course."

"That's kind but not necessary," Ryan replied. "Deputy Lauren Jackson lives close by and is going to park her patrol car in front of the house when she's off duty. I don't think there's an ongoing threat."

"Will the deputy be present?" Charlie asked.

"No," Paige answered, glaring at Ryan. "We'd appreciate someone actually watching over us."

"When Monica makes a statement like that, I usually acquiesce," Charlie said.

Ryan gave Paige a wry smile.

"Thanks," he said to Charlie. "What's the man's name?"

"Clint Broome."

"Is he related to Norris Broome?" Ryan asked.

"Nephew. Have you met Norris? He's retired from the sheriff's department."

"Yes."

A young blond woman knocked on the doorframe of the parlor.

"Dinner will be ready in a few minutes, Mr. Drummond," she said in an accent that sounded Russian.

"Thanks, Nataliya."

The woman left.

"Where's she from?" Paige asked.

"Ukrainian refugee. Her husband was killed in the war with Russia. Monica and I sponsored her to come to the US. She helps around the house."

Before dinner, Monica gave Ryan and Paige a tour of the house. Then they sat down to a meal of chicken Kiev. The chicken wing remained attached to the breast and was covered with a frilled paper napkin. Next to it was grilled asparagus, mushroom risotto, and garlic bread. Charlie sat at the head of the table to Ryan's right. Monica, a quiet brunette who looked at least ten years younger than her husband, sat at the other end. Nataliya took Sandy and Captain to a fenced-in backyard.

"This chicken is amazing," Ryan said after the first bite.

"Thank Nataliya," Charlie replied. "She's taken Monica and me on a culinary journey around the world. Her Indonesian dishes are stunning."

"But her Ukrainian roots run the deepest," Monica said.

Ryan finished eating before anyone else.

"Where's the bathroom?" he asked.

"On the other side of the staircase and down the hall," Charlie said. "It's not in the most convenient location. I'd be glad to show you."

"I'll be fine. Excuse me."

Ryan passed through the foyer and around the staircase into a long hallway. He opened a door, assuming it was the bathroom, but it turned out to be a working office with modern decor. Just inside the door a glass bookcase contained photos in frames. One photo, of Charlie and his sister as adults, caught Ryan's eye. They were standing in front of a sign that read "Drummond Enterprises." Printed across the bottom of the picture was the date and the words *Cheryl Drummond, CEO* and *Charles Drummond, COO*. The photo was taken less than two months before Cherie's death. Ryan picked up the picture to get a closer look at Cherie's face. The last image he'd seen of the young woman had been so horrific that he wanted another one to replace it. Cherie was smiling. Charlie looked businesslike and serious.

"The bathroom is the next door on the right," Nataliya said.

Ryan jumped.

"Sorry," he said, backing out of the room. "I took a wrong turn."

After Ryan returned to the table, he continued to think about the photo.

"Save room for Kyiv cake," Monica said. "With hazelnut meringue."

"A meringue cake?" Paige asked.

"You'll see," Monica replied.

Nataliya cleared the plates from the table. Ryan turned to Charlie.

"I opened the wrong door and saw your office," he said. "Very modern."

Charlie leaned over and spoke softly. "That's what I prefer, but Monica loves Victorian. I carved out a small space for myself."

"I couldn't help but notice the photo of you and your sister in front of the company headquarters."

"Yes," Charlie sighed. "That was taken to go along with an article in the local newspaper. It was right after my father named Cherie CEO. I'd already been serving as chief operating officer, running the day-to-day affairs of the business, for a year or so."

"You were both so young."

"My father had no interest in the business my grandfather built. He couldn't wait for Cherie and me to graduate from college and take over. Neither one of us was really ready, even though she had an MBA from Wake Forest. When it all fell on me, I had to learn quickly."

Charlie was silent for a moment.

"Another picture was taken that same day with Marty in it," he said. "I threw that one away."

Dessert arrived. It was as good as advertised. Forty-five minutes later, Ryan, Paige, and Sandy retraced their steps toward the car.

"I think Sandy had a good time," Paige said. "According to Monica, Captain desperately wants friends. The four of us may go on a walk together soon."

"I think Monica needs a friend."

"Yeah, I felt that too. I asked her if she knew Madge or Vicki or Candy. She didn't."

Ryan opened the rear door of the car. Sandy jumped in.

"What did you think of the house?" he asked.

"I'm glad I saw it," Paige replied. "It satisfied my curiosity, but it had a dreary feeling."

Pulling into the street, Ryan told her about Charlie's home office.

"They have totally different tastes in architecture and furnishings."

"What about you and me?" Paige asked.

"I guess we'll find out when we have an unlimited budget."

They turned onto Hamilton Street.

"Are you really okay that I wanted to accept Charlie's offer for extra security at the house?"

"Yes, that was my pride putting up resistance. I should have agreed immediately."

Thankfully, the last two days of the week were uneventful. Sunday morning, Paige took extra time getting ready for church. Ryan, who was waiting for her in the kitchen with a second cup of coffee, looked up and smiled when she entered the room. He was wearing casual slacks and a polo shirt. She'd selected one of her most flattering dresses.

"You look great," he said. "I thought this church wasn't formal."

"It's not, but if they're going to hand out what I wrote in the Sunday school class, I want to look nice."

"Right," Ryan agreed. "Make sure you bring your favorite pen so you can sign copies."

"Ryan!"

"Okay," he chuckled, holding up his hands. "I'm just trying to figure out how to be married to someone who's famous."

They parked in the same area as before and made their way to the classroom. Lauren Jackson was handing out name tags.

"Have things been quiet at your house?" she asked, leaning forward. "I was glad when I heard that Mr. Drummond was sending Clint Broome to watch over you."

"Very quiet," Paige replied.

Vicki waved from across the room and motioned for Paige and Ryan to come closer. Paige grabbed Ryan's hand and pulled him along.

"I'm about to explode!" Vicki said when they came closer. "We're not going to give out your testimony until the end of the class. Otherwise, people would be reading it instead of paying attention to the lesson."

Candy joined them. She also had a smile on her face. In her hands was a stack of the papers with a clear plastic cover on the front of each one.

"Here it is," she said, handing a packet to Paige. "But don't let anyone see it yet."

Paige looked down. The cover included a border and a nice font for the title. The interior type size was also good. The Bible verses were italicized.

"Looks good," she said to the other two women.

"Great," Vicki gushed. "I've read it so many times that I almost have it memorized."

Vicki and Candy moved away. Ryan leaned down.

"This is a bigger deal than I realized," he said.

"They're just being sweet."

"No, it's more than that for them."

They settled into their seats. The format of the class followed the same pattern as before. During the prayer time, Paige and Ryan were once again part of a small group with two other couples. This time it included Vicki and her husband, Bruce. Although she'd been praying regularly at home, Paige kept quiet. Ryan didn't say anything. After the prayer session wrapped up, Candy stepped to the podium at the front of the room. She called for everyone's attention and held up Paige's testimony in her right hand.

"We have a real treat for you," she said. "Paige Clark, a new visitor to the class, has written the most beautiful testimony about a recent encounter she had with the Lord. Paige is a professional writer for a big company, but what made me fall in love with what she's written is the way she reveals her tender heart. It's my understanding that a man in prison wrote a letter that had an influence on what she experienced."

Candy then read a paragraph about God coming to live in us just like a mother carrying a baby. Paige could feel the power of what she'd written. It was something she'd never felt before. She involuntarily shivered.

The class ended. Several people thanked Paige. Candy came up with her hands almost empty.

"Only three left!" she exclaimed. "Based on the title and the little bit I read, several people asked for multiple copies because they want to give one away."

"I'd like two," Ryan said. "One for myself and another for a friend."

Candy quickly handed them to him.

"Who's your friend?" Paige asked after Candy moved on.

"A guy in prison."

———————

On Sunday evening pockets of men huddled together across Unit C. It was a sight Joe had longed for but in the depths of his heart was never certain he'd see. Close by the guardroom a group included Ned Walker. Deshaun was speaking. Joe made his way to the group.

"At first, I played the blame game and told guys that I wasn't guilty of the crime that landed me in here."

"I've done that," one man said.

"Me too," another added.

"But when I owned up to my sin, I was surprised how it made me feel," Deshaun said. "For the first time since I saw the blue lights flashing in my front yard, I felt like I could stop running. I'd been caught by the law but set free by God's grace."

As Deshaun continued to talk, every word proved the work of the Holy Spirit in the young man's life. Even with the tension he felt about Ned, Joe experienced a surge of joy.

"Does anybody else want to come clean about a lie they've been holding on to?" Deshaun said. "It doesn't have to be about why you're locked up. Like Joe once told me, there are all kinds of prisons. Most of them don't have bars."

Joe looked around the circle. Deshaun's challenge caused the men, including Ned, to find something interesting about the floor at their feet. Ned looked up and met Joe's eyes.

"What about you?" Ned asked Joe. "Have you confessed what landed you in prison?"

"We know Joe's story," Deshaun jumped in. "He's the one who's led the way for a bunch of us—"

"I'll confess if you do," Joe said, keeping his eyes on Ned.

"Deal," Ned quickly responded.

Joe took a deep breath. "I'm in here for murdering a young couple outside a nightclub where I was performing with my band. My sin was so terrible, it really makes me appreciate the gift of God's forgiveness."

"You admit you killed that young couple?" Ned asked.

"Yes, and a jury found me guilty," Joe replied.

"Did everyone hear that?" Ned asked.

"Yeah, we're standing right here," Deshaun said with a puzzled look on his face.

"And I confess to stealing the car that got me locked up," Ned added. "I tried to claim at trial that someone loaned the car to me, but I stole it and intended to sell it to a guy in South Carolina who dealt in hot vehicles." Ned stopped. "Is that good enough? I want to do it right."

"God knows the honesty of your heart," Deshaun said.

Ned nodded and looked at Deshaun.

"You know, it does feel good to get that off my chest and quit pretending," Ned said.

"Yeah, it's amazing how that works," Deshaun replied.

After Ned spoke, another man named Hank, with tears in his eyes, admitted to multiple instances of unfaithfulness to his wife.

"That's bothered me a lot more than what landed me in here," he said. "I knew I was guilty of the crime, but I've been carrying the other stuff all bottled up inside me for over two years. My wife doesn't know or suspect anything. She's stood by me and is waiting for me to get out next summer and come home. But I'm not sure how I'm going to look her in the eyes or face my three kids."

Joe spoke: "For tonight, the important part is to get right with God so you can ask for his help with the rest. Do you want to do that?"

The men stood in a circle with Hank in the middle. When Hank finished praying, Deshaun said, "Amen."

Joe opened his eyes. Ned was gone.

"Where's Ned?" he asked.

"I don't know. My eyes were closed," Deshaun said.

Another man spoke. "There's something in my past I've never admitted to another person," he said. "But my heart is about to beat out of my chest, and I've got to confess it in case God can forgive me."

"He not only can, but he will," Deshaun said.

CHAPTER 36

M onday morning, Paige glanced out the kitchen window.
Clint Broome, the security guard assigned to them by
Charlie Drummond, sat in his car in the same spot where Lauren
Jackson left her vehicle when off duty. Earlier, Clint had joined
Ryan and Paige for a meeting with the security company and had
given great advice regarding the type of system best suited to the
house and their needs. Installation would begin the following
Monday. Ryan had cleared everything with their landlord. Clint's
presence and the planned home safety measures eased Paige's
anxiety.

Paige checked the time. Tom should be in surgery or in the
recovery room. She'd prayed with Ryan before he left for the office, but a second prayer couldn't hurt. She rested her hands on
the sides of the sink and offered up a silent petition.

Her phone vibrated.

"Tom's out of surgery," Ryan said. "Not sure if they were able
to do everything they wanted to or not."

Paige stepped away from the sink and sat in a kitchen chair.

"But he's alive," she said.

"Yes, not many people die these days during heart surgery, but I know he was at risk. Whatever the result, there's no telling when he'll be back to work. Maybe never."

"I hope you're wrong about that."

"Yeah."

As soon as the call ended, Paige's phone vibrated again. It was Madge Norton.

"You've been busy since we first met," Madge said when Paige answered. "I just finished reading your beautiful testimony and had to call to tell you how much I enjoyed it."

"Thanks."

"How's the pregnancy going? I read how the Lord used the baby to speak to you."

There was something reassuring to Paige about bringing Madge up to date on all that had happened. She even told her about the brick and the bullet. Madge, who had been very interactive during the conversation, was silent for a moment.

"I'm going to pray for you and Ryan," she said in a serious voice.

Hearing the commitment of support from Madge, a mature Christian, meant even more to Paige than the equally sincere promises from Vicki and Candy.

"And not stop until the Lord tells me to," Madge continued. "Don't hesitate to call me, anytime at all, if you need anything."

It was the beginning of a new week, and Ryan and Nancy agreed to stop locking the office door. Additional news from Karen confirmed that the doctors weren't able to complete Tom's surgery as they'd hoped. He was going to receive ongoing treatment from the heart failure division of the clinic.

"Nothing will be as it should until Tom comes back," Nancy said with a sigh.

Ryan went to his boss's office and stared at the empty chair behind the desk. It had only been a few days since Tom jumped from one project to the other so quickly that it was hard for Ryan to keep up. He walked over to the credenza where Tom kept photos of himself at different golf courses. There was a knock at the door.

"Your receptionist wasn't at her desk, so I came on back," Wyatt said. "I heard about Tom's surgery. How is he doing?"

"The doctors weren't able to totally correct the problem. The extent of his recovery is uncertain."

"When I heard about the surgery, I knew I needed to see you as soon as possible."

Ryan braced himself. He couldn't believe the older lawyer was going to revisit the offer to come to work for his firm on the morning Tom barely survived surgery.

"I owe you an apology," Wyatt said. "I was totally out of line at lunch the other day when I mentioned you coming to my firm. It was a spur-of-the-moment thing. Well, not exactly. I've heard about the good job you're doing with clients. Anyway, there's no excuse for my timing, and I'm sorry."

"It really bothered me. I'm a young lawyer, but I'm loyal to Tom and wouldn't want to do anything to hurt him or Karen."

"I totally understand and respect that," Wyatt replied, clearing his throat. "With that in mind and to prove my good intentions, I'd like to give you some friendly advice about loyalty to one of your best clients."

"Who?"

"Charlie Drummond. This Joe Moore matter is becoming a bigger and bigger negative."

Ryan pressed his lips together tightly. He couldn't repeat anything he knew about Charlie's comments to Tom.

"Regardless of what Charlie might say," Wyatt continued, "your representation of the man who murdered his sister is going to have an impact. Before I talked to you the other day, and after Tom's heart attack, Charlie contacted me about retaining Belk and Banner. I told him you were a capable young attorney. He agrees but is troubled by what he hears around town about Moore."

"What would he expect?" Ryan blurted out in frustration. "That we open a file, do nothing, and close it?"

"I've probably said too much," Wyatt replied. "I meant it as friendly advice."

The thought flew through Ryan's mind that Wyatt was lying. Nothing during dinner at the Drummond house gave Ryan a hint that Charlie was upset about Joe Moore or might take his business elsewhere. But if true, Ryan wanted to be professional about it.

"I'm sure Charlie will talk to me directly," Ryan replied with more confidence than he felt.

"Absolutely. He's always been straightforward."

Wyatt left. Ryan sat down in one of the chairs that faced Tom's desk. This news would have deeply upset his boss. And it would be devastating for Ryan if a third job collapsed, especially with a pregnant wife. For the first time in a couple of weeks, Ryan felt a familiar panic rise up from deep within.

It was a cloudy day as Joe and Ray walked side by side toward the garden. A guard trailed along behind the group. Joe saw him, but Ray hadn't noticed.

"Might get another drop or two of rain later today," Joe said, sniffing the air.

While they walked, Joe told Ray about Ned's confession the previous evening. Ray was using the hoe in his hand for a walking stick.

"I'm not sure Ned was sincere," Ray said, hitting the ground with the hoe. "Nothing about him seems honest to me."

"He's in prison. Honest people are hard to find."

"You know what I mean. I didn't see or listen to him last night, but there's always been something sneaky about him."

"Yeah," Joe sighed. "I wasn't convinced myself."

Ray glanced over his shoulder at the guard. "Why the extra security? Do they think someone on the crew is going to try to climb the fence in broad daylight?"

Joe had decided during breakfast that the threatening note was too big an issue to keep hidden from his friend.

"Joe!" Deshaun called out. "Wait up!"

Joe and Ray stopped while the young man jogged up to them. Deshaun held up his right hand. A bandage was wrapped around his index and middle fingers.

"Sliced myself bad on the rusty faucet for the spigot at the rear of the unit."

"What were you doing there?" Ray asked.

"Filling up a five-gallon bucket for one of the guards who told me to clean up a mess in the bathroom. Blood from my hand went everywhere, and he sent me to the infirmary. While I was there, I saw two guards come in with Ned Walker between them."

"Did you find out what was going on?" Joe asked.

"No, but I stuck my head out the door and saw them take him into the main office. Maybe the warden wanted to see him. Anyway, I thought you should know so you can be praying for him."

"Will do," Joe replied. "And you shouldn't be here on work detail. That hand needs to stay clean and dry."

Deshaun grinned. "Oh, I'm not going to do anything except sit under one of the shade trees and eat fresh strawberries. I can eat them with my left hand and keep the guard who's tagging along today company."

The three men continued toward the garden. With Deshaun present, Joe wasn't going to say anything to Ray about the note. After announcing the morning work assignments, Joe moved off to the rows of bean plants. During the lunch break, he unsuccessfully looked for an opportunity to talk privately with Ray.

Prison life is as public as a subway train. A positive aspect of that reality was the chance to eavesdrop on the conversations flowing back and forth among the men. Today much of the talk had to do with the move of God at the facility. Spiritual activity no longer required the efforts of a few men like Joe and Ray. It had taken on a life of its own. During the lunch break, Ray poured a cup of water from one of the plastic containers and sat next to him. Joe commented on how well Deshaun was handling himself in his day-to-day life.

"It's what we prayed for," Ray confirmed. "Deshaun has been studying his Bible a lot. He's coming up with great answers to questions."

"And the feedback from his wife has been positive."

"Yeah."

Joe leaned back on his hands.

"What do you think is going on with Ned Walker?" Ray asked in a soft voice. "Are you going to drop in on your buddy Warden Gunton and ask him?"

"Probably."

"Seriously?" Ray asked.

"He'll talk to me."

Ray glanced sideways at Joe. "What are you keeping secret?"

Three men were within earshot of where they were sitting.

"Nothing I can talk about now," Joe said. "Later."

Paige and Ryan sat at the table in their kitchen. Neither of them had eaten much supper. Ryan told Paige about the conversation with Wyatt Belk. It helped to share the burden.

"After Wyatt broke the news about Charlie, I checked the accounting records. Forty percent of Tom's revenue last year came from his representation of Charlie and his companies. That's way more than I expected. Without that, Tom barely made enough to cover overhead. Basically, it was his profit."

Paige knew the implications for Ryan and her without him spelling it out. She felt completely deflated.

"Our life here is falling apart," she sighed.

A knock at the front door interrupted their conversation.

"I'll get it," Paige said.

Through the newly repaired sidelight glass, she could see Clint Broome standing on the front stoop. The private security guard bore a strong family resemblance to his uncle Norris.

"I'm heading home for supper," Clint said. "I should be back in an hour and a half, and then I'll stay until ten o'clock."

"That's not necessary. Why don't you take the rest of the night off? You've been here since lunchtime."

"That's up to Mr. Drummond—"

"I can't give you orders, but Ryan is here, and we'll be fine."

"Well, it would be nice to watch a baseball game on TV with my friends," Clint said slowly.

Paige waved her hands. "Go. Ryan loves baseball. He'll understand."

Paige returned to the kitchen and told Ryan that she'd sent Clint on his way.

"I agree," he said. "I already feel strange about Clint being here if his boss isn't going to be a client of the firm."

"Maybe you should take the initiative and speak directly to Charlie. The uncertainty is stressful."

"Not if the reality is worse."

Ryan woke extra early in the morning. He rolled over onto his favorite sleeping side and closed his eyes, which was often a successful strategy to grab another thirty minutes of sleep. Not today. Paige remained asleep. Ryan had debated the previous night whether to inform Paige that Joe wanted to drop the case, a decision that would potentially have a big impact on retaining Charlie Drummond as a client. But Ryan remained deeply conflicted. He simply wasn't sure what to do and when to do it. He slipped out of bed and took Sandy into the backyard. The day threatened to be hot. Sandy let out a woof at the sight of a squirrel wanting to steal breakfast from one of Paige's bird feeders. The squirrel hopped onto a nearby limb. Ryan's phone vibrated as he received a text from Norris Broome.

> Sorry to hear about Tom's situation. Do you have
> time to meet today around 11:00 a.m.? I had the

> witness statements in the Moore case transcribed
> so I could double-check for accuracy.

Ryan knew he could either reply that he was no longer represent-ing Joe or agree to show up.

> I'll be there.

The detective replied:

> Bring anything you want to go over in the Moore
> case. Since I'm no longer a Blanton County
> employee, no questions are off-limits.

Ryan fed Sandy and brewed pots of both regular and decaf coffee. He was pouring his first cup when Paige entered the kitchen and rubbed her eyes.

"I can't believe you didn't wake me up when you left the bed," she said.

"I'm very quiet."

"No," Paige said with a shake of her head. "Quiet isn't in the lex-icon of your behavior around the house. I think this stage of the pregnancy is like a sleep aid."

"I'm going to run by Norris Broome's house later this morning," Ryan said.

"Be sure to tell him how much we appreciate Clint looking out for us."

———

At the office, Ryan was surprised to see Nancy sitting at her desk. It was an hour before she normally started the day.

"Coming in early was the best thing for me to do," Nancy said before he could say anything. "I want to reassure clients that you're on top of things and will be here to serve them until Tom returns."

"If he's able to practice again."

"I'm trying to be optimistic."

Ryan went into his office and picked up where he'd left off the previous day. He tried again, without success, to reach Shana Parks. His phone buzzed.

"Danny Milton is calling," Nancy said.

It was almost time to leave for his meeting with Norris, but Ryan accepted the call.

"When you get a chance, please let Tom know I'm rooting for him," the acting DA said. "He made a contribution to my campaign from the hospital."

"He believes you're the person for the job."

"I also wanted to let you know I received a verbal report from the lab that tested the DNA evidence in the Moore case. They found Moore's DNA on the handle of the knife and the blade along with DNA from the two victims on the blade."

Ryan wasn't surprised. It was an additional reason to drop the case.

"There was also DNA from another person that's been submitted to CODIS, the Combined DNA Index System used by the FBI. They'll run it through a pool that contains over fifteen million profiles. It's something that couldn't be done at the time of the original trial. I'll let you know as soon as I hear anything else."

"Okay, thanks."

On his way out the door, Ryan stopped by Nancy's desk. He could see a pile of tissues in her trash can.

"It's been quite a morning," she said. "A lot of people have called to let me know they're praying for Tom."

"Any updates from Karen?"

Nancy shook her head. "No. But I wouldn't expect anything."

"I'm on my way to meet with Norris Broome and should be back in a couple of hours."

CHAPTER 37

Joe left the administration building. In the dining hall, he saw Ned enter and casually make his way to the food line. Ray and Joe sat beside each other. No one else was close by. Joe turned to Ray.

"Okay, I'll tell you what's going on," he said.

Joe told Ray about the note left in the consultation room, his conversations with Warden Gunton, and the absence of clear evidence from the surveillance cameras.

"I had no idea those cameras used a fish-eye view," Ray said. "I guess it gives a wider angle."

"That's not why I'm telling you about this."

"I know, I know." Ray tapped the table with his right index finger. "We don't know why Ned was dragged into the warden's office, but if there was proof he left the threatening note, he wouldn't be eating in the dining hall. Warden Gunton would have thrown him into lockdown in the disciplinary unit."

"Yeah."

"But I don't care about evidence and proof," Ray continued. "Ned's up to something and it has to do with you. After what Max told us about the guy getting stabbed at Central Prison, you've got to be extra careful."

"I know."

Joe told him about what had happened at Ryan's house.

"Whoa," Ray said, his eyes wide. "A bullet? This isn't just about keeping a close eye on Ned."

"That's why I told my lawyer to drop the case. There's no way I can put him and his family at risk."

"But he's obviously onto something."

They sat in silence for a few moments. Ray closed his fist and laid it on the table.

"Ned knows something. In the old days I'd catch him off by himself and, with a few friends, interrogate him in a spot where the guards wouldn't hear him calling out for help. I'd get to the bottom of this." Ray added, "But those days are gone."

"Yeah, those days are gone."

———

Paige did her best to stay on task all morning with her work schedule. Fortunately, the concentration and focus needed to be an editor could drive distractions into a corner of her brain. It was close to noon when she stood and stretched her hands high over her head. When she did, she was aware that her stomach didn't go as flat as before. Paige placed her hand on her abdomen.

"You're welcome to take up all the space you need," she said.

Sandy was already heading toward the door to the backyard. Paige followed. The midday heat was a wall of hot humidity that discouraged her from joining her pet. Paige stepped back into the house. The front door chimed. Leaving Sandy in the yard, Paige went into the foyer. Through the newly repaired sidelight, she could see Charlie Drummond standing on the front porch. Paige opened the door.

"Mr. Drummond," she began.

"I thought we settled that the other night at dinner. It's Charlie. I'm sorry to drop by unannounced but wanted to talk with you for a minute."

"Of course. Come inside. It's too hot outside today."

Paige led the way into the living room. "Please, sit. I have to let Sandy in."

Charlie sat in a side chair. While getting Sandy, Paige tried to guess the reason for the unexpected visit. It was especially surprising given the news Ryan had received about the businessman possibly taking his legal work away from the firm.

Sandy trotted into the house. As soon as she saw Charlie in the living room, she started barking.

"It doesn't matter that she's met you," Paige said. "She barks like that when Ryan comes home from work."

"Good watchdog."

Charlie held out his right hand so Sandy could sniff it, then patted her on the head. Paige sat on the couch.

"But you need more than a good watchdog," Charlie said. "I heard you sent Clint home last night before the end of his shift."

"Yes, Ryan was here."

"That shouldn't change the need for safety and protection."

Paige felt like a schoolgirl getting scolded by a teacher. "I really appreciate your concern—"

"Which is greater than you realize," Charlie cut in.

"Why?"

Charlie leaned forward. "Because I believe the threat to you and Ryan is real, and you should be extra cautious."

"What do you know that we don't?"

"It has to do with Joe Moore."

Paige realized she was holding her breath. Charlie continued, "Ryan probably told you that I didn't initially oppose him representing the murderer. Moore's family was going to hire someone, and I'd rather it be an ethical attorney than one who'd falsely manipulate the situation. Not that Ryan needed my permission. In my heart and mind, I know Moore is guilty and trust the justice system to keep him where he belongs."

"You're sure he's guilty?"

Charlie looked directly into Paige's eyes. "Absolutely, one hundred percent. But for the first time since the murders occurred, I'm having to consider the possibility that Moore didn't act alone. If that's true, someone doesn't want Ryan to continue what he's doing."

"Why are you telling me this and not Ryan?"

"Talking to you is talking to Ryan, which I can't do because of attorney-client rules. Ryan made it clear early on that my input wasn't welcome and I didn't have the right to ask him questions about the case."

"That doesn't sound like Ryan."

"I know what I heard. Anyway, there were other people who had a motive to kill Marty Brock that night, but those leads were never fully investigated because the evidence against Moore was so strong. Years ago, I asked Norris Broome if there were any loose ends. He reassured me he'd followed through on every lead. But there's always been one fact without an adequate explanation. It has to do with the amount of money in Marty's possession earlier that night. It was several times more than they found on Joe Moore."

"Does Ryan know about this?"

"He should. I mentioned it when Detective Broome interviewed me, so it's in the file. Earlier on the day he died, Marty sold me a utility truck and a backhoe to use on one of our farms. I paid Marty in cash when he came by the house to pick up Cherie for their date. The last time I saw Marty alive, he had eighteen thousand dollars in an envelope stuck in the back pocket of his jeans. I told him to take the money home and put it in a safe place, but he ignored me. The deputies found three thousand dollars in Moore's pocket when he was arrested. The rest of the money was never recovered."

Charlie stopped, and his face hardened. "Marty never should have taken Cherie to that club, a known drug den, especially carrying that much money. Detective Broome concluded the rest of the cash probably ended up with a drug dealer who stole it from Moore. I know that's an option, but now I wonder if that's what really happened. Moore wasn't the only person desperate to buy crystal meth that night, and eighteen thousand dollars would buy a lot of drugs."

"Do you know the names of any suspects?"

"There were other people arrested that night on drug charges. They should be checked out. I don't have a list of their names, but the sheriff's department recently promised to review the entire file at the district attorney's office. If anyone with known drug connections was involved in the murders and is still living in the area, they could be the ones trying to shut down what Ryan is doing. There's going to be an article in tomorrow's edition of the newspaper about the sheriff's department opening a fresh investigation."

"How do you know that?"

"I've talked with the sheriff directly and discussed the new investigation with a reporter who's writing the story. She's also going to reach out to Ryan. In my opinion, the best option for him would be to hold off any independent investigation and let the sheriff's department complete its work. That route would lessen the risk of harm to the two of you." Charlie leaned forward. "And to be totally honest, if Ryan backs away from Moore, it would make it easier for me to continue to use him and Tom to perform legal work for my companies. Dragging all this up has been tougher on me than I anticipated, and it's hard to think about the law firm representing me and also working to get Moore out of prison."

A sick feeling washed over Paige.

"I hate to dump this on you," Charlie continued with a sad look in his eyes. "But I wasn't sure how else to communicate with Ryan. I know what it's like when a beautiful young couple has their lives cut horribly short, and I don't ever want to see that happen again."

———————

Ryan pulled into the driveway of Norris Broome's house. Before he reached the front door, the former detective stepped outside. He had a thick folder in his hands.

"Let's sit on the porch," he said.

They sat in matching white rockers. Norris handed the folder to Ryan. "These are the witness statements. As I mentioned earlier, I paid to have them transcribed."

"You didn't have to do that."

"It was the right thing. Anyway, I didn't see much that will help you. You can review it for yourself, but the evidence points to Moore as the murderer who acted alone. We both know motive isn't relevant, but the logical conclusion is a robbery for money to buy drugs that turned deadly."

Ryan involuntarily shivered as he thought about the crime scene photos.

He nodded. "Yeah. I'm probably not going to pursue filing a motion for appropriate relief."

"It's none of my business, but why?" Norris asked in surprise.

"You know I can't tell you that."

"Right, right."

The former detective leaned back in his chair for a second before rocking forward. "I don't know where that puts you related to the primary information I wanted to pass along to you today. My contacts at the sheriff's department indicate they're going to reopen the investigation into the murders."

"That's news to me."

"The request came from someone with a lot of power and influence, Charlie Drummond. For years he's had questions about why there's a discrepancy between the amount of money Marty Brock had earlier in the day and the cash in Joe Moore's possession."

"I saw that in the transcript from the trial. I believe you testified about it."

"Correct. When drugs are involved, cash has a way of disappearing. I never uncovered anything relevant to the murders in the money trail. Charlie is more interested than anyone in making sure everyone responsible for his sister's death is brought to justice. I hate the fact that he's still grasping at straws after all these years."

Ryan paused for a few moments. "Why do you think someone threw bricks at our homes and shot at my wife?"

"I have no idea. I'm moving on."

Ryan looked down at the folder with the translated witness statements.

"I'm not sure I'll need this," he said.

"Keep it."

Ryan returned to the office. As soon as he entered the reception area, Nancy spoke. "A reporter from the newspaper called three times wanting to talk to you. I refused to give her your cell phone number."

"I know why she's calling. Anything else?"

"Yes, Shana Parks called. I put her through to your voicemail."

Ryan listened to Shana's message. It was a simple acknowledgment that she'd received his request to talk. He entered her number. She answered on the second ring.

"I spoke with your uncle yesterday," Ryan said. "He insists that we drop the case. I was about to send you a bill for my services, but based on his decision, I'm going to refund the balance of the retainer."

Shana was quiet for a moment before saying, "I'm surprised and confused. I thought we'd worked through his objections."

"I don't have Joe's permission to explain all that's involved, but we discussed his options in detail, and he told me to pass along to you that he's not going to change his mind. He doesn't want me to pursue the motion for appropriate relief. However, there is some good news that's come out of this."

Ryan told her about the sheriff's department reopening the investigation.

"Ultimately, I believe that's likely to have a greater chance of success than anything I could do," he said.

"I'm not so sure," Shana said. "My family doesn't trust the system down there. That's one reason we hired you. What if the sheriff's department is doing this to convince you to stop an independent investigation?"

Ryan paused. It wasn't an angle he'd considered.

"I doubt that's the case," he said.

"But it's a possibility, isn't it?"

Ryan didn't want to give a flippant answer.

"It's certainly possible," he said slowly. "But, in my opinion, unlikely. Regardless, that doesn't change the instructions I received from your uncle."

"And you're not willing to continue the investigation without his permission? Mr. Clark told me Uncle Joe's consent wasn't required. What does he say now?"

"Tom recently had a serious heart attack. He's out of the office indefinitely."

"I'm so sorry to hear that," Shana said. "Does my uncle know?"

"Yes, Joe's been praying for Tom."

"Okay, I'll pass this along to my mother. I know she's going to be disappointed."

CHAPTER 38

Joe worked steadily in the garden. Physical labor was a good antidote to mental tension. The hoe hit the ground, sending tiny bits of weeds and dirt scooting off to the side. The roots for the weeds were concealed beneath the surface, but with accurate force and pressure they could be dislodged and removed. While he worked, he prayed.

Throughout the day, the guard assigned to the crew remained on duty. The young Black man had the most boring job at the prison. He occupied himself by walking around the garden, heading to the fence line, circling back in the direction of the barracks, and returning to the shaded area where the men ate lunch. Several times he stopped to chat with Deshaun, who came up beside Joe.

"Barry is getting in his steps today," the younger man said to Joe. "I wonder how many it counted on his phone."

"What do you mean?" Joe asked.

"Cell phones can count the number of steps that a person takes in a day."

"How do they do that?"

"No idea," Deshaun chuckled. "Sometimes I forget that men like you who've been in here a long time have missed out on what's going on in the real world. Some things on the outside are good; others are bad."

"I really like cinnamon raisin bagels with cream cheese," Joe replied.

Deshaun rubbed his hoe against the soil. "Do you want me to ask Barry about Ned? He might tell me."

"Yeah."

Later, as the men made their way back to the toolshed, Deshaun came over to Joe and Ray.

"Barry says they brought Ned in to be questioned about something, but he didn't say why," he said.

"Okay, thanks for trying."

Deshaun moved away.

"Secrets are hard to keep in this place," Ray said. "I wonder how long it will be before people find out about the note left for you in the phone room."

"Maybe I should go straight to the warden about Ned," Joe said.

"Do it. Warden Gunton is your best buddy. Next to your lawyer."

After he showered and changed into a clean uniform, Joe made his way to the administration building. The guard at the front door waved him past. In a way, Ray was right. Joe had extraordinary access to the warden. Elle was on duty.

"May I see the warden?" Joe asked.

"Sorry, he's not in."

"I was wondering about Ned Walker. I heard he had a meeting with the warden earlier today. Do you—"

"Sorry, I can't tell you anything."

Joe stopped in his tracks.

"There's nothing you can tell me?" he asked.

"No," Elle said, then smiled. "But I have a piece of lemon cheese-cake for you if you'd like it."

Elle reached down and retrieved a bag from the floor at her feet. She held it out to Joe. Joe opened the bag and caught a whiff of lemon.

"This is better than news about Ned," he said.

"I'm glad," Elle replied.

———————

Joe made his way to the dining hall. Moving down the line, he received a double portion of okra and tomatoes. Ray and Deshaun were sitting at their usual table with a vacant chair beside them. Joe joined them.

"The okra and tomatoes are okay," Ray said as soon as Joe sat down. "They'll be better later in the season. How did it go with the warden?"

"He was out, and Elle wouldn't tell me anything." Joe placed the bag on the table. "But she gave me a big piece of lemon cheesecake."

Joe divided the cake into tiny slices and passed them around the table.

"Deshaun knows about the note left for you in the phone consultation room," Ray said in a low voice.

Joe pressed his lips together. "How?"

"From the same guard who just told me why Ned was dragged into the warden's office," Deshaun explained.

———————

After Charlie Drummond left, Paige muddled her way through a work meeting. A sharp knock on the front door caused Sandy to leap off the couch. Paige cautiously approached the door. Through the sidelight she could see Clint Broome's car in front of the house. A middle-aged woman with closely cut brown hair and wearing dark slacks and a white top was standing on the front porch. Paige cracked open the door.

"Are you Ms. Clark?" the woman asked in a clipped accent that revealed she wasn't from the South. "I'm Dee Henderson from the newspaper. I'm trying to contact your husband. I stopped by the law firm, but he wasn't in, and he's not responded to three voicemail messages. The receptionist wouldn't provide his cell phone number."

"He's usually prompt about getting back to people."

"When are you expecting him to be home?"

"Usually around six o'clock."

Paige saw Clint get out of his car. She waved to let him know that there wasn't a problem. The reporter turned around.

"Who's that?" she asked.

Paige ignored the question.

"Wait here, please," she said. "I'll see if I can reach Ryan and let him know you're here. I'm sure he wants to talk to you."

"Why are you so sure about that?"

"I'll be back in a moment."

Paige closed the door and called Ryan.

"A reporter from the newspaper is here," she said. "Do you want to talk to her at the house, or should I send her to the law firm?"

"I just got back to the office a little while ago. She's left messages, but I've been too busy to call her back. Tell her to meet me here."

"I will," Paige said. She continued, "Charlie Drummond came by the house earlier to see me. He told me there's going to be an article in the paper about the sheriff's department reopening the investigation into the murder of his sister and her boyfriend."

"I know. Norris Broome told me."

"Charlie also wants you to stop representing Joe. It was very uncomfortable listening to him—"

"He shouldn't have talked to you, but it's not going to be a problem. Joe wants to drop the case."

"Why?" Paige asked in surprise.

"We'll talk later."

Paige returned to the front door. "My husband will meet with you at his office. He just got back there."

The reporter turned to leave, then stopped and faced Paige. "Is it true that someone recently fired a gun at your house?"

"I'd rather you ask my husband any questions."

"Will do. I took a few photos of the house while you were calling him."

Nancy buzzed Ryan to let him know the reporter had arrived. He went out to greet her.

"I'm Ryan Clark."

"Dee Henderson."

The reporter glanced around. "Nice office. I've not been here before. The only time I tried to interview Tom Clark, he refused to speak with me."

Ryan led the way to the conference room, where they sat across from each other. The reporter placed her phone in the middle of the table.

"Do I have your permission to record our conversation?" she asked.

Ryan took out his phone and laid it beside hers. The reporter nodded. Both of them started recording.

"For background purposes, please tell me about your educational and professional background and how you came to practice law in Cranfield."

Ryan provided the information without revealing the reasons for his unstable employment history.

"Do you represent a man named Joe Moore who is currently in prison for committing a double murder twenty-six years ago?"

"Yes, but I'm withdrawing from representation."

"Why?"

"At the request of my client for reasons that I can't share due to attorney-client privilege."

"Does it have anything to do with the sheriff's department re-opening an investigation into the possibility that Moore isn't guilty or didn't act alone?"

"No comment," Ryan said, then smiled. "I've always wondered what it would feel like to say that."

The reporter didn't change her expression. "Was the decision to withdraw from representation influenced by the incident at your home when a brick was thrown through a window followed by a gunshot that narrowly missed your wife?"

As he listened to the question flow from the reporter's lips, Ryan stiffened.

"No."

"Is that 'No comment' or 'No'?"

"No."

"Do you believe there may be a connection between the incident at your home and your representation of Mr. Moore?"

"No comment."

As soon as he said the words, Ryan was concerned how the reporter would spin his answers in her article. "No comment" could be cast as an affirmative response. He never should have responded to the previous question with a simple "no." Henderson gave a satisfied nod.

"Is it true that Tom Clark represented Moore at trial?"

"Yes."

"Did Mr. Clark harbor doubts about Moore's guilt?"

"You'd have to ask him that."

"Why did you and Mr. Clark recently decide to represent Moore?"

"I can't discuss that due to attorney-client privilege."

"Have you been communicating about this matter with a former detective at the sheriff's department named Norris Broome?"

"I've spoken with Mr. Broome."

"About the Moore case, the incident at your house, or both?"

Ryan hesitated. "Both, but not in an official capacity. He's retired from the sheriff's department."

The reporter reached over and picked up her phone.

"Thanks for talking to me," she said.

They walked in silence to the reception area. Sue was standing beside Nancy's desk. The reporter left.

"How did it go?" Nancy asked.

"Not very well. I thought I could control the conversation but failed. The most important news she'll print is that we're no longer representing Joe Moore. He's asked me to drop the case."

Nancy smiled broadly, then covered her mouth with her hand.

"That's unprofessional," she said.

"But understandable," Ryan replied. "You've been professional about the situation since Joe's family hired us. You'll read about it in the article, but the sheriff's department is reopening the investigation into the murders."

Ryan returned to his office. Sue followed him.

"I know what Nancy thinks, but how do you feel about this?" she asked.

"Part of me is relieved and another part is frustrated."

"You can take some satisfaction in causing the sheriff's department to reopen an investigation."

"Yeah, I guess that's where my focus needs to be."

Sue left and Ryan logged on to his computer. He had an email from Danny Milton:

> Still waiting on the test results for the additional
> DNA on the murder weapon in the Moore case.
> Do you still want to know the results when they
> come in?

Ryan held his fingers above the keyboard for a few seconds before responding:

> Thanks, but no need.
> I'm no longer representing Moore.

CHAPTER 39

Here's what I found out," Deshaun said. "Someone claimed Ned was stealing scraps of the sheet metal conduit used in the air-conditioning and heating systems and turning them into shanks. They dragged Ned into the warden's office but let him go about an hour later."

"Why did they release him?" Ray asked. "And who saw him stealing metal conduit?"

"I don't know, but whatever Ned said must have satisfied Warden Gunton."

"It doesn't satisfy me," Ray said with a glance at Joe.

"Or me," Deshaun added. "Do you think Ned left the note for you in the phone room?"

Joe shrugged. "Maybe. If Ned was making homemade knives, he may have been trading them for something valuable. Someone who was caught with one would help the guards trace it back to Ned. The warden wouldn't let that pass."

"I didn't hear that Ned was selling them," Deshaun said. "He could have been making them for himself."

"That's what Max would claim," Ray said to Joe.

"What does Max know about Ned?" Deshaun asked.

Ray told Deshaun about the attack at Central Prison.

"That's bad stuff," Deshaun said with a slow shake of his head. "Ned doesn't look very tough to me."

"A knife in a man's hand is an equalizer," Ray commented.

"Equalizer?" Deshaun asked. "Where did you come up with that?"

"I've been trying to improve my vocabulary while I'm locked up in here."

Ray and Deshaun continued talking, but Joe wasn't listening. He suspected that Ned was the author of the note and viewed Joe as a threat, either to himself or to someone outside the prison. But a stubborn, nagging doubt lingered in Joe's mind. And he didn't know what to do about it. Deshaun's voice interrupted his thoughts.

"Joe, I've got your back," the younger inmate said. "And if you say the word, there will be a lot of men standing with me."

"I know," Joe said. "But don't say anything to anybody. Not yet."

After the meal, the three men made their way back to Unit C.

"I believe the Lord is going to meet with us tonight in a powerful way," Deshaun said when they reached the door. "That's what I was praying all day while we were in the garden."

"Amen," Ray responded.

Deshaun headed over to his bunk. Joe and Ray stayed behind.

"I can't let what's going on with Ned distract me," Joe said. "Deshaun is right. We're on the edge of something big that could sweep across the entire prison."

Ray rubbed his arms. "The anointing of the Holy Spirit just came all over me."

Joe spent the time until the meeting sitting on his bunk and praying. He heard a commotion near the entrance to the unit. He stood and moved to the right for a clearer view. Two guards came running up to the scene. A crowd of men had formed and started shouting.

Through an opening in the swarm, Joe could see Deshaun holding Ned in a headlock with his bandaged hand while trying to frisk him with his good hand. At the appearance of the guards, Deshaun released him.

"Check him out," Deshaun said and nodded toward Ned, who was panting and out of breath.

"He tried to choke me!" Ned explained.

Deshaun pointed at Ned. "Search him! He's been making contraband weapons."

One of the guards stepped forward. Ned stood with his arms stretched out while the man frisked him.

"He's clean," the guard said.

Ned gestured toward Deshaun. "What are you going to do about him?"

The guard turned to Deshaun. "Morgan, stay away from Walker. If you do that again, we'll put you in a disciplinary cell."

"Yes, sir," Deshaun said.

Deshaun, followed by a group of men, headed toward a far corner of the room. Joe hurried over to Ned.

"You can join my group," Joe said.

Ned shook his head. "No way."

Joe reached out and put his right arm around Ned's shoulders. Normally, that sort of gesture in prison would result in a quick rebuff, especially after what had just happened. Ned stood still.

"Please," Joe said, removing his arm.

Ned looked at Joe, who saw something in the other man's eyes he couldn't easily identify: sadness, mixed with fear, sprinkled with confusion. But it wasn't anger or aggression.

"Okay," Ned said. "But don't expect me to say anything."

"Agreed."

Ned stayed until the end of the Bible study and prayer meeting. He remained silent. Other men poured out their hearts and souls to the Lord. It was one of the most extraordinary gatherings that had taken place during Joe's time in prison.

"God is in this place!" said one of the men who'd never come to a meeting before.

Heads around the circle nodded in agreement. One of the guards emerged from their room and signaled to Joe it was time to end the meeting.

"Yes," Joe said. "And he wants to meet with each and every one of you in a way that's just right for you. See you tomorrow."

The men picked up their chairs and began moving away.

"Thanks for staying," Joe said to Ned.

"Why did you put your arm around my shoulders?" Ned asked.

"Because I felt God's love for you come up so strong inside me that I couldn't stop myself."

After Ned left, Deshaun came over to Joe.

"Like I said at supper, I've got your back," the young man said, flexing his right bicep.

"And I appreciate you looking out for me," Joe replied. "But I don't want you to get thrown into a detention cell because of it."

"It would be worth it if Walker gets the message that he'd better not bring any junk in here."

"He got the message," Joe replied. "But it was different than the one you gave him."

———

Paige never imagined she would be waiting at a convenience store for delivery of the local newspaper. A man brought in a stack of the papers and placed them on the counter beside the cash register. She purchased the top one and sat in her car to read it. The article about the Moore investigation was on the front page under the headline "Murder Case Investigation Reopened."

A mug shot of Joe Moore at the time of his arrest was pictured. Beneath it was a photo of Cherie Drummond and Marty Brock standing in front of a tree. Paige turned to the page where the article continued. There was no photo of their home. The reporter provided a summary of the original investigation and the trial. Paige already knew that information from the appeal to the North Carolina Supreme Court. Then followed a statement from the sheriff's office:

> The murder of Cheryl Drummond and Martin Brock is subject to ongoing investigation. No specific information will be provided at this time. Anyone who has information they believe may be helpful or relevant should notify the Blanton County Sheriff's Department.

More facts about the status of Joe's incarceration followed. Ryan wasn't mentioned until the next-to-last paragraph on the inner page:

> Moore's family recently retained local attorney Ryan Clark to represent him. It's unclear what sort of relief Clark was seeking on behalf of Moore since no pleadings have been filed in court. Clark claims he is no longer serving as legal counsel in the case and would not provide a reason for his withdrawal. Acting district attorney Danny Milton referred all questions about the matter to the sheriff's department and stated, "There is no statute of limitations for the crime of murder in the State of North Carolina. The

District Attorney's Office stands ready to prosecute any and all individuals criminally responsible for this heinous act."

There was no mention of the brick or bullet. Paige placed the paper on the passenger seat of her car and phoned Ryan.

"Have you read the newspaper article?" she asked when he answered.

"Yes. What did you think?"

"It was okay, maybe better than I expected. How about you?"

"It made me seem like an attorney who didn't know what he was doing. First, I take the case for no apparent reason. Then I drop the case without explanation."

"The ethical rules wouldn't let you say anything."

"Yeah, but the whole thing doesn't sit right with me."

Paige bit her lip. Aspects of Ryan's thought process about the Moore case had been frustratingly hard to understand or accept.

"Ryan, once the sheriff's department reopens the investigation, there's nothing for you to do," she said. "We don't know if there is a connection between Joe and the attack at our home, but it's best if no one believes you're a threat to them. Even with a new security system and Clint Broome sitting in front of our house, we're not one hundred percent safe. Publicizing your withdrawal is the best way to keep us out of danger."

"Yeah, you're right."

When Paige arrived home, Clint Broome's car was gone. Paige hoped that everything from now on would be peaceful and calm.

"Walk slowly," Ray said to Joe as they left the toolshed. "Let the other guys get ahead of us."

The two men hung back.

"What was going on last night with you and Ned?" Ray asked. "You pull him into your group like he's your best friend after Deshaun made sure he wasn't carrying a knife. Then you go over and eat breakfast with him this morning."

"God's working in my heart," Joe replied.

"This makes no sense."

"It would be stupid to ignore the threat from Ned," Joe said. "I'll keep a close eye on him anytime we're around each other. But I couldn't resist the love of God that rose up inside me for him after Deshaun turned him loose last night. It was so strong—" Joe stopped.

"Go on."

"I had to do what I did. Ned didn't pull away or treat me like I was crazy. He was surprised, or at least that's the way he looked at me. He knew something was going on, even if he didn't know what it was. He didn't say anything during the meeting, but he didn't bolt either. He listened."

"You're reading a lot into your interaction without anything being said."

"And I could be wrong," Joe acknowledged. "But I had to reach out to him. Jesus said to love our enemies. This is my chance to do it."

"I don't know," Ray said, worry evident in his eyes. "There's real danger here. If Max is right, Ned could try to stick a knife in you."

Joe glanced sideways at his friend. "If something happens to me, will you remember this conversation?"

"Quit it!" Ray said so loudly that a couple of men walking in front of them turned around.

They reached the garden. Joe spent the morning working alone. Whenever anyone came near, he moved away. He wanted to sort out his thoughts. The Bible was filled with stories of people who did what appeared to be foolish things that turned out to be right in the eyes of the Lord. Who would have thought that sending out the Israelite marching band to circle Jericho and then blow their horns would be God's idea of military strategy? Compared to that episode, demonstrating God's love to Ned Walker seemed mundane. At lunchtime, Ray collected his sandwich and went to sit beside Joe.

"Are you going to take a nap with your head on a rock like Jacob?" Ray asked.

"I was planning on it, and if a doorway to heaven opens up, I'll let you know. It would be nice to see a bunch of angels."

"Quiet about that seeing angels and going to heaven stuff." Ray took a bite of his sandwich. "I thought all morning about you and Ned and kept getting a sick feeling in the pit of my stomach. I'm not going to let you out of my sight."

CHAPTER 40

On his way home, Ryan received a call from Charlie.

"What did you think about the article in the newspaper?" the client asked. "Were you satisfied with it? I provided quite a bit of guidance to the reporter."

"Mostly. I've never been a quitter, and it was tough reading the part about withdrawing from the case, even though it's the truth."

"It was the right call. Above everything else, I want the best for you and Paige."

Not wanting to drive Charlie away from the firm, Ryan decided not to confront him about his conversation with Paige. Ryan gritted his teeth.

"Thanks, I appreciate that," he managed.

"Any updates on Tom?"

"No. But if he's out of the office for a long time, or even permanently, I hope I can continue to represent you."

"Business is business," Charlie replied cryptically. "Talk to you soon."

Ryan turned onto Hamilton Street. When he hugged Paige, she felt stiff in his arms.

"What's wrong?" he asked.

"I don't think you really need to ask that question. The past few weeks have been really difficult."

Ryan leaned against the kitchen counter. "I just got off the phone with Charlie Drummond. I got the sense he pretty much dictated the newspaper article."

"Normally, I would advocate for journalistic freedom, but not in this situation," Paige said. "I'm glad Charlie stepped in."

"I also made a pitch to keep his business at the law firm."

"With you no longer representing Joe, that has a much greater chance of happening."

They ate a salad with grilled chicken for supper. Paige didn't speak.

"What can I do to help you get out of your funk?" Ryan asked.

"Are you accusing me of being in a funk?"

"Observing, not accusing," Ryan said defensively.

"What's the difference?"

"Your perception."

Her salad half eaten, Paige left the table. Sandy followed. Ryan stared after them.

Paige sat on the edge of the bed. Sandy nuzzled Paige's leg with her nose. As she stroked the dog's head, Paige's phone vibrated. It was Lauren Jackson.

"Sorry to call during dinnertime," the deputy said. "Do you have a minute to talk?"

"Yes, I just finished eating."

"First, I want to tell you how much your testimony meant to me. I've read it several times. I first read it in between the Sunday school class and the church service. I tried to thank you but couldn't find you."

Paige felt a twinge of guilt for leaving early.

"And when I got home, I prayed the prayer. Since then, I've really felt closer to God."

Paige's guilt increased.

"I'm glad," she managed.

"I also wanted to call because I read the article in today's newspaper. It made me consider the possibility of a connection between the shooting at your house and your husband's involvement in the Joe Moore case."

"I hope that's not true, but like the article said, Ryan is no longer representing him."

"The Moore case is the other reason for my call. Something happened that upset me. Is Ryan available?"

"Yes."

Paige took the phone to Ryan, who was sitting on the couch. "It's Lauren Jackson."

Paige turned to leave the room as soon as Ryan took the phone from her.

"Hello," he said.

"I told Paige how much her testimony meant to me," Lauren began. "But I need to pass along something off the record about the reopening of the investigation into the Joe Moore case."

"Okay."

"My husband's hours were recently cut way back at work, so anything I tell you has to be kept between the two of us. I can't risk losing my job."

"Agreed."

Lauren was silent for a moment. "I don't believe the sheriff's department is serious about a new investigation."

Ryan sat up straighter on the couch. "Why?"

"Something the detective in charge said to the sheriff when neither of them knew I was around the corner but close enough to overhear their conversation. I can't repeat the detective's words, but it was clear that nothing is going to be done."

"Did either one of them give a reason?"

"No, and I wouldn't feel right trying to find out. I'm nervous about saying anything, but it troubled me that you've not been told the truth."

"Thanks for letting me know."

After ending the call, Ryan went into the bedroom. "May I join you?"

"Yes," Paige answered softly. "What did Lauren tell you about Joe's case? She seemed upset."

Ryan repeated what Lauren told him.

"Does that make any difference?" Paige asked.

"It bothered her, and it bothers me. I need to tell Joe. It wouldn't be right to keep this from him. I should also check with Norris Broome. He may be able to confirm what Lauren said and find out the reason behind it. And I may call Danny Milton, although I don't think he's in the inner circle at the sheriff's department. Nancy told me the sheriff is supporting Scott Nelson for the DA job."

"Lauren told me she's concerned the attack on the house is somehow related to your representation of Joe. That keeps coming up regardless of how many times we try to push it to the side."

"I know."

"I can feel you wanting to jump back into this situation, but I need a promise from you," Paige said. "If Joe still wants you to drop the case, will you give it up?"

Ryan looked directly into her eyes. "Yes, I promise."

During supper, Joe kept watching Ned, who was sitting across the room with some of the men from Unit G. He still felt the love of God for a lost soul. There was no limit to the distance Jesus would go to recover a wayward sheep. Toward the end of the meal, Ned carried his tray to the drop-off window and then headed toward their table. He leaned over between Joe and Ray.

"Any chance you could work in a harmonica lesson this evening?" he asked.

"Sure," Joe replied. "Are you coming to Unit C for the Bible study?"

"Yes, but will you swing by Unit G for the harmonica lesson? We can go from there to the Bible study."

"Yes."

Ned left. Ray turned to Joe.

"Why did you agree to meet with him at Unit G?" Ray demanded. "You won't be surrounded by people like Deshaun and me. Ned might try to get you off by himself."

"I'm supposed to go the extra mile to rescue Ned."

"Whose responsibility is it to rescue Ned? Yours or God's?"

"Both. He uses people. I'm not afraid."

"It's not about fear; it's about safety and being smart. It seems like you want something bad to happen to you."

"I don't," Joe responded. "But I believe this is one of those situations in which it looks foolish to obey God but it's the right thing to do."

"I'd ask where that is in the Bible—" Ray started.

"But you don't have to, because it's there from beginning to end."

"Yeah, I just hope you're not being presumptuous."

"Impressive," Joe said with a slight smile. "If you get a chance, use that word in a sentence with Deshaun later in the evening."

"That won't be hard if we're talking about you."

———

A strange peace rested on Joe as he took a harmonica from the box beneath his bed. He slipped out of Unit C and made his way across the exercise yard toward Unit G, which was at the far western side of the prison. Men were shooting baskets and loitering in the exercise yard. As he got closer to Unit G, the number of men decreased. Joe reached the building and went inside. Not knowing where Ned bunked, he looked around the room. A lot of men were moving through their evening routine. He saw Lonnie Mixon, who led the main prayer meeting in the unit. It, too, had evolved into multiple groups. Joe went over to Lonnie.

"What brings you here?" the large man asked in his deep bass voice.

"Looking for Ned Walker."

Lonnie glanced around. "I haven't seen him since supper. His bunk is over there in the last row."

Joe walked in the direction Lonnie had pointed but found no sign of Ned. Joe stopped beside a prisoner he'd seen before but not met who was holding a Bible. Joe introduced himself.

"Oh, I know who you are," the man said. "You're the leader of everything the Lord is doing around here."

"That's not exactly true. Have you seen Ned Walker?"

"He was here a minute ago. Grabbed a harmonica and took off. Said he was going to play out back."

"Thanks."

Joe exited the unit and walked around to the rear. The sun was going down and the buildings cast long shadows across the ground. There was nothing behind the unit except an open expanse of scrubby grass with the high security fence beyond it. A man stepped out of the shadows into the fading light. It was Ned.

"Glad you found me," he said. "I was about to come looking for you. No one should bother us here at this time of the evening."

"Where can we sit?"

"I thought we'd stand."

"Okay."

Joe reached into his pocket and took out his harmonica. "Let's begin where we left off last time," he said. "I'll play a melody line, and you come along underneath."

Joe raised the harmonica to his lips and blew a few notes. Ned's right hand went into his pocket. But instead of a harmonica, he pulled out a homemade knife that gleamed in the fading light.

———————

Paige went into the living room to read. Restless, Ryan took Sandy outside. Sitting in one of the Adirondack chairs, he called Norris Broome. The former detective didn't answer, and Ryan left a message. He then phoned Danny Milton.

"You're working late or looking for a tennis match under the lights," the acting DA said when he accepted the call.

"A match under the lights is a good idea," Ryan replied. "We should play one evening when it's cooler."

"Just let me know."

"I hope I didn't interrupt your supper."

"No, I'm still at the office. What can I do for you?"

"It's about Joe Moore. I assume you read the article in the newspaper."

"Yes, and you mentioned in your email that you were no longer representing him. But I understand that you couldn't reveal the reason why to the reporter."

"You do?"

"Yeah, one of the detectives at the sheriff's department sent over the affidavit from a prisoner at the facility where Moore is being held. Within the past few days, Moore confessed to committing the murders in front of a number of prisoners. With that in hand, there's no way you'd get any traction for an MAR."

"I knew nothing about this," Ryan replied.

"I assumed you did. Otherwise, why did you drop the—" Danny stopped.

"I withdrew because of serious danger to both Joe and my family," he said. "Are you aware of the attack on our home?"

"No."

Ryan told him what happened. "And two days ago, someone at the prison left a threatening note for Joe and me. I've not seen the note, but basically it said that if we didn't drop the case, both of us were going to be killed. Joe took the note to the prison authorities, who've tried to identify the author. So far, they've come up empty. I withdrew from the case and publicized it in the newspaper so that whoever is behind the threats would back off."

"Who knows about these threats?" Danny asked.

"No one except Joe and me. I didn't even tell my wife about the note because she's stressed out enough already. An inside source told me about the decision by the sheriff's department but not the reason."

"Ryan, I'm going to demand an investigation be opened into who's threatening you and Moore. That's where immediate action has to be taken."

"No! It will just increase the danger to my family."

Ryan paused for a moment to calm himself. "Can you tell me the name of the prisoner who signed the affidavit claiming Joe confessed?" he asked.

"Not unless you're representing Moore."

"Was it someone who grew up in Blanton County named Nathaniel Daniel Walker?" Ryan asked. "I believe he's in jail for car theft."

Danny didn't reply.

"Okay, I'm going to assume that's a yes," Ryan said. "Walker is the prime suspect as to who left the threatening note."

"I'm not going to comment, and don't assume anything by my silence. But you can't dump this information about deadly threats in my lap and expect me not to act on it. My job is to uphold and enforce the law. I'll be discreet and bring it up with a detective I trust. Even though the sheriff and I are on different political sides, his first loyalty is to his job. They know how to conduct a confidential investigation. It's done all the time."

"Even if you're right, that doesn't make me feel safe."

"Trust me. In the meantime, don't talk about this with anyone else."

"Norris Broome has been helping me from the time I first spoke to him. A brick was also thrown through a window at his house."

"Okay. I'll keep you informed. Call me anytime. Day or night. Please."

The call ended. Ryan didn't move from the chair. He still wasn't sure what to say to Paige. He picked up his cell phone to make another call.

CHAPTER 41

Ryan was spending a long time with Sandy in the backyard. Paige closed her book and stared at the blank TV screen. Opening her laptop, she began to type her thoughts, beginning with how she felt and why: "Everything that's been happening makes me wonder if what I wrote about the God who heard me before I knew who he was came from inside my head. Does God really care and act?"

Paige stared at the words. She was discouraged, but after a few moments passed, a seed of hope appeared at the edge of her consciousness: "Or is there hope even when it's impossible to see? Is that faith?"

Paige stopped. She had to be honest: "I have no idea what either one of those words actually means."

She took several deep breaths before typing, "But I do know one thing—even in my confusion and questioning, you are with me."

The last four words Paige typed caused tears to suddenly appear in her eyes and roll down her cheeks. She didn't try to wipe them away. Sandy came dashing into the room and jumped up beside her on the couch. Paige heard Ryan's footsteps.

"Sorry," he said before he came into view. "I was on a phone call."

Paige wiped her cheeks.

"What's wrong?" he asked.

Paige read what she'd written.

"It's like the night you prayed after reading the letter Joe wrote to Doc Garrison," he said.

"Yes," Paige said, encouraged. "And I'm still in the midst of experiencing it."

"That's fine. I'm going back to the office for a couple of hours."

"Now?"

"Yes, I'm traveling to the prison early in the morning to talk to Joe, and I need to be there by nine o'clock."

"What I told you earlier about Joe—"

"I heard, and I promised."

———————

Ned pressed the edge of the knife against Joe's neck in the area of his carotid artery.

"Keep your hands to the side," Ned said. "Any move and you're going to bleed out. I know how to use this."

"I'm not afraid to die," Joe said.

"Nobody believes that kind of talk. You know what this is about, don't you? Did you read my note?"

"Yes, and I told my lawyer to drop the case. I don't want him or his wife to get hurt."

The pressure of the knife lessened. "How do I know you're telling the truth?"

"You have to decide that for yourself," Joe said. He added, "You know you're not going to get away with killing me."

The pressure from the knife increased again. "That's my problem, not yours. If I didn't have a plan, we wouldn't be standing here."

Joe took a shallow breath through his nose and exhaled.

"What did you feel when I put my arm around your shoulders last night after Deshaun roughed you up?" Joe asked.

"Nothing."

"That was God's love flowing through me to you."

Ned grunted. He removed the knife so it was three or four inches from Joe's neck.

"I signed an affidavit that you confessed to the murders in front of five other men," Ned said.

"From what I said in the prayer meeting the other night?" Joe asked. "That was clever, but you didn't have to do it. Getting out of prison isn't my number one goal. It's reaching men like you for God."

"You can believe if you want, but it's not for me."

"It's for everyone."

The knife blade pressed against his skin with more force. Joe felt a sting. He'd been cut.

"Enough with the preaching! You're making me mad!"

"If you step away now, I'm not going to say anything about this to anyone."

"Why should I believe you?"

"Because you know I tell the truth."

Ned was silent for a few moments before he spoke. "Close your eyes!"

Joe shut his eyes. The pressure of the knife blade lifted. Joe silently counted to ten, then opened his eyes. Ned was gone. Joe touched his neck. His finger came away wet with blood. But it wasn't serious. He'd done almost as much damage when he first started to shave with a razor. Then Joe began to tremble. He wasn't afraid to die, but that didn't mean he was immune to the power of a deadly threat.

———————

Paige handed Ryan an envelope on his way out the door in the morning.

"I wrote another letter to Joe Moore," she said. "Will you deliver it to him?"

"Of course."

Ryan stopped at the only coffee shop in Cranfield for a grande that he sipped as he drove to the prison. It was a bright, sunny morning, and the sun's glare through the windshield made him squint. Reaching the prison shortly after 8:00 a.m., he entered through the visitor gate and, after passing through another level of security, finally stood at the rear of the administration building. The guard on duty checked with the office and buzzed him through. Another guard escorted him to the attorney consultation room where he'd previously met with Joe. Along the way, they passed several prisoners. The guard left the door unlocked. Ryan sat on the far side of the small table and waited. Five minutes later, Joe entered.

"Why are you here?" Joe asked before Ryan could say anything.

"There are several things I need to tell you. But first, here's another letter to you from Paige."

Joe took the envelope from Ryan but didn't open it. "Tell her I was really blessed and encouraged by what she wrote the other day and her testimony. She's a special person. I'd like to meet her someday."

"Maybe that can happen." Ryan opened his mouth to speak again, then closed it for a moment. "What's that on your neck?" he asked. "Did you cut yourself shaving?"

"No."

Ryan wondered about the wound but decided not to dwell on that now. He explained what he'd learned about the nonexistent investigation by the sheriff's department. When he reached the part about the affidavit from a prisoner claiming Joe confessed to the crimes, Joe interrupted.

"That was Ned Walker."

"He was at the top of my list."

"I remember when it happened," Joe said. "Ned made sure I admitted to committing the murders in front of witnesses during a Bible study. He was obviously setting me up. Last night, he also admitted that he left the threatening note in this consultation room."

Ryan put both hands on the table in front of him.

"We have to find out who he's working for," he said excitedly. "Have you told the warden about this?"

"No, and none of it changes what I told you the other day about dropping the case. There's no use continuing any attempt to get me out of here. It's not going to work because I'm in here for reasons other than a murder conviction."

"Do you mean God wants you in prison?"

"He's had me here for his purposes, and I believe I'll stay until he says it's time to leave."

The door opened, and a man in a prison uniform entered. Joe jumped up and stood between him and Ryan.

"Nothing has changed!" Joe said, holding out his hand. "He's only here so I can tell him once and for all that I don't want to pursue the case."

The other man had his right hand in his pocket.

"I've not slept all night," the man replied. "When I went to the warden's office this morning for my work assignment, I saw on the schedule that your lawyer was coming to see you. When he passed me in the hall a few minutes ago, I knew what I had to do."

Joe grabbed the man's right hand and jerked it from his pocket. The hand came out empty. Joe patted the pocket.

"Joe, there's nothing in my pockets," the man said. "And I'm not going to hurt anyone."

"Why are you here?" Joe demanded.

"I'm willing to answer any questions your lawyer has for me."

Joe took a step back and turned sideways. "Ryan, this is Ned Walker."

Ryan's eyes widened. The inmate looked like a man who'd lived a hard life. His face was riven with deep creases, and his eyes were bloodshot and red.

"Sit down," Ryan said.

Joe pulled another chair close to the table and positioned himself between Ryan and Ned.

"I came close to killing Joe last night," Ned said.

Ryan pointed to the side of Joe's neck. "You did that to him?"

"Yes." Ned nodded. "Joe may think I spared him because he promised to drop his case. That's not true. I didn't believe him. It would have been easy and quick. A cut in the right place, and Joe would have bled out. But when it came to it, I couldn't force myself to kill him. My hand wouldn't move. It was like it was frozen or something. After I let him go, I went to my bunk and spent the rest of the night tossing and turning. I felt like I was going crazy."

"Why did you want to kill Joe?" Ryan asked.

"To protect my brother, Larry," Ned said with a long sigh. "He got in touch with me a few weeks ago and told me what you and Joe were doing. Larry was scared to death you might uncover something that would lead to him."

"Is Larry the one with cancer?" Joe asked.

"Yeah, and he's in bad shape."

"Did your brother kill Marty Brock and Cherie Drummond?" Ryan asked.

"No!" Ned replied emphatically. "He just thought it was a drug buy. He'd sold drugs to Marty Brock a few times. On the night Marty and the Drummond girl died, Larry got word from one of his contacts that Marty had a big wad of cash. Larry was promised a cut of the money if he set up a meeting with Marty at a local drug house. I don't know exactly what happened, but both Marty and the girl ended up dead."

Ryan wasn't convinced. "If it wasn't your brother, then who killed them?"

"I don't know, and Larry never told me. He said it was better if I didn't know what happened."

"Who contacted Larry and promised him money if he set up a meeting with Marty?" Ryan asked.

Ned pressed his lips together tightly. Ryan waited. Several seconds passed.

"I can't prove it, and Larry never told me directly, but I believe Mr. Drummond was involved. Larry was working for him at the time of the murders, and Mr. Drummond is the one paying for Larry's cancer treatment. I think he wants to keep Larry quiet about what he knows."

"Charlie Drummond?" Ryan asked in disbelief.

"Yeah. About ten years ago, Larry was drinking one night and started talking about the night of the murders. He told me Mr. Drummond was mad at Marty. Mr. Drummond's sister had jumped over him in the family business, and then Drummond found out that she was going to marry Marty, who planned on kicking Mr. Drummond totally out."

Ryan remained skeptical. "Who told Larry this? Mr. Drummond?"

"Maybe," Ned said with a quick nod. "But I never could see Drummond talking like that to Larry. I think it had to be somebody else, but I don't know who, and Larry never mentioned a name."

Ryan looked at Joe. "There's a better chance Charlie Drummond is paying Larry's doctor bills because he's a generous man."

"I don't trust the man," Ned said. "Larry sold him drugs, but Drummond didn't always pay him."

Ryan shook his head. He wasn't buying Ned's character assassination of Charlie Drummond, but he had to ask another question: "Did Charlie Drummond threaten you or Larry, saying that if you didn't silence Joe, Charlie would cut off Larry's treatment?"

"I haven't met or talked to the man, and Larry didn't tell me that."

Ryan sat back in his chair. "Setting up a meeting with Marty might be a drug offense, but it's not murder," he said. "How did you and Larry end up at the nightclub the night Marty and Cherie died?"

"I don't want to talk about that," Ned said, shaking his head.

"Both of you were arrested."

"Yeah, on misdemeanor drug charges. All we had to do was pay a fine."

"What are you leaving out?" Ryan pressed.

Ned shifted in his chair, then tapped the table several times lightly with the fingers on his right hand. "If I tell you, are you going to turn Larry over to the police? He's in bad shape, but with treatment, there's a chance he'll make it."

"I can't promise you anything—" Ryan started.

Joe spoke: "Ned, the reason you're sitting in that chair is because the Lord convinced you to tell the truth, not for us, but because you need to clear your conscience."

"Our mama was a God-fearing woman," Ned said, anguish evident on his face. "She wanted Larry and me to follow her example. Neither of us did."

"Until now," Joe said.

Again, Ned was silent for several moments.

"Okay," he said. "Here's what happened, the best I know. According to Larry, whoever killed Marty and the Drummond girl dumped the bodies behind the nightclub. I asked him how they died, and he said it was a setup at the drug house. Larry was freaking out when he got to the nightclub. A few minutes later, the cops swarmed in. I dumped the pills in my possession on the floor, but a deputy saw me. Larry and I claimed the pills belonged to both of us so the charge against us would be less. Splitting the amount made it a misdemeanor."

Ryan was stunned. This was the kind of information that could justify a new trial for Joe.

"Larry has always been torn up over this," Ned continued with a sad look on his face. "If any of it comes out, do you think he could be charged with some kind of murder?"

"I can't give you legal advice," Ryan responded.

"But you're a lawyer."

Ryan shook his head. "I'm sorry. I can't because Joe is my client. Larry would have to have his own lawyer."

Ned stood to leave. "I don't have anything else to say."

"We'll talk later," Joe said.

"Just a minute," Ryan said. "I want to be clear about one thing. Are you saying Joe didn't have anything to do with Marty's and Cherie's deaths?"

Ned looked down at Joe. "I can't swear to it, but I believe that couple was dead before they got to the nightclub."

CHAPTER 42

After Ned left, Joe and Ryan sat in silence.

"What do you want me to do?" Ryan asked.

"Ned would have to be willing to speak up in court, right?" Joe asked.

"Yes, but because what he just told us is inconsistent with the affidavit he provided the sheriff's department, Ned's credibility would be attacked. Everything he told us is supposition. It would be necessary to corroborate, or have other evidence that backs up what he's saying, for it to be given much weight by a judge. Larry is the key. If he comes forward and says what Ned told us is true, it would change everything."

Joe scratched his forehead.

"This has hit me so fast," he said. "I'm not sure what to say or do."

"Joe, if you're not guilty, then it's wrong for you to be locked up for even one more day."

"I've got to get my head around believing that. But even if Ned isn't a threat to me in here, that doesn't mean you aren't in danger out there."

"That's true," Ryan acknowledged. "Which is what I have to

figure out. My pregnant wife believes this trip is the last contact you and I will have about your case."

"Is there anyone you can trust with what Ned told us who can do something about it?"

"That's a short list. I believe I can trust Danny Milton, the acting DA. And there's Norris Broome. He doesn't report to anyone but himself, but he's retired and doesn't have any power or authority. Still, I'd like to bring him into the loop. As a former detective, he might have an idea of how to move forward in a way that minimizes the danger. Remember, he's been threatened too."

"Minimize isn't the same as eliminate."

"I'm not going to pretend there isn't risk, but I have to try to convince someone to run down this information and see where it leads."

"Okay," Joe sighed. "Talk to the DA and Detective Broome if you think that's the way to go."

"And let me know immediately if Ned mentions anything else."

Joe looked into Ryan's eyes. "I don't want anything bad to happen to you or your family," he said.

"I'll be careful."

After Ryan left, Joe walked across the exercise yard. In the distance was the high fence. The razor wire looped along the top glinted in the morning sun. Joe had never resented the fence. Today was different. The fence no longer had justice on its side.

Paige was in the middle of a meeting when Ryan unexpectedly entered the living room.

"Why are you home?" she asked.

"I need to talk to you as soon as possible."

"I'll be finished in around fifteen minutes. Take Sandy into the backyard. It's been a while since she went out."

Ryan left with the dog. Paige's boss asked one of the participants a question, which led to a discussion not on the agenda.

"Paige, are you following along?" Sara asked. "You need to be the one to organize this so we can include it in the proposal."

"Uh, yes. I'll access the audio from the meeting and have something to you by four o'clock this afternoon."

"Make it three o'clock," Sara replied.

"Will do."

Ryan returned with Sandy. He silently pointed to the watch on his wrist.

"I know, I know," Paige replied. "I can't exit this call until I'm sure nothing new is going to be discussed. Fix something to eat for lunch and make enough for me."

Ryan left again. Paige tapped her finger impatiently against the edge of her keyboard. Finally, she was able to log off and go into the kitchen. Ryan was almost finished eating his sandwich.

"Peanut butter and jelly with potato chips?" she asked.

"I was in the mood for it."

"Did you see Joe?"

"Yes, and I gave him your letter. He's appreciated the feedback you've given him."

"How did he take the news that you're no longer representing him?"

"About that," Ryan said slowly. "There have been some new developments that have to be tied up. It shouldn't take long."

Paige sat down.

"I thought you were going to quit," she said morosely.

Ryan spoke rapidly: "I was, but a man in the prison has a brother in Blanton County who could possibly clear Joe's name. It's not definite, but I have to follow up on this lead. Don't worry. I'm going to be totally discreet. I'm only talking to Danny Milton and Norris Broome about it."

Paige didn't respond.

"Do you have anything to say?" Ryan asked.

"Yes, but I can tell that what I think or say isn't going to make a difference."

"That's not true. Keeping us safe is my number one priority. But there's also the issue of justice for Joe."

"Finish your sandwich and go," Paige said with a wave of her hand.

Ryan drained the rest of a glass of milk, kissed her on the cheek, and left the house.

Paige took one bite of the sandwich Ryan had fixed for her and threw the rest in the trash bin. Before returning to her computer, she armed the security system and called Lauren Jackson. The deputy didn't answer. Paige left a message asking her if she'd be willing to park her car on the street in front of their house for a few days.

As she waited for some information to come up on her computer, Paige thought about Joe Moore. If he was truly innocent, he should be freed. But Ryan was in over his head. The sheriff's office would be the best place to provide any new information. She sent Ryan a text message making that suggestion. He replied immediately:

> The sheriff's department has already terminated the investigation. That's something I'll discuss with Norris Broome.

Surprised at the news about the decision by the sheriff's office, Paige wanted to ask for an explanation but didn't have time for a back-and-forth conversation.

———————

Ryan was faced with a small mountain of phone calls and emails that needed an immediate response. He took a moment to stop by Sue's desk and tell her what he'd learned from Ned Walker.

"That's a bombshell," she said. "Feelings of guilt can do more than most people realize."

"Yeah. My dilemma is what to do next."

"You could call Mitch."

"Great suggestion. I hadn't thought about that. He offered to help if I needed it."

Sue picked up the phone. "I'll see if Mitch is available."

"I'll take it in my office."

A minute later, Sue buzzed him. "Mitch is out all day in depositions in Asheville. I left a message for him to call."

Ryan phoned the DA's office. Danny Milton was also unavailable. Ryan then called Norris Broome. The former detective answered on the third ring.

"Any chance I could come by to see you?" Ryan asked.

"I'm busy most of the day, but things open up this evening around six o'clock. That might be too late for you."

"No, I'll see you then. It's important."

———————

Joe was in a daze as he made his way to the garden with the other men. Ray came alongside him.

"Where were you during breakfast?"

"Meeting with my lawyer. He drove down early this morning."

"What?" Ray exclaimed.

"Yes."

"Why?"

Joe took a deep breath. "Stuff has come up in my case that he wanted to tell me about."

"It must be big if he made the trip to tell you in person."

"Yes."

They took a few more steps.

"I'm waiting," Ray said. "You're going to tell me eventually. You always do."

"Not this time," Joe replied. "Except I'm no longer worried about Ned Walker. The Lord is moving in his life."

"That's big news. What happened?"

"It's always better to hear directly from the person, but I believe with all my heart that Ned wants to get right with the Lord. Don't ask him about it, not yet. He'll share what he wants to when the time is right. Until then, I'm going to come alongside him the best I can."

They reached the garden plot. Joe took a moment to look over the large cultivated area. From humble beginnings a few years earlier, it now produced a significant harvest of fresh vegetables and fruit. Often there was enough to feed the entire prison.

Hoeing the green beans, Joe began to consider the prospect of leaving prison, a notion he'd never entertained because it wasn't possible. He'd often said that God could use a person regardless of where they lived. That remained true. But if the Lord opened the front gate so that Joe could walk out as a free man, it meant Jesus had someplace else for Joe to serve. Joe suddenly felt both excited and apprehensive. He wiped his sweaty hands on the front of his uniform, leaving dark red-clay streaks.

During their lunch break, Joe didn't try to take a nap on his rock. Too much was running through his mind. Instead, he sat on the scrubby grass. Ray and Deshaun joined him.

"I've been thinking all morning," Deshaun said after he took a long drink of water. "I believe we should ask the warden for permission to have a big open-air meeting in the exercise yard."

"Warden Gunton checks with Joe before he makes any important decisions," Ray joked.

"I'm serious," Deshaun replied.

"Okay, okay," Ray said. "I think it's a great idea. There are a lot of guys who for one reason or another don't go to chapel."

"I'd be glad to bring it up," Joe said. "But I think we need to get Chaplain Jim on board first. It wouldn't look right if we went behind his back."

"That makes sense," Deshaun said.

Both Joe and Ray nodded. Deshaun got up and moved on.

"Butch Anderson could lead a few songs with his guitar," Ray suggested. "And you and Ned could play your harmonicas. The last time you jammed together in front of Unit C was really good."

"I'd like that," Joe replied. "I'll bring it up with Ned. I hope he'll come over to Unit C this evening."

"Don't you think it could wait until tomorrow?" Paige asked Ryan when he called to tell her that he was going to work late, miss supper, and try to catch Norris Broome at home.

"This thing with Joe is eating away at me, and I want to get it off my plate," he said. "And I'm so amped up that I'm not very hungry."

"If you're not hungry, you're sick," Paige said, hoping to lighten the tension that had been between them.

"No, I'm fine. But I have a plan. I'm going to ask Norris's advice about the best way to contact the brother of the man I talked to this morning. Maybe even ask him to go with me."

"Whatever you think is best."

Paige started to mention that she'd reached out to Lauren Jackson but could tell Ryan wanted to end the conversation.

"I'll give you a pass on being here for supper," she said. "But you have to promise something special tomorrow night."

"You got it. See you later."

With Ryan not coming home for supper, Paige decided to take a walk. She'd taken Sandy out earlier, and the dog tilted her head and gave Paige a puzzled look when she saw the leash.

"You're so smart," Paige said, rubbing Sandy's head. "Yes, we've already gone for a walk, but we're going to do it again."

Retracing their steps from earlier in the day, they crossed paths with multiple people Paige had never seen walking before. They turned onto Washington Avenue. Approaching the Drummond house, Paige slowed. Only one of the expensive cars was in the driveway, which made Paige suspect Charlie hadn't come home from work. Pulling Sandy closer to her, Paige walked up to the front door and rang the doorbell. Captain barked. Monica cracked open the door and scooped Captain up in her arms. She was wearing a nice cream-colored dress and heels.

"Sorry to bother you," Paige said. "I didn't realize you were just going out."

"No, I'm just waiting for Charlie to come home. Would you like to come inside? Now that Captain has seen Sandy, he's going to be disappointed if they don't get to play together for a few minutes."

Paige entered the house and unhooked Sandy's leash. The two dogs sniffed noses and then trotted off toward the rear of the house.

"Captain is probably going to show her where we keep the treats he can get to," Monica said. "Come into the parlor."

Monica sat in an armchair. Paige sat in its twin beside a small antique table.

"Sandy and I were out for a walk and wanted to stop by and say hello," Paige said. "We really enjoyed dinner the other night. I'd like to invite you and Charlie to come over. It wouldn't be nearly as fancy."

"Don't let that stop you," Monica replied with a forced smile. "I spend way too much time alone. Charlie has so much work to do that it's not unusual for him to get home after I'm asleep in bed."

"Ryan has been keeping long hours since Tom's heart attack."

"How is Tom doing? Charlie hasn't mentioned him for the past few days."

"He made it through surgery, but recovery will be difficult."

The two women sat in awkward silence for a few moments.

"We appreciate Charlie asking Clint Broome to look out for us recently," Paige said.

"I don't know what you're talking about."

"Oh, we had an incident at our home, and Charlie sent Clint over to keep watch."

"What kind of incident?"

Paige told her. Monica's eyes widened, and she glanced past Paige toward the foyer.

"That's horrible," she said. "Aren't you afraid to go out for a walk?"

"No, Ryan and I believe we're safe now."

"I hope so. I know what it's like to be afraid."

Nataliya stuck her head into the room.

"Mr. Drummond called and asked me to bring supper to him," she said.

"Where is he?" Monica asked.

"At the Devon property. There's lobster salad in the refrigerator, or I can—"

"I'll be fine," Monica said. "Go ahead."

Nataliya left.

"The Devon property is a farm we bought on the west side of town," Monica said, shaking her head. "The house is undergoing renovation, and it's taking a huge amount of Charlie's time."

"Are you involved in the project?"

"Not much."

A second moment of awkward silence followed. Paige cleared her throat and stood. "I guess I'd better be going."

"Stop by again. It gets lonely in this big house."

Paige called Sandy, who came running with Captain trailing along behind her. Sandy licked Paige's hand in greeting.

"Your dog really loves you," Monica said.

"We're inseparable."

Paige felt sad as she and Sandy walked away from the house. Money hadn't brought marital happiness to the Drummond household.

Arriving home, she fixed a pesto pasta salad that she knew Ryan didn't like and settled in for a quiet evening. She had a new book she wanted to start.

CHAPTER 43

It was cloudy and overcast when Ryan pulled into Norris Broome's driveway. Ryan walked up the front steps and knocked on the door. There was no answer. He knocked again and heard footsteps approaching. The door opened. Norris was wearing blue overalls, a white T-shirt, and a cowboy hat.

"Come in," Norris said. "I was working at the back of my property until a few minutes ago."

The inside of the house had a distinctly masculine feel. Several large buck trophy heads with impressive antlers hung on the wall. The floor in one corner was covered in a black bearskin with the head attached and the mouth gaping open. A spacious living room was situated to the left.

"Are you married?" Ryan asked, sitting on a dark leather couch.

"No, divorced years ago. Law enforcement work kills marriages.

"Would you like a water or something stronger to drink?" Norris asked. "I have just about anything you could want."

"No, thanks. You're a serious hunter."

"That's just a few of my trophies. I have a room that includes a few exotics, which some people don't believe should be hunted. I've been all over the world."

"Who goes with you?"

"Different people. Most of the trips are organized by Charlie Drummond."

"I didn't know Charlie was a big-game hunter. I didn't see any mounted animals at his house when we ate dinner with him and Monica the other night."

"He has them elsewhere. What's on your mind?"

Ryan shifted on the couch. "I wanted to talk to you about the sheriff reopening the Moore case. I understand from Danny Milton that it's not going to happen because a prisoner named Ned Walker signed an affidavit that Joe recently confessed to the murders in front of a number of fellow inmates."

"That's news to me," Norris replied.

"Do you have any influence with the sheriff to convince him to continue the investigation?"

"Not really."

"There's significant new evidence that I believe would help persuade him."

"What kind of evidence?"

Taking a deep breath, Ryan plunged into what he'd learned from Ned Walker. Norris shook his head several times.

"I remember Larry and Ned. They were petty drug dealers. But I don't recall them being in the club that night." Norris was silent for a moment. "I never considered that Marty and Cherie might have been killed elsewhere."

"Do you think there's a possibility Ned is right?"

"No, but I can understand why you're interested in finding out everything you can."

"That's not all Ned told me, and I hate to even bring this up. He claims Charlie Drummond felt threatened by Marty's relationship with Cherie because of the impact it could have on Charlie's position within the family business."

"How?"

"Cherie had jumped over Charlie in the company leadership structure, and according to Ned, Marty planned on marrying Cherie and completely removing Charlie from the business."

"How would Ned Walker know that?"

"I wondered the same thing, but he seemed sure of himself."

"Are you going to talk to Charlie about these allegations?" Norris asked.

"I don't want to, but maybe someone should."

"Who?"

"I thought you might mention it to the sheriff, and I'll discuss it with Danny Milton. They can take it from there."

Norris didn't respond. Ryan continued, "Obviously, Larry's testimony would be key to creating doubt about Joe Moore's guilt, and I'd want to interview him."

"From what you're telling me, Larry is a suspect. I doubt he'll confirm what Ned told you. Talking to him would be a waste of time."

"You may be right, but I can't leave this alone until I can pass it off and be sure it's going to be thoroughly investigated. Ned's credibility is shaky, but I believe there's enough to convince Danny to act. Who knows? According to Ned, Larry has cancer. If asked the right questions, he may confess or reveal who actually committed the murders."

"You're definitely going to talk to Milton about what Ned told you?"

"Yes, that's the plan. I tried to call him earlier today, but he wasn't available. After that, I'll also contact Larry. Is there a chance you'd consider going with me to interview Larry? You have way more experience doing that sort of thing than I do."

Norris closed his eyes for a moment before speaking.

"You're not recording this conversation, are you?" he asked.

"Of course not."

"What I'm about to say needs to be off the record. Shortly before Cherie died, her father promoted her to CEO of the family business."

"That's not a secret. Charlie mentioned that the other night at dinner."

Norris continued, "The relationship you've described between the Drummonds and Marty Brock is partly accurate. Marty intended to push Charlie aside once he and Cherie got married."

"You don't think there's a chance Charlie was behind the murders?" Ryan asked in shock.

"No, but with what you've told me, I think there's a good chance the DA will pressure the sheriff's department to launch an investigation. And where that investigation goes will be impossible to predict or control. Encouragement from me won't be necessary."

"Still, a word from you would help."

Norris was silent for a moment. "No, and I have to make sure none of that happens."

"What do you mean?"

"Who knows you're here?"

"Just my wife. Why?"

Norris leaned over, opened a small drawer in a side table next to his chair, and took out a large pistol.

"Give me your phone," he said, pointing the gun at Ryan's head. "It's time for you to come with me."

"No!"

Norris raised his index finger to his lips. Ryan closed his mouth.

"Quiet," Norris said. "Not a word."

The former detective took Ryan into the kitchen and bound his wrists behind his back with a black twist tie.

"Why are you doing this?" Ryan asked.

"Outside," Norris said coldly.

They reached the white pickup. Norris opened the rear door and placed his hand on Ryan's back. Ryan resisted. Norris roughly pushed him forward.

"Get in! I'm not going to repeat myself."

Ryan stopped. "This—"

"Has already passed the point of no return for you and your wife."

"My wife! She doesn't know anything that I told you! Please, don't do anything to her!"

"She knows you're here."

Norris pushed Ryan into the truck and made him lie face down on the floorboard.

"Don't try to raise your head or look up," Norris warned.

The truck engine started, but the truck didn't move.

"I have Ryan Clark," Norris said. "He's not dropping the investigation, and things are about to get out of control."

Ryan moved his head enough to see that Norris was on his cell phone. He listened as Norris summarized their conversation.

"I went along with you manipulating the situation, but that's no longer an option," Norris said. "We need to end it."

Another period of silence followed. "I'll take care of everything. You just make sure the crypto is in my account within the next thirty minutes."

Norris listened for a longer period. "No, Charlie! This time it's going to be taken care of my way! You've let these loose ends hang around too long! If you're scared and want to leave town until it blows over, do it! But I'd better see that money in my account before you get on a plane! All of it!"

Ryan sucked in a quick breath. Norris was talking to Charlie Drummond.

"Good," Norris said in a calmer voice. "And that includes Larry Walker. Even if his brother takes out Moore, Larry is a dangerous liability."

The call ended. The truck began to back out of the driveway.

"Now you understand why there can't be an investigation," Norris said. "Charlie Drummond has had me under his thumb ever since he bribed his way out of his first arrest for drug possession when he was a teenager. If he were hauled in for questioning as part of a new investigation into the death of Marty Brock and his sister, he'd likely crack under the pressure and blame me or someone else."

Ryan didn't speak. The truck increased speed once they reached the highway. Norris made another call. This time on his Bluetooth.

"Time to act," Norris said.

"Are you sure?" the man asked. "I thought everything was over."

"No, I have Clark. He and Moore talked to Ned Walker, who told him enough to cause a big problem. I just spoke with Charlie, and he gave the okay to take care of this my way. Once Clark is dead, I'll go to Larry Walker's house. Clark's wife knows he came to see me. Take care of her. She trusts you."

"Now?"

Ryan realized who was on the phone. It was Clint Broome.

"No, Clint! Don't do it!" Ryan yelled.

Norris abruptly ended the call.

CHAPTER 44

Joe saw Ned making his way toward him from across the dining hall.

"Coming over this evening to play harmonica?" Joe asked.

"I haven't been able to think about harmonicas today," Ned replied. "I'm worried about my brother."

Joe stepped out of the line, and they moved to a more private spot.

"I ran my mouth too much to your lawyer," Ned said. "I need to let Larry know what I've done so he doesn't get caught off guard."

"Do you want my lawyer to contact him?"

"No, he didn't sound like he'd be willing to do it, and Larry won't trust him."

"What about a member of your family? The aunt you mentioned."

"I lied about her. Larry is the only one I've been communicating with."

Joe thought for a moment. "There's the retired detective who worked my case. He's been helping my lawyer. He might be able to find a way—"

"It's not Norris Broome, is it?" Ned interrupted.

"Yeah. My lawyer is going to ask his advice about how to proceed."

Fear flashed across Ned's face. He leaned forward and spoke in an intense whisper. "Broome can't know what I told you and your lawyer this morning! Larry is afraid of him. It may have to do with dirt Broome has on Larry or the other way around. Whatever the reason, Larry always told me to steer clear of him."

Joe looked at the large clock over the exit to the dining hall. It was three minutes before five o'clock.

"I can try to call my lawyer," he said.

"Do it!"

Joe left the dining hall and jogged across the exercise yard to the administration building. The guard on duty held up his hand.

"Closed for business, Moore."

"It's an emergency. I need to contact my lawyer."

The guard gave him an annoyed look, then moved to the side. "Make it quick."

Joe walked rapidly down the hall to the office. Inside sat an older woman who normally worked in another area of the prison.

"Where's Elle?" Joe asked.

"Has the day off."

"I need to call my lawyer," Joe said.

"Not today," the woman replied gruffly.

"Is Warden Gunton here?"

"No."

"Will you call him and tell him that Joe Moore—"

"I'm not going to bother the warden you've turned into the governor of North Carolina."

Joe stared at her for a moment.

"Leave," the woman said, waving him away with her hand. "Come back in the morning and put in your request."

Joe slowly trudged across the exercise yard to the dining hall. Ned was sitting at a table with other men from Unit G. He got up and came over to Joe. "They didn't let you make the call, did they?"

"No," Joe said dejectedly. "I have to wait until tomorrow morning. But I'll be there first thing."

"That may be too late," Ned replied.

Joe felt a sense of dread. He wasn't sure if it was coming from Ned or himself. The heaviness stayed with him throughout the evening. The meetings in Unit C continued to grow with more and more men participating. Joe wanted to enjoy what God was doing, but he was worried. Ned didn't show up.

For the third time, Paige checked her phone for a text from Ryan. She knew he was a man on a mission but wished he'd let her know his status. Laying aside her book, she sent a short text message:

ETA?

The text showed immediate delivery, but there was no answer. Ryan had the discipline to ignore his phone in the middle of something important. Paige usually considered that a good trait when he was talking to her, but a bad one when she wanted to reach him quickly. She turned on the TV and began randomly flipping through channels until she found a nature documentary that seemed interesting. She continued to check her phone for a response from Ryan. A text message from Clint Broome popped up:

> Got a call from your security company. There's a
> problem with your system. Turn it off and wait for
> me to arrive. I'm on my way over to reboot it.

Paige went to the central control station. All the lights were green. Puzzled, she turned it off, waited ten seconds, and turned it back on. The green lights returned. She picked up her phone and texted Clint:

> Everything looks fine. I turned it off and on. Why
> did the security company contact you?

He replied:

> Gave them my cell phone as a backup in case
> they couldn't reach Ryan. Almost there. I'll knock
> on the front door.

Paige's fingers flew as she typed a response:

> I've not been able to reach Ryan. He's working
> late and was going to see Norris.

Paige fixed a cup of hot tea and returned to the living room. Three minutes later she heard a knock on the front door. Sandy jumped off the couch and began barking.

"Hush," she said to the dog.

Sandy ignored her. Tea in hand, Paige went to the front door. She could see Clint through the side glass. He was wearing a dark shirt and pants with a ball cap on his head. She unlocked the door and opened it. Without being invited in, he quickly entered. Sandy continued to bark.

"Can you tell your dog to shut up?" he asked.

Paige put her free hand on Sandy's head.

"Settle down," she said to Sandy, then turned to Clint. "What do you think is wrong with the security system? It seems fine to me."

"Come with me so we can check the control panel."

When they reached the box, none of the lights were on.

"Power to the system is out," Clint said.

"It was on a few minutes ago."

"But not now."

Clint, who had his back to her, turned around. He held a gun in his hand and pointed it at her chest. Paige put her hand over her mouth and screamed. Sandy began to bark furiously. His eyes wide, Clint took a step back. Paige threw the hot tea in his face and ran into the bedroom. Slamming the door, she locked it and then immediately went into the master bathroom and locked that door. Clint slammed his fist against the bedroom door and started kicking it. The doors in the house were solid, but Paige could hear the wood beginning to split. She raised the small window and pushed out the screen. Standing on the toilet, she managed to lift herself onto the sill. With all her weight on her abdomen, she thought about her baby but wiggled forward until she slid headfirst out of the window onto the ground below. The neighbors had a fence that prevented her from running toward their house. Instead, she crept along the wall and peeked around the corner at the front door. When she did, she saw Lauren Jackson ringing the doorbell.

As the truck accelerated, Ryan closed his eyes. He unsuccessfully struggled against the constraints on his wrists. He tried to pray, but all he could muster was a doubt-filled plea that Clint Broome wasn't as cold-blooded as his uncle and might spare Paige.

As they left the main highway, the road became bumpy. The truck stopped, and Norris turned off the engine. Without saying a word, he opened the driver's door. Ryan braced himself for the former detective to drag him out of the vehicle. Instead, silence followed. Minutes passed. Then the door opened.

"Is there—" Ryan started.

"Shut up!"

Norris stuck a rag in Ryan's mouth. He pulled him out of the truck and made him stand. Wobbly, Ryan leaned against the side of the truck. The setting sun cast a faint light through the thick cloud cover. Ryan could make out a dilapidated mobile home. It was Doc Garrison's place. Norris pushed Ryan toward the trailer. Ryan spit the rag out with his tongue.

"What are we doing here?"

"Because you dragged Doc Garrison into this mess. He'd kept his mouth shut for years. Everything that happens tonight is on you!"

Norris then hit Ryan in the back of the head with a large plastic jug filled with an unknown liquid. Ryan stumbled and fell to the ground. Norris roughly jerked him up. They reached the trailer. Norris dragged him up the three steps and through the front door. Doc was sitting on the sofa. Norris had already been there. The older man's hands were tied behind his back and his feet were also bound by ties.

"What does he have to do with this?" Ryan asked.

"He signed his death certificate when he talked to you," Norris replied. "Charlie thought he wasn't a threat. I disagree."

"I didn't tell him anything!" Doc cried out. "I told him to leave me alone! I swear!"

"You're lying!"

Norris tied another rag around Ryan's mouth and then did the same to Doc. The older man looked at Ryan with terror in his eyes. Norris pushed Ryan onto the raggedy sofa beside Doc and bound Ryan's feet with longer ties. Norris then went to the old gas stove and turned on one of the burners. Grabbing a couple of dish towels, he soaked them with the liquid from the jug. Ryan could see that it contained vegetable oil. Norris laid the towels on the burner. Within seconds the cloth caught fire and flames shot up. Still holding the bottle, Norris stepped back and tilted the bottle so that oil splashed onto the floor.

The door to the bedroom burst open, and Rex came charging out. Bounding across the room, he crashed into Norris, causing the former detective to stumble forward toward the fiery stove and spill some of the last contents of the bottle onto his clothes. Seconds later, Norris was on fire. Slapping his burning overalls with his hands, he ran toward the door with Rex chasing after him.

Ryan slid off the couch and wiggled across the floor toward the door. Doc wasn't following. The older man shook his head and tried to kick a small table beside the couch. Ryan managed to stand and hop to the table. On top was a pair of toenail clippers. Ryan leaned back enough to grasp the clippers in his fingers. They were already opened. He unsuccessfully tried to position them to cut the twist tie that bound his hands. When he realized that wasn't going to work, he motioned for Doc to lie down. Sitting beside the older man on the couch, Ryan used feel to position the clippers to cut the plastic tie on Doc's wrists. Just as the clippers seemed in the right spot, they slipped from his fingers and fell into a crack in the couch. The flames spread from the stove to the wall and to the ceiling in the kitchen.

CHAPTER 45

N o!" Paige screamed. "Run!"

Lauren turned toward her as the door opened. Clint emerged from the house with the pistol in his hand. He pointed it at Lauren and looked toward Paige. When he did, Lauren grabbed his right wrist and sharply twisted it so that the weapon fell from his grasp. In a single move, she brought Clint's arm down and stepped forward so that his face was pressed against the floor of the stoop. The deputy lodged her leg against the back of Clint's elbow. With her other foot she kicked the pistol from the stoop into the grass.

"You're breaking my arm!" Clint cried out.

"Go to my car!" Lauren called out to Paige. "There are handcuffs on the console!"

Paige ran across the yard toward the patrol car. Sandy came out of the house. Paige glanced back to make sure the dog hadn't caused a problem for Lauren, but the deputy still had Clint locked down. Paige grabbed the handcuffs and returned.

"Fasten one onto the wrist I'm holding," she said.

Paige hesitated. She didn't want to come near Clint.

"I can't," she said.

"Then I'm going to have to break his arm."

"Do it!" Clint cried out.

Paige put the handcuff around Clint's wrist. When she did, she came in contact with his skin, which made her feel sick to her stomach. She stepped back. Lauren clicked the handcuff shut and quickly grabbed Clint's left hand. Within seconds, he was lying on his stomach with both hands secured behind his back.

"I didn't want to have anything to do with this," Clint said. "I wasn't going to hurt Paige, just scare her."

"Where's Ryan?" Paige demanded. "I haven't been able to reach him."

"Norris has him. He's taking him to Doc Garrison's place. I want to cooperate."

"Get his gun and put it on the front seat of the patrol car," Lauren said to Paige. "I'll use the radio to contact one of the detectives."

Paige gingerly picked up the handgun by the end of the handle and took it to the car. Lauren verbally gave Clint his Miranda rights.

"I told you. I'm going to cooperate!"

Lauren put Clint in the rear seat of the patrol car.

"Do you need to see a doctor?" she asked Paige.

"No, I'm coming with you to the sheriff's department. If you hadn't shown up—"

"But I did."

Lights flashing, Lauren sped away. Paige reentered the house. The bathroom door was destroyed, with shards of wood hanging at odd angles. Paige rested her hand against the wall. With each breath her fear for Ryan increased. Putting Sandy in the laundry room, Paige grabbed her purse and keys.

Ryan desperately tried to cram his hands into the crack between the cushions. He managed to grab the clippers and position himself so he could cut the twist tie from Doc's wrists. He placed the clippers on the plastic tie, closed them, and Doc's hands came free. Doc grabbed the clippers and cut the ties on his feet and then Ryan's hands and feet. Both men ripped the gags from across their mouths. The trailer was beginning to fill with smoke.

"Get out!" Ryan shouted.

Instead, Doc stumbled toward the bedroom. "Gotta get my gun," he said.

"No!" Ryan shouted.

Doc ignored him. Not wanting to abandon the older man, Ryan moved closer to the door and waited. The smoke thickened. The walls of the kitchen and the roof of the mobile home were on fire. A few more feet and the door would be engulfed in flames. Doc appeared, waving his pistol in his hand. Ryan helped steady Doc, who handed the gun to Ryan.

"You shoot him!" Doc said.

"Let's get out of here!"

Ryan led the way. In the light from the fire, he could see that Norris's white pickup truck was still there, but he saw no sign of the former detective. Rex came running up to them from the direction of the Eastside Music Barn. The dog excitedly jumped around his master.

"Behind the club," Doc said to Ryan. "If Broome wanted water, there's a hose and spigot."

"Then we're going the opposite direction," Ryan said.

The flames were shooting higher into the air. Ryan and Doc circled behind the burning trailer into a large field.

"Lie down on the grass," Ryan said. "I don't want him to see us."

Ryan could hear Doc's labored breathing.

"Once I'd talked to you the first time, I was afraid they'd come after me," Doc said. "Broome warned me that if I wanted to stay alive, I'd better keep my mouth shut."

"Why?"

"I know more than I told you."

While the trailer burned, the two men and the dog lay flat on the ground. Ryan desperately wished he had a phone so he could call and warn Paige. Then, in the distance, he heard the sound of a fire truck. A minute later, the trucks streaked past the club. Ryan started to jump up, but with a surprisingly strong grip, Doc held him down.

"You were right," Doc said. "We can't take a chance on Broome seeing us!"

"I've got to call my wife. Broome sent someone to kill her!"

Ignoring Doc, Ryan jerked away and ran around the trailer as the first of two firemen emerged. One of the men saw him and motioned for him to come closer. Two other firemen exited one of the trucks.

"Is anyone inside?" the first fireman yelled.

"No, we got out. But the man who set the fire intended to kill us. He's still in the area. Give me a phone. I have to call my wife."

Ignoring Ryan's question, the fireman started looking around. "Where do you think he is?"

"Maybe over behind the long building. Do you have a phone?"

"The sheriff's department is on the way."

Ryan grabbed the fireman by the shoulders and shook him. "I need a phone!"

The man roughly knocked Ryan's hands away. "Stand in front of the truck where we can watch you."

The fireman joined the other firefighters as they dragged the hose toward the mobile home that was now completely engulfed in flames from one end to the other. Ryan stood in front of the truck and watched as they connected hoses to the tanker truck. Doc Garrison appeared from the field. The fireman who'd talked to Ryan turned toward him and grabbed the old man's arm.

"Did he set the fire?" the fireman called out.

"No, he was inside with me!"

Then, in the flickering light from the flames, Ryan made out a figure crawling toward the white pickup on his hands and knees.

"There he is!" Ryan yelled out to the firemen.

They ignored him. Taking the gun from his pocket, Ryan started running. As he came closer, he could see that most of Norris's clothes were burned off his body, and the exposed skin was bright red.

"Hold it!" Ryan ordered.

Norris managed to turn his face toward Ryan. The former detective didn't speak but collapsed on the ground about three feet from the truck. Ryan cautiously approached. There was no sign of Norris's gun. The burned man raised his head a couple of inches and tried to speak, but no intelligible words came out of his mouth. Ryan heard the sound of another siren. It was a sheriff's department car. Leaving Norris where he lay, Ryan ran over to the car and waved his arms. Two deputies got out. One of them pulled out his gun and pointed it at Ryan.

"Stop right there!" he shouted. "Drop the weapon! On your knees with your hands behind your head!"

Ryan dropped the gun and got on his knees. He clasped his hands behind his head. Doc Garrison approached.

"That's my gun," the older man said to the deputies. "We thought we might have to protect ourselves from Norris Broome. He wanted to burn us to death in my trailer."

The two deputies looked at each other. "Where is Broome?"

"Over by his truck," Ryan said. "His clothes caught on fire."

One of the deputies picked up Doc's pistol while the other approached Norris.

"Broome is in bad shape," the deputy called out. "He needs medical help."

"I need to call my wife," Ryan said to the deputy standing closer to him.

"Are you Ryan Clark?" the man asked.

"Yes," Ryan replied in surprise.

"Your wife is fine," the deputy said. "She's on her way to the sheriff's department."

Every bit of adrenaline-fueled energy suddenly gushed out of Ryan. He collapsed, lay on the ground, and stared up at the night sky.

CHAPTER 46

Ryan and Doc sat in the rear seat of the sheriff's department car as an ambulance transporting Norris Broome to the hospital roared away.

"I'm taking both of you in so you can give statements to one of the detectives," a deputy said.

"It's been a while since I was in one of these," Doc commented, glancing around. "The seats are nicer than they used to be."

"Are you sure your dog will be okay?" the deputy asked.

"Yeah, he don't mind being tied up for a few hours so long as he has a water bowl. You're not going to put me in a cell, are you?"

"That's up to the detectives."

They rode in silence for a few moments.

"How did you know who I am?" Ryan asked.

The deputy looked at Ryan in the rearview mirror.

"Lauren Jackson called in a report letting us know Broome had abducted you and might be bringing you here," he said. "She's with your wife at the sheriff's department."

Ryan looked out the window of the cruiser. Moments later, tears formed in his eyes and rolled down his cheeks. Everything looked peaceful and calm when they arrived at the sheriff's department. The deputy escorted them inside the building. Paige and Deputy Jackson were standing to the right side of the waiting area with their backs to them.

"Paige!" Ryan called out.

Paige turned around. They rushed toward each other and embraced. The deputy on duty spoke.

"Take your time," he said. "When you're finished, let Deputy Jackson know."

Ryan and Paige parted.

"What happened to you?" he asked.

"No talking."

They kissed and held each other again. When they finally separated, Ryan looked over at Lauren Jackson, whose face was beaming.

"Detective Carpenter needs to take a statement from you," Lauren said. "He's already talked with Paige and me."

Reluctantly, Ryan released Paige's hands.

"This way," Lauren said.

"Have they arrested Charlie Drummond?" Ryan asked when they entered the hallway. "I believe he may have been behind all this."

"Not sure. I know at least two cars were dispatched to his house. Detective Carpenter will fill you in."

Ryan followed the deputy down a hallway into a small, spartan interview room. Detective Carpenter was not much older than Ryan. The stocky detective had short blond hair and blue eyes. He stood and shook Ryan's hand.

"Glad to see you," Carpenter said.

"He asked me about Mr. Drummond," Lauren said.

"Okay, have a seat."

Ryan sat in a plastic chair. Deputy Jackson left.

"We haven't located Charlie Drummond yet," the detective said. "He wasn't at his residence when officers arrived to bring him in for questioning. According to his wife, Drummond never came home this evening."

A knock sounded on the doorframe and a deputy stuck his head inside the room and announced, "We found Drummond's car at the farm his wife mentioned, but he wasn't there. Most likely he changed vehicles and left. Based on what his wife told us, we assume the housekeeper is with him."

The deputy closed the door.

"I'm sure he had a contingency plan in case this happened," Ryan said.

"And law enforcement agencies all over the US are going to be looking for him."

———————

Joe had just sat down to eat breakfast when a guard came into the dining hall and walked over to him. "Moore, the warden wants to see you."

Joe pushed his tray toward Ray and stood to leave. "Eat what you want."

"I'll fix you a sausage biscuit and bring it with me," Ray called after him.

Joe hadn't seen Ned in the dining hall. He entered the administration building. Elle was on duty.

"Good morning," she greeted him with a smile. "Go in. The warden is expecting you."

Warden Gunton was staring at his computer monitor. He glanced over at Joe.

"Sit down, Moore," he said. "I'm reading the news reports from Blanton County. None of this is official, but there were multiple arrests last night that seem connected to you and your case."

"Does it mention my lawyer, Ryan Clark?"

"Yeah, he was abducted by a former detective named Norris Broome but wasn't harmed."

"Norris Broome?" Joe asked in shock.

"Broome is in the hospital with severe burns and is under arrest. They're also looking for a person of interest named Charles Drummond. He's a wealthy man with some kind of connection to what happened."

"I was convicted of killing his sister and her boyfriend."

Warden Gunton turned in his chair and stared at Joe for a few seconds. "But you didn't do it, did you?"

"No, sir."

The warden tapped his fingers against his desk. "The threatening note left in the consultation room—"

"I know who wrote it," Joe said.

"What's his name?"

Joe took a deep breath. "I'd rather not answer that. He came forward and confessed to me because the Lord convinced him that he needed to tell the truth."

The warden shook his head. "Moore, you may be getting out of here, but I wish you'd stay until this whole place believes and acts like you and your buddies."

"That means a lot to me." Joe took a deep breath. "I'd like to contact my lawyer."

"Of course. I'll ask Elle to see if she can track him down. From what I'm reading, a lot of people will want to talk to him."

A knock sounded on the door.

"Yes!" the warden barked.

The assistant stuck her head inside the office. "Mr. Moore's lawyer is on the phone and wants to speak with him."

"Ask and you shall receive," the warden said. "Isn't that in the Bible?"

"Yes, sir."

"Transfer the call to consultation room B," the warden said.

Joe returned to room B. It seemed like much more than twenty-four hours had passed since he'd been there with Ryan and Ned. He picked up the phone.

"Have you heard what happened?" Ryan asked.

"The warden was filling me in."

"Broome tried to kill me and Doc Garrison. He tied us up in Doc's trailer and set it on fire."

"Doc Garrison?" Joe asked in surprise.

"Yes, and I believe the truth about what happened the night of the murders is beginning to come out."

Joe leaned his elbows on the table to steady himself. "Go ahead," he said.

"Here's what I know so far. Doc and Larry Walker convinced Marty to come to a drug house for a supposed meeting with a major drug supplier in Raleigh. No one knew Cherie was going to be with him. Doc stayed outside the house while Larry went inside with Marty and Cherie. When Detective Norris Broome and another man arrived, Doc got scared and took off. Back at the Eastside club he saw you, barely conscious, dragged out of your car by sheriff's deputies. A few days later, Larry told Doc that Norris and another man killed Marty and Cherie, then forced Larry to take the bodies to the club and dump them near the back door. Doc didn't know what really happened, but he always doubted you were involved."

"Did Doc tell that to the sheriff's department?"

"Yes, he met with the same detective who interviewed me."

Joe paused to absorb the news. "And your wife?" he quickly asked. "Is she okay?"

"She's—" Ryan began but stopped.

Joe could hear the lawyer trying to control his voice.

"She's okay," Ryan managed. "Broome sent someone to kill her."

Joe swallowed. "Thank God, both of you are safe," he said.

"Yes."

"Will you let Ned Walker know that his brother is okay?"

"As soon as I see him. He's been terribly worried."

"With good reason. The police are also trying to locate Charlie Drummond. He's fled the area with his housekeeper."

"Do they think he was behind his sister's murder?" Joe asked in surprise.

"Based on what Doc said, Marty may have been the target, but Cherie was in the wrong place at the wrong time. Also, Broome has been taking bribes from Charlie Drummond for years." Ryan paused. "One thing is more and more clear."

"What's that?"

"You're an innocent man."

CHAPTER 47

After finishing a three-set tennis match, Ryan and Danny Milton sat beside each other on a bench and leaned against the fence surrounding the tennis courts. It was late on a Thursday afternoon. Ryan wiped his head with a towel and took a drink of water from a plastic bottle.

"Thanks for letting me win the third set," Danny said.

"I didn't let you win. You wore me out in the first two sets, and I didn't have enough energy left to keep chasing down those sideline shots you were hitting."

Danny also took a long drink of water.

"Now, for business," he said. "We took Larry Walker's sworn statement four weeks ago. He corroborated what Doc Garrison told us about luring Marty Brock to the drug house. When Broome and another man showed up, they forced Marty and Cherie into a back bedroom and killed them. Broome told Larry to dump the bodies behind the Eastside Music Barn. If he refused, Broome was going to charge Larry with the murders. Broome and his accomplice put the bodies in the back of Larry's pickup truck. Broome drove Marty's Corvette to the club. Before they left the bodies behind the building, Joe stumbled out the rear door of the club. Recognizing an opportunity, Broome choked Joe unconscious and then ordered his accomplice to cover Joe with the blood of the victims, put the murder weapon in his hand, and stuff some cash in Joe's pocket. Broome and Larry watched while the other man followed orders."

"Any leads on the identity and location of Broome's accomplice?"

"Broome gave us a name, and we're working on it. He claims the guy was a professional hit man and is the one who actually committed the murders, but it was Broome's DNA that showed up on the murder weapon. Broome also contends his accomplice died in an armed robbery in Atlanta twenty years ago. Other information Broome provided checked out, including the money paid by Charlie Drummond through a shell company. That's how Broome bought that big house and farm."

"Did Drummond hire Broome and the hit man to kill both Marty and Cherie?"

"Broome claims the contract was on Marty. If that's true, it makes the whole situation even more tragic."

Danny again wiped his head with a towel.

"Here's the latest news," the DA said. "After reviewing Walker's statement, Broome's lawyer confirmed this morning that his client will accept a plea deal for life imprisonment without parole in return for dropping the request for the death penalty. Do you think Mr. Moore will be good with that?"

"Yes. As long as someone is breathing, Joe believes it's never too late for a person to change."

"Except for an ugly scar on the right side of his face, Broome has recovered well from his burns. He'll plea to both murders, along with the charges related to your abduction and the attempt to kill you and Mr. Garrison."

"Still no word on Drummond?"

"No, the FBI agent I spoke to last week thinks he may be in the Ukraine, which doesn't have an extradition agreement with the US. No one is giving up the search."

Ryan took a drink of water.

"Are you ready to set up a meeting with Judge Brinson to discuss a consent order granting my MAR?" he asked.

"Yes. I'll send over a draft of the findings of fact and conclusions of law by the end of the day tomorrow for you to review."

"Joe's been patient. He understands there's a process." Ryan was quiet for a moment. "Oh, one other thing. It doesn't matter much at this point, but did Norris admit to throwing the brick through the window and firing the gun at our house?"

"No, that was Clint. The sentence for all his crimes if he pleads guilty is still being negotiated."

Danny stood up. "How's Tom?" he asked. "I heard he was back in the office."

"Part-time. Monica Drummond hired us to clean up the mess with her husband's companies. Tom is going to focus on that. Monica is devastated but should be okay financially."

Ryan and Danny walked toward the locker room.

"One last thing," Danny said. "Do you think we should enter the country club doubles tournament?"

"As a team?"

"Yes, the first-place prize is a nice grill, one of those ceramic smokers."

"No one would want to play us," Ryan replied.

"Yeah, and if a team took a game from us, they'd brag about it all over town."

———————

The day before Joe's MAR hearing in Blanton County, he gathered together the men on the garden crew and bequeathed the rock he used as a pillow to Ray. Joe then shared his heart to the men who'd labored with him in both natural and spiritual fields. Tears of friendship and brotherly love flowed freely. Joe knew there were more tears ahead but none sweeter than those of the men he would be leaving behind.

His last stop of the day was Warden Gunton's office. Elle cried when she saw him. Joe stepped up to her desk.

"Would it be okay if I called you once I'm on the outside?" he asked.

"You know the answer to that is yes," replied the woman who had been so kind and respectful to him. "The first thing I'd like to do is invite you to visit my church. I've told my Sunday school class all about you, and they can't wait to meet you in person."

Elle handed him a slip of paper with her phone number on it. Joe put it in the front pocket of his uniform.

"Calling you when I get a new phone will be at the top of my list," he said.

"It'd better be," Elle said, wiping her eyes with a tissue.

"Is the warden available?"

"Yes, go in."

Warden Gunton stood when Joe entered the room. Never before had the warden greeted him in this way.

"If I didn't have a conflict in my schedule, I'd drive you to Blanton

County in the morning myself," the warden said. "I'd like to be in that courtroom."

"Hearing you say that is enough for me," Joe replied.

"Any word on whether the governor is going to issue a pardon?" the warden asked.

A pardon would be required for Joe to receive compensation from the State for being wrongfully imprisoned.

"It's in the works, but I don't know when or if he'll sign it."

"I hope he does."

The warden came around his desk and shook Joe's hand.

"Joe, I know how much the men in here mean to you," the warden said. "And as long as I'm in charge, you'll have access to meet with them beyond what anyone else enjoys."

"Thank you, sir. I'll be back."

That evening, Joe held a meeting with the men in Unit C. When Joe finished speaking, man after man stood and spoke about how much Joe meant to them. The two who touched Joe the deepest were Deshaun and Ray. Joe's friends then presented him with a handmade certificate of appreciation signed by men from all over the prison. As he glanced down at the names, Joe's vision blurred with tears. He held up the certificate.

"This is the most important thing I own," he managed. "I'll never forget you or stop praying for you."

Paige had transitioned into full-blown maternity clothes. Ryan was standing in front of the bathroom mirror straightening his tie. Paige was in the bedroom waiting for an opportunity to fix her hair before they left for the courthouse.

"Why are you taking so long to get ready?" she asked.

"I want to make sure my tie is perfect for the photographers."

Paige edged her way into the tiny bathroom and pushed him to the side.

"Your daughter and I need a turn," she said. "Especially since there's no way I'm going to look perfect."

"You're beyond beautiful," Ryan said as he kissed her cheek.

It had taken months for a hearing to be scheduled that would lead to Joe Moore's release from prison. The wheels of justice turned slowly, even when the destination seemed certain. Paige put the finishing touches on her makeup. She joined Ryan in the kitchen as he was finishing a second cup of coffee.

"The courtroom is going to be packed, but Nancy and Sue are getting there early to save a seat for you directly behind Joe's family."

The previous evening, Joe's family had hosted a dinner at the McKnight home. Danny Milton was there, along with Lauren Jackson, her husband, and Detective Carpenter, the officer who had pulled together all the evidence needed to legally support Joe's release. Tom and Karen had been able to come. Tom's health continued to slowly improve.

"Are you sure Tom won't be in court?" Paige asked.

"He's going to pass on the publicity."

"What about Doc?"

"Yeah, he should be there. He says he's no longer afraid to show up at the courthouse and claims he's going to be in church on Sunday."

Four TV station vans and a small crowd of people were assembled outside the courtroom. Several people were holding signs that read "FREE MOORE NOW" and "JUSTICE FOR JOE." One woman holding a sign was being interviewed by a news reporter.

"Any idea who those people are?" Paige asked as they slowed down to turn into the municipal parking lot.

"Most likely from a post-conviction justice project. It's a way to attract attention to their cause. They didn't have anything to do with Joe's case, but there are prisoners who can thank similar groups for their freedom."

Two reporters spotted Ryan and came up to him with microphones in their hands and camera operators trailing behind them.

"Mr. Clark, what do you have to say about the case? Do you believe Judge Brinson is going to order Mr. Moore's immediate release?"

"We believe the judge is going to take appropriate action based on the totality of the evidence," Ryan replied as he made his way forward.

Questions continued, but Ryan didn't reply. Inside the courthouse they got in line to pass through a metal detector.

"You sounded like a real lawyer on a TV show," Paige whispered.

"Is that a compliment?"

"I'm not sure."

The courtroom was buzzing. Holding Ryan's hand, Paige made her way to the seat Nancy and Sue had saved for her. Ryan stopped to speak to Joe's sister and niece before greeting Danny Milton. Joe wasn't present yet.

———————

It had been over two and a half decades since Joe sat in the holding cell behind the main courtroom at the Blanton County Courthouse. Ghosts of ancient shame still inhabited the atmosphere. He stared down at his newly shined black shoes, closed his eyes, and commanded the old accusers to leave. Shame and guilt no longer had the right to shoot their arrows at his soul.

A stocky deputy appeared in front of the holding cell.

"Follow me," the young man said. "The judge is on the bench."

Joe stood straight as he entered the courtroom. It was packed with people, just as it had been the last day of his original trial. As soon as Joe appeared, a group of people began to clap. Joe saw his sister and niece. Barbara looked so much like their mother that it caused Joe to do a double take. In a way, their mother was present. Her tenacity about his innocence set in motion the events that had brought him to this moment.

Out of the corner of his eye, Joe saw Judge Brinson sitting on the bench. The judge had aged a lot since Joe last saw him. He rapped his gavel and called for silence in the courtroom. The applause died down. Joe reached the table where Ryan waited for him and sat down.

"Call *State v. Moore*," said the judge. "Motion for appropriate relief."

The DA handed a thick file to the judge.

"Your Honor, as Mr. Clark and I discussed with you in chambers, the State consents to granting the motion and Mr. Moore's immediate release from custody. You have a proposed Findings of Fact and a Consent Order before you."

The judge turned to Ryan. "Counsel, do you have anything to add?"

Ryan stood and cleared his throat.

"Your Honor, on behalf of Mr. Moore and his family, I want to thank Mr. Milton and the Blanton County Sheriff's Department for all their efforts to see justice done today," Ryan said and sat down.

"Mr. Moore, would you like to say anything?"

Joe stood and took a yellowed slip of paper from his pocket. "The last time I was in this courtroom, my mother gave me a piece of paper. On it, she wrote a Bible verse, John 8:36: 'If the Son sets you free, you're free indeed.' That wasn't true for me then, but it became true while I was in prison. I'm grateful for the reason we're here today, but more thankful for what God has done in my life since I last stood before you. That's all."

The judge signed the order, then looked at Joe.

"Mr. Moore, the goal of every legal proceeding is the determination of the truth. Tragically, that doesn't always occur. It's my privilege to correct the injustice done to you. No one can give you back the years you've lost, but I hope the years before you will be filled with those things only an innocent man or woman can enjoy. As you've said more eloquently than I could, you are going to leave the courtroom a free man."

The courtroom erupted in cheers. Judge Brinson leaned back in his chair. Joe shook Ryan's hand and hugged him. Joe turned around to Barbara and Shana, who were both crying. Joe leaned across the wooden railing. Tears running down his cheeks, the three of them embraced.

———————————

Ryan watched Joe's celebration with his family, the image forever etched in his mind. When they separated, Shana turned to Ryan.

"Thanks again for risking your life to help Joe," she said.

"Risking my life wasn't on purpose."

"But you didn't run from the challenge."

Ryan wasn't as certain of his hero status as Shana, but he could see deep appreciation in the young woman's eyes. Paige came up and Ryan introduced her to Joe, who shook her hand.

"Thank you for the influence you've had on my life," she said.

"Praise God," Joe replied. "It's one of the reasons all this happened."

That evening, Paige and Ryan were sitting beside each other in the backyard. Sandy, her nose to the ground, was sniffing around.

"Now that Joe's case is over, how do you feel?" Paige asked Ryan.

"It's going to take me a long time to process everything. Nothing can ever happen to me in the practice of law to top it."

"Good," Paige quickly replied.

"Yeah." Ryan smiled and reached out for her hand. "I want my future highlight moments to be ones with you and our children."

"Children? I haven't finished making our baby girl, and you're talking about more."

"Just a figure of speech."

They sat in silence for a few moments. Paige said softly, "Ryan, I know I brought this up not that long ago, but I want to try again: Are you still dealing with guilt over your father's death?"

"Why do you ask that?"

"Today was about Joe being released from guilt he didn't deserve. I feel the same way about you and your father."

Ryan didn't respond.

"Would you talk about it with Joe?" Paige asked. "I believe he might be able to show you a way through."

"I'll bring it up with him," Ryan said after a few moments passed. "He's counseled a bunch of men in prison who've struggled with guilt."

Paige retrieved Ryan's hand and squeezed it.

"Thanks. You're going to be a great dad to our little girl," she said.

Ryan returned the pressure to Paige's hand.

"And to all five of our children," Paige continued.

"I wasn't trying to suggest—"

Paige interrupted with a smile on her face. "But you gave me the right to say whatever I want."

———

Ryan and Joe were in the car on their way to LPCC. Ryan glanced over at Joe, who was sitting in the passenger seat with his eyes closed.

"Are you praying?" Ryan asked.

Joe opened his eyes. "No, grabbing a short nap. The carbs from that big lunch we ate before leaving Cranfield caught up to me."

"Are you looking forward to seeing Elle after the meetings at the prison?" Ryan asked.

"Yeah, she's more amazing than I ever imagined."

They drove in silence for several miles. Ryan glanced over at Joe to make sure he was still awake.

"Paige says I should talk to you about my father's death and how I feel about it."

"Is Paige usually right?"

"Yes."

"Go ahead. I'm awake."

Joe listened without interrupting as Ryan retold the story of his relationship with his father and his sudden death.

"I don't want to become a father with all these negative thoughts and feelings still stuck in my head," Ryan said.

"Bringing something into the light is half the battle," Joe said. "The next step is to forgive your father."

"I've tried to do that."

"And yourself."

Ryan opened his mouth, then closed it. Paige had suggested the same thing, but Joe's two simple words touched a live place in Ryan's spirit.

"How do I do that?"

"Ask God to help you. Then be quiet for a minute before saying anything else. He'll take it from there."

"Right now?"

"Yes. You don't have to close your eyes to pray and talk to the Lord. And I'll feel safer if you keep your eyes on the road."

Ryan gripped the steering wheel tighter with his hands.

"Lord, help me. I want you to forgive me and help me forgive myself for all my wrong thoughts, words, and actions toward my father." Ryan took a calming breath. "How's that?"

"Sounds good to me. Now wait."

Ryan had judged his father, often for good reasons, but being right didn't solve the problem; it simply created more bricks for the wall that divided them. And Ryan's faults and failures had made the wall higher and thicker. Suddenly, a new understanding bubbled to the surface of Ryan's consciousness. He saw his father and himself in a new light, the light of God's presence in the midst of all that happened between them, whether good or bad. And if God was there, it meant that the ability to love and forgive and heal was also present. Ryan took one hand off the steering wheel and placed it on his chest.

"Something is happening in here," he said. "He says, 'I love you. I forgive you. Your burden is gone.'"

As soon as the words left his lips, Ryan felt a massive weight lift from his soul.

Joe nodded. "Sounds like the Lord at work to me."

"And it's real!" Ryan exclaimed.

Joe smiled. "More than anything else in the world."

ACKNOWLEDGMENTS

Special thanks to all who contributed to the creation of this story: Becky Monds, Jacob Whitlow, and Deborah Wiseman. And to my wife, Kathy, who never stops believing in me.

DISCUSSION QUESTIONS

1. Ryan's legal career had a rough start. How do Ryan's early career obstacles shape his decisions and his character now?

2. What part does Joe's faith and authenticity play in his leadership role in the prison?

3. The story is set in North Carolina. Is the South and its culture a "character" in the book?

4. "Waiting" is a theme in the story. Where do you see the people in the novel coping with waiting in diverse ways?

5. Early in the novel, Paige says, "Law school does something to a person's brain. It teaches you to separate the real world from the legal world." Do you see this at work in the plot and in the decisions Ryan and other attorneys make through the book?

6. There are a number of strong female characters in the book. If you had to describe Paige, Shana, Myra Moore, and Lauren each with only one word, what you would choose for each?

7. In the prison, Ray says, "Anything that celebrates evil in the past doesn't have a place in the present." What do you think about that in the world today?

8. Family is a constant in the book – Ryan's relationship with his father, family conflicts with the men in prison, Joe's mother, sister, and niece, and finally the truth about the Drummonds' relationships. What key plot moments involving family impacted you most?

9. How does Ryan change and grow through the book? Do you see a different man by the conclusion?

10. What character in the story do you feel the most connected to in this novel?

11. If you had to pen a testimony of faith for one of the characters, who would you choose and why?

ABOUT THE AUTHOR

Photo by David Whitlow, Two Cents Photography

Robert Whitlow is the bestselling author of legal novels set in the South and winner of the Christy Award for Contemporary Fiction for *The Trial*. He received his JD with honors from the University of Georgia School of Law where he served on the staff of the *Georgia Law Review*.

Website: robertwhitlow.com
X: @whitlowwriter
Facebook: @robertwhitlowbooks

LOOKING FOR MORE GREAT READS? LOOK NO FURTHER!

THOMAS NELSON

Since 1798

Visit us online to learn more:
tnzfiction.com

Or scan the below code and sign up to receive email updates
on new releases, giveaways, book deals, and more:

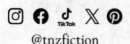

@tnzfiction

ALSO AVAILABLE FROM ROBERT WHITLOW

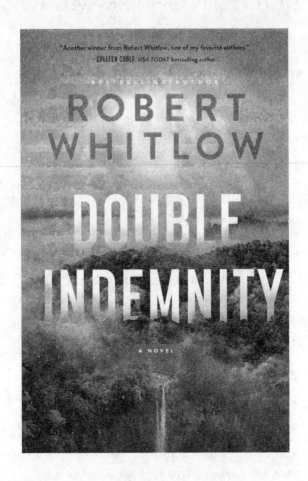

"*Double Indemnity* is another winner from Robert Whitlow, one of my favorite authors. The taut suspense builds until the likable pastor is falsely accused of murder, and his new girlfriend, an attorney, has to solve the case. Highly recommended!"

—Colleen Coble, *USA TODAY* bestselling author of *The View from Rainshadow Bay* and the Annie Pederson series

AVAILABLE IN PRINT, E-BOOK, AND AUDIO DOWNLOAD